...AND THIS IS
THE CURE

ALSO BY ANNETTE LAPOINTE

Stolen
Whitetail Shooting Gallery
You Are Not Needed Now

...AND THIS IS
THE CURE

ANNETTE LAPOINTE

anvil
PRESS

ANVIL PRESS / VANCOUVER

Library and Archives Canada Cataloguing in Publication

Title: ...And this is the cure / Annette Lapointe.
Names: Lapointe, Annette, 1978- author.
Identifiers: Canadiana 20200290541 | ISBN 9781772141511 (softcover)
Classification: LCC PS8623.A728 A73 2020 | DDC C813/.6—dc23

Book design by Derek von Essen
Author photo by John Galaugher
Represented in Canada by Publishers Group Canada
Distributed by Raincoast Books

The publisher gratefully acknowledges the financial assistance of the Canada Council for the Arts, the Canada Book Fund, and the Province of British Columbia through the B.C. Arts Council and the Book Publishing Tax Credit.

Anvil Press Publishers Inc.
P.O. Box 3008, Station Terminal
Vancouver, B.C. V6B 3X5 Canada
www.anvilpress.com

PRINTED AND BOUND IN CANADA

For John

This book was written in Treaty 8 Territory,
on the traditional lands of the Beaver people,
where I am grateful to live and work.

～ I ～

Ativan Sea

I had to fly home in the middle of the night.

The last flight from Pearson to Winnipeg came in at 11:56 p.m., and by then I'd been in transit for something like five hours. Six-and-a-half if I included the airport traffic in Toronto, sitting in the back of a cab playing elaborately cheerful Pashtun pop music. Quiet airline agents had escorted me to the special screening line reserved for the elderly and disabled, and for emotionally fragile minor celebrities. I'd walked up with something like confidence, then crumbled when I realized I hadn't sorted my purse out for air travel. It was loaded with the small, basic contraband items that kept me locked in conversational loops while my flight boarded, and called for me a second time, and then left without me. They confiscated my jackknife and screwdriver set, and a nail-care kit loaded with metal edges, two lighters, and a handful of loose pills half-crushed against the lining that I might have been able to persuade them were antihistamines, or something else innocuous that hadn't come into my possession at a 2 a.m. concert last summer, the last time I'd wanted to carry that purse before the current moment.

They were so polite. I was treated with the respect of a prosperous white woman, even as they called up the police records that included my two arrests for indecent exposure, my unprosecuted but well-known assistance of runaway cultists, the bar fights and riot grrrl battles and mental health reports after I'd stood on the railing above the CP Rail Yards and suggested that I might be better off neither a mother nor a living woman. Nobody commented. The nine years since working for Public Broadcasting had gradually turned me into a respectable figure for a polite nation.

They asked me to sit down. There might be a short delay.

I cried.

The airline agent was still hovering wordless at my elbow. I stared at the small number of extra pills in my purse and wondered if I could level out in time to fly. If I took everything right then, before it was confiscated, I might have a chance. I'd need more, though, later.

No one was home to bring me more. Eden was still out of the country, coming back on his own sleep-walk itinerary of boats and airports and five days in Miami. That long, then, before he could come back, find my pills, express ship them to me.

I tried to explain, very calmly, that I hadn't been planning on flying, but my possessions, my pills, were important. I couldn't just throw them away.

What came out was, "And this is all going to be on the fucking *news* tomorrow just like it's happening to somebody I don't even *know*."

I missed that flight, but they let me take my pills, and a doctor on site gave me two Ativan out of her own purse and wrote me an authorization for them on the back of a business card. CATSA agents scanned my shoulder bag carefully and determined that it was so clean that it probably wasn't even mine. It wasn't, but I didn't confirm that. I needed those clothes, that hairbrush, the Lady Speed Stick stuffed down the side. The airline workers hissed. My phone buzzed so many times that the agents had asked me, calmly, if I wouldn't mind turning it off.

I asked them to just, please, call and confirm. I didn't know the number. The Winnipeg Police Service. I thought that, contacts-wise, they could probably manage.

They did. Then they called someone to put my contraband in storage until my return trip.

Agents had been working for me with the fervor of people who saw a public relations coup building around them. CATSA released me. They held my next plane.

There were so many pictures. If I lived in a bigger country, in an American or British version of the world, it would have been tabloid fodder. *Here is Allison Winter*: teary eyeliner, black wool coat smeared with city grime, sharp-edged hair and makeup still in place from a photo shoot I'd done earlier in the day to promote *The Cure*. Studio girls had carved out an on-camera version of me that matched the radio voice.

"I like your show," the security agent said. "I podcast it in the car while I'm commuting."

"Thank you. That means a lot."

"What's on tomorrow?"

I stared at her. Past her at my own reflection in the security glass. "Um. A best-of. It'll have to be. I won't be back by morning."

"Right. I suppose that was obvious."

"I have to get my plane."

Toronto to Winnipeg was a regional flight, but Winnipeg was enough of a hub to merit regular-sized planes. When I was a kid, you had to walk out onto the tarmac and climb up stairs. Not anymore. There are digitally-coordinated gates, and a fast link-up to Pearson, where space collapses and parts of Canada flow into other countries and you can fall asleep and wake up on the other side of the world.

The airline was so, so sorry I'd been delayed. When I reached the gate, they informed me that they'd bumped me into first class.

"You don't need to."

"Sometime, say you had a good flight with us."

I stared at the woman. She was middle-aged and wearing green eye-shadow that went horribly with the red-white-and-blue everything else. She looked tired.

I said, "I'm flying tonight because there's been a death in the family and my daughter's all alone. It's not going to be a great flight no matter what. Give first class to someone else."

"Too late."

"I'm serious."

"So am I. You're in first class because someone upstairs noticed your name and said you should get to be in first class, and they told me to tell you. I know it's not your style. I listen to your show."

I hadn't realized first class was an option on regional flights. The space was tiny, and the other seats were occupied by men in polo shirts and ironed slacks. Because first class boarded before the others, people travelling in the bodies-stuffed-together back seats had to come through after, laden with unchecked bags and purses and shopping bags and coats and garments that wouldn't fit in the overhead bins. We were delayed twenty minutes while they worked out whose bags went where.

While I was waiting for them to sort it, the Ativan kicked up to the next level and I fell asleep. They woke me up on the Winnipeg tarmac. "Ms. Winter. We've arrived."

Words fell out of my mouth: "Thank you. I appreciate that."

III⦿III

I went to the Health Sciences Centre, looking. They told me she wasn't there. I asked again.

I must have sounded stoned. I was stoned, still riding the Ativan low, but I was trying. They called security, and then the city police, who checked my identification and their attitudes.

"I'm so sorry, Ms. Winter. We'll take you to her."

It had been years since I'd ridden in the back of a police car. They were more polite to me than when I'd last been there, but the smell was hallucinogenic, and I travelled with them on an Ativan sea that I thought lasted for hours but only covered a handful of blocks through the winter city.

Hanna was in a terrible hotel room in some nameless tower a couple of blocks from the Hockey Centre. I'd spent years visiting rooms like this with recording gear, a junior producer visiting mid-range bands who'd graduated from the Motel 6 by the airport. When I'd been touring, we'd never climbed this high, but working in radio I got used to hotels, thought they'd be my life until the universe soaked itself in blood and I crawled out of it a smoky host instead of a struggling minion.

Hanna said, "I'm not going with her."

I still talked to bands, but now it was in studio or in better hotels, where we hung out on mirrored mezzanines or in their polished suites. Network photographers captured charmingly off-kilter pictures of us. We interviewed and swapped stories and chord changes.

I made it a point of pride that I'd never fucked anyone in a hotel room that looked like this. I had in the motels of our touring days, and in a few awful campers. In a few hotels in world cities, where no one knew who I was, I could get away with it. But not this. The brown-ness. The worn wall-to-wall carpets. The stale not-cigarettes smell.

The woman sitting with Hanna said, "You don't have to go anywhere right now."

I said, "Can I get a 'Hi mom?'"

Unbecoming

Claudia's parents and Ethan's came to Hanna's room in the early morning. I was asleep. I'd curled up on one of the beds with my clothes and the lights on. Hanna had stayed at arm's length, watching me with wide little-girl eyes while I slipped below the tranquillized surface. That whole night, she stayed in the chair by the window. The social worker slept on the other bed.

She was still there because Hanna had explained to her that if she left, Hanna would act out her trauma by killing me.

"Nobody would convict me. I'm in shock."

I said, "You're eleven. They couldn't even charge you."

"No one's killing anyone," said Maegan the social worker. I got to watch her regret her choice of words. Like she'd bitten down on something very, very cold. "Oh my god."

"That's an obvious lie," I said. Couldn't help myself. Underneath my voice, Hanna said, "Too late."

Maegan looked so relieved that there was knocking.

She shouldn't have let them all in at once. They were all crying. All. Claudia's very nice geology-professor father and Ethan's father and both the mothers. They'd been crying all night. They weren't going to stop.

They had their own escort. I recognized Wayne, Ethan's lawyer. He'd handled the custody arrangements for Hanna so that Claudia wouldn't have to write the agreement up herself. We'd thought that might be a conflict of interest. Wayne wasn't crying, but I thought maybe he had been. He and Ethan, I remembered, had done two years of university together. They'd been friends for a long time.

Wayne had introduced Ethan to Claudia.

It occurred to me that, if I needed a scapegoat, I could probably make people believe that everything was his fault.

While I identified the lawyers in the room, Ethan's mother descended on Hanna. Pressed wet tears into her hair. "Oh baby."

"Grandma."

"Shhh. It's going to be alright." Rocking her back and forth just like Hanna was the one crying. Like she wasn't icy-calm and frozen in the arms of a woman whose shell had cracked open to let all her misery and fury spill out on whomever she touched.

Wayne said, to the air high up in the room, "The news people want to know if you have something to say."

"Them!"

"They were there all last night. At the hospital. They were at the *house*! Why are they so hungry?"

Wayne said, "Winnipeg's small. It's a small town. People have already heard, and something like this always garners attention. You don't have to talk to them, but it might make people feel better."

"Is that why *she's* here?" Pointing at me. Fragile, bronze-nailed finger. I couldn't remember Claudia's mother's name.

"Go away. We don't want to talk. And you may *not* record us. Go now."

I said, "This is my room."

Hanna said, "This is my room." Her grandmother rocked her harder.

Maegan said, "We called Ms. Winter because of Hanna. She came in late last night. Try to remember that this is her loss, too."

Ethan's father turned away from Maegan. I thought he was going to walk out the door, but he turned a hard left just before the map of fire exits would have struck him and locked the bathroom door. The fan didn't suppress his howling as much as he must have wished it did.

I said, "Do you want me to make a statement?"

"Tell them to leave us alone!"

"I can tell them that."

Wayne said, "They were asking about you, actually, Alli."

"Why?"

"Because Winnipeg's a small city and you're famous. Sort of."

He wasn't wrong. "I'll talk to them. Eleven o'clock. What time is it now?"

"Eight."

My skin creaked. I was shellacked with hairspray and thick foundation and wet mascara runoff. Lingering tranquilizers tugged at the boundaries of reality. I said, "Are they serving breakfast downstairs?"

"Probably."

"I'm getting coffee."

Maegan said, "Take Hanna with you."

"I don't want to go with her."

"You can stay here if you'd prefer."

It sounded like a threat. I think someone said something similar to me, shortly before I abandoned all desire to visit rural Manitoba ever again.

"I'll go."

Elaine released Hanna when she pulled away. Watched her walk to the hotel room door. To me, she said, "Do you think you can manage yourself and her both?"

She sounded so calm, almost non-toxic. Her shell had fused together as soon as she turned toward me.

I'd written chapters about that woman. I had inventories of reasons why things were her fault. All of them had been excised early in the editorial process. Notes in the margins included the words *juvenile* and *unbecoming*, but more centrally: *if we print that she will sue you.*

If I'd been a slightly different girl, closer to fully ignited when I left her house and Ethan because he was in it, and walked out into the snow, I would have burned it down behind me.

Instead, while we were downstairs, I arranged for my own room. I had no idea how to book it under a name other than my own, but I told them I wasn't taking calls, and that I'd call their corporate office if they gave my location out to anyone at all.

"Shall we assume that your family is an exception to that rule?"

"You should not."

The breakfast they served guests was cold, juice and coffee and lemon-poppy-seed muffins congealing in individual plastic wrap. There was a small fridge with cups of yogurt in it.

Guests might have been an exaggeration. Most of the people eating in that shadowy breakfast room were kids and teenagers, quiet and miserable and stuffing their faces, dressed with a grubby sameness I recognized. This was the place, then: the infamous nameless hotel where they stashed foster children between placements. I'd read the stories as they came out over the newswires. The year they were all displaced so the rooms could be opened up for a championship football game. The three sisters who'd lived here for eighteen months.

Outside, lurking, then, were the others. The people waiting for little girls to walk out the door and turn into street food.

Hanna studied them. She'd gathered up food in both hands, stuffed a spoon in her pocket. I liked her style.

I said, "Let's go back upstairs."

"I can't."

"We'll leave your Grandma Elaine for a while. New room. Come on."

:::●:::

Hanna turned on the new room's television. It didn't get any interesting channels. She left it on anyway and sat on a bed eating Froot Loops dry out of a miniature box, scooping them with her fingers.

I showered off the thick layers of travel. Hotel soap dissolved while I scrubbed at my face, and at the end I was still marked by the waterproof makeup of the previous day. I sat in the bathtub with the water steaming down against me and tried to digest breakfast. Assemble words.

There was no robe, and the towels were minimal. I had to pull my old clothes back on before I could go out. I filled both plastic bathroom tumblers with water and attacked the coffee machine, trying to decode it without turning my back to the girl on the bed.

The machine was a pod system I hadn't seen before, and the instructions were missing. In their absence, I ducked down to look for a barcode reader that might tell me which way to slip the crenellated plastic into its berth.

I said, "Hanna, are you okay?"

"What do *you* think?"

"Physically. *Physically* are you okay?"

"I've been inspected and everything. They took my clothes. These are other ones." She chewed thoughtfully. "I have this, like, random bag of my stuff. No computer. Can I have your phone?"

It was on the bed, next to my purse. I unlocked my phone and handed it to her.

"Where are the games?"

"In the folder marked *games*."

She examined them. "These are awful games. I'm going to need different ones."

"Which ones?"

"Just give me your password."

"It's my thumbprint. Show me what you want."

She didn't show me, but she held the phone out for my print with the screen covered, and I didn't think it was worth wrestling her for it. The code would wear off in half an hour, and I could assess the financial damage then.

The coffee spat into a chipped mug, and I decided this was a victory. With it in hand, I went up two floors, negotiated with Maegan, and collected my bag without going in.

I needed clothes.

I didn't have a go-bag of my own. It was the strongest evidence at work that I wasn't actually a journalist. The people who'd come up through field reporting kept bags under their desks all the time, just in case. In case they got spattered with something at a scene, or they had to fly to Jordan, or they were out three nights in a row and needed to file a story on-camera before they went home to bed.

Hosts are not journalists. Not as such. Junior producers on pop-media beats also aren't journalists, though they keep extra eyeliner in their desks, and maybe underwear.

I hadn't had a bag when I got the phone call, and I hadn't been able to sort myself enough to go home. Instead, Linda Jansen from the news desk brought me hers. She'd said, *we're about the same size,* like it was a careful, critical assessment. I'd been grateful. Taken it without even asking what she had packed.

I remembered Linda coming back from Guatemala. How disappointed she'd been that no one had threatened her life while she was down there, like it was a sign she hadn't done her job well enough.

Black T-shirt. Black jeans. J. Crew sweater that was better quality than I expected though a size smaller than I'd have liked. The underwear was all cheap stuff that any woman could afford to lose: La Senza panties and a Fruit of the Loom bra that might stretch enough to fit. Deodorant. A basic hair brush and smoothing oil to off-balance the damage cheap hairdryers could do to your scalp.

My purse was still a war zone from the night before. I couldn't find anything in it. I poured its contents out on the bed and dug.

"Shit."

"What?"

"I didn't pack my makeup." I hadn't needed to. I'd gone in to work in the pre-dawn bare-faced, ready to be constructed.

"That's got to be a serious problem for you."

"I have to go to The Bay. Give me my phone back."

She stared at me. Held the phone against her chest.

"Hanna. Give me back my phone."

"No."

"Hanna, I need my phone."

"I need a lot of things. My dad back. My mom. Lots of things that aren't you. You go away."

"I'm your mom," I said.

"You don't even have makeup on. You're not my mom. You're not even whoever you usually are."

~ 3 ~
The Cure

The progression of events up to now is approximately this:

My name is Allison Winter. I was born in Manitoba in the 70s, to parents who were getting ready to go forth into the world and witness for Christ and the Anabaptists.

We did that for years. We came back to Canada, and then to Manitoba, during a lull in my parents' ministries. I didn't go to school except at our kitchen table, but there were other people around, and I was allowed to go outside by myself, which later my parents probably considered a mistake but by then it was too late.

I married Ethan Hoeppner in an after-supper ceremony at our church, on the grounds that I was pregnant, and that this would be the best decision for all of us. We would be supervised thereafter, and assisted in child-rearing until Ethan finished high school, and then we would carry on. Our family, early constituted, would make us adults, members of the community. We were already members of the church. He'd been baptized in the same church we were married in, three years before. I'd been baptized in Burundi, while my parents were on mission.

From the perspective of our church, we were adults. Our parents were less than impressed with us, but they signed the necessary documents. My birth certificate got "misplaced" so that they could certify that I was sixteen, which I wasn't yet.

That marriage lasted two weeks. I walked out of his parents' house, down the highway into town, and found the police station. I told them that I was fifteen, that I'd been forced into marriage, that my parents had left the country, that I was now the government's responsibility. Later, I moved into Winnipeg and joined a punk band.

I divorced Ethan in 2002. I hadn't seen him regularly in a decade, but he wasn't free to marry until I signed the papers. I signed them. Ethan married Claudia Hardee. I had Hanna, and then other things happened, and after that I handed Hanna over to Ethan and Claudia. Surrendered to in-patient treatment with raw places scratched all over my body and one still-intact daughter who'd just acquired a very nice family.

I started doing radio in the early 2000s, in the intervals when The Innocents weren't on tour. I knew sound equipment, and I was reasonably competent. They liked my work. Said I had a radio voice. After I was on my own, out of the band and out of the hospital, Rosemary in the Winnipeg office recommended me for a junior producer job in Toronto. I did eighteen months filling in for a half-dozen people, the oldest, most junior producer running segments for anyone who needed one or running sound boards if someone called in sick. I met Jay Beaton. He pushed me up against the sound booth wall after his show and said, "I'd really like to hate-fuck you."

I have problems with judgement. For instance, I decided that was an appealing come-on. I took him up on it, and I got to be a regular producer and writer on his show, *The Cure for Ordinary*, which was a break it was widely agreed that I didn't deserve.

They had no idea.

Then Jay went down in fire and blood and police lights, and we had to go to air on sixteen minutes' notice without him, so I sat down behind the microphone and went out live, nationally, on what was then the third most popular show on Canadian Public Broadcasting.

They put me on the radio because I was sacrificial. I'd been doing music journalism for a few years, and I sounded clean enough to wash the worst toxic ooze out of the studio, but no one thought I'd last more than an episode or two, and when they cleaned house in Jay's aftermath, I'd go too.

They re-launched Jay's show under my name that October.

The Cure, with Allison Winter airs weekdays nine to ten thirty ante-meridian, rolling across the time-zones, broadcasting from the city of Toronto.

Good morning, Newfoundland and Labrador.
Good morning, Maritimes. It's good to hear you.
Beau matin, Québec. Je t'aime.
Good morning, Canada.
    (O world, I shall be buried all over Ontario)
Good morning to the prairies and the mountains and the glorious Pacific.
Good morning to the high Arctic. Are you listening, you beautiful people? Are you
out there on the third coast?

Ethan and Claudia stayed in Winnipeg. They bought a house in glossy Lindenwoods. Claudia's son from her previous marriage lived with them on weekends. They were stable. They had the kids on soccer teams. They took them on vacation to Florida at spring break and let them appreciate the wonder that is Disney World, and then took them north to witness one of the last shuttles launched from Cape Canaveral.

I sent postcards. They sent me regular pictures of Hanna. I even visited a couple of times, in controlled situations where Hanna clung to Claudia and made it clear which one of us she considered to be her mother.

I didn't resent Claudia. This sounds like a lie and actually isn't. Claudia saved my life. Claudia looked like me, but she had a career in tax law and a close relationship with her parents, and she loved Hanna. She loved Hanna more than her own child.

More than she could have loved her own child.

I have it on excellent authority that Claudia never *once* stood over Hanna's crib and thought, *Don't throw the baby out the window.*

Claudia never solicited strange men for kinky sex in online forums and pursued them into luxury hotels to follow up on the idea. She was never arrested too drunk to remember her own name.

Claudia never got stoned with The Jesus Lizard.

Claudia never even really processed *how* someone could do those things. Someone who was a parent. Not, maybe, a good parent. Not a responsible or stable parent. She did understand, at least on paper, that years of unmedicated bipolar depression made me very, very difficult to live with.

Manic-depressive woman totally not fun when she's not manic.

Claudia never quite adjusted to my ability to make jokes about it, either. She and Ethan decided, and they politely informed me, that my autobiography (bestselling, the first thing to give me real money in the bank) was not going to be acceptable reading for our collective daughter. Not until she was older, and they'd talked about Allison's problems with her, and she was ready.

Hanna wasn't ready for her step-brother to develop quiet symptoms of his own. Claudia and Claudia's ex dealt with him, and talked to him, and suggested that if he wasn't going to take his medication, he shouldn't come by the house.

I had a certain amount of sympathy for him. It's hard to stay on your meds. The first months, it's like something chewing on your brain. These days, I do okay. Nobody whispers in my ear. I only ever very briefly thought members of my family were dangerous. The only one I was ever scared of enough to attack was Hanna, and I stopped myself before that happened in any permanent way.

Hanna's stepbrother came to his mother and stepfather's house in the middle of the afternoon on a Tuesday. He argued with his mother. He hit his mother — Claudia — with a kitchen chair. He hit her with it a large number of times.

Sometime after that first incident, Ethan came into the kitchen, encountered his stepson, and was stabbed repeatedly with a kitchen knife.

The stepson was in the house for three more hours, as the police measured it, before he killed himself.

Hanna was in the basement. She didn't, at any point, call the police. When they asked her, she said she'd had her headphones on. The neighbours found her when they came to investigate why the front door was open and found Claudia fatally beaten in the living room, Ethan stabbed in the kitchen, and Claudia's son from her first marriage naked in the bathtub, where he'd cut his wrists.

~ 4 ~

True Love's Kiss

The Bay in downtown Winnipeg was a massive stone building hulking out of the nineteenth century into the twenty-first. It was the last of the great department stores. Eaton's had died and been demolished while Winnipeg was still recognizably my hometown. The Bay lingered, massive and ancient like a sulking trace of the colonial process. I was surprised, abstractly, that it was still there. The Bay kept contracting, and every time I read a story about The Bay and Winnipeg, it was about possibly-maybe selling the downtown building. It could become a government office, or part of the adjacent university. It might make expensive condos for people who valued original marble floors over natural light.

The cosmetics department still lurked in a haze of perfume on the main floor. In that sea, the MAC counter stood out, black in the land of pastels. I'd have taken a trip to Sephora over this single-kiosk experience, but the only one in Winnipeg was a long cab-ride away in a city with no subway system.

It was too early in the day for anyone to be as fully contoured as the girl behind the counter. Her shading and shaping almost completely erased the natural outline of her face. I felt naked in front of it. My skin was dry in patches from the hotel soap, and bare. Uneven.

There were lines there, the kind that cameras amplify.

Department store lights were almost as unkind as cameras. I closed my eyes and tried to re-centre. To find my riot grrrl certainty of the irrelevance of makeup.

Makeup wasn't important, except that I needed it very badly.

I let her sit me on a stool and sponge colour-corrector under my eyes.

"How bold do you want to go?"

"I don't. I just need foundation, powder, eyeliner — black, please — and highlighter. Whatever you have in a nude eyeshadow palette. Lipstick."

I watched her do the math. Two hundred dollars, more if I wanted brushes. "Why don't you test the shadow colours and I'll try to match you on the rest?"

I missed the previous decade's makeup shades. I'd developed an affection for MAC in a period of vivid eyeshadow and glittering metallic liquid eyeliner. It provided a kind of mask. It was a cultural passcode, too: the right eyeshadow could open doors, or reassure bands that I didn't take myself as seriously as the word *producer* indicated.

That over-the-top style cycled out before I wore out my paint pots, and I was genuinely disappointed. It was replaced with a subtler aggression: light and dark shaded foundation shaping women's faces into pixie-pointed chins and cheek-bones, narrowing their noses and hollowing their cheeks.

Eyes neutral, smoky, nothing that could be identified as a colour but a dozen shades of it.

Grow out your eyebrows. Define them with pencils. Brush powder through them.

The only remaining colour explosion rests on your lips. Line them, expand them, colour and layer them. Shed all your metallic shades from last decades and replace them with matte liquids, sticky and easily transferable.

Every meal you eat is going to look like it's bleeding. But what business did you have eating, anyway?

I said, "Definitely lipstick."

"Neutral?"

"Dark."

She gestured to the rack. I'd forgotten that this year's collection was coded to a Sleeping Beauty reboot. I wasn't sure how I could have forgotten that. I'd talked to the star, though not about the fairy-tale movie. She was working with a charity for children separated from their parents by war. They'd built a massive database of undocumented people, to reassemble the broken families, she said. DNA records to link them all together. She was so thin, we had to find her an extra pillow for her chair. Huge eyes like an insect.

Her signature colour was, apparently, True Love's Kiss. Clean, bright red, with an amplified finish.

▮▮▮●▮▮▮

I looped back through the Portage Place mall, trying to avoid Winnipeg's winter for as long as I could. The city was achingly cold, and I was so tired, though the girl at the store had done my makeup in return for the multiple hundreds of dollars of product I'd put on my credit card, so I looked less undead than depthless and otherworldly.

The mall was still a gathering place for people living in subsidized housing towers and staying in the Mission shelter to the east. They filled tables in the food court while office workers lined up for their coffees and breakfast sandwiches. Dropped their eyes as I walked past them.

I reached the end of the mall. I had to go back outside.

The city moved, though differently from Toronto. Only a few panhandlers sat in the wind, holding out empty coffee cups for change. I had a handful of coins stuffed in my pocket for them, but I ran out before I reached the end of the human line that ran east along the commercial strip towards Portage & Main, the advertised coldest point in Canada. Outside of Indigenous Media Systems, there was a man curled up, face to the wall, in a sleeping bag.

It was so cold. I thought that he must be dead. That I should check.

I didn't.

I was navigating in an unfamiliar city without my phone. I had to guess at which turns to make to reach the fashion stretches of The Exchange, lurking north of the downtown in its glossy, refurbished industrial buildings.

I needed a car to do this in any kind of comfort, but I'd carved Toronto into my surface like graffiti, and I wasn't going to surrender to driving. Winnipeggers and aliens drove cars. I walked. Down the street, past more crouched panhandlers, and across single-direction streets to the plate-glass world of clothes for people who didn't buy their clothes in shopping malls.

I thought about the state of my credit cards. How much damage I could do.

It wasn't quite nine, yet. Most of the stores were closed until eleven, when the hipsters woke. I kept walking. Jewelry shone next to a Thai restaurant.

One shop open.

Aspiring fashion designers still working this far west tended to pick up echoes of Brooklyn and last year's *Project Runway*. Romper-dresses hung in shallow rows next to parachute pants.

"Are you okay?"

"I'm cold is all." Frost on my eyelashes. Numb fingers.

. I found a button-down shirt and a dark sweater. Black pencil skirt. No tights. I'd have to go back to the Bay. I wasn't sure I had time.

She rang me up. I counted the dollars of the flight, the hotel room I'd secured this morning to escape from the gaze of my childhood mother-in-law, the makeup palette in a tiny carrier bag. These clothes. I said, "Can you call me a cab?"

"Sure." She dug a phone from her pocket.

The snow outside billowed. I'd lost track of where I was. I went down into it, caught the cab, then realized we were headed in the wrong direction. North. He looped me most of the way to the North End before doubling back. By the time he pulled up, I figured I was four, maybe five blocks from where we'd started. If I'd been better-oriented, more awake, I could have walked and saved myself the money.

The hotel didn't look better in full daylight. There were two camera crews setting up in the lobby. A guy from local radio, not the Public Broadcasting affiliate, with a recorder. I'd worked with him. "Allison?"

"You can't see me, okay?"

"Allison, can we talk?"

"I'll be down in twenty minutes."

"Come on, don't be a bitch. We go back!"

I turned around. Under the makeup, I could feel frostbite's low burn. I said, "I am fucking *bereaved*. I'll be down in twenty minutes. And no. *We* cannot *talk*. Tell the station if they want to talk to me, they have to send somebody else."

Behind me, he said, "Cunt thinks she's really something. You read her book? That memoir-thing. You'd think she'd spent her whole life walking on broken glass."

⁑⦂⁑

I did go out and talk to the local press, but whatever they were looking for, I didn't provide it. The local television news ran a fragment of the footage at noon and again at six. I must have infuriated them, because they all pointedly left out my name.

I went back to sleep after, pressing my contoured face into the flat hotel pillows. Hanna had fled by the time I woke up, joining her grandparents two floors up. My phone was there, battery depleted, like a sad, starved animal.

While it charged, I watched television again. Late afternoon. Time for the news.

I was tagged in the lower third of the screen as a friend of the family. Pieces of my voice on different commercial stations drifted across the radio when I called up each channel on my reclaimed, still-charging phone. Two networks, including mine, posted raw video of the press conference to their sites. I scrolled to the bottom of my home system and was relieved to find that comments had been disabled.

On the commercial network's site, comments were active. I read most of them.

They weren't, for the most part, about me. There was a long thread about the layers of crazy that fermented in society, and what should be done with the people who were. There were layers of reference in the comments. The man who'd killed the boy on the cross-country bus came up more than once. That degenerated, finally, into people who claimed they'd known the victim (the boy on the bus, not the woman in the living room or the man in the kitchen or even the boy in the bathroom) and that those who hadn't should just shut the fuck up about it.

There were a couple of references to a thing I'd first read in an alt-weekly paper out of Seattle: *if you're thinking about committing a murder-suicide, do the suicide part first.*

People who'd skipped to the end of the article and missed crucial details suggested either castrating the killer or waiting for the trial. Other commenters chimed in on the impracticality of both options.

The comments weren't all not about me. There weren't any good ones, any kind ones. A couple about my current fuckability and a few about my love of media attention, even when it was not about me, and some expressing some variation on *stuck-up-bitch.* Suggestions as to what they'd do with my body if they could get their hands on it, the previous comments on castration notwithstanding.

My work email piled in, refusing to be ignored. The administration was very, very sorry for my loss, and when was I coming back? Tomorrow? Friday? They were just trying, they assured me, to establish a schedule. Who they hired to cover for me depended on how long I'd be gone.

It occurred to me that if I wanted to, I could just leave, go home to Toronto, and back to work. I'd been waiting, but I wasn't sure for what. For someone to decide if more action needed to be taken. For someone to plan a funeral that I could attend. I hadn't talked to anyone since the press conference. I'd made coffee in the room, filled it with sugar, and given up on food.

I phoned Toronto. I said, "Can I work from here?"

"You mean, over the phone?"

"There's a station down the street. They might have room for me."

"You want Ellie to fly out to meet you?"

Ellie was my senior producer. Her voice ground out over the radio like the second coming of Tom Waits and she looked like a math teacher. Tall and odd, like a stick-insect with dense glasses. She wore discount shirts in pastel colours. Did great things with sound and watched the timer like a hunting insect. We hadn't missed a cue in almost a year. She was keeping count on a board.

"Will she come?"

"You're under stress. We could bring in a substitute host."

They had a roster of people who came in when I was on vacation. Mostly semi-retired pop singers, with a smattering of adults who'd hosted children's television shows when they were kids themselves. Friends, generally, but predatory. I had a good job. Any of them would have been happy to take it over temporarily and keep it forever.

"I don't know how long I'm going to be."

"We'll get you a sub."

I looked at the room. "I need to work. This isn't taking enough of my time. I have the notes for the next shows on my phone. You know we can do it."

They told me to wait. I took another shower. Soon my room was going to be a wasteland of single-use hygiene products and damp towels. I piled them in the tub, then added the pillowcase with foundation traces of myself on it like the shroud of Turin.

Toronto called me back. "Go down to the office. See what you need to get set up."

⦂⦂⦂⦂

I wasn't wearing my own clothes. Except for the funeral look I'd picked up that morning, everything I had was Linda Jansen's. She was one of the cadre of very serious journalists who worked out of the Front Street building. They shipped out to war zones and kept notebooks in their pockets and, as far as I could tell, all went to J-school together, or else had worked together at some formative phase of their careers.

We'd gone to the same university.

"I never saw you there."

I said, "I was on tour a lot. My university terms were sort of here and there. I did some college radio."

Linda said she'd worked at the university paper. Gone on from there.

A little bit friendly; a little bit brittle. Not that she *wanted* to host on air. It would have kept her from going into the field. Still.

Still, she gave me her go-bag since I didn't have one.

This weirdness of wearing another woman's underwear. Her panties, her bra. We weren't the same size. Her hips must have had that flare mine didn't. The jeans adjusted, but the panties underneath sagged off my ass. Her bra was too tight against my ribs. My left breast pushed up towards the centre, creating a kind of double cleavage while it tried to get loose. I buried the escaping mounds as best I could under my coat.

Sleep had offset the worst of the winter chill. I told myself I didn't need to call a cab.

Went outside. Crossed two streets and went down Portage Avenue to survey the field.

~ 5 ~

Radio Country

The few months I'd worked out of Winnipeg Public Broadcasting, I was freelance. I'd done more work for the college station, where all you had to do to get on air was show up and not swear constantly and have arcane taste in music. I sounded calmer than most of their on-air voices. I could manage a microphone without hissing. When Public Broadcasting needed someone to interview The Bee Collective, our station manager gave them my name. They gave me a recorder. Told me to watch my language.

The Bee Collective was three boys in thick glasses and too-short jeans playing synth and banjo. They weren't local, but they had an in with the Winnipeg scene, where they were just weird enough to qualify for indie cred. They were friendly and forthcoming. They liked me okay. I liked them.

We talked in a bar after sound-check, in the dead period of the afternoon. I'd done that once or twice from the other side of the reporter-musician divide.

We got a bit drunk, after.

I fooled around with the drummer in the bathroom. He was such a tiny fucker. He weighed maybe half what I did then. Two-thirds of me now. All bones and tiny shoulders and long hair, and he kissed like a demanding teenager. Dragged my jeans down around my knees and proved it was almost/not quite possible to eat pussy on a girl wearing jeans in a bathroom stall.

The Winnipeg Public Broadcasting office was where I'd left it. They had new carpet. They had a poster of my made-up face in the foyer, listing *The Cure*'s airtimes in central standard. An office manager dispatched baby broadcasters over the city's geography.

They had two radio booths — one for the AM band, one for FM — and a soundstage for the television news. Most of the staff worked out of vans, moving around the city. They checked car accidents, watched traffic, recorded highlights of collegiate varsity sports. They covered provincial and municipal politics and reported on scandals. There'd been one camera for me in the hotel lobby, but two for the street in front of the house where everyone died. Cycling news footage showed earnest young reporters talking to Ethan and Claudia's neighbours. Talking to Claudia's ex before he retreated behind his door. An extra crew ventured forth to interview selected experts.

Police have no comment on the killer's motivations. They have acknowledged him to have a history of violence. He had two previous arrests for common assault, both at bars in St. James. He is not believed to have visited his mother's house regularly. Neighbours and friends continue to speculate what brought him there for yesterday's terrible confrontation.

Ellie had emailed Winnipeg my requirements. Just a raw studio, if I wasn't staying. A competent producer — they could bring in a freelancer, if they needed to. Our roster of interviews could all be done over the phone, though we'd have to start unspeakably early. Two guests would sit in my Toronto studio, listening to me across time zones. Three others were dialling in.

To meet the Atlantic and Newfoundland air times, I'd have to be in the studio by five. I keyed a wake-up into my phone.

Producers scrambled around me. Writers were emailing script fragments and monologue options for the morning. Student interns stared from between the blind slats.

Like the Queen walking into a barely-remembered embassy and demanding to hold court on the morrow, I wasn't sure if they were delighted or planning to kill me as soon as my back was turned.

"Allison." Rosemary was still on-site. She'd done her weekly show earlier that same day. She had a tablet in one hand, and a list of questions. "Are you set?"

"Yes. Thank you."

She paused. "Do you want to appear on the TV local tonight, maybe do an interview? At eleven?"

It was — I checked — 10:10. I needed to be asleep already. I hadn't talked to Hanna in hours.

It occurred to me that her grandparents must have taken her. They'd have collected Hanna and checked her out of the hotel and taken her home. Given her a bath and whatever they gave kids to help them sleep, now. Nyquil or Benadryl or something comparable. Or, knowing Ethan's parents, warm milk and psalms.

I said, "Maybe tomorrow."

"I'm going to hold you to that."

"I'll be dead by then, and you won't be able to make my corpse do shit."

"What?"

"I said, 'That's really kind of you. Have a good night.'"

"Yes."

"Okay."

I walked back. It occurred to me, three blocks in, that I should have called a cab. I hadn't walked downtown Winnipeg at night in years, and my shell was thinner than usual. People staggered out of bars and wrestled with each other in the bus mall.

It wasn't the bus mall. The busses had moved. Where had they gone? The abandoned street was half shut-down, and guys were shooting up in the alleys, and I was walking in the dark.

I left for a few years and they shifted the whole city.

Hanna was watching television on my bed when I let myself in. She said, "Nobody got me dinner."

"Where are your grandparents?"

"Crying. They had to go lie down."

I tried to remember if I'd eaten. I said, "What do you want?"

"Chicken fingers."

"Do they have to be from somewhere in particular?"

She wrinkled her nose. "I like the A&W ones."

I didn't know if there was an A&W in walking distance. If I took out my phone to check, she'd steal it from me. I said, "If I order room service, will you eat whatever shows up?"

The prices were extortionate. I tried to remember when I'd last eaten room service, and it was more than a year ago, and on a trip that I wasn't paying for. I'd have taken her down to the hotel's restaurant, but then I'd have had to eat down there, and also it was closed.

They brought her deep-fried chicken tenders of some description, with plum sauce and fries that had obviously come out of a freezer. The pesto-laced panini under my own tray-cover reeked of garlic and melting mayonnaise.

"I'm going to bed."

"Allison?"

I looked over.

"Can I wear something out of your bag? I kinda stink."

I had my shirt halfway over my head. "Where are your clothes?"

"At home."

"Nobody got you any?"

"Uh-uh."

I rubbed my eyes. She had four grandparents on site. "Do you have pajamas?"

"Uh-uh."

"Toothbrush?"

"Yes."

"Where'd you get it? I don't have one."

She stared at me, blankly. Up close, her face was crusted with salt and what had to be snot. She didn't cry anytime I could see her, but I hadn't seen her much. "Come on."

I ran her a bath. Housekeeping had replaced the toiletries, at least, so I could pour in the body wash and make bubbles. Piled up towels on the toilet seat and found her a cheap robe wrapped in plastic. "Try to clean off," I said. I left her to it. Peeled off my clothes in the room and studied the single queen-sized bed. Its spread was sticky.

I was half-asleep in one of Linda's not-big-enough T-shirts. Hanna said, "Allison?"

"Mmm."

"I need help washing my hair."

The clock said 12:03. I had to be up in too few hours. When I focussed an eye on her, Hanna was wrapped in a towel in the pooling light of the bathroom, hair still dry.

This little girl. I'd been trying to remember how old eleven was. She was taller than I'd expected, and she stared at me like a teenager, but underneath the towel she had a child-body. Breasts completely absent in a way I had trouble processing. Naked crotch. The water in the tub was greasy and cold, and I had to run her a new bath.

"In."

She sat and turned her head.

"How do you usually do this?"

"We have an elephant shower." Pause. "It comes down in a trunk so I can get my hair wet."

Telephone shower. I said, "Lie back into the water."

"I'll drown."

"It's not that deep." She hunched her shoulders. Tried to lean back without releasing a single muscle. "Here." I put a hand at the base of her skull. Let her lean back just until the water brushed her hairline, then used my other hand to cup liquid and soak her scalp. Like dyeing a friend's hair in the sink. Get her wet, lather her up. Wrap her head. Wait. No. Just wash and rinse. Did little girls condition? The hotel shampoo left her with tangles I could feel against my fingers, so apparently conditioning wasn't something that could wait for her to hit puberty. It meant we had to go through the process again.

She stood, finally, with sloughed-off hair and soap clinging to her legs. I said, "Just towel off. You can deal with it in the morning."

Only, dry, she was still tangled and staring at me. I gave her one of Linda's shirts. Found a comb in the bathroom's toilette-kit and tried to work the knots loose.

She said, "My mom uses No More Tangles."

I didn't say anything. Tried not to rip strands loose from her scalp. Finally draped an almost-dry towel over a pillow on the sticky side of the bed and said, "Sleep. I have to be up for work in three hours."

"You're leaving?"

"Just down the street."

"Can I come?"

She'd never wake up for it. I said, "We'll talk about it." Turned out the light. Groped for body-length covers in the tangle of bedding.

This huge bed. I slept in one half the size at home. Before I was asleep, Hanna crawled across and butted her head into my shoulder. Stayed there, snoring.

Good morning, Iqaluit. It's currently -17 and overcast, but you'll reach a high of -4 today, they've promised me. How are your polar bears?

We're in radio country, people. I'm coming to you today from the early, early hours of Winnipeg, Manitoba. They've kindly made space for us here, and we'll be talking to some fantastic people. Jamaica Hind comes to us from Chicago, and Marilyn Bowie will be in to talk about music education, something close to my heart. Almost half the country has no provincially-set music curriculum, and in schools where budgets are tight, that means no music education at all.

Tell me, what's music ed like where you are? Our phones are open across the time zones. Labrador, I'm talking to you. Tell me who's singing in your town.

Yeah, hi.

Hello Jaikin. Am I saying that right?

You bet.

How's music ed where you are?

I'm in Rabbit Bay. We have elders who come in, sometimes. And there's an electric piano.

How many kids in the school?

I don't know. A hundred, maybe? Some of them are boarding. We have a good drum circle.

Do you think there should be a cross-country music program?

I think they wouldn't know how to drum in, like, Saskatchewan. I don't know if they'd be interested. I think they might like different music.

What music do you like?

I like hip-hop, mostly.

You like A Tribe Called Red?

I like Jay-Z.

Good to know. Thanks so much for calling.

And maybe Jaikin has a point, no? It's a big country. Would a national music curriculum mean air-lifting upright pianos into Cambridge Bay?

- I vote for national drum circles.

That's an idea. Rosemary, you're my new favourite person. It seems like a place to start, drumming.

So here's what we're going to do, radio people. Are you drumming? Is your school? Are your kids? Is your church? Is your drum circle the best in the country? Send us a video. We'll watch them all, and we'll post the best ones on our site.

- You should bring them down to play in studio.

I'll talk to the powers that be, Rosemary. Depends on the size of the circle. And how far. Did you map Rabbit Bay for our listeners?

- Rabbit Bay is on Baffin Island, Allison.

Did I say I didn't know where Rabbit Bay was?

- I took a guess.

You're not my favourite anymore.

Anyway. I know they're not Jaikin's favourite, but here's Polaris nominees and Juno winners A Tribe Called Red. This is "Trap Heat." I'll be here on the other side of the news, in ten minutes.

Hanna occupied most of the couch in the waiting area outside the studio. She'd nested there with her coat, my coat, and my phone. Asleep when I came out, and cradling my phone like an animal. Someone had covered her with another coat, full-length and soft with synthetic fur.

"Hey."

She whimpered. I waited for her to wake up, ten, fifteen minutes. When she didn't, I shook her. "I'm finished."

"Oh."

She sat up in my T-shirt and blinked at me. "Can we go home?"

"Sure. I'll get my purse."

"No, I mean." She stood up and wiggled her pants back into place around her non-existent waist. One hand still holding my phone. She had it against her breastbone. The case was visibly sticky.

"What?"

"I want to go *home*. I want my clothes and my stuff and my phone, okay?"

I stared at her. "I don't think I can do that."

"Why not?"

I didn't have all the details. I'd listened, more or less, before the press conference, to a brief, highly sanitized account of Ethan and Claudia's deaths. A police volunteer had handed out tissues. Hanna had stayed in the hotel room with Maegan the social worker while the adults were routed away to review the facts. They said if we wanted more information, later, it would be made available to us.

It had been, by my count, three days. Two and a half.

"Did they tell you what happened?"

Hanna looked away from me. "I want to go home."

I said, "I'll talk to someone."

:::●:::

They give you a pamphlet when someone is murdered. How to access community supports. How to access the court system. Compensation for victims.

I was left imagining a compensation form. *Please provide receipts for all expenses related to your loss. Itemized lists will expedite this process. All claims are subject to verification. Sign and date.*

I'd had to call four people to find someone who would admit that the house was, as it were, released. The police were finished with it. They'd been finished with it for hours or days. Only, I didn't have keys. Hanna didn't have keys. Ethan's parents, I thought, had keys, but I couldn't imagine asking them.

I called Maegan. She wasn't in. I keyed my way through her voicemail to reach a central desk. Explained who I was. What I wanted.

It took ages. A woman, maybe sixty, interceded on my behalf with the powers of bereavement, and finally brought me the keys at the broadcast office. I hadn't gone back to the hotel yet. I needed to check out. Find out how long, exactly, I could keep broadcasting from Winnipeg. Three days? I had a band-in-studio show booked for next Wednesday. Dossiers for a week of guests on my desk in Toronto.

Ellie phoned me halfway through the afternoon. "We're going to get you a sub-host, Allison."

"You don't need to." Thinking about booking a flight home. How it was harder when airlines demanded you buy round-trip tickets, and you always needed to know *when* in advance.

"You lost your . . . you're dealing with family stuff. It's *okay.*"

"Ellie."

"Allison. I promise I won't let them replace you this week, okay?"

I said, "I need to work."

"I'll send you some dossiers. Upcoming guests."

"They have to be readable on my phone."

"Okay."

"Don't let them replace me."

"I won't. We'll get someone good to sub for you, though. I'll see who's in the building. Perfect world, who do you want?"

"Lindsay Avon."

"I think she's on tour."

"I don't think she wants my job, either. That's why I want her."

"I'll ask. Otherwise, you know. I'll ask for someone who has a better job than yours. Just to be safe. Are you okay?"

"I want to go home."

"Oh, lucky girl, you are home. You wrote a whole book about it, remember?"

~ 6 ~
The House

I set my phone to navigate the trip, and we changed busses at the new Confusion Corner station. It was blue and raised above the ground, reminding me of filmic Japanese train stations, which I suspected was the point. Less dingy and exposed than the old exchange. Less snow-bound. Nobody was going to write songs about this place for years, but it shone. It echoed like the aftermath of a war. A guy asked me for spare change, asked Hanna when I ignored him. She crowded up to me, like she'd never been asked for money before.

On the bus, though, she settled in a seat-pair across from me, out of arm's reach, and looked pointedly out the window. I watched her for a while, then crossed the aisle and sat down, crowding her in.

We swept through the early-60s low-rise coziness of Grant Park. A Mennonite-run retirement community stared across the street at a Jewish Seniors' complex that rose higher, distinguished by its rounded modernist design in the midst of generic architecture.

It looked just like Winnipeg, albeit south Winnipeg, the land of middle-class white people, that I'd visited but never fully lived in.

"Are you poor?" Hanna asked.

I turned to her. "Why do you ask?"

"You don't have a car."

"I live in Toronto."

"We're on the bus."

"The bus works fine."

"The bus doesn't really go where I live."

"The map says we can get practically there."

"You'll see."

She wasn't wrong. After it left Grant Park, the bus looped through a min-iature walled city surrounding a frozen synthetic lake. We ran down one side — the wrong side, my phone informed me — then waited ten minutes at the Wal-Mart exchange before doubling back. The next bus, according to the phone, would be along in just sixty-five minutes.

There were no sidewalks. If anyone took the bus out of that miniature city, they were underage and agile enough to scramble over the snowbanks along the curb.

Hanna jumped. I staggered after.

The side streets curled crescents within crescents, punctuated by non-sequential house numbers. Postal confusion was forfended by central mail delivery points. Cars pulled up, children emerged, emptied the boxes, and climbed back in. We were the only people walking.

The house itself had a double garage emerging gravidly from the two-storey hulk behind it. Off-white siding, almost blue. The buried lawn had been wrecked by tire tracks. They cut through the snow, pushed it back, strewed street dirt and other fluids into the white banks. Nobody who'd staked out the house had cleaned up after. At least the police service had locked the doors when they were finished.

The key I'd been given didn't fit the front door lock. Hanna said, "Nobody uses that door. Come on."

So we came through the garage. Beside the paired parked cars, Hanna keyed a nine-digit code and the house door released without any key being applied. She pushed at it. I caught her arm. "Hanna, where does this go into?"

"Kitchen."

"We'll use the front door. Do you have a key anywhere?"

"It's *open*."

"Humour me."

She huffed. Reached upwards, scrambling finally to scale the raw garage shelving, and retrieved a plastic box from a high level. Flipped it to reveal a key taped to the bottom.

"Let me go first."

"There's nobody *in* there."

She was right and she was wrong. I should have left her at the hotel. Laid her in her grandparents' arms, spirited away with a list of wishes, come back with all her chosen possessions and no girl walking into a crime scene.

It was a very white house. I wasn't sure how much blood there was.

None, in fact. Not in the living room. Not, from a quick glance, in the kitchen. I didn't look behind the butcher-block-topped island. Hanna was already loose, running upstairs with her shoes off, quick as a kid returning to her own space.

Straight to her room.

I looked around.

The kitchen smelled like a school janitor had been through: it reeked of some powerful disinfectant. The floor was very clean. Just the floor, though. There were bread crumbs on the counter and kitchen-grit around the sink and the sponge in the drying tray stank. The trash in the bag under the sink stank more.

I crouched to pull it out. Up close, there were dark marks on the cabinets. Just small ones, but blood, unmistakably.

The broken chair was gone. They were one short at the dining island

I got down on my knees. The floor was so clean. My kitchen floor had never been that clean, not for five minutes in my whole life. It was warm, too. Heating coils lurked under those tiles. No forced air here to blow the dust around. I lay back on it and felt my back tighten and release as my spine realigned itself to the level surface. Stared at the ceiling. Its small dark spots of moisture and dirt, and the occasional brighter spots. Brown, brown, brown. Red.

I studied the ceiling and tried to decide if there was anything more substantial stuck to it. Bits of hair. Brains. Blood clots. Skin.

That last one didn't alliterate.

The bar chairs next to the island called to me. I pressed my heels to the floor and pushed, slid across the slick clean space to stare at their bottoms. Dark-stained wood, white cushioned seats. I wouldn't have chosen them. They looked, I thought, both expensive and tacky. Something you'd buy in a set at a big-box home store to fill a gigantic house. In five years, you'd donate it or sell it on Kijiji and get a different set. New colours.

How big was the house? I'd only seen it from outside, and most of that had been car housing. How far back did it go? Did the foyer, with its bevelled windows and two-storey ceiling, eat into the living space, or did they have it to spare?

I went back and stood in the foyer. Tilted my head back, expecting a chandelier. Instead, there were spider plants hanging over the second-storey view.

Ethan's, I thought. He'd grown them in his teenaged bedroom, encouraged by their weirdness or the name. They'd been smaller, but that was years ago. More than two decades. These could be their descendants, or the same plants. Inheritors. I had to know.

Up the white-carpeted stairs for a closer look.

There was a plastic watering-can on the mezzanine.

Mezzanine.

It was a nice house. In Toronto — or, realistically, Mississauga, because I didn't think Toronto proper had beasts like this — it would run just about 1.4 million. Less in Winnipeg, but how much less? They had money. Double income, one-and-a-half kids, two cars. Photos in artful black and white of the three of them (the half-child was invisible) on vacation. Somewhere tropical but not beachy.

Inland Hawaii. Maybe Costa Rica.

"Hanna, where were these pictures taken?"

No answer. Her door was shut. Music came through it harmonizing boy-band vocals on a synth-pop track.

I'd learned a few songs by earlier incarnations of this layer of sound. I knew the Jonas Brothers' "Love Bug." I knew a couple of Hansen tracks. This was One Direction, though. I didn't know the band, really, but given her age, it had to be them. Their music was fundamentally the same as the Backstreet Boys and the New Kids on the Block, and Take Five, and the Bay Street Rollers, and the Monkees. I hadn't had that, at her age.

I wondered if I was jealous, or grateful that I'd missed this saccharine stage in my musical development.

Hanna's bedroom had a poster for *Frozen* on the door. Blue-toned stars and the snow queen.

Master suite to my left. A king-sized bed lounged in a field of hardwood, and silky, heavy curtains covering the windows, still closed. Claudia's work suit lay crumpled on the bed. Ethan's jeans on the floor to one side.

He hadn't changed back yet. He died in his work clothes, still wrapped in sweat and low-grade stress.

The master bath had a door, at least. I'd seen houses where the tub was simply in an alcove, the toilet hidden behind a half-wall. The better for erotic bathing, sexual adventures leaping from water to mattress. Scented candles and Turkish towels.

Jesus, the bathroom.

He'd done it in here, not in the main one. The other child. He'd died here. The disinfectant smell was overpowering. Insufficient. The tub was stained with blood. The bathmat was stained with blood. The towels were all in pools on the floor, mouldering, undisinfected.

I shut the door. Not slammed it. Shut. Very gently. No sound.

When you have a baby, something chemical happens to your brain. Hormones flood your system, demanding fundamental behavioural changes, and guaranteeing that the tiny being you've just forced out of your body will become the centre of your universe.

Oxytocin is the foundation of love, and it's triggered by labour. It heightens the mother's sense of smell, so that she buries her nose in her sticky, slick infant's head as soon as she can reach it.

Vasopressin is more ferocious. It lets you look at the creature lying against your clammy, exhausted body, and inform it, *I will die for you.*

Prolactin feeds the baby and lulls you to sleep.

The hormones didn't entirely work for me. The other women I encountered in my hours in the hospital had knife-like attachments. *This is my baby. Do not touch it. Do not take it. I will cut you.* Softened by exhaustion and the routine lull of hospital and family, but still very much present. I didn't get that, the urge not to let go of her. Hanna never ceased to be terrifying, a dependent, almost-blind, almost-boneless creature. She haunted my sleep.

I handed her to anyone who held out their arms. I'd happily have killed things for her, but I would have preferred her to stay home, in someone else's custody, while I did it. It meant, I thought, that I would have been better off on the other side of the process. I'd have made a decent, if absent, father.

Kara and Mary-Beth were with me when Hanna was born, but they had other things going on, and no one, really, can help you mother.

I tried. I think I really did.

When she was just past a year old, I gave Hanna over completely to Ethan and Claudia, and they were so *happy* about it. It was like all the hormones I'd been missing had followed after Hanna in a cloud and flooded these other, better parents as soon as they had the baby in their arms.

I wasn't alright. I'd first handed our daughter to Ethan so that I could go into a psychiatric stabilization program. They needed to re-adjust the medications that pregnancy and childbirth had stopped, and the moods that hormones had ruined. I'd been dysthymic for weeks, and I could see the edges of my life running up towards me like bad animation.

This particularly: I always expected Claudia to be angry at me. I did, in fact, sleep with her husband. He was my husband first, but I hadn't done a good job of keeping him, whereas Claudia had selected him as a sane adult who enjoyed his company as well as his body in the dark.

I suppose they must have hashed it out between them, in the months between our divorce and Hanna's arrival.

She took the baby out of my arms, smelled her head, and said, "Take care of yourself, honey." To me, as if she didn't want any part of my skin to come off.

:::◉:::

Hanna wouldn't come out of her room. I'd retreated to the living room, but Hanna was upstairs. I climbed back up. Found the guest bedroom (had it been his, the stepson's, when he visited?) and stretched out on the bed. Stared at the ceiling.

The phone rang, and I answered the landline by the bed out of habit before I realized the ringtone was mine. There was no name showing up, and I considered not answering. The ringing stopped. Started again. I picked it up.

"I have a request to make of you." Elaine's voice was blunt in the way of squared-off firewood: efficient and full of potential splinters.

"I'm listening."

"The woman from social services said Hanna wanted to stay at the house. Is that correct?"

"I could probably get her to leave. There'd be a scene, though."

"Say yes if you mean yes, Allison."

"Yes. Hanna wants to stay."

"I can't go in there," Elaine said.

I nodded. Remembered she couldn't see me and made a throat-sound, the one I made on-air to signal nodding.

"My son died in that house."

"You could talk to Hanna. Ask her to come out. I'll take her the phone."

"I want you to stay there with her."

For how long? I needed to know, badly. I had been considering *The Cure's* upcoming guests until Elaine phoned me. Carefully, using the hotel phone, on the number that she didn't have until, I suppose, the social worker gave it to her.

"Just. I need you to stay with her. We need you to. Until she's ready to leave."

I said, "They didn't clean the bathroom."

"I'm sorry?"

"It's really bad."

Elaine paused. Choked. I thought she'd hung up on me. I went to dial her back and found the line still open. She said, "I can't, Allison. You have to."

:::●:::

Hanna wasn't a waif. She was half an orphan with half a mother, but she had a family network worthy of any Mennonite Manitoban girl. She had two living sets of grandparents.

She had two uncles on Ethan's side, and three aunts. An aunt on Claudia's. Nearly all of them would be married by now. There would be cousins. Second cousins. She wasn't alone; she was related to half the province. People had children on human schedules, one stage after the next, all photographed and posted to social media for extended family. Ethan sent me a few of the pictures, to keep me in the loop.

One layer out from those postings, there lurked my own family. Ethan's family lived in the same town they did, just north of Winnipeg. Unless something changed, they still all went to the same church.

If I let myself become too visible, they might come for me.

Hanna had cousins. Godparents. Layers of family. She had the tangential relatives of her half a brother.

I couldn't remember his father's name. The other survivor, who was he?

Claudia's computer, in her office in the basement, was turned on. It had windows open and every application running. Everything with a detail of her life was still on display. That wasn't like her. Claudia put away her laundry when it was done and her shoes when she came in the door. I guessed it was the police who'd made this mess. They would have wanted to know everything, in case the scene wasn't what it looked like. In case there was . . . what? Someone else? A mysterious, highly systematic killer?

In Claudia's Facebook, her friends and relations spiderwebbed outwards, all linked to her profile page. That first look didn't take me to her ex, but it took me to her son.

His page was ugly. It was covered in comments from everyone he'd ever met. Some of the posts were as psychosexually tangled as the comments on my single press statement. Some of them were worse, because they were adoring. Girls he went to high school with couldn't believe it. They could not believe that someone so beautiful could be gone from this world.

Oh, Collin? How could you do such a thing? Hurt yourself? Didn't you know we loved you?

I worked backwards. Collin's last name. Back through Claudia's network to David, whose page was locked.

I opened her contacts. Found David. Keyed all his details into my phone.

I killed the computer, window by window. Shut it down. Unplugged it.

Turned off the lights.

She squeaked, caught in the dark.

"Hanna."

"I'm hungry."

I sighed. "What do you want?"

"Toasted cheese."

"Go nuts."

She stood there, in the doorway. Not allowed in here, I thought. Then, deliberately, carefully, she said, "Will you please make me a toasted cheese sandwich?"

"If there's any food in the fridge."

There was. Three kinds of cheese, each in a press-and-seal bag to keep it fresh. Havarti, parmesan in a hard block, aged cheddar. White, sliced bread. I dug for a knife.

"I want plastic."

"Huh?"

"Plastic cheese. In my sandwich. And mustard."

I stared into the fridge. Processed cheese slices, individually wrapped, lurked in the back. "Do you want tomato soup with this?"

"Why would I want that?"

"Tomato soup goes with grilled cheese."

"I don't want soup. And I don't like tomatoes."

She ate the sandwich. I realized, watching her, that I'd failed in my slicing responsibilities. I should take the sandwich back, cut it twice, on the diagonals. Since I didn't, she ate it whole. Got down from the bar stool, crossed to the fridge, poured herself milk. Retrieved a pickle from the massive refrigerator jar.

"I'm still hungry." Pause. "Can I make myself something?"

"I think you can officially make yourself anything you want."

The pizza pockets were buried in the chest freezer in the basement. Everything else was carefully packaged; these were open and partially freezer-burned. Hawaiian flavour. Hanna microwaved them. Dug into a shuttered cupboard, dragged a chair over and climbed that, found chips in a clear Old Dutch bag on the top shelf. Barbecue.

"Can I eat in my room?"

"Sure, why not?"

I waited until she was gone. Milk in one hand, pizza pockets on a plate, chips under her arm. The music she deafened the world with turned back on.

In the opened pantry, I found more chips. In the wicker basket next to them, I found dark chocolate, for cooking.

I made myself grilled cheese with the other cheeses. Carved away blue spots off the cheese bricks and threw them into the stinking trash. Took it outside.

The garbage bin, I discovered, lived in the garage, and had to be put out front. Garbage cycle five (highlighted on the fridge) had its pickup on Tuesdays, this month. I'd missed it. Everything would have to stink, outdoors, until next week.

I took my food and went upstairs.

Hanna's door was shut. Music loud. I couldn't hear her voice. If she'd found her phone, she wasn't talking on it. Texting, I thought. Kids texted. They did it secretly, in class, behind doors. If I was going to reach her, I needed Hanna's number.

Downstairs. Boot up Claudia's computer.

It asked for a password.

Four tries. Right answer: ClaudiaEthan.

Hanna's cell. Its number. Find-it code. Access code.

Dishes needed to be washed. I couldn't find soap. The dishwasher stood empty, spots ugly on the stainless-steel door.

I typed, *Hanna, are you okay? Do you need anything?*

im ok

My phone capitalized and punctuated automatically. Hers had to. Had she gone in, fixed it so it wouldn't?

Your grandma says you can stay here if you want.

Ok

I still needed my things. I needed, if I was going to stay here, to check out of the hotel.

I needed a shower.

The main bathroom was massive, clean of blood other than menstrual traces in the trash, tampons under the sink.

I stayed in the shower a long time. When the water ran cold and I turned it off, I discovered that the towels smelled like Ethan.

I fell asleep in the bathroom, with my cheek against the towel. Wet. Naked. Later, I woke up with the lights off, in a world coloured by a small Disney-themed night-light. Hanna had dragged other towels loose from the cupboard and built herself a bed beside me.

~ 7 ~
Mythos

L ike Hanna, I was not an orphan. After a fashion, I suppose I orphaned myself. I found an official representative of the state, and I expressed that I would *not* be returned to my family. I had a perfect weapon in this campaign.

They made me get married.

I'm fifteen.

They made me.

This wasn't supposed to be possible. There was a law on the books that you had to have parental consent to marry if you were under eighteen. That a family court judge was required to sign off on an order if you were under sixteen. Still, before the internet, looking up details like that was a problem. The regional library might not have had a complete set of rules. The church might not.

Your church might say, *Yes, you can and should get married.*

I might have said, *Yes, I think this is a good idea.*

Yes, I want to.

I want to get married.

It might have been my idea.

You don't have legal volition at fifteen, though. You can't be the person who ignores the rules, who adjusts Allison's birthday when copying information onto the marriage license. Makes her two years older. Not a legal adult, but close enough.

That sort of crime brings not only social workers, but the police.

I hadn't expected that.

I wanted to leave, but I had no experience at running away from home. I'd read about it, but all the accounts were either fantasies of a not-quite-pastoral quasi-England, or urban narratives with cities that swallowed little girls.

You can run away like Jane Eyre across the moors and meet your cousin, learn German, and not marry him even though he's perfectly nice, if a bit imperialistic in his intentions for the Indian subcontinent. I could have run away across the fields and met my own cousins, who'd have given me dinner and driven me home, and my parents would have been very reasonable about it. Told me that if I needed to go somewhere, they would be happy to drive me.

Except, they'd gone off on their own missionary ventures, though not to India. They'd packed up and left without me.

The room the police interviewed me in felt like a classroom. A blonde woman with gorgeous shoes talked to me softly for a couple of hours, about Ethan and my baby and how much I understood about sex, really.

I told her about childbirth. About working with my mother to deliver babies on two continents. About the baby my mother had with me in lurking attendance.

A year later, I might have given her different answers. By then I'd read the complete *Joy of Sex*, complete with the details about navel-fucking and how to do it on a motorcycle.

In the end, she studied me like she wasn't sure whether to lock me in a box, and I said, "Please don't make me go home with them."

"Do you think they're going to hurt you?"

I thought, *Lie.*

I couldn't imagine anyone believing it. Ethan's parents were as wholesome as anyone I could imagine, and they'd already successfully raised kids who could speak for them. They'd agreed to take care of me, since I couldn't travel with my parents. Since I was pregnant. Since I'd married their son. Since I'd walked my whore body into their house.

I said, "If you send me back, I'll run away again."

I said, "If you send me back, I'll kill myself."

One of those. I'm fairly sure I said one of those things.

The best part, later, was telling people they put me in the mental hospital. Not exactly true, but part of the necessary mythos. They did send me for a three-day assessment. The girls on the ward with me were anorexics and cutters, and the one girl with emergent schizophrenia simply didn't talk, just drew for hours on yellow legal pads with luminous ball-point pens. I was allowed to wear my own clothes.

I was a little disappointed.

I threw up on my clothes, carefully. They put me in scrubs while my clothes were washed. They brought them back and I threw up on them again, and that was the end of wearing my own clothes.

We were being watched, for our own safety. After I vomited, they shifted me to the room with the bulimics. We didn't go to the bathroom on our own. We ate in groups.

I missed the cutters. Three of them: Adeline, Amber, and Kelly. They had marks not just on their arms but all over their bodies. Amber's belly was crossed with red, healing lines that puckered with recently-cleared infections. Adeline wore socks all the time because she'd carved up the soles of her feet. I didn't show them my arms, which were only scratched in comparison. I didn't know much about how to do real damage to myself. It hadn't occurred to me, before, that you could repurpose so many household objects. It was something that I might have learned if I'd gone to public school.

Kelly had carved patterns into her thighs with her geometry set. Not, she said, to make it hurt. She'd just been bored. Her fingernails had been chewed more or less off. That, she said, hurt. Hospital gloves on her fingers. Blood traces inside them.

There was a lot of crying. They were always crying.

Always *crying*.

This is the joke: they caught me in a completely level phase. Not manic. Not dysthymic. Not bottomed out. I was well-spoken, unexpectedly well-read, polite. Church girl on the run. Too calm to be borderline, too intact to be depressive.

Years later, when I wrote about this, I was disappointed not to have been more picturesquely mad. Borderline Personality Disorder would have been so *apt*. So very *do-it-with-a-rock-star*. I could have pulled it off: the screaming performances, the clinging, the weeping, and the rage. Those were the traits of a girl who flees her husband and her parents and lands in a tangle of orphans and lesbian separatists.

I got worse and better. I met Billy, who gave me a crooked *we both know you're smarter than they are* look. And gum.

49

The only time I remember crying, that week, was in the janitor's unlocked closet, sitting by the antiseptic-reeking mop bucket. Waves of *what did I do?*

Billy worked there. He'd come in looking for something. I said, *My baby died.*

He said, *Do you want another one?*

God. Yes.

Yes?

I said it out loud. Like I thought he'd have one in his backpack. He had gum and cigarettes, and I shared one with him in the stairwell.

He said, *You think they're going to let you out?*

I don't know. Maybe?

If they do, I'll help you.

He wrote his phone number on my belly, just below my bra-line, while I held up my shirt. I looked down, later, and I couldn't read it upside down. In the metallic half-reflective bathroom, it was only slightly clearer. I wrote what I could make out on my arms as many times as I could to get it right.

They observed me for longer than seventy-two hours, but after a week they decided that, except for the vomiting, I was fine. For the vomiting, they injected my hip with Gravol and declared me cured, then sent me packing.

When I got loose, all my writing was smudged. Numbers were missing.

I slept at the group home and dug through everyone's pockets for loose change while they were showering. Earned an immediate reputation as a kleptomaniac.

I went through fourteen quarters, later, getting Billy's phone number right. Trying to reach him.

I didn't know Billy's last name. I couldn't remember his voice anymore. He was ragged-haired and blonde. He smelled like cigarettes and something else that I couldn't identify yet.

This stupid girl in a phone booth, at a strip mall in Charleswood, saying, "Is Billy there?"

"He's out."

"Oh."

"You want to leave a message?"

"Tell him Allison called."

Like it meant something. *You know, Allison, the girl with the fewest cutting marks. The one who made out with you in the stairwell and sat in your lap and thought about whether she could carve another baby out of your body. Whether she could keep pulling parts out of boys' bodies until she got it right.*

Little heartbeat.

I had the number right. I needed more quarters.

"Billy?"

"Hey, yeah. Where are you?"

He had a car. It was a shitty car, but he was old enough to drive, and the staggering bronze Reliant smelled like him.

He thought he was a bad man.

He bought me stuff. McDonald's, which I'd only had a half-dozen times in my life. He wanted to know about where I was from. Was it really a cult? Did I have sex with the devil? Did we sacrifice babies?

Is that what happened to your baby?

I climbed out of his car on Portage while it was rolling-stopped at a light and walked back into suburbia, to the group home where they stored girls who weren't domesticated enough to assign to artificial parents.

We had bunk beds. Girls filled this anonymous detached ranch house, two to a room, three in the basement. I was new, so I went downstairs. Bottom bunk.

"You're late."

"Was he cute?"

I said, "He made me mad, so I killed him."

"Sure. We'll see it on the news?"

"Baby-killing Satanists. We know how to hide the bodies. Why we never get caught."

"Whatever, Jesus-girl."

Billy came back. Sat outside. Got me to come out into the scrabbling humidity and told me about the water-child ceremonies in Japan.

You want to save your baby's soul, right? So you get a stone doll and you make it a hat.

It sounded like a lie. I walked into the back yard, climbed the fence into the woods and he followed me. I said, "If you touch me, I'll sacrifice you."

"I was *joking* about you being a Satanist."

"I know. You don't think I look like one. It's why no one suspects me."

He kissed me. Pulled me down to lie in the wet, insect-ridden grass by the fence. "Hey. Hey, I think you're pretty."

You think I'm stupid. But I let him put my hand in his pants. Kiss him and let him come in my hand. Hot and wet between my legs, too.

I don't think he'd ever been to Japan, just, maybe, he'd read a library book about it or heard a story from someone. He wasn't all that smart. He believed me when I told him I could haunt him, now, because I had the traces of his spirit he left on me.

He laughed while I drew a pentagram on the fence in semen, but when he thought I was gone he tried to rub it away. Cut himself on a half-protruding nail and wound up smearing blood over the mess.

I like to think he got lockjaw. For sure, he would have thought it was me, following him and cursing him whenever he tried to sleep.

⁖⁖⁖

Mostly, no one kept track of us. The group home had a staff, but as long as we didn't start fights or fires, they were content not to monitor us too closely. No one was sure what to do with me, anyway. I'd never been to a recognizable school. *Home-schooled* wasn't a concept most people had yet, and none of the local high schools would take me until I'd been assessed. The waiting list for educational assessment was months long.

I stayed home and read for days at a time until my roommate was suspended from school. She made it clear that if she had to be home, I had to be elsewhere.

I started walking.

It was a long way into the city proper. I caught busses when I could get on with packs of girls and disappear when they wanted the fare, or I hitch-hiked. I must have had a charmed skin not to be killed.

I walked for hours.

The city's core was closer to what I'd expected real life to look like. I hung out there for hours, until I was exhausted, and I could bum a quarter from someone to call home. *I got lost.*

You're fifteen years old. What do you mean you're lost?

I have never, ever before been in a city. Lies. I'd been to cities most of my roommates couldn't pronounce. Hamburg. Cairo. Bujumbura. Dar es Salaam and Kigali. Lagos. I'd spent six weeks once in Minneapolis, some of it by myself. *I don't know how to get home.*

The staff sent a car for me, sometimes, or paid for a cab, but twice they sent the police to collect me. Other kids already cuffed in the back hissed at me while they took me away, back to suburbia.

So, you think you can manage to stay home?

I didn't run away. I got lost. I'm new here.

Where were you before?

I lived in a cult. In Neuenheim. Before that in Africa.

The first time, the police officers reached out to me. Rubbed my arms and told me I was safe, that Jesus was with me now. The second time, one of them sneered.

I'm from Neuenheim, too, and you're a sick, sad little girl.

I waited until he was gone and the house door was shut to say, *One of us is.*

••••❘❘❘

I kept leaving. I wore other girls' raggedy clothes, jeans that were too short until I ripped out the knees, and then they were too long, pooling around my feet. I found somebody's abandoned green church-going tights to layer underneath. Ugly T-shirts. No bra. Tank tops when I could get them, and sweet little-girl clothes when I couldn't. One of the house-managers bought me a bra, polyester out of a box and the wrong size, and I left it on the bathroom floor.

They assessed my education. We went downtown and I did a battery of tests, and they said I had odd deficits, but not as many as they could have predicted, and that I could go to school.

You run away from home and they make you go to *school.*

I went with hair in my eyes. Cheap runners. The polished Charleswood girls wore oversized Mondetta sweatshirts and slinky panties that they showed off in the locker room.

I couldn't stay there. They'd have devoured me.

And if they didn't kill and eat me, the Christians would have come for me. I could see them, planning their campus ministries and circling in for recruitment. They were always blonde.

I had to shed my aura of salvation before they caught me.

I stood in the basement with the group home's oldest girl. We washed my hair with Kool-Aid. At the end, I was red and sticky as cheap sugarless candy.

At school, I wrote on my arms with magic marker. A picture of the Cheshire Cat, drawn from memory. A cupcake with a happy face.

Eat me.

All teenaged girls, I think, love *Alice in Wonderland* at some point.

I made it through two classes with my improvised ink before a teacher noticed. Grabbed my wrist and pulled me up. Sleeve up, arm exposed.

The first instinct I had was to scream, *I don't know you, you're not allowed to touch me.*

He took me to the vice-principal's office. They made me scrub my forearms, first with hand soap and then with diluted industrial cleaner. Then they tried to rub the pictures off. My work still echoed there, under the skin, vivid in the raw red:

Eat me.

The scratch-marks on my arms were still there, shedding their scabs, getting uglier. Begging infection.

They sent me to the nurse's office, where I was informed that, due to budget cuts, they didn't keep bandages of any size and I'd have to keep looking. Thence to the Home Economics room, where scraps from the last class' sewing projects were repurposed. *Wrap her up. Cover it.*

Allison is a lot of trouble. Look at this mess.

It was the sort of thing they suspended girls for, but someone had written a note in my file. *Allison is a Very Nice Girl who's had a Hard Time. She was home-schooled. She is Christian. She will be very, very good if you don't scare her.*

I wondered where Kelly the cutter went to school when she wasn't in the hospital. She'd carved patterns into her skin, in class, and nobody'd said anything for a week. Maybe I could go to school there.

I wasn't suspended, but I took myself out. I stayed home, sitting in the basement bathroom when my room wasn't safe. I read my textbooks, worked through them. Wrote out answers to the end-of-chapter questions. Put together an essay of sorts on the battered Young Adult novel they'd handed me for English class. It contained nothing with words longer than six letters. Simple ideas.

I didn't find Kelly anywhere I looked in the city, but I met gutter punks, and they all told me the same thing. *Fuck school. Go to the library. You might learn something.*

Go downtown. Start looking for the girls you want to be with.

Keep walking.

Downtown Winnipeg was tangled with old stone storybook churches. Guys sat beside their stone fences and drank beer. Suggested I might like to suck them.

Come on, pretty. Fuck, you look like a lollipop, c'mere girl.

Guy who followed me for two blocks. *Nobody can hear you.*

I whirled on him. I was furious, and there was traffic everywhere. It wasn't like we were alone. *Everyone can hear me. You have no idea.*

Gonna fuck your corpse, little bitch.

I stared. I didn't think I could stand him off. He was too dirty and sick of the world to be scared of Satanists.

I said, *I'll give you AIDS.*

Fucking dirty bitch.

I kept walking. He didn't follow.

Out of downtown. Westward.

Flyers covered the light posts on Sherbrooke Street.

I didn't go home. I stayed up all night. I went to the show.

I came to the door with five crumpled dollars and they just pushed me in without taking my money. One more girl in the club. The bouncer had metal all through his face.

I learned the mosh pit by feel, how to move with the crowd, scream back at the stage. To drive out an elbow every time I felt a hand on my breast.

It occurred me that if they were bigger, I could weaponize my tits. Let them swing free and knock out assholes who got too close. They'd need to be huge. Covered in metal. Sharp.

The crowd pushed.

Jump forward. Climb the stage.

You can climb up on anything when your guts have already been ripped out. I had raw places on my arms from where steel wool had tried to take the words off my skin.

You are very, very, very angry. You can do whatever you want.

Jump from the speakers. Dive from the stage.

A hand went down my pants. I stood there in the middle of the room. Spit at all of them. Staggered to the back. I had five dollars, enough for one-and-a-half Cokes, room temperature and maybe spiked with something.

Jump before anyone else touches you.

Go outside if you're going to throw up.

That was how I met Kara. I was puking out of adrenaline and smoke-sickness. Kara came out of the club behind me and spat on the pavement, blood and saliva and what might have been something thicker. She was working on a black eye. We looked at each other.

"You want to go for a walk?" she said.

"I don't know where I am."

"That's perfect. Come on."

She'd come by skateboard, but to keep me company she walked. We wandered for miles, over the train yards and into the wilds of the city's metal-sharp north end. In through the back door that was unlocked for us, and up the stairs to Kara's bedroom. In the morning, we both went down to sit at the plasticky dining table and eat Cheerios.

If you do this right, you can move right in. You can stay here forever.

⇜ 8 ⇝

Octopus

Eden called before it was really morning, and I had to grope for my phone on the bathroom counter. It was almost dead. I crawled into the hall, and got to my feet there, holding a clammy towel around myself while he talked.

He'd come back the night before, slept through the afternoon and evening, and woken up in the small hours, realizing finally that I wasn't there.

"Where are you?"

I said, "You haven't checked your messages?"

"I have seventeen messages. They aren't all from you."

"I think they might be."

I thought about being back in Toronto with Eden. He'd have come to my room, burrowed in beside me and mouthed my hair for a while. He always wore pajamas like a kid in a 50s movie, all plaid and buttons.

Our house without me must smell, I realized. I'd left food thawing on the counter. He wouldn't have noticed, yet.

"What's going on, Alli?"

I said, "How was Miami?"

"Hot. It's like another planet down there. You should go with me next time. How come you aren't here? It's early for you to be at work."

"I'm in Winnipeg."

"What?"

I was too tired. Couldn't assemble a full explanation. I'd left him at least a dozen messages, progressively more and then maybe a bit less hysterical. *I have to go to the airport. There's been an accident. A murder. Three murders. Two murders. I'm so cold. I won't be home. Clean up the kitchen. Come find me, please please please. Take your meds. Find my meds. Come home and pick up your messages. Call me.*

"It's on your messages. Too early, here. I have stuff to do. I gotta sleep."

"You sound bad."

"Yeah."

"Did you take your pills?"

I tried to think what day it was. I'd had a handful of tablets in my purse, but they were gone. I needed to call my pharmacy in Toronto, the corner-shop one with the senior-citizen clientele. Ask them to fax everything to Winnipeg. I had to find a pharmacy in Winnipeg to have them fax it to.

I couldn't possibly do all that. The sheer complexity made it impossible.

"I just need to sleep," I said.

"What time is it there?"

Don't look at the table. "Four something? I need my glasses."

"Okay. Go back to bed."

"Yeah."

"I'll stay on the phone with you."

I couldn't believe how sore I was. In the still-lit bathroom, Hanna was sleeping on the floor.

"Can I put you down for a sec?"

"Sure."

I laid the phone on the master bed, face up. Withdrew and then came back and listened for a while to him breathing over the digital distance.

I couldn't possibly pick Hanna up. She was going to be so cold.

Pink comforter from her bed. Pillows. I found a couple of stuffed animals and tucked them beside her. Turned off the light, left the fan on. When she was tiny, disruptions in sound would throw her out of sleep, make her scream until I couldn't hang on to my own skin. One time I let the vacuum run for two hours just to keep her still.

Eden was still there. I could hear him breathing even before I spoke.

He said, "I'm going to stay on the line with you until you fall asleep."

"You'll know?"

"I'll hear the snoring."

"I don't snore." Pause. "Never mind. Okay."

I curled up in that huge bed, wrapped around the tiny phone. In the background, I could hear Eden's fingers on his silvery computer keyboard. Sorting footage from the southernmost edges of the United States to be merged into a music-video project for an American band, ambient electronica with money behind it to pay for whatever he was planning next.

He said, "The water was so warm I kept forgetting I was actually wet."

"That sounds amazing."

"Too many people, though. It was insane. If they'd wanted footage in full daylight, I'd never have been able to manage. And I think something bit me. I've got red marks on my arms."

"Sunburn?"

"Just night shoots, remember?"

"Good."

"I met this guy, at the hostel where I was staying. He talked for, like, two hours about how much he hates the Keys. Said he moved there and his daughter was hit by a car and killed the first week. And it'd been a year since then, and nothing better had happened. I couldn't figure out why he just kept staying. Like he thought the place should make it up to him. I don't know if he actually had a daughter. I mean, he was sincere, intense, but he was sort of detached, too, like he was angry but not grieving, and he'd invented the daughter just to give himself a reason to be mad.

"I can't imagine having kids, you know? I think you'd have to be scared all the time. If I had to be as angry as he was, I wouldn't be able to cope.

"Alli?"

"Yeah. I know."

"Go to sleep."

I listened to him typing. Silent images, high definition. I thought he was probably lying about the state of his skin. He'd be sunburned. Some of what he'd had to do — find a hostel, scout the beaches — would have been in daylight, and he always forgot his sunscreen. If he admitted it, though, we'd have to fight about it, so he just presented he wasn't in pain. He went on with things, his hairy back and shoulders livid and peeling. If he slept in my bed while I was away, he'd lose the damaged skin into it. All its rags would still be there for me to clean up when I got back.

Claudia's mother woke me up. She was there, really there, standing over me and my dead phone in the bed.

"You didn't answer. I even called the land line."

I sat up. The still-damp towel balanced across my chest. The rest of me was naked.

"I'm sorry. We . . . it was a hard night."

She nodded. Sat down on the bed beside me, then leaned over and took a pillow and buried her face in it.

"I can't."

Hanna appeared in the doorway. "Grandma?"

Margaret started to sob.

"Hey, hon," I said.

Hanna stared.

"Can you give me a sec so I can get dressed?"

"I woke up in the bathroom."

"I know. I'm sorry."

"Where'd you go?"

I said, "The phone rang." Eden. How many hours ago had that been?

"Oh."

"Give me a second?"

I didn't have any clean clothes. I needed laundry, more clothes, more underwear. I thought of raiding Claudia's drawers, but her mother wouldn't stop crying behind me.

I pulled on my jeans without underwear. My shirt was unholy. I found one of Ethan's and pulled it on instead. "Okay."

Outside, Hanna said, "I'm hungry."

I tried to think where we were. Where food came from, relative to the suburban tangle surrounding the house. What did kids eat? Cereal? Did she want pancakes?

I said, "I think I have to take Hanna out."

"Don't leave me here." Margaret was frantic. She stared up at me. She'd put on makeup, I thought, just like she didn't know tears would melt it.

"Come with us."

She dragged air under her ribs. Stood up. "I'll just wash my face."

Long seconds before I realized I hadn't told her not to use the master bath.

She was on the floor, screaming into her hands, by the time I got there. Hanna zipped up behind me, so close I knocked her jaw with my elbow when I leaned in to pull the woman on the floor away from the mess.

"Hanna get *out.*"

This voice I'd never used before. She got out, but when she reached the landing, I heard her start to scream. I hadn't known a human animal could make a noise like that.

Margaret stared at me. She said, "How could you *sleep* here?"

I said, "There's another bathroom," as though that explained it.

I was the last one out of the house. The other two would have left with the doors wide open, and burned the place behind us, and I thought they might change their minds about that, later, after they'd eaten.

To reach food, I had to drive. I had to load Hanna and Margaret into Margaret's ancient Crown Victoria. They cried separately. Hanna's screams had settled down into little kid sobbing. Margaret cried at an odd, off-key pitch that grated on my nerves.

It was a beautiful day. It had no goddamn right to be.

The phone told me there was an A&W two hundred yards away, but we couldn't get there from here.

Navigate. Go.

We ate grease. It saturated the paper wrappers of the breakfast sandwiches and left fingerprints on the coffee mugs. Hanna swallowed her first bottle of juice before her sandwich and wanted another one.

Juice was expensive. Twice as much as coffee, and it came in tiny, foil-lidded cups. Almost everyone in the restaurant was dressed in work clothes. Old people sat in the corners, having coffee with their tanked oxygen.

I said, "Just, like, give me three or four juices. We'll need them."

"How many?"

"Three or four."

"Please give me a number." The woman at the till was Filipina, probably. Pretty and tiny. I wondered if she'd be forced to leave the country on the day she couldn't bear fast food work anymore. There were so many thousands of people willing to move to this bleak city to serve layers of egg and sausage to half-awake, fractured citizens. How did anyone imagine that, living in the mango-and-refuse scented suburbs of Manila? Did she live in the Filipino enclave in the north end and commute by bus in the pre-dawn? Did she have kids?

Were they here with her, or did she have to leave them behind?

How did you explain to a child that you were leaving their equatorial universe to go feed a troubled, frozen country?

I said, "Four, then."

"Eleven ninety-seven."

"On Mastercard."

Margaret had gone to the bathroom; Hanna was alone at the table, picking apart a potato patty with her fingers and tracing a new universe in oil on the plasticized tabletop.

"You okay?"

Hanna nodded.

Behind me, Margaret said, "We need to do something about the house."

I didn't think she meant *we*, not really. She wasn't going to be the woman who cleaned that bathroom. She hadn't seen the kitchen yet.

"There are services," she said.

"Oh."

"But they will make a mess. First, we need to find the things."

I stared at her.

"We need clothes. Photos." She paused. "Bank records." Her eyes were swollen almost shut. She hadn't slept, I thought. Where was her husband? Had she left him in the hotel room? Would he get out of bed?

Deep breath. "We need to plan the funeral."

The *we* she meant was me.

"Elaine didn't think she could go to the house. I said I would come. If we can gather enough things, I won't have to go again."

It was more complicated than that, I discovered. Both husbands had fled. Marshall, Ethan's father, had gone back to the farm. The cattle needed feeding; the neighbours wouldn't keep doing it forever. My family would be lurking there, across the fields, to see if he'd returned. They'd be watching the roads. Thinking about the tragedy. Not, if I was lucky, thinking at all about me.

▮▮▮

The funeral director's office had an aquarium wall. The tank was stocked with plants and undulating water but not, so far as I could tell, fish. Hanna shot up to it as soon as I turned away from her. Hands on the glass. The director flinched, then visibly forced his irritation into a box. Decorous people, who understood the process of death, didn't, presumably, bring children to these meetings.

I said, "Hanna, do you want my phone?"

"I've got mine."

She was taking pictures. I wondered if anything would translate through the glass' smudged reflections.

The director was younger than I was. He looked about twenty-five, actually, and had a car-salesman edge. Someone, at least, had told him not to wear black suits. On the street outside, I'd seen three guys his age in black suits, jumping through traffic with coffees in both hands. They looked like gangsters. Black suits and purple shirts, vividly clashing neckties. In Toronto, they'd have some kind of model of how men were supposed to dress, but in Winnipeg, they were making up their adult wardrobes out of their own imaginations. At least one was wearing black running shoes with his suit. His pant-legs were too long.

The funeral director's pant-legs were too long, too. He was telling me about caskets. He used words like *respect* and *bereaved* and *tasteful*.

I said *cremation*.

He was disappointed. I wondered what the cost difference was. I said, "They're not in any condition to be seen."

"Oh, we can fix that." He lit up. "They'll look beautiful. Don't you think people should have a chance to say goodbye properly?"

I'd been to funerals while we lived in Burundi, but those took place as soon after death as possible. I'd been to fewer than four in Canada, all for people from the music scene. Only one was open casket. The mortician had covered his tattoos with thick makeup, and I didn't recognize him in there. I'd never seen him with a naked face.

I tried to imagine conveying that to a boy who wanted to sell me an upper-mid-range casket for the price of a used Toyota.

Hanna said, "There's an octopus in here."

She wasn't wrong. It was pale blue, with a long, skirt-like body, wrapped around a chunk of coral in a shady corner of the tank.

The director said, "There are two, actually. That's Frank. Edna's probably in the grass."

"Is she blue, too?"

"Not if she's hiding. She likes to pretend she's a plant."

He knelt in front of the tank. "They're Caribbean Reef Octopi. I just introduced Frank, so he's a bit stand-offish. I'm kind of hoping they'll get together."

"Would they have babies?"

"I really hope so. They'd have about two hundred."

Hanna stared at him. "Would they all fit?"

"No. I'd take some of them home after they hatched. They get big really fast. But a lot of people in town would really like an octopus."

"Why?"

"They're super friendly."

"No way."

63

"Seriously." He went to the closet and retrieved a step-stool and a box from a mini-fridge. "Come on up."

The tank reeked of ocean when he lifted the lid. I thought about a different version of the universe, one where I'd gone with Eden to Florida and swum in the sea while he filmed. I could have met the angry man who hated the Florida Keys.

"There."

"Omigod."

Hanna's hand was barely submerged, but the octopus had her. A blueish pale tentacle traced up her wrist, exploring. Hanna caught her breath, half-ready to scream.

"Oh wow. He's not usually that ready to shake hands with strangers."

"Does he know lots of people?"

"I used to keep him at home. One of my friends, Frank decided he didn't like him, and he'd come up and spit water at the guy every time he came over."

Without turning around, Hanna said, "Allison, I want an octopus."

"We'll talk about it." I sounded like a mother.

"You can stay there for a minute, if you want," said the funeral director. He stepped back beside me. Leaned in, quietly, and said, "You're *the* Allison Winter, aren't you?"

I sighed.

"I saw you at an all-ages show, on the last Innocents tour. Oh my god." Pause. "That's your daughter, isn't it?" He grinned. "*Barefoot and Pregnant*. God, that album was genius."

Paused again.

"Sorry."

I said, "Do me a favour. Just cremate them."

"Is it that bad?"

"I don't know. But I don't want to look at them, and anybody who felt differently shouldn't have put me in charge."

He nodded. "Don't laugh at the urn collection. I'm serious. One of the ones you can get is a glass dolphin that you put the ashes inside."

I tried to picture that.

"It's like something from a flea market. People love it. Especially for kids who die, you know? If they don't want angels, they always want dolphins."

"You're a little goth, aren't you?"

"Naw, totally punk. But I don't get too scared of the dead, and this is a good business."

He let Hanna stay talking to the octopus while we worked through the papers. Costs, designs, service. I said Margaret would call him about the service. I was just in charge of, well. The bodies.

I said, "There might be one more. But I haven't got hold of his dad yet."

The director said, "Can I suggest?"

"Sure."

"Have the son's funeral separately, and make it private. I'm afraid I've been following all this online. It's a circus. There are going to be a lot of upset teenagers at his, if they find out when and where it is. If they get too over the top, you'll have the old folks losing it."

"I'll tell his dad."

"Jesus. You guys had a bad week, huh?"

I looked at Hanna. Thought about the bathroom. Said, "Do you know anybody who cleans up houses?"

He nodded. "Oh yeah. That can be really bad. Nobody expects the mess death leaves behind. It's worse than what we do. If you give some of those guys an autograph, they might cut you a deal. But they'd probably want you to sign one of *those* pictures."

The ones from *Boxed*. I'd posed for them in 1998. They were immortal online.

I said to him, "Tell them I have tattoos now that they can't even imagine. If this is going on my credit cards, I want the discount."

~ 9 ~

Naked Pictures

There are naked pictures of me on the internet.

It doesn't, in the large scheme of things, bother me. I posed for those pictures. There are earlier ones, too, that we took with Polaroids and photocopied into zines, but they don't scan to digital very well. The quality was so bad, you couldn't see anything even at the time.

I wrote a border around them in sharpie. *My skin belongs to me.*

I am not a good girl.

I wrote a song called *Fuck Your Friday Panties*. It was moderately popular.

By the standards of the internet, the pictures aren't that shocking. They're maybe one step up from Janis Joplin's 1967 nudes. In her day, you couldn't take pictures showing pubic hair, so she covered hers with her hands. I like her face in those pictures. She's so obviously young, not especially pretty, tangled in her hair and her necklaces. I like how people were scared of her.

In mine, I'm wearing eight-hole lace-up Doc Martens and nothing else except earrings. I didn't shave in the nineties, so you can see the hair spreading across the tops of my thighs and slipping out from under my arms.

You can see the cutting scars, too. We worked to get the lighting just right for that. In the end, I remember, we enhanced them with lip-liner. The pictures were shot on film, and they're just a touch out of focus. You can't tell how much of the damage is enhanced.

The negatives wandered off. They're probably still being traded on eBay.

By the time I joined Public Broadcasting, three different hosts had naked pictures on the internet, and one had done an unsimulated sex scene for an indie movie. No one cared.

Almost no one. Jay printed the pictures of me out and left them on my desk.

This sticky note next to them said, *I hope you shave now.*

Jay did shit like that. I threw away the note and replaced it with one that said, *Not as much as you'd like.* Left it on my desk, not his, but I think he saw it, and the note disappeared.

There were texts, later, but they only featured naked pictures of Jay.

Jay Beaton was a stunning asshole. The riot grrrl in me wanted to kick his nuts in. He tried to kiss me outside the Black Parrot following after-show drinks, and I did knee him, hard, but I missed. Later, I told him he must not have any balls at all, if I could miss his with a shot that close up, and he took a picture of his sack and sent it to my phone. He said he wore a cup for nights out, to fend off bitches like me.

Both before and after Jay was arrested, the women in the office shared stories like this about him. Jay was famous around Toronto for his fast hands and his willingness to take abuse if he was allowed to give more in return. He liked having female junior staff and male senior producers. He was funny on-air and a dick the rest of the time. I slept with him on three nonconsecutive occasions.

That's not in the book. The sheer lunacy of having done it aside, fucking Jay made me look stupid. I went with him more or less willingly, and I went back, and that wasn't the sort of detail I particularly wanted to share.

I kept his texts. Documented them and backed them up and printed out pictures and mailed them to him after he went to prison.

He sent me a picture of my bruised back in his bathroom in return.

i'll put ur cunt online

I made a bet with myself that he didn't actually have pictures of my cunt, and as far as I could tell, later, I won. He didn't post anything.

There are other photos. Eden took hours of footage of me, digital and analogue, but he developed his own films in the basement. He says there isn't a decent film lab left in Toronto, outside the universities, and he doesn't want students working on his stuff. The wall outside the darkroom is covered with black and whites of me in the house, partly or completely naked, and pictures of himself, nude, taken in the mirror. He said the ones I took lack depth of focus.

He might be right. I take pictures with my phone, mostly. If anyone decides to hack me, it's Eden's ass that will end up online.

～ 10 ～

Transcona

The geography of Winnipeg told me most of what I needed to know about David before I ever found him. To meet David Wilson, Collin's father, I had to leave the suburban tangle of Lindenwoods and cross most of Winnipeg's sprawl. Traverse bridges, follow traffic arteries I'd never taken before.

I lived in Winnipeg for fifteen years, but I didn't own a car during that time. I couldn't find my way to Transcona without a map.

I did an interview at one point with a poet who was in love with Transcona, who celebrated it in strange little books filled with doodles and 1980s strip-mall memories.

That version of Winnipeg fit like a Venn diagram with my own version, overlapping only at a few small points.

It wasn't always part of the city. A couple of years before I was born, Winnipeg devoured the town of Transcona, one of a half-dozen villages that legally vanished and functionally continued to exist as places slightly separate from the city around them. And, in spite of having been legally devoured, Transcona didn't appear to agree with Winnipeg. The city had stopped growing in that direction, leaving an odd almost-place that slouched on the rim of urban life.

I was filled with the urge to pull into the nearest mall and play Ms. Pac-Man, preferably on a two-player, table-top system that could double as a lunch table.

I wanted Sprite and crinkle-cut french fries.

Here it was 1982 forever.

The poetically-immortalized strip malls were punctuated by small, forget-table restaurants with Coke signs and garbage cans spitting takeout foam boxes onto the ground. It was too cold, but I kept expecting wasps to buzz against the windshield.

Maybe I should have gone to David's house by bus, to get the full Transcona experience. (The poet said, *You're not in Transcona 'til you've been on the bus for an hour fifteen and transferred twice. Some guy should pee on your leg for full credit.*) But riding the bus even once out of Lindenwoods was agonizing. Crossing the city with Hanna in tow seemed impossible.

Hanna had eaten, recovered, and come back to the house like she'd never been too horrified to stay inside it. She expressed her contempt for the bus mostly with sighs. While I was mapping routes and corralling change for our fares, she said, "We have cars, you know."

I didn't answer.

"Do you know how to drive?"

"Yes."

"Then why aren't we driving?"

I had a list of reasons. I wasn't sure to whom the cars presently belonged. What the police would think when they wanted registration, when they inevi-tably pulled me over for driving while insane. What personal artifacts would be left in the consoles and glove boxes that might set Hanna off, or me. How should one behave herself in the cars of the dead?

Against that was the pressure of the hours-long bus trip, the rotting cold outside, the possibility of being stranded, there, downtown, or at David's, for extended periods if the busses failed to show. They had before.

If I drove, I could leave Hanna at the house, let her play with her phone and be back in under an hour with what I needed. She didn't ever need to step outside.

I gave in and searched the kitchen.

There was something on the front a drawer that I chose to believe was left over from a previous spaghetti night.

I found car keys. Both cars were in the garage, shining softly under their dust layer, and I couldn't at first be sure which one I held the keys to. Pressed the fob, but the wrong way, so that the garage exploded into sound.

Hanna appeared behind me. Took the fob out of my hands and turned off the alarm. She said, "Take me with you."

"Not this time."

"I want a slurpee."

"I have to go do some awful stuff."

Hanna said, "Everything is awful. Buy food, okay?"

"What do you eat?"

"Take me with you and I'll show you."

Hanna knew the city better than I did. Unlike me, she'd lived there her entire life. Her gestation in Europe's low-rent clubs didn't appear to have left any clear psychic geography. She rode in the back of the car, the way kids apparently had taken to doing since I last was one myself. Played with her phone, and with a plastic, lavender compact that proved to be a fairly advanced game system that sang softly until I begged her to wear headphones.

My phone informed me that it knew where we were going.

We drove north and east. In eight hundred metres, we turned right. We took the exit. Changed lanes. Turned right again. Then left. I had no idea where we were. If the system glitched, it could hurl us into whichever river we were presently crossing and I wouldn't even consider changing course.

Transcona, I discovered, was a matrix of convenience stores. I stopped at one and bought Hanna a slurpee. A poster reminded me that Winnipeg was the slurpee capital of the world.

I wasn't prepared for David's house. I'd looked at it on Claudia's computer, on Google earth: an off-white bungalow, practically the definition of *house*. It was mid-block on an ordinary street.

Outside, offline, it was surrounded by flowers and candles. Stuffed animals sat in carefully-arranged plastic nests to keep them away from the muddy snow. Several signs created on poster board with glitter glue edged the property. From the car, I couldn't make anything of them.

Up close, they were grotesque.

We ♥ U Collin
R.I.P. well miss you
Collin Wilson 1997–2015 nevr forgotten

Pictures of him had been printed out on cheap inkjet paper and pasted in. Most were class photos or half-focussed cell phone portraits.

> *Collin martyr we wont let them h8 u*

They were everywhere. The rubber trash bins by the fence overflowed with culled glitter creations.

Girls turned down the block towards me, their arms full of poster-board and candles. I'd stopped being able to read the tribal allegiances of teenaged girls from just their clothes. They didn't read as goth or punk, not biker skanks or metal-heads or even Christian sweet spirits. I was left staring at aliens in skinny jeans.

The sun had mercifully stopped shining, but my eyes ached all the time. I'd bought huge-lensed sunglasses at the 7-Eleven. Behind them, I wondered if the girls could see me at all.

Evidence suggested not. They pushed around me, stepped up to the memorial snowdrift, and added their items. Turned back to the street. One extended an arm with her phone held horizontally.

"Hey, Collin. I miss you so much."

"You were beautiful."

"They say terrible things about you. We know it's lies. This is for you, baby."

They were talking to the internet, either live or recording for later posting. The girl retracted her arm and they reviewed their speeches. Nodded. Pocketed the phone and walked on.

I considered leaving.

The screen door framed a sheet of printer paper with *Please Don't* written on it in purple market.

I rang the bell.

I waited for a long time in the snow. Turned back to look at Hanna in the car. She stared back at me for a while before returning to her game. I rang the bell again.

It occurred to me that he must be at work, like an ordinary mortal.

From the side of the porch, David said, "I know you."

I turned.

"I mean. We haven't met, but . . . I think you're Allison Winter? Is that Hanna?"

"Yeah. "

"Does she want to come in?"

I had no idea. I looked over, turning my head ostentatiously. Hanna shook her head without looking up.

Inside, David gave me coffee in an off-white mug that reminded me of diners in the form they had just after I first came to the city. The coffee was generically good. There was a pod-brewer on the kitchen counter.

He said, "I take the signs down every night. I want you to know I didn't ask them to do that."

I nodded. I wished I'd kept my sunglasses on.

"I . . . I'm so *sorry*."

Like everyone I'd talked to for days that I had any reason to know by name, he started to cry.

"I suppose I'm the ambassador," I said. "From Hoeppner country. They want to know what you're going to do."

"What? Nothing. I mean, what would I do? *Sue*?" He thought about this, still crying. "Jesus. They're going to sue me, aren't they?"

"I'm pretty sure they can't sue you." For what? Parenting badly, I had to hope, wasn't a litigious offense. "I mean, with his body. We're trying to plan the funeral."

"Oh."

"Have you decided?"

He shook his head. "I wasn't going to do anything. I told them I wanted him cremated, if they ever give him back to me. Do they give bodies back, do you think, after something like this?"

I had no idea. They might simply keep all the dead monsters in an underfunded government storage facility, floating in yellowish liquid for future study.

They wouldn't. It would have been discontinued years ago due to funding cuts.

"The funeral director talked about it like he assumed they'd release the body. He suggested that we not have," pause, "Collin's funeral at the same time as Ethan and Claudia's."

"It never occurred to me that you would."

Someone else rang the bell. David went to the door, peered through the fisheye, and walked back. "Ignore it. It's girls."

"What's wrong with them?"

"I don't know. Their coming here has something to do with his Facebook page. I can't look at it anymore."

"Don't read the comments."

"So I'm learning."

I paused. "Did he tell you why? Collin. Do you know?"

"No." David finished his coffee and walked away without apologizing to make more. He brought back a second cup for himself, and a second one for me in a fresh mug that sat beside my first one. "He had problems, you know?"

"How long?"

"Years. He disappeared for six weeks earlier this winter, and when he came back he'd lost a fingertip. Frostbite, most likely, but I'm not totally sure he hadn't just cut it off. He wasn't allowed over there, you know."

"Claudia and Ethan's?"

"Yeah. They fought. But she'd ease up, give him money. I think she had coffee with him sometimes while he was disappeared, like maybe he showed up at her office and she didn't tell me.

"The police went through his room again, this week. I haven't gone in there since." He looked at me. "Would you?"

#

A few times while I was a teenager, Kara and I tried breaking into people's houses. There weren't so many security systems, then, and in the north end you could open a lot of doors with just a credit card. We picked houses with no one home. Watched them for an hour or two. Then we went in, usually at the back.

I liked to watch TV and pee in their bathrooms. If there was loose money lying out, I took it, but mostly I took food, earrings, small objects from side tables. Kara lifted pictures from photo albums, which, in retrospect, was the most alienated Gen-X gesture she could have enacted. I wish I'd thought of it.

Let ourselves out the back, and shut the door behind us. We weren't ever caught.

I'd thought about that, earlier, in the Lindenwoods house, and I thought about it in Collin's bedroom.

His room smelled like a teenaged boy. When I was younger, I'd thought it was body odour and spoiled food, because I hadn't learned what semen smelled like yet. I didn't want to touch anything soft.

He had posters, a few books, a computer. Notebooks on the floor, though some were clearly missing. The posters were mostly of Juggalo bands.

He had anime girls, naked and splayed out, on the closet doors.

Inside the one door, there was a small, high-gloss print of The Innocents' *Fuck Your Friday Panties*. The one where we're filthy and angry and I'm topless, half out of my jeans and kicking at the camera.

I stared.

Without moving, I said, "David."

Nothing.

"DAVID!"

He came, silent on the wall-to-wall near the door, not entering.

"Tell me that's not me."

"I'm sorry. Yeah. They sell those around town, I think."

I said, "I don't know what you're going to do with this stuff. I'm sorry." Thought. "Maybe? There are these moving companies you can hire. They say, if there's moldy fruit in the bowl when you tell them to pack, you'll have moldy fruit at the other end. They don't sort, just box. You could hire them to pack everything and . . . maybe store it?"

"I can't have any of this in the house."

"Not here. In one of those locker places."

"For how long?"

"How the hell should I know?!" Angry at him, suddenly. I was afraid that if I moved the poster, one of my nudes would fall out from behind it.

I wanted to know what his chair-wielding, blood-smearing son thought about me.

Did he think about Hanna?

"I don't know," I said. "One year. Seven years. However long it takes 'til you can deal with it. Have you talked to somebody?"

"No."

"Have you gone to work?"

"No."

"What have you done?"

"I've talked to the police. I let them take things out of the house. I clean up the yard. I have no idea what I'm supposed to do. I keep pretending he's just taken off into the city, again. We weren't doing well, living together. I told him he had to move out, or take his meds regularly. He didn't, usually. He hated them."

"You have to work really hard on it to stay medicated all the time."

"I know. I read your book."

My first two years of pills were awful. I lost my upper emotional register. I shit blood. I had to keep reminding myself that if the meds weren't working, I had to tell someone. That no one could tell what my level of insanity was just by looking at me.

I went off them for long periods and thought about all kinds of things.

I thought about jumping off one of the bridges, maybe Osborne, in the deep winter. If I didn't die on the Assiniboine river ice, I could break through and go down into the water and disappear.

I thought seriously about wrapping my arms around Hanna so she'd go first, crushed in the half-second before my own impact.

I thought about that now and said, "Excuse me." Walked into the bathroom and locked the door.

∷◦∷

David was smarter than I expected. He found my phone. Tracked recent calls. Pressed the right buttons for Eden to answer him.

At the bathroom door, he said, "Allison, do you have your pills with you?"

I flushed the toilet a few times. It made an enormous noise in the tiny space. I wondered whether his bathroom tiles had always been faintly brown, or if their colour was a function of age and fecal dust.

"Allison. I need you to tell me that you're okay."

"I just need to sit here for a while."

"Eden says, do you have your pills?"

Silence.

An almost-analogue crackle shot out as the speaker phone activated. Eden over a huge distance. "Alli. Come on."

"I ran out."

David said, "Okay. Thank you."

I liked bathrooms. I like them. They're closed spaces, and the private ones in houses are usually a little warmer than the surrounding rooms. The hot water pipes radiate all the time. The humidity rises. Bath mats lurk warm, bacteria-filled, and welcoming on the floor.

I curled up. Tried to sleep.

Couldn't.

I got up again. In the medicine cabinet, there were pills in carefully-marked bottles, but none of them overlapped with mine. The schism between bipolar depression and manic psychosis. Except lorazepam. Guardian of the sleepless, ender of convulsions. Tiny, half-milligram pills. I took three. Curled back up and dozed.

Later, David forced the bathroom doorknob with a screwdriver and a kitchen knife. He pulled me upright without forcing me to wake up completely and walked me to bed.

Woke me later, with coffee, fresh again. "Allison, I need you to get up."

"No."

"Yes, please. I need you to get up. We had your prescriptions faxed over to the drug store, but I can't collect them without your consent, and since you haven't been there before, they won't accept your consent without your physical body. So we're going to get your coat, and we're all going to go to the drugstore."

I chewed on *we*.

He said, "Hanna's in the living room. I ordered her a pizza."

:::❦:::

I took my pills while David watched. Drank water. Opened my hands and my mouth, shook my head with my face to the floor and my mouth open to show I'd swallowed. I did that in the Superstore pharmacy while the south Asian tech watched and passing families stared.

"Thank you."

"Any time. Always glad to illustrate compliance."

"Okay. Do you want anything before we go home?"

"No."

"I told your husband I'd make you eat."

"He's not my husband."

"Boyfriend. He said you stop eating, when things are bad. So, what do you want?"

"Let me sleep and I'll tell you later."

:::❦:::

I slept in David's bed. Hanna curled up beside me and watched the old, deep television propped on the bureau. David was elsewhere. He checked on us, gave me water, gave me pills.

Drugged sleep travels outside of time. Days collapse, but minutes stretch out infinitely. I wondered why Hanna didn't go to sleep. Half-roused and asked her, and she said, "You said that five minutes ago. It's not late. Leave me alone."

I was not sane again immediately, but I was level by morning. Whichever morning it was.

David was opening new boxes of coffee pods. His trash was full of them. He said, "Thank you."

"Jesus. Why?"

"That's the most things I've done in a row since I found out."

"Oh. Well, glad to help. And, yeah, I'm so sorry."

"Well, it's a shitty situation. But take your meds. I know you don't have what he had, but take your pills so none of the rest of us have to be that frightened again for a bit."

I hadn't gone off them in four years. I felt sick. Not hungry, but aware of my stomach gnawing on its own lining.

"I'm hungry."

"For what?"

"Terrible Chinese food."

He looked at the stove clock. "Bit early. I might have something in the freezer, though."

David microwaved portions of simulated take-out food, and I read the nutritional information and considered leaving, taking Hanna, not coming back, or ever eating again. In the mirror, earlier, I'd had the sharp cheekbones that a makeup artist had had to create with shading the previous week. If I skipped eating for one more day, the jeans I bought next would be markedly different from the ones I had at home.

David said, "Eat and I'll give you the keys back."

It was amazing. MSG and sodium and oil and sugar. He had handfuls of paper-wrapped takeout chopsticks in a drawer and gave me a pair.

He had green tea in an actual pot.

Hanna padded in wearing her T-shirt and panties and mismatched yellow and pink socks. "Can I have some?"

"Of this, sure. Do you want a big shirt to wear?"

"Thanks."

She didn't want the microwaved food, though she drank two cups of tea. He gave her a selection of dry cereals and a carton of almond milk.

Still drunk on not-enough pills, I said, "You're not the worst parent in this family. Not even close. You know?"

"If I cry again, it's going to scare Hanna."

"Do they know where we are?"

"Everyone knows. And I called the funeral home." He drank coffee. Watched me. "Oh. Shit. To be clear, when I said, *everybody knows*, I mean I called Margaret and Elaine and I talked to somebody named Maegan, and I think you know I talked to your husband."

"He's not my husband."

"He keeps a list of your meds and he knows what pharmacy you use."

Eden's smell hit me. He wasn't there, but his presence was odour-based and could re-create itself out of fragments of perspiration and body-wash.

"I need to go home."

"I'd tend to agree. Oh, and your husband said he'd called your work. They're doing okay. Lindsay Avon's good on the radio."

"Yeah. She's a doll." I arched my back. "And I don't think she wants my job, so, you know, that's nice."

David nodded. "Did you really want to go to the funeral?"

I shook my head.

"Then don't. God knows I won't. I don't think funerals are actually good for the things people think they are, and your mortician friend wasn't joking. The girls are planning to make a scene. The police are thinking of going. You could say goodbye later, you know?"

Hanna finished her cereal. "*I* want to go."

"You can. Your grandma and grandpa are going to be there."

She nodded. Chewed on a scrap of corn and sugar. Paused. "Are you going to make me go with them?"

"You don't have to go to the funeral. You said you wanted to, though."

"Go home with them. I don't want to. Or are they going to come live in the house?"

I thought about trying to explain lawyers, and probate, and wills. I didn't actually know what became of houses when their owners died. If it was insured or whether it was lurking there, waiting for the next mortgage payment to fail.

Hanna said, "Can I go with you?"

I said, "Maybe. I'll ask. Why do you want to?"

David said, "Never ask that. If they say they want to go with you, you say yes. You say yes."

~ II ~

Probate

Cleaners were already at work on the house, two young guys with a corporate truck. I didn't remember booking them, but they had my name on their paperwork, and I was prepared to accept that.

They said to me, in the kitchen, that they didn't usually clean such nice places. "Mostly apartments, the kind where if somebody's died there, it's not the first time."

I was present to identify the patches of mess I'd been unable to deal with. Hanna had come barrelling through the door before I had it fully open and fled to her bedroom. She was still there.

I had to find a place to be. There were untouched rooms. I chose the basement. Deep, colourless carpeting down there. Two offices. Claudia's files, I realized, were likely confidential. Someone should come and take them. Ethan's were odder. Most of the papers were shuffled randomly, and I didn't know what an engineer's business documents would look like. Whether anything on paper was secure, whether either of them had worked on paper at all.

The boxes in the cluttered family room were easier to parse. One was full of sparkly layers that I thought might be dance costumes. I tried to think when Hanna had quit dance. If she had. How many carefully-registered activities had she missed so far?

I wondered how long she'd been out of school. It was something concrete. I phoned Margaret.

"I don't know, dear."

"Margaret. Who's going to take her?"

There was a pause on the phone. "I'm not her blood grandmother. You know that."

"But they must have talked about it."

"Not to me, I'm sorry."

I thought of calling Elaine. Elaine didn't like me.

I tried to focus my eyes. Looked around the home office, at the multi-channel landline phone stuck to the desk. This remnant of some earlier technological age. It still worked. I tried to think who to call.

Business card stuck to the wall. *Office Manager.* Long law-firm name.

I called. The main office directory for a law firm popped up, and I keyed in the four-digit extension. Reached the woman whose card I'd found. She wanted to know if I was at the house right now.

I said I was.

She came over. She had a list of codes and keys, and she stared at the man chemically laundering biohazards from the living room carpet. He turned to me. Said, "I think this chair's not salvageable."

"Then throw it away."

The woman shook her head. "It's in probate."

"It's covered in blood."

"Leave it where it is."

She took over the home office, shutting the door in my face. I retreated to the couch and read dossiers on my phone. Periodically, she came out to ask me things that I didn't know the answers to. When she went back, she left the door open, and then I had her to look at, at least. She growled softly while she worked. It wasn't aggressive. Her chest vibrated arhythmically, as if she were thinking through her breastbone.

I dozed on the couch. The manager woke me. Held out her phone.

"Mr. Cardinal would like to speak with you."

I took the phone. Studied its glossy surfaces for top and bottom and tried it against my face. Flipped it when the only sounds that emerged were warped by skin and distance.

Wayne said, "Have you been paying for the death things yourself?"

"Yeah."

"You didn't have to."

I tried to imagine approaching Ethan's parents with a collection of receipts and suggesting ways of splitting the costs. Shook my head. Breathed.

"Most of it should come from the estate."

"Oh."

He asked me for documents. I said I'd see what I could find.

"I do need to talk to you."

"In person?"

"Properly, yes. It's about Hanna."

I remembered Wayne in Claudia and Ethan's then-living room, witnessing the papers that I signed granting full custody to the very nice, high-functioning adults.

"Please tell me they named a guardian for her." Someone to manage the house. Who would deal with the grandparents and the funeral director. Wayne, I thought, must be the executor. His problem entirely, this tangle of people who wouldn't step into the fray.

"There'll be a trust fund. I'll liquidate the house, unless you want it."

"I don't think I could afford it."

"It would have been sold, the assets divided automatically, but. Collin." Wayne paused. "Is David planning to contest?"

"Contest what?"

"The inheritance. Half of the family assets would have passed to Collin. An even division between Collin and Hanna, you see. They thought it was fairest. Actually, Claudia was working on setting up a trust for Collin. She worried he'd be . . . you know. Homeless."

Wayne spoke like a lawyer, calmly explaining the too-intimate details of this other family's life. I found myself detaching. Listening like a radio host. If he paused, I'd ask something open-ended and let him talk further. Vaguely, I thought, I was going to have to sit through an editing session, later, to make the thing coherent.

"Is that common?"

"Oh, yes. Claudia found that, I think, eighty per cent of men with Collin's diagnosis spent periods of their lives homeless. She wouldn't be able to force him indoors, but at least he'd have the assets to pay for an apartment."

"That seems wise."

"I thought so. She even brought Collin in to talk about it." Shaky breath. "I knew him when he was a baby, you know? Years before she and Ethan met. He was a happy kid. She used to study with him in one of those bouncy seats."

"I should phone David."

I said, "Yeah."

"I'm not sure he knows what do to. But I'm technically Hanna's lawyer, now. If he contests, we'll be opposing."

"That must pose a serious conflict for you."

Wayne said, "You do radio voice really well. It barely sounds like you at all."

"Yeah. Sorry. I'm tired. Why didn't you call a week ago?"

"I called Elaine and Marshall. They told me they were taking care of it."

That paused me. "If there are two funerals for the same bodies . . ."

"I'll ask them. It's like them, to make plans and refuse to tell you." He hung up.

I handed the phone back to its owner. She was lurking by the stairs, scream-ing with her body that she wanted to leave. While I talked to Wayne, she'd crept around corners and peered into other rooms, and come back stiff. Took her phone and let herself out like a discontented fairy.

It occurred to me that I could take a shower. It would give me time to think.

My phone rang.

The funeral home needed a word. His parents had planned Ethan's funeral, separate even from Claudia's. Two funeral homes had claimed the body. One secular, one Mennonite. The director called me.

I said, *Tell them they can have him. Send them the bill for what you've done so far and tell them to go to hell.*

I thought, *The witch is coming.*

Wayne called back.

I said, "They've taken Ethan's body."

"I heard. You have bigger problems," he told me. "Take Hanna and go home."

He'd received notice, in the last ten minutes, of an application for custody from Elaine and Marshall.

"They're moving fast." Like wolves.

Wayne said, "It stands in conflict with the will. Their application is spuri-ous. There's no reason a court won't grant you custody. And since it's non-urgent, it might be a year before this comes to trial.

"Anyway. There's a chance that Elaine will try to accelerate the process. And this is one of those weird things where possession actually is nine-tenths of the law. You need to establish that you're acting in accordance with a legal contract between yourself and the deceased, and then you need to change jurisdictions." He paused. "Is Hanna okay?"

"Hanna said she wants to go with me."

"That's useful. I'm glad to hear it. How fast can you get back to Ontario?"

"What about the house?"

"I'll deal with the house."

I said, "You're a prince."

"I get ten per cent of the estate. It's more than my student loans. I'll be fine."

I went upstairs. Elaine was already on her way, I thought. She'd be coming here, to the house, to make her demands.

The witch in the wood coming for the baby.

My phone helpfully offered me an airline booking page when I opened the browser. Either I'd been looking at it before, when I was half-dozing, or targeted advertising was getting better.

I needed my wallet.

Hanna was curled up on her bed. She had a tablet laid on the comforter. Her fingers traced the patterns of some kind of basic puzzle game. Periodically, a chat window overlaid the game screen.

"Have you got a suitcase?" I said.

"I don't know."

I looked in the master closet. There were suitcases. I brought one back. Brought two.

I said, "Pack."

"Where are we going?"

"Toronto."

～ 12 ～

Punchline

I met Eden in the punchline of a *New Yorker* cartoon. Which is to say, we met in the lobby of our mutual psychiatrist's office.

I left Winnipeg when a job listing popped up in Public Broadcasting. Production assistant for *The Cure for Ordinary*. Pop cultural background essential. At least eighteen months' experience in sound design.

I moved to Toronto.

The time zones shifted around me. The light moved. I was farther south, deeper into the lake effect climate, inhaling hydrocarbons at a density I hadn't experienced before. Toronto was, after Winnipeg, impossibly huge. I needed an apartment, a sense of direction.

I found those, mostly through friends. People who knew me from print articles, or radio, or The Innocents. I slept on a couch in a band house for a week before I developed any kind of more permanent home.

I spent six months seeing whatever doctors were available at the walk-in clinic where I waited for five, six hours for someone to meet with me for five minutes. They looked at my pill bottles, prescribed more of same.

I said to one, "I'm thinking about cutting myself."

She said, "Don't do that."

"Can I get some help with it?"

"I'm hesitant to change your dosage. This isn't really my field."

I went on a waiting list. I cracked a little around the edges.

Jay, it turned out, liked cracked girls.

I'd been warned. Even while I was still writing my application and lining up references, women came up to me sideways. They said, *Watch out for Jay Beaton.*

He's an asshole.

He's got fast hands.

He really, really likes being in charge. Are you sure you want to work for him?

I'd wanted out of Winnipeg. I'd surrendered Hanna to her much nicer new parents, and my apartment without her was empty. I was out of psychiatric care, I was stable. I could, conceivably, ask to take her back.

I needed not to. And I needed not to work in the same downtown business district as her other, better mother.

I nodded to all those women. Told them I believed them. Carried on.

Jay was funny and not handsome. He wasn't quite as ugly as a face made for radio, but he was strange-looking. Still, he had a liquid broadcast voice and he worked it. He got the interviews. He asked the hard-but-not-too-hard questions. He explicated cultural trends in an engaging, helpful tone that appealed to Public Broadcasting listeners.

I was taking not-enough Effexor. Jay sat down at my desk next to me. He said, "Do you want to fuck sometime?"

I went home with him. He lived in a high-gloss condo, thirty-one floors up, with the inevitable view of the lake, and nearly reflective black-finish wood floors.

There were blown-up prints of photos on the wall of Jay talking to David Bowie, U2, David Foster Wallace. The focus on the last had been heightened, so that light shone out of Wallace's trademark bandana.

I liked the obscurity of the image. Wallace hadn't died, yet. Meeting him was an elegant, not-quite-esoteric possibility.

I said, "You don't have one of Pynchon?"

"I keep the empty frame in my bedroom. It's very special to me."

Jay leaned in, bit at my jaw. He tugged a little at the skin.

"You're going to leave a mark," I said.

"God, I hope so."

He moved me to stand in front of the floor-to-ceiling windows. It was icy. Night. The apartment's lights created an almost-mirror. He stood behind me.

"Take your shirt off. Over your head."

I did.

"I like this," he said. My ribcage. I hadn't been eating. There was a hollow between my bottom rib and my hipbones. "I like the bones in your back. You look good."

He knelt, then, leaned in, and bit me there. Teeth into skin over the unguarded core organs. He dug in. I jerked away, pushing out. He hung on.

This was sex with Jay. He didn't break the skin, but he liked to go close. Bring blood up to the surface and then discuss what might bring it out.

I said, "Do my arms."

He leaned in to my bicep, gnawed at it.

"No. The insides."

These hollow blue lines lit them up. I'd been working long hours without access to daylight, and my veins were showing. The melting body fat left new matrices of blood and tendon visible. I was more than passingly aware that without a body fat cushion, if I did cut myself, I'd go too deep too easily. Lose permanent sensation in my fingertips.

I'd shifted to cutting my thighs. There was more flesh left there under the skin.

Jay pushed me up against the window. Flipped me to face him, so that my shoulder blades snapped back into myself, away from the chill on the glass. "That's cold."

"I know."

Pushed my left arm above my head. Wrist against the glass. He leaned in. Bit me.

His chest was close against my face. I wasn't sure I'd be able to breathe. His teeth dug deeper, shifting my tendons so that my fingers curled up and suddenly slackened.

It didn't exactly hurt. There were thin scars there, but the skin wasn't particularly sensitive. The pressure on my arm's internal structure felt more like a bad electrical current, something damaging pushing the wrong way against pieces of myself I still needed if I was going to walk out in the morning.

Arms or legs, I thought.

I could live without my legs. My arms connected my fingertips to my brain. Writing came out there. Music did.

This grinding of the internal structure of my forearms. I felt one of his teeth catch on the protruding tendon, and he broke off. Shook his head.

He stepped back behind me, into the reflection. Snow behind it. It blurred my edges while I pulled at my belt and let my jeans fall. They crumpled around my knees, catching on my trouser socks. I had to step forward, just a couple of inches, to get myself free.

I'd taken to wearing a bra at the office, largely because I was cold and it added another layer. Buying bras again after years of not wearing them had been a strange transition. While I'd been ignoring them, they'd transformed into brilliantly coloured bowls of contoured foam. Electric blue with orange straps. There were bins of these in every lingerie department, in every mall kiosk catering to girls. They made everything nipple-less and excessive.

I'd had to go back hunting into the matronly depths of the Bay, looking for anything like the soft cups I remembered. I found sports bras, nylon creations by Warner's and WonderBra, and the barely-there layers by Calvin Klein that I adopted and resented. If I'd learned to sew when everyone else did, I could have made my own and done a better job.

Later, when I discovered American Apparel, I grabbed handfuls of poorly-made half-sheer pornography simply because they were cheaper than the brand-named shit I'd been buying.

Jay loved it. The minimalist bra, the panties shifted down my hips and curled from the day, the half-sheer knee socks.

He said, "Leave it on."

Turned me around. Pushed me forward against the glass. My palms ached almost instantly, and I shifted to my forearms. No conservation of heat, but at least relieving the pressure. Jay dragged his teeth down my spine, bit my protruding ass on his way by. Said, "Up."

I stood on my toes. He was taller than me, too tall for this, really, but he said *up* and it sounded like a good idea. My skin vibrated, and I was soaking wet, the first time my body had offered that up to me in over a year. This stupid, filthy idea, and if I leaned forward farther my breasts would freeze along with my arms.

He pushed the panties aside without taking them off. Behind me, he was still almost entirely dressed. Just his slacks open and his shirt unbuttoned. He had to be hard, but I couldn't see it.

He was, hard enough to rub his tip across my labia and soak it further.

I said, "Condom."

He said, "I can't believe you don't shave."

"You don't know anything about me at all."

"That's true."

"Condom."

He hissed. "Well. Stay there. On your toes."

Stepped away, out of the room. I dropped on my flat feet, stood up, arched my back, and rubbed feeling back into my arms.

"I said to stay there."

I thought about going home. I thought about going out for the night, getting very drunk and crawling onto a dick I wouldn't have to work with in the morning.

"You have the most amazing bitch face."

"I really thought you'd be less drama outside of work."

Jay grinned at me. He said, "Yeah. So, at the windows or on the couch?"

"Condom?"

He held it up.

I said, "Put it on."

He did. He'd softened, slightly. Enough that he had to pinch the latex edges to keep them from slipping after he'd rolled it on.

"Okay. I'm going to say windows. I reserve the right to change my mind."

"You can try."

"I can kick you from behind. You'll be amazed."

Jay slid up behind me. I could feel him stroking himself. I said, "Be careful. If you rip it, I'm done. I'm going home."

He nodded. Pushed a finger under my panties and pulled them to the side, slid a finger in. Teased at my vulval mouth like he was going in and then didn't.

"You like that?"

"You do. So fuck me."

He was too tall, and my calves ached from balancing on my toes, but I liked the angle. He pushed in hard, harder than the last few, harder than Ethan had at any point in his too-sweet life.

"Jesus."

"Don't."

"Fuck."

"Better."

Thrusting in hard for a minute, maybe two, until my calves gave and I slipped. Hit my forehead on the glass.

Spinning in the room that I gradually realized was the drifting snow. Vertigo looking down at the city.

"Are you okay?"

I said, "Maybe couch."

We finished there, with me in his lap, shifting and losing my balance as dizziness set in and then twisting to regain my equilibrium. My arms were bruising. I thought, vaguely, that I should ask him to bite my thighs. Later.

Next time.

No next time. This vertiginous space wasn't somewhere I wanted to fuck ever again.

He came, shifted out from under me, and laid me out on the couch.

"Don't fall asleep."

Water poured out in another room. I rubbed my forehead and then my eyes. The headache that came with medication and exhaustion was moving in, just held at bay by the sexual tension built up in my abdomen.

From the bathroom doorway, Jay said, "Finish while I watch."

I had my head towards him, but he could, maybe, see in the reflection. I was wet and aching, and it only took a few passes with my fingertips to release all the remaining tension. Not coming, exactly, but enough like it that I suspected he couldn't tell the difference.

"Nice. Do you want a drink?"

I hadn't had a drink for six months at that point. I wasn't exactly sober, but I was powerfully deterred by the crushing migraines that emerged where my brain's disrupted serotonin met alcohol.

Aversion therapy. I either had to quit or move to something harder. I didn't live through the 90's club scene to take up heroin after I'd graduated to adult professional status.

"No thanks."

"Do you want me to call you a cab?"

He made it sound like chivalry. I thought about asking to stay, just on the couch. I hadn't looked at it much, before. It was squared-off black leather, like an elevated waiting-room sofa. Chrome legs. My skin stuck to it. I was still cold.

He walked across the room with his pants still undone and turned on the TV. "I want to watch the news. Figure out some material for tomorrow's show before I go to bed."

I'd been dismissed. I considered explaining to him how terrible he was at sex. Only my half-concussion stopped me, garbling the words. Later, I wondered what would have happened. If he would have slapped me, as he'd apparently slapped other women. If he would have opened the glass doors, walked my dizzy, under-wear-clad body onto the terrace, and tipped me over.

Falling for hours in the snow before I reached the ground.

I called my own cab. Went home and took a couple of prescription-strength Tylenol and slept too late the next day. When I studied myself in the mirror after my shower, I was prepared for the bruise on the side of my neck and the damage to my forearms, but not for the rest. The blood called up when my face hit the glass had slid downwards in the night had been pulled by gravity into the orbital sockets of my eyes. The right was worse than the left, but both were obvious.

I went in to work anyway. Late, possibly still almost-concussed. I refused to wear sunglasses.

When someone asked, I said, "Jay happened."

I wrote monologues for him that afternoon. Pieces that he could use at any point in the next five or six weeks if the nightly news didn't generate more urgent material. Extra points for metricality, clever wordplay, little poems that emerged at unexpected points.

Jay really did assign them points. Four of us wrote him monologues, and he'd rate them and send us back our scores.

Later, two girls from the office awarded me a Bad Decision Dinosaur mug. Just a little reminder. It came with a card that had a picture of Jay on the front, a circle around his face, and a line drawn through it. Written inside,

> *No no no no no no no no no no*
> *Not this. Not this*
> *Just say NO to Jay*

I ignored Jay the next time he suggested I come home with him, and I started taking more of my pills. It was a complicated process. My early rounds of medication had been actual pills, hard and easily snapped in half. The current ones were caplets. Taking more, but not simply doubling or tripling the dose (sleeping late, sleeping for a day-and-half, vomiting) meant opening the pills. Cutting the powder inside with a knife.

I had no idea what would happen if I snorted it. In the end, I licked my fingers to wet them, picked up the powder on the tips and sucked it off while I watched television on my own shitty couch in a low-rise neighbourhood that separated the new glass downtown from the suburban wastes of the strange, amalgamated megacity.

I liked how no one pretended it was all just "Toronto." There was a street at which Toronto ended and Etobicoke began. A line at which Mississauga emerged from the tangle of streets. Oakville was separate, and Burlington and Richmond Hill.

I was waiting for new medication. If I took four pills at once, I'd likely manage to put myself in the hospital, but I'd been to Urgent Care with a co-worker after she fell on the ice outside the broadcast centre, and I didn't like my odds of being seen before I vomited, or ran naked and photographed through the city, or drifted into slow, permanent overdose.

I took three mental health days in a week. Human resources called me to ask if I was ever coming back. I told them I was waiting for a medical opening.

"How long?"

"They said six, maybe seven months."

"We'll talk to someone."

There were no inter-layers of government whereby Public Broadcasting employees could command medical appointments, but someone in one of the other production units had family who saw an actual, living psychiatrist. That person called someone, said I was family, and could they make an opening for me, please?

There was a telephone chain linking me to Eden even before we met, through medications and bad decisions and snow.

:::◉:::

I have a strong, clear memory for trauma, but far less for happy accidents. I spent a long stretch of that winter walking in the city. I'd come to Toronto without a car, and I stayed that way. I was learning the transit map slowly, but when the system turned me around, I just got off and wandered. I wore base layers that made my clothes fit again.

I liked "base layers" as a euphemism for long underwear. It sounded like I might take up mountain climbing or snowboarding, some alpine sport during which I might overheat and need to peel down to some lighter version of myself.

If I remembered to layer, the cold felt like a distant relation that I didn't need to engage with. If I forgot, I froze. The front skin of my thighs ached all the time. I'd get to work and rub my hands frantically along my bare legs in the ladies' room, trying to chafe my blood into re-circulating.

Other days, I stood outside like that. Considered taking up smoking.

Smokers everywhere, outside every building, illegally close to the doors, automatically accepted me into their circles, but when I didn't light up, they shifted uncomfortably until I left.

After that, on my breaks, I walked, ranging out from the broadcast building into the city. Homeless guys waiting on stoops got to know me. I'd buy them coffee and stand around with them while they warmed up and I froze.

The psychiatrist's office was seventeen blocks from work, north past the University of Toronto campus and into a grey-treed street of big houses that had ceased to be residential. Doctors and architects and real estate offices barely advertised themselves on their converted doors. It would have been discreet if there hadn't been so many of them crowded onto the low-key, matte-metal nameplates.

I walked there. Booked an extra hour off work to cover the distance. Inside, I paced the waiting room.

Dr. Maggrah asked me to stop. "You don't need to perform. I'm perfectly aware that you're distressed."

"I just needed to move around."

"Make an effort to keep still."

Make an effort. It sounded eerily familiar. That joke about psychiatrists: if it isn't one thing, it's your mother.

He gave me a scrip and a regimen. Ten days to wean off my current pills. "You'll be tense," he said. "You can take these if it's bad. When you're down to a quarter of your current dose, you can shift to the new medications. Expect to feel a significant result in two to three weeks."

Dismissed.

I made it just over a week, and then I pushed a computer monitor off the desk at work and cried. After that, I stayed home.

The new pills gave me migraines for three days. I called for an appointment on the fourth day. I was lucky: they had an opening eleven days hence.

I was still in the early years of my medication cycle, and I wasn't inured to the period when taking the pills was worse than not taking them. I paced through my terrible, almost-bare apartment gathering up sharps, put them in a bag, and took it down to my storage locker in the basement next to the laundry. This nylon sack full of my leg razors and nail scissors and the paring knives from the kitchen.

I could hit my thighs without breaking the skin. Punch my hips.

The headache shifted before my appointment. I was dizzy, eyes unfocussed.

He adjusted my dosage. We made me a regular appointment on Thursdays, every two weeks for three months. Suggested I see my family doctor for B12 shots.

I didn't have a family doctor.

Oh, well. Yes.

I came for my third regular appointment and the door was locked. It was still snowing, grey and dirty. I checked the address, checked my calendar, tugged at the door. Then pushed aside the snow and sat down on the stoop to wait, like a kid.

That was how I met Eden.

He sat next to me for a while. I'd seen him twice. He had a Starbucks tea that he clutched with both hands. Blew on it and didn't drink.

"Can I talk to you?"

"No, please."

He didn't talk again. Sat down next to me.

Twenty minutes passed before someone came out of the office downstairs and realized that the door was locked.

I'd missed my appointment. Eden said, "Take mine."

I stared at him.

"I can get another one. It's just a check-in. I know you need it."

"Do I look that bad?"

"I heard about the computer. What did it ever do to you?"

I hadn't been paranoid before. Mania had pushed me up onto stages and strange, gorgeous men and elaborate shopping trips, and then fled. Depression had carved at my skin and become steady company. At some earlier point in my life, I'd had equilibrium, and I couldn't remember where I'd put it.

"I'm sorry," he said. "That sounded creepy." He paused. "My uncle works with you. He mentioned it."

"You know who I am."

"Oh, I knew before. You're Allison Winter. I'm a fan."

I said, "Take your appointment. I have to go back to work."

He handed me his tea and went inside.

When I came for my next appointment, he was already in the waiting room. He handed me a sugarless green tea, the mate for his, and sat very still while I paced.

I met him again in the hallway at work. He was carrying a backpack.

"We're doing a show. You should come."

He gave me a flyer.

It was written in blue ballpoint ink, hard to read, on lined white paper.

> I know now that I am totally punk
> and I will show you after the dance
> Film and spoken word
> Gladstone hotel, February 12

I went to the show, and I wore a punk T-shirt. Afterwards, he came up to me and hugged me like we'd been friends all our lives.

~ 13 ~

Mirror World

Hanna was angry. I finally asked her, "What did you think was going to happen?"

It wasn't a fair question. She'd made it fairly clear what she expected: that I would move into the Lindenwoods house. The house, now cleaned by grubby post-murder experts who had carried the write-off furniture out to the garage, was reverting to its silver glory. It was a beautiful space, in its way. Very contemporary. Silver carpeting and dark wood and thoughtful, muted paint colours. A few carefully-purchased paintings, all watercolours. Original.

They had heavy silverware of a kind I hadn't seen before.

Hanna's room, really, was the issue. She'd lived in it, from her perspective, her entire life. When she grew too big for her crib, they bought her a twin-sized bed. When she got too old for a Dora the Explorer comforter, they bought a Friendship is Magic one. When she grew too sophisticated for that, Claudia bought her a duvet and then they shopped together for the cover. Pops of Marimekko-style pattern. The pink was both preteen-girl appropriate and subtly sophisticated enough that it had probably been Claudia's suggestion. The walls were decalled with a press-on vinyl forest and animals.

They'd hung twinkle lights from the ceiling around her bed. It suggested a canopy without quite creating one.

It was a mess.

I tried to imagine how to begin to pack a room like that. Would clothes and books be enough? How many stuffed animals constituted quorum? Her electronics were small enough to go in a carry-on, at least, but the room was dense with her possessions. They ruined the carefully-curated design. There were papers and notes. Small toys from McDonald's. Hair clips.

Hanna stared at the two suitcases. They were big enough that she could have curled up tightly in one.

They were inadequate.

"I'm not leaving."

"You said you wanted to come live with me."

"I guess."

I paused. "Do you want to live with your Grandma Elaine?"

"If she'll come here."

"There's no *come*, Hanna. There's only *go*."

She turned into a storm, then. Impossibly angry. She tried to articulate it for a minute or two, but it descended into screaming beyond words. Tried to push me out of the room, and when I wouldn't go, she left. Locked herself in her parents' bedroom, where the bathroom was again a sterile oasis.

I'd booked tickets for us to Toronto. We'd need an hour, maybe an hour-and-a-half at the airport. A courier had brought papers from Wayne asserting Hanna's guardianship, but I had to find other things: her school and health records, whatever identification a middle-school girl owned, the things not in her room that she couldn't function as a citizen without.

The bedroom door would have unlocked with a twist of a table knife. I could have told her that, when social workers came for you, they gave you a garbage bag for your things, if you had things. Every time you moved, they gave you a garbage bag. It might rip and spill your underwear onto the street. It might leak small objects.

She was crying so hard.

I packed. I sorted clothes and objects that looked heavily used. Her backpack had a few school papers in it and more of the odds and ends I associated with her. I added the electronics I could find, chargers and connection cables.

Everything else would come later, or not at all.

While I was at it: what level of "everything?" Were the light fixtures important? Could the wall decals be replaced? Which objects outside the room were hers?

Where in the name of God and the Pixies was I going to put it all?

I went back. Found another bag and stripped the duvet, folded and added the cover. Two more stuffed animals. Some runners with LEDs in the soles that I found at the back of her closet.

In the basement, the boxes of dance costumes lurked. Closets revealed ice skates, dance shoes obviously too small, sports rackets and bats.

Ethan's home office wall featured a trophy case. All Hanna's.

She swam. She was a Dolphin, a Porpoise, a Sunfish, a Mermaid, a member of the Neptune club.

I went back upstairs. To the bedroom door I said, "There's a couple of pools pretty close to us in Toronto. We'll get you set up at one right away."

Through the door, "I swim at Pan-Am."

"I know. That's a great pool. We'll find you a good one." I checked my watch. 6:30. We needed to mobilize. "Hanna, please open the door."

I didn't hear her move. The doorknob, I realized, lacked the angled slot that would let me twist the lock back.

I studied the space between door and jamb. Went downstairs and got my wallet. Credit cards still worked.

I said, "If you hate it, you don't have to stay. But I bought plane tickets. And you can't stay here by yourself tonight." She stared at me, a ball of puffy-faced misery. "Have you ever been to Toronto?"

"No."

"It's pretty good. We can go to some museums or something."

"When are we leaving?"

"I'd like to leave in an hour." Realistically, we had two, but I hadn't yet shifted her as far as the door.

She stalked out. Examined the suitcases in her room, then snapped from place to place gathering up further objects. They made a dizzying heap on the bed. "I need another bag."

It meant four bags, plus her carry-on and mine, in the foyer. I realized, suddenly, that I didn't know what to do with the house keys. The car keys I'd simply returned to their drawer. Wayne's office was across town, and closed.

I called a cab.

Cars drifted by the house, but none of them were taxis. I waited and watched the clock, and finally went outside to look down the block. The neighbours had returned for the night. Most of the protruding garages had their doors shut and light trickled thinly from behind heavy curtains on the matched front picture windows. Brighter spills came down from upstairs.

I wondered if the taxi was lost.

Periodically, for days, the neighbours had watched us. No one had approached, but cars slowed if we were outside. People walked their dogs past the driveway and paused as if it were the animals' idea.

Lights flicked on over porches as smokers surreptitiously stepped out to light up and study me.

Their lurking meant I didn't notice the woman on the street at first.

I craned my head past her. No lights approaching at all.

She stayed there, hands in her coat pockets. Boots and a long coat and no dog. She watched me as if I might be contagious.

I said, "Can I help you?"

"I'm sorry."

"No worries." She could stare if she wanted. I'd be gone in minutes. My phone buzzed in my jeans pocket; when I retrieved it, the cab company wanted to know where I was. They were waiting outside the house. Ten minutes, now.

"You're not here."

They were on the other side of the lake, in the mirror-world version of this cul-de-sac.

"I'm going to be late. I'm going to the airport. Do I need to call a different company?"

It was an empty threat. Winnipeg only had two cab companies, and one of them was perpetually booked. The few independents were clinically unreliable.

The city needed an influx of roving drivers from some distant country. Somalia or Bhutan.

Five minutes. Promise.

"Alright."

She was still there. "Hello," I said.

"Hello, Allison."

"I don't think I know you."

"I didn't think you'd forget me."

I stared at my mother. Hanna had come out of the house to see where I'd gone. I said to her, "Can you get the bags down the steps? The cab's going to be here in a second."

"No. They're heavy."

"Try, please."

My mother said, "I'm so sorry, baby. I'm so, so sorry."

I said, "I have to go. If there's something you want, you can talk to the lawyers. Elaine has the number, I'm sure."

She watched me go back to the house. Hanna hadn't budged the suitcases, and in the end, I had to haul them out myself to where the driver could reach them and load the trunk. She stood there while I hoisted my own bag and pushed Hanna to the car.

I went back and checked that the door was locked. I could mail the keys to Wayne later. Express, if he wanted to pay for it.

My mother stood there in the snow while we left.

Hanna was dead walking by the time we got home, killed by hours in security and in the air and more hours on the ground moving from the airport into the city. She was conscious, but she shivered uncontrollably. When I tried to talk to her, she complained that she was hungry.

We found a still-open Subway en route, and the driver waited, ticking up the meter, while I bought her a sandwich.

She had nothing to say about the house. I called, "We're home!" to it, but if Eden was there, he didn't answer. I'd texted him in the cab; he hadn't answered that either.

It was almost two in the morning. I left Hanna's bags at the bottom of the stairs, blocking the door, and walked ahead of her to the landing. "The bathroom's there. I'm in here. You can sleep in there. We'll get you set up tomorrow."

The guest room, to the extent that we had one, was choked with objects. If we'd been more organized, they might have been boxed, at least, but as it was, they towered against the walls, overwhelming any daylight sense of the space.

I left her there. Brushed my teeth and padded back to my bedroom. I'd found a T-shirt and panties, in deference to the company in the house, and I was almost folded into bed when Hanna opened the door. "Can I come in?"

"What's up?"

She crawled across the foot of the bed and curled up by the wall. "I'll be quiet."

Too exhausted. I'd been awake for eighteen hours. "Fine."

Except it meant I didn't sleep. Hanna curled into her night shirt and fell asleep almost instantly. She'd left even her phone behind.

Soft child-breathing. Her hair needed washing again, because I kept forgetting that she needed to be reminded.

I rolled over and she kicked me.

I lay on my back. Breathed and worked on tracing the path of the breath out of my lungs and through the air around me, a blank mind that reaches for sleep. Nothing. The house shifted softly as the night went on, and finally I heard footsteps on the third floor, clarifying as Eden came down the stairs.

"Allison?"

"Hey."

Hanna was asleep. I walked away from her into the hall.

"I didn't know you were home."

"I texted you."

He looked around himself. "I don't know what I did with my phone. I'm sorry. Should I have come to meet you?"

I tried to imagine Eden navigating transit all the way to Pearson. He'd have been lost until morning. "No, it's okay."

"You got someone in there?"

Hanna muttered in her sleep.

I said, "No. Not really. Can I curl up with you for a bit?"

He leaned in, then, and wrapped me in bear arms. Up close, he smelled like two or three unshowered days and the faint spiciness of layered deodorant.

He didn't turn on the lights in his room. The curtains were open, soaking the room in yellowish streetlight.

"C'mere."

He'd stripped. Lain down on top of the covers in a half-spoon, waiting for me.

It was the first bed I could remember that didn't smell foreign. Eden hummed softly while I eased back against him. "What?"

"I think it's R.E.M. Is it bothering you?"

"No. You can sing if you want."

He sang *Try Not to Breathe*. It drifted across keys without grating my nerves. "I'll try not burden you."

"I missed you."

"Mmm." He shifted. "Are you at work tomorrow?"

"No. Next week. They know."

I fell asleep almost instantly. Woke up in the dark with a vague assurance that it was morning. Eden's alarm clock was out of my range of vision. I disentangled myself. Walked to the bathroom. Clock on the radio there said 6:40. Past time I was up; too early to rouse anyone else.

Hanna was still asleep.

Downstairs to the main floor. I got a glass of water in the kitchen, drank it standing up, then padded back to my office.

Hundreds of emails waited. Documents to be reviewed. Guests to be prepared for. Story ideas and bands fishing for coverage.

I put on headphones and the Public Broadcasting feed. Started the first of the missed shows.

That music.

Good morning, Canada. Happy Friday. This is The Cure.

～ 14 ～

Rabbit

The house in Toronto wasn't mine.

I'd once tried to calculate how long it would take me to buy the house, or just initiate the process. The real estate sites told me that, conservatively, I was looking at about one-and-a-half million dollars. A ten per cent down payment, then, would be one hundred fifty thousand. A monthly payment, with historically low interest rates, of a little under seven thousand dollars every month, would carry on for the rest of my life.

The house was more or less Eden's. He'd grown up in it, and when his parents had relocated to other cities and climates, they'd assigned it to him. He didn't own it, but neither did he have to pay the property taxes. A trust was established for that. It provided for the monthly bills and costs of being human, and an allowance that let him make under-funded art films without succumbing to starvation or cold or the economic necessities plaguing the rest of his generation.

Hanna had a trust fund. They had that in common.

The house was so fully his, so not mine, that it wasn't my legal address. For the past five years, I hadn't had one. My last recorded address was that: my last recorded. Necessary mail went to the office, was answered, and went out again. Bills arrived electronically. When they'd asked for my address so I could vote, I decided against it. Voting.

A certain number of documents probably went to my old apartment and were swallowed by the void, but they hadn't so far disrupted the course of my life.

I'd needed to move.

Eden whispered, *Just move in here.*

We'd been tangled on his bed, not asleep, and I was looking at apartment listings on my phone. I needed an anonymous building, close to work, with door security. I'd lived in a low-rise box with almost no furniture for three-and-a-half years. Six months had passed since officers had come to the office, warrants in hand, and taken Jay out with them, minutes before we went to air, and charges pending.

I couldn't stay where I was. People were following me. Buzzing at all hours. Waiting for me outside the door.

Just move in here.

It wasn't quite a question. Not quite, *Will you move in with me?* He had space. His parents' things were boxed in two of the bedrooms off the landing. His bedroom was the same one it had been his entire life.

I said, joking, "Which room can I have?"

"Pick one. We'll put the boxes in the basement."

He moved a few of them himself, even. It was an oddly focussed action for him. I had friends from work help me pack my old apartment.

"Not much here."

"Live to work, Alli?"

I said, "The rock and roll lifestyle doesn't have room for couches."

And then, because of course we did, we went out for martinis.

I was drinking again, carefully, socially. After years of abstinence, I'd reverted to a teenager's tastes. Chocolate raspberry-tini, liqueurs and vodka swirling together like candy across my tongue. Mango pineapple.

"The word," Ellie told me, "on the street is that you're a real estate whore."

"What?"

"I mean, sorry. I know you and Eden are sweet together. But it doesn't hurt that he's got that house, does it?"

I hadn't been prepared for the insularity of Toronto's arts community. Eden's familiarity and overlap with the indie film-and-music scene didn't quite eclipse the presence of his family's money. His father's shift into publishing, and then out of it in time to avoid the print collapse, was legendary. His mother, originally an artist, worked as an art dealer, now in Montreal and New York. There were two uncles left dominating Toronto's cultural hegemony, and no cousins to inherit the cultural capital.

Eden wasn't the city's most eligible bachelor, but it was a popular joke.

He was quite mad, of course. Crazier than I was, and more vividly aware of it than anyone else I'd met. His work was shaped around the currents of his brain chemistry.

Cam Restly, running the Laneway Press and talking to me at a book launch party at the Gladstone Hotel, had called Eden *The Luminous Rabbi of the Annex.*

It stuck. That version of his name showed up in occasional poems at public readings. It blinked through social media. In my head, he was just *Rabbi. Luminous.* Outside my head, I called him *Rabbit.*

•••◐•••

How much money Eden had was a lingering question. He was constantly hustling to fund his film projects, taking small, irritating jobs to pay the epic bills. He spent the year after I moved in with him partnered on a project to create a reality-based wedding show filmed around southern Ontario.

"The Americans like Ontario," he told me. "They say it looks like everywhere."

I picked that up, turned it into a monologue: *Does the nowhere of perfect America actually look like Canada? The clean streets, the schools without bulletproof glass, the friendly neighbours, the sprawling suburbia spreading between one major city and another? Could we reasonably tell whether we were in Mississauga or Airdrie? (It's in Alberta people, look for it just north of Calgary on your map or your app.)*

Why do we build these generic spaces? The architecture of a century ago is markedly different from Halifax to Montreal, distinct in Winnipeg from the structures of Vancouver.

Ah, but after World War Two, were we too scared to go home? We'd been shaken up, relocated, and wherever we landed, we built up a country of anywhere. This loss of place representing our loss of home.

Do you know where you are when you wake up?

When we migrate across the country, can we notice?

Feel safe where you are, Canada, but try to look beyond the cul-de-sacs. Instead of nowhere, know where, be sure.

Good morning, Canada. This is The Cure.

•••◐•••

Eden's show took him mostly to the outer circles of Toronto. First- and second-generation immigrant families planning massive, community-based weddings made marvellous low-budget spectacles, and the wedding parties loved their automatic celebrity status.

Here comes the bride. She has a degree in Commerce and Operations Management from McMaster University, and she's shown here with her beloved Bichon Frisé, Tiffin.

The groom is a debonair fellow, just starting out in pharmacy.

Together, they have amassed a tentative guest list of one hundred twenty.

Their parents have created a further, supplementary guest list of three hundred ten. Four hundred thirty people in all, or approximately everyone either of them has ever met.

The budget is conservatively estimated at fifty thousand dollars.

Let's begin!

Eden said, "It's not cinema verité, but I think it might be more moving to film than to watch."

"Did they let you taste the cake samples?"

"The catering trip was amazing. Why doesn't anyone I know get that kind of food when they get married?"

I thought about this. We were lying on the aged Persian carpet — retrieved by his father from cosmopolitan Tehran in the mid-1970s — in Eden's office on the third floor, contemplating the ceiling. "Do the people you know get married?"

"You got married."

"Doesn't count."

"How was the food?"

"We had soup, after. There wasn't a party."

"Hmm. Anyone else you know?"

"Katie got married at the Pop Underground festival?" Not a question, but when I wasn't paying attention, my voice quivered into up-speak. This rising intonation that years of Riot hadn't bred out of me. *Is this appropriate? Do you understand what I'm saying?*

"I didn't think riot grrrls got married."

"We didn't make it a habit. Patriarchal construct and so forth. But Katie and Trick wanted to get hitched, and we thought we could make a joke out of it. We found the dress at this Goodwill in Portland. It was from the 70s, all stiff and satiny, and we helped her take it apart. Got her a blood-red veil and army boots."

"These days, that's practically fashionable. There's a whole subculture. I can show you the websites," he said.

"Katie would like that."

"Mmm. It's a bit craft-y for really hard-core feminism."

"We've talked about this."

"If feminists like cupcakes, why don't you ever make me any?"

"I only eat them. You know how to cook. Anyway, when Katie and Trick got married I think we just barbecued, and the vegans ate hummus."

Eden said, "You should do a show about the changes in weddings."

"That's not really our thing. *Walk Out* does the theme shows."

The Cure was not about quirky documentaries. We did commentary, short and sweet, with music, timely references, and interviews with interesting people.

And, in fact, Jay Beaton had already covered it. When *Oh Mommy!: Blood, Girls, and the Wedding-Industrial Complex* came out, he did an interview with the author in the first half-hour of the show. We did a play-out to the news with The Whip's indie-folk ironic cover of "White Wedding," and after the world update, a *Cure for Ordinary* panel: *What do weddings mean now?*

We were short of panellists that day, so they had me sit in, as Riot Grrrl Alli Winter rather than as my production-assistant self. I told the story about Katie's wedding. Jay dubbed it the first angry anti-wedding.

"Did they live happily ever after?"

"No. It's hard to stay married while you're on tour. He got both parrots in the divorce, and I think they still go on vacations together."

"That's a nice story."

Jay said, *True love, Canada. What's it for? Call us and tell us.*

We pulled that show from the archives a few weeks later, when Jay shot his ex-wife. It was an ongoing problem, that we'd say something off-the-cuff, a little funny, that would explode afterwards. The website team simply made certain files inaccessible during periods of scandal.

All of Jay's files went into the grey zone of sound recordings. They stayed there through the media coverage and through his trial. While he was waiting for sentencing, he threatened to sue us for suppressing his work. He hired new lawyers, a publicist. He talked about it on American television, always by remote video-link because he wasn't allowed to leave his apartment.

It wasn't the sort of thing you could actually sue over. I don't think he wanted to, so much as he wanted to make the point.

He irritated the judge, though. Jay's trial had a partial publication ban on it, because of unspecified items found in the victim's house, and the judge announced that the "end-run" around the ban was a violation in spirit.

Jay was sent to Collins Bay Penitentiary, no contact with the press under penalty of judicial review. Journalists Without Borders protested. The sentence was appealed.

Jay developed his own libertarian free-speech cult, an odd creature in Canada though through the one-way mirror to the south, it had cousins and offshoots that looked more familiar. They built Jay a webpage and an archive, and acquired his show recordings through applications under the Access to Information Act. They sent angry boys to interview him every six to eight weeks, and posted transcripts within hours of each conversation.

That kind of anger finds ways of spreading. It's viscous and sticky. I took over *The Cure* and got it all over me.

Allison Winter is a media tool suppressing Jay Beaton's essential cultural contributions.
Allison Winter is a frigid cunt who hates men.
Allison Winter is part of the feminazi conspiracy.

Jay's minion-boys came to talk to me at work. I declined to meet with them.

I had no comment on Jay. No comment on Public Broadcasting's position. No comment on the screamed-out *whore* on the streets of Toronto.

They published as much personal information about me as they could: phone number, address, bra size. They doxxed me. It was how I learned the word.

The information they published wasn't complete, but there was enough. They had all of my work contacts, and some of the information on my family, and pictures of me, and my arrest records in Windsor (1996, indecent exposure), Seattle (1999, disturbing the peace), Vancouver (simple possession), Winnipeg (disturbing the peace). They posted my cell phone number (the first of six times I changed it). They posted my address.

I needed to move.

They re-published my email and changed phone number, but my new address wasn't listed. Legally, I didn't live anywhere. My former building, sad brick thing that it was, was hit with balloons of red paint and a surprising number of used condoms.

It seemed like a good idea to never, ever tell anyone where I was. Eden didn't argue.

I went back to work. Finished a show cycle. Took a day off.

I went to Collins Bay. I wasn't on a list of friends or family members, so I had to approach Jay as a journalist. He thought that was funny.

"Did I do something specific to piss you off?"

"I built that show."

It wasn't strictly true, but close enough. Jay ignored his writers and production staff, treated them as extensions of his own brain, except when he was prowling for sex, or angry.

"I didn't fire you." *I didn't make you butcher your wife.*

"You changed the name."

"We changed it. Yeah."

"You pulled my shows."

"That was the legal department. Not my choice."

"What do you want, kisses?" It was sarcastic, hostile, but the guard growled at us that no physical contact was permitted. "I've already seen her pussy, thanks."

"I want to know why you decided to sic your adolescent pit bulls on me. You were always smarter than this men's rights bullshit."

He said, "Fuck you. Really. Fuck you, Allison, right back to the fundie hole you crawled out of."

His boys eased back, didn't follow me nightly, but all my numbers had to change, and it took a legal injunction to remove the original doxxing documents from the website. I got hate mail at work, but the mail room filtered most of it, sent the worst to legal or the police.

My personal, domestic life was something I had to bury. I subsumed most of it under Eden's long-established presence in the scene. His house, only half-possessed and held in trust, shielded me. His house phone was a landline that he kept years after everyone else converted to cellular. His name sat on the utilities and the tax rolls.

They still found us, occasionally.

We got attacks, but nothing worse than rotten fruit or dog shit.

I cleaned it up myself, when I could. When I didn't catch it, I'd come home to find Eden doing the cleaning.

"Do you want me to move?"

He blinked at me. "Why?"

"Well." Pointing at the mess.

"I like this house."

We had circular conversations where I tried to ask if I should leave, and he just asserted that he liked the house, and was staying, and that seemed to be the end of the question.

He wasn't moving. He hadn't asked me to.

He left, sometimes, but I was expected to stay.

I bought the groceries. When my bank went more fully digital, I figured out how to pay utilities that weren't in my name. It created continuity. Eden went off for weeks to film. I walked in at night to find him packing for a trip to Greenland. Flight at 8 a.m. No warning.

I said, "Keep warm. Text me."

You couldn't text from Ilulissat, as it turned out. He did almost a year of periodic circumpolar photography, and I got used to fragmentary emails sent via satellite, poorly spelled and affectionate.

i saw you in the snow on worley street your back stiff that time i remember you steaming furious at the space between the lights. late for pills production caffeination falling to critical levels i remember catching you at the bus stop and exchanging lips with yours you better be still there when i get home

E

~ 15 ~
# *Hi-Fi*

I'd been off *The Cure* for thirteen broadcast days. Each show ran for seventy minutes of airtime, interrupted by news broadcasts. I could accelerate that by skipping the music, which compressed it to fifty-five minutes per episode. I'd need another weekend, maybe a week of conscious work, to catch myself up.

I had to be back on air in thirty-eight hours.

I listened. Took notes. Travelled through the spaces of sound.

At some point it was fully daylight. My office was at the back of the house, and it lit up only slowly. Grey light seeped in. I needed caffeine.

Coffee at home was Eden's responsibility. I'd been drinking coffee since I was a teenager, but in our first months living together he'd quietly disapproved of my coffee-making techniques. I bought cheap, big cans of ground coffee and made fast pots whenever I wanted them.

I apparently did it wrong.

The coffee maker had to go. The coffee-pod system that ran the broadcast offices where I spent so many hours a day wasn't allowed through Eden's door, even after he insisted that the door was also mine. Pods that I picked up on my way home could stay in the mud room by the front door, but they weren't allowed in the house proper. If I left them there for a day or two, Eden would pointedly go in and out through the back.

Eden ground his own beans. He went to the market and bought small batch-es. Stored them in glass. When he got up, he came downstairs into the kitchen in pajamas and measured beans into an antique burr grinder and paced the morn-ing, grinding them and listening to the radio.

I was still aching from the late-night Winnipeg flight. The aftermath of travel felt like the flu, or withdrawal.

Eden wasn't in his bedroom, but he was home. I found him upstairs, in his office at the top of the house. He said, "Are you hungry?"

I thought about it. "Yeah. You're offering?"

"Sure."

Hanna was curled asleep in my bed. Tiny creature. I pulled the door closed.

Eden said, "She woke up a while ago. I got her some cereal, and then she wanted to go back to bed."

"Thank you."

He made eggs and toast. I thought about taking a shower.

There was music everywhere.

New albums had come in from bands whose releases were weeks away, and who would appear on the show four or five days before those records dropped. At some point, there'd been a fashion shift, and instead of the music arriving on a flash drive or an iridescent disk, it came on vinyl.

Couriers brought the records to work, put them in my office. I carried them home, two or three at a time, on my back, along the subway and on the bus and through the city to Eden's house.

Everything came home like that: indirectly. When I commuted, I covered my tracks. I doubled back sometimes. Changed busses. I left work out of differ-ent doors, at different times. I only used the front if I was travelling with other people.

I wasn't sure whether I still needed to travel that randomly. I hadn't been threatened by anyone I wasn't related to in months.

Hanna came downstairs. She sat at the dining room table, hopefully, with her feet swinging. I tried to remember the last time we'd eaten in there.

Eden cleared her a place. Set down a placemat before the plate and fork.

I said, "Do you drink coffee?"

"I drink juice."

We had pomegranate juice in the fridge.

"What kind of juice is that?"

"Red," I told her.

"Okay."

Eden looked at me pointedly. I took my own plate to the dining room and sat with it laid on top of a record sleeve.

Crumbs drifted downward. I checked which album it was and concluded that it wouldn't be much worse after the damage from breakfast was done than it was already. I drank my coffee. Pulled my feet up in front of me.

Hanna said, "This house is like some kind of time-travelling house."

"Oh?"

"Like, it looks like houses look in old movies or something. Why don't you have a TV?"

"It's upstairs."

"There's books everywhere. And what are these?"

"Records. They've got music on them."

"Music goes on your phone."

"Thank you for the reminder."

Eden came in. He'd made more toast and found marmalade in the fridge. He went out, came back again with a plastic jug of something vaguely artificial-looking.

"What's that?"

"Peach nectar, I think."

I said, "One of your secret vices?"

"Well, I don't remember buying it, but I'm pretty sure powdered drink mix made completely of chemicals doesn't go bad. Have at."

Hanna looked at her untouched pomegranate juice.

I said, "If you don't want it, pour it down the sink."

She did. I heard her rinse the cup. She came back and poured chemical sugar into the tumbler instead. Drained it, filled and drained it again, and sat down with a third glass.

"Did I sleep for a long time?"

Eden said, "I think about eleven hours."

"That's a lot?"

"It's pretty impressive."

"So, who are you?"

"I'm Eden."

She said, "Who *are* you? Why do you live with us?"

"I've always lived here. I came with the house."

"Seriously?"

"Seriously. I live with Alli."

Hanna studied him. "Are you dangerous?"

"No. I'm crazy, but I'm not dangerous."

"Okay."

He left. Hanna said, "Is he dangerous?"

Eden, to be fair, looked dangerous. He'd cultivated a look that was usually worn by men in posters warning little girls to be careful.

I said, "Eden is my boyfriend."

Hanna nodded. "He's the guy who called you at David's."

"Yes."

Pause. "Can I phone David?"

I nodded at her phone.

Hanna shook her head. "My phone doesn't work anymore. Just the games are still there."

"Okay. I'll deal with it." I dug my phone out of my pocket. "Do you know his number?"

"Yes."

She dialled. Paused with her finger over the green 'call' icon. "I can do this by myself." Walked upstairs, away from me.

I sat on the landing. Hanna pushed the guest room's door closed, pointedly, and I couldn't hear most of what passed between them. When she fell silent, she didn't give the phone back.

I realized that her phone had been on her parents' plan. It was dead.

I sat on the landing working with my show, drafting, making plans for upcoming shows. Some of the albums I had to review, I already knew I wasn't going to like. I had fewer hours, could I just write them off, send them back unlistened, labelled *no*?

It wasn't fair. I wasn't fair.

I went back to the living room and put the first of the unloved albums onto the hi-fi. Gave it twenty minutes before I declared it dead and loaded the next one.

The third pick out of the pile was better than I expected. I jotted questions about it, a reminder to look up the band, a possible invitation for them to perform a live session in studio.

I took a shower. Scrubbed the dead skin away from my eyes and forehead.

Hanna behind the door was talking again, covering the distance though I didn't know to whom.

I knocked. She didn't answer. The clock downstairs said it was 2:40 in the afternoon.

I went to work.

The Cure's website led with a canned statement saying that Allison Winter was away dealing with a family crisis, but that she'd be returning soon. That she thanked everyone for their kind wishes.

They'd reorganized around my absence, moving papers and data away from my workspace and into others' so that my desk was eerily clear. The surface had been cleaned, but only once, and there was a faint dust-haze above the gloss. The wireless keyboard had gone into deep-sleep mode.

They rustled near my arrival without quite making eye contact. For radio people, it was late. The broadcast day started at 5:45 a.m., with every evening repeating the morning broadcasts. If I waited long enough on any given day, I could turn on the feed and hear myself arriving, hours before.

"You're off until next week."

"I'm fine."

Ellie snorted. "You look fine. I mean that we've got guest hosts booked into next week. If you cancel, they'll be pissed."

She meant the hosts. We had a string of backup hosts, mostly musicians, who could use the pay.

"Okay. How long 'til I'm back?"

"You can go on Wednesday, if you like."

I said, "Until then, why don't I do production?"

"You realize we're fully staffed?"

"We haven't been fully staffed since three rounds of government cuts ago."

She shrugged. "You can be a martyr if you want to, but you're getting paid not to work right now, so you might as well stay home. When did you even get back into town?"

"Last night."

"What about the little girl?"

"She's home. I mean, home here."

"What are you going to do with her?"

I had no idea. I needed to make a list of what children needed.

What had I been doing when I was her age?

We'd been in the mission fields. Sub-tropical. I'd been barefoot most of the time, risking sunburn. Living that pre-Ethan life.

Ethan flickered through my brain and slid back into the dark corners. He looked good. There was almost no blood on him at all.

I said, "I need to talk to someone with kids."

"I'll ask around," she told me.

:::!:!!

It was too late in the day to deal with most of the list they gave me. What did children need? Schools, school clothes, after-school lessons. Day care. Transport to school. Transport to lessons. Packed lunch. Shoes: they grow out of shoes constantly. Permission slips, pocket money, a schedule posted next to the door so they could check what they had to do today. *What lessons are coming? What instrument do you need to carry? Is your homework in your bag?*

Children need vaccinations. Unless you're one of those people who doesn't do that.

I said, "I have her records. She's had her shots. Completely up to date. Like a puppy."

"What grade is she in?"

I thought about it. "Five? Maybe six?"

"You need to know that."

"I have it written down."

"Is she in band? They start band in grade five."

"This is arcane. What do I need to know *today*?"

"School. She needs to go to school. Have you applied to anywhere good?"

I said, "She's been in public school all her life."

"I think you . . . might want to make some adjustments. I could call some people." The woman sitting across from me worked in administration. She had a suit on, and she didn't look like she could operate a sound board. Her perfume smelled vaguely of an MBA. "Where do you live?"

I avoided the question.

I said, "I'll make some calls. Tomorrow."

She didn't get up to leave, so I did. She could, I decided, have my office if she was so attached to it. Her perfume might fry the acoustical equipment, but her department was responsible for replacing our gear, so the damage would remain her problem.

It was dark outside, or deep twilight. Spring was going to come, one of these days. The lingering snow-dirt felt familiar, though. It was the purest manifestation of Toronto that I could imagine.

There were buses, but I decided to walk home. Twice I checked my pockets for the phone I'd left with Hanna. I tried to remember if I'd told Eden where I was.

It wasn't a walk the perfumed monster in my office would have made, but I wasn't sure that she owned shoes with traction. Her car — she'd have a car, she was commuting from somewhere with elaborate yards and complex school zoning — would lurk underground, something elegant and clogged with kids' bags, waiting for her to return.

A car wasn't on her list of utter necessities, but she must have assumed I already owned one. The walk reminded me why I didn't. The streets were car-solid, barely moving with downtown's fluid population. Drivers would be commuting into the mid-evening. I took the subway, usually, and then the bus. In the summer I could bike or walk. Skateboard on the days I was feeling young and resilient enough. In the early hours of the day, moving on the slight downhill grade towards the lake, boarding gave the same pleasure it had when Kara and I took it up.

These days, I wore a helmet. I didn't have even one safety pin put through my face.

I tried to imagine groceries and failed. A dozen blocks from home I picked a storefront and walked in, ordered take-out, and sat until the curries were packed and ready. The last half-mile smelled like korma and car exhaust.

Eden came down to eat, following the food-smell. Hanna took longer. She had my phone, battery exhausted, and she held it out. I said, "I'll get yours working."

"Okay."

She picked at her food. I offered her a samosa. She sniffed it suspiciously. I gave up, went to the kitchen and poured her cereal in a bowl. From the dining room, she called, "No milk."

"Okay."

Her dry chewing left me vaguely nauseated. Why she'd chosen stale cereal instead of sweet, MSG-loaded hot food was beyond me.

Eden offered her bites. She refused. He waited until he'd decided she was sure, then ate hers.

I poured Hanna a glass of peach nectar. When she demanded more, I said, "That's pure sugar." Not my mother's voice, but maybe Elaine's, a wind of indirect disapproval.

Hanna stood up and got herself tap water.

I said, "What did you do, before? After school, I mean."

"Swimming."

I said, "We'll get that set up."

~ 16 ~

Equilibrium

We tried different pools. The University of Toronto's aquatics complex, two community centres, a health club. The civic website claimed there were sixty-one indoor pools in the city, though when I mapped them I realized they meant *all* of Toronto, a name they'd stretched to include the amalgamated sprawl.

Schools were less hit-and-miss. They didn't take children on a trial basis, and unless you'd prepared years of records, children were assigned entirely on the basis of house number. We typed in numbers, we came up with a school.

Hanna was in grade five. She was not in band. She played soccer, but only at school, not on a team.

She swam three times a week. She'd been doing it for years.

I'd tried to parse the schedules of swimming clubs and failed. Every organized activity for little girls began in September or October. In March, there were no gaps in the roster for late arrivals. Until the next cycle began, she could only do things alone.

That wasn't true, or not absolutely, but I couldn't imagine how we'd get back and forth to Etobicoke, the nearest club with year-round admission.

Our neighbourhood pool was in the basement of the ancient Jewish Community Centre. It had stood since the district was last Jewish, after the Second

World War, when Eden's family had arrived and settled. His name helped me make arrangements with the centre. And it was close to her school. We didn't even need bus fare.

I thought about letting Hanna go by herself. I remembered walking farther than that at her age, but the school didn't feel that was acceptable. Other girls were collected in SUVs and ferried from place to place. Boys piled into vans. The few pedestrians came and left with accompanying adults.

I asked Eden whether that was normal.

"I think for rich white people it is."

I'd thought of *rich* applying to different neighbourhoods than ours, but I hadn't tried to buy a house in the middle of Toronto, recently, either. We were miles from the nearest family-friendly condo high-rises. Refugees and new arrivals lived in the city, but elsewhere, far from us.

I reorganized my work day so that I could meet Hanna after school and walk the seven blocks with her. I had a bag full of work, a commitment to get things done remotely. I spent nights and weekends in my home office, and I was mostly keeping up.

After that first day, I didn't mention Hanna at work again. No one there had ever seen her in the flesh. She might not have existed. I wondered how long I could reasonably keep her invisible. There were show hosts with children, but not many, and most of those were men. Women with children worked in kids' television production. *The Cure* met broadcast standards, but it wasn't "family friendly."

Hanna didn't listen to the show. She was at school when it aired. Her musical taste ran below our demographic. She followed the universe on her phone. She'd never in her life voluntarily turned on a radio.

If she was invisible to the broadcast centre, I was invisible to her. She didn't say *thank you* to anything without a prompt, and she once walked into me sitting blankly in the dark, trying to sort my thoughts, and simply informed me that we were out of juice. She tramped through the city two steps behind me or three steps ahead, avoiding my company. In the locker room, she selected her own locker and placed her own combination lock, half a row down from whichever one I chose.

I hadn't been in the water in years, and it emerged that I was a terrible swimmer. Hanna distanced herself from me and swam endless laps at the opposite end of the pool while I struggled through laboured breaststroke lengths. The woman who swam in the next lane, two days out of three, was massive. She moved through the water like a seal, quick and smooth and perfectly buoyant. That sleekness made it hard to flinch at the ripples of fat pressed beneath her swimsuit.

In the showers, where she let her body loose, I could choose whether I wanted to look at her or away.

I'd been good at this, once: being naked around other women and treating bodies as just-bodies. I'd written songs about it, given rants about it that appeared in zines next to ink-smeared dark photos of my own nakedness. I needed to re-centre myself in that other self, who existed where it was more normal for women to swim, who hadn't been fantasizing about what I'd look like in publicity photographs if I lost another four or five pounds.

I made an effort. I didn't hide in my towel while I changed. I didn't deliberately look away from women whose bodies swelled outwards, or whose joints had buckled so permanently that they had to rest half-nude on the benches between garments while they dressed.

Hanna's locker-room routine was aggressively modest. She'd gather her things and change in a toilet stall while I stripped at the bench. Orthodox women around us de-layered and re-created their bodies for aquatics, guarded by the promise of a women-only afternoon session.

Hanna never let me wash her hair again after that first time. Her body had become almost entirely invisible. She stood in front of the mirror and struggled with the snags in her own hair, flinching away when I offered to help.

The woman beside us, straightening her wig, said, "Have you tried No More Tangles? It works for my girls."

"My mom uses spray-on conditioner," Hanna said, without turning. Vaguely in my direction, "You should get some."

I said, "There's perfectly good conditioner in the bathroom."

Perfectly good came out again in Elaine's voice. She tasted like tonsil concretions exploding against the roof of my mouth.

The Jewish Community Centre had a *perfectly good* pool, but Hanna made it clear she didn't like it. Without a swim team and a coach, what was the point? Just swimming for its own sake.

"Can I do something else?"

"I thought you liked swimming."

She considered. "It's loud in my head."

"All pools are loud. It's the acoustics," I said, absently. We were waiting for the bus, both ragged-haired and irritable. It was far enough home, after swimming, that I'd decided against the walk. Hanna's backpack smelled like her lunch was rotting in it. She rejected most of what I packed for her. Her school didn't have a lunch program. I tried to remember what I'd eaten when I was her age, but when had I ever eaten bag lunch?

My childhood lunches were mostly soup and crackers, eaten at the table with the rest of my family, in whatever country we were in at the time.

Hanna said, "If I think too long, I feel like I'm going to throw up."

I tried to think of an answer to that. The bus came. We stepped on, showed my pass, and found a grip-bar to balance against. Hanna held her proof-of-age card in her hand, but no one asked for it.

No seats at that hour. We stood in the human press and I counted blocks.

Go home. Make dinner. Work before bed.

It was more schedule than I'd had in years.

Before Hanna, Eden had needed to phone me to remind me to go home. I didn't always. I kept club clothes in my office. I had an office, an actual one with a door and windows that could be covered, and I changed in there. Shifted from work to night life. My phone fed me possible shows.

I went to see the Headstones or Neko Case, stayed out all night, came in to work still flying on caffeine and after-party energy, and did whole shows before I collapsed. Slept on my office couch and showered at the gym and made the afternoon planning meetings with time to spare.

It wasn't required. There was nothing in my contract that said I had to work eighty hours a week. I did it because it was fun. I could sleep in my office. I could sleep at a half-dozen friends' places, downtown and close to everything.

It was something I'd thought about. My friend Lucy's condo was the sort of place I'd have bought for myself if I hadn't landed with Eden. The book money would have covered a down-payment.

The downtown was full of these single-human spaces. One bedroom plus den, four hundred square feet. They sounded dystopian, but not all of them were. Lucy's apartment was beautiful. Almost-black floors gleamed. Red enamel cabinets. Cats on the kitchen island and on the couch, all the time.

She had glass walls, less ostentatious than Jay's, but striking.

She took me with her when she bought the couch. This elephant-grey sectional, futuristically modular.

"Why do I need to be here?"

"I want to see if you can sleep on it."

"I can sleep on anything."

"Still." She made me lie down on it in the store. The two sections came apart and re-aligned as a bed. She found a throw made of carefully re-purposed saris and billowed it over me.

"Picture yourself sleeping like this."

The tag on the blanket whispered, *$113. Do not wash.*

I flinched, but she bought it. She bought throw pillows and the ferociously expensive sectional and flawed-glass light fixtures for the corner space. She said, "It's not your credit card."

Nested in that tower, she could work, go home, and trust that there was too little in her box-apartment to take over her life, and that the robot vacuum would handle the floors. As long as she never had children, she could live there indefinitely, clean and perfectly efficient, magazine-organized and digitally-managed at every hour of the night.

Off the bus and walking, Hanna said, "It's not the pool noise. I just have too much time to think. So I don't think I wanna swim anymore."

She walked ahead of me to the house. Vanished upstairs into the guest room and stayed there until I'd cooked and prodded her to come down and eat.

The dining table had been unearthed a few times since I'd moved into the house, usually for dinner parties. It made a convenient potluck surface, after which people could free-range and seat themselves on whatever levels made them happy. I ate at my desk. Eden ate there, or in front of the TV.

I'd cleared it again for Hanna. In the absence of a kitchen table, she needed somewhere to eat. If I let her eat in front of the TV, she stayed there for hours, dishes abandoned at her feet. She stepped on plates and broke them. Glasses upended themselves according to the forces of entropy and spilled their contents towards exhibition catalogues without any apparent concern.

If she ate in the living room, I was going to have to clean.

My domestic laziness had me setting the table for dinner every night. When I surveyed the mess, a few days after we landed, I realized we were going to need different, non-vintage objects in order to survive. Plastic, table-protective placemats. Glasses for milk.

I bought a lot of milk. Hanna drank a little and I drank the rest in the middle of the night, unwilling to let it spoil.

Eden drifted down while we were eating. He looked at the table. "No room for me?"

"I thought you were working. I was going to bring you something later."

"Can I sit down?"

"It's your house."

He sighed. Went to the kitchen and gathered himself a plate.

I wasn't a great cook. Websites showed elaborate, family-friendly meals that I couldn't reasonably aspire to. The things I knew how to cook well, I was fairly certain that a child wouldn't eat. That sense of failure regressed me to adolescent cooking patterns.

I cooked enough for five to seven people, consistently. Meat cooked separately from basic vegetables and a starch. Usually rice, sometimes potatoes. I did pasta twice a week, using sauce from a jar. Red every time.

Salt and pepper. Glass of milk.

The vegetable, if I didn't have time to plan, was peas and corn. Cooked together from separate frozen bags.

If I was ambitious, I put mushroom soup on the meat.

Eden sat down with us. He prodded the chicken and took a bite. "What did you put on it?"

"Lemon juice. It burned a bit. Sorry."

"It's okay. It's good."

Hanna said, "MayIpleasebeexcusedfromthetable?"

Reflexive. "Yes."

Gone.

I sat with Eden and chewed. When I heard Hanna's door close, I said, "Remember when we tried having sex on here?"

He nodded. "I twisted my knee."

"I ruined a book."

"I should clean up." He looked around. "You cooked."

"Don't worry about it. I'll clean up. You do what you're doing."

He shook his head. I got up, and he said, "Alli, come on. Sit down."

I sat.

"You look like you think I'm going to yell at you."

I'd never heard Eden shout. He operated on a scale that ranged from low-key ecstasy to sharp anxiety, almost entirely turned inward. A massive, friendly cat with a digital camera.

"Sorry, Rabbit."

"And now you're apologizing. What's up?"

"I keep channeling the ghost of my ex-mother-in-law."

"I thought she was still alive."

"She is. Doesn't mean she can't haunt me when she puts her mind to it."

"Okay." He waited. "Alli."

"What?"

"While you were in Winnipeg, did you do something *really* dumb? Something like going home?"

My eyes screwed shut. There was a lurking headache I thought I might be able to ward off.

"No."

"Then?"

I said, "I saw my mother."

"Where?"

"Outside the house. As we were leaving."

"Was she spying on you?"

"No. I don't know. Maybe. It's not like it ever happened before."

He nodded. "You should talk to someone."

"I'm talking to you."

"Someone sane." Pause. "Not that I'm complaining, but do you know Hanna's room smells really awful?"

Hanna's room did stink. If she wasn't eating the lunches I packed her, I wished she'd at least throw them away.

"I'll clean it up," I said.

"I bet she could clean it up herself. Are you going to see Lost Girls tomorrow night?"

"They're playing Saturday. I'm interviewing them tomorrow."

"Think they might be hurt if you don't show up?"

I said, "They're magnificent bitches, and they don't run around with hurt feelings because some chick they used to know blew off their concert. There'll be hundreds of old riot grrrls there, begging to get their homemade T-shirts signed."

"You said you might play with them."

"I didn't promise."

"Alli. Take your meds and go see your friends."

I'd taken my pills carefully for not quite eight weeks, and I was as close to equilibrium as I could be in Hanna's orbit.

"Go introduce me and I'll cover for you. Me and the tiny person can go to a movie."

"She isn't that tiny."

"She's a mite. Go play. Wear a sweater. It'll give you an extra layer to peel off when you can't resist climbing up on stage."

～ 17 ～

Restorative Justice

I studied Hanna slumped next to me in the moulded plastic office chairs. She'd been crying. Like me, when she cried her face turned red and she immediately became furious.

I'd always done that. I wasn't always sure whether I was angry at myself for crying, or whether I cried simply out of pure rage.

I remembered talking to a woman, an aging sound producer in the Winnipeg office. I asked her if she thought men cried in the bathroom. I'd been crying in the bathroom, but I'd also spent long minutes in ladies' rooms around the building peeing and ignoring the quiet sobs and nose-blows from adjoining stalls.

She said, "No."

"Men must cry."

"Oh, they cry. I've seen my husband cry, and he's a stoic. But men don't cry out of anger, so they're much less likely to cry at work."

I thought about that for years. *Men don't cry out of anger.* If I'd learned it earlier, it would have become a song. It was a revelation, the explanation for decades of humiliation and male discomfort.

He thinks you're sad.

He doesn't know you're crying because you want to kill him.

129

They were coming back. I got up, crouched in front of Hanna. I said, "They don't understand that you're mad. Hold onto the mad. Stuff it inside. Grind your fingers into your palms, or your legs if you have to. You can scream as soon as we're out of here."

She stared at me. Nodded.

They came in.

Because Hanna was under twelve, her vice principal informed me, they had decided not to involve the police. That said, they wanted me to understand how seriously they were taking the incident. The girl's parents were furious, legitimately, and had demanded a formal apology and a restorative justice process before Hanna returned to the classroom.

I looked at her. "Why." Not exactly a question.

"We take violence very seriously, Mrs. Winter."

"*Ms.*"

"If we had realized how disturbed Hanna was, we would have requested a psychiatric assessment before she joined us."

There was a distant, journalistic part of my brain that recognized that the woman's horror was genuine enough. Hanna had flattened not one but two classmates. The boy had lost a front tooth. The girl's nose was broken, apparently the result of more than a dozen rapid-fire blows to the face.

I said, "I want you to acknowledge that she was provoked."

"We don't accept violence here, regardless of provocation."

"What do you propose?" Journalist voice.

"A two-week, out-of-school suspension. Her return will be contingent on a therapeutic assessment, an Individual Behaviour Improvement Plan, and a formal apology from Hanna to the students involved."

I nodded. "I expect you'll send me a document to that effect."

She hesitated. "I had assumed you wouldn't want a paper trail."

"Do you expect me to find a therapist and complete this process in two weeks without official forms?"

"Very well."

I said, "Hanna, let's go."

Leaving furiously would have been easier if we'd had a car. It would have created an iron cage in which we could race away from the mess and both shriek once we were out of sight.

I said, "Keep walking. Grind your teeth."

Hanna nodded. Her face was scarlet. She didn't look at me.

I stopped. "Hang on." Thought about it. "Empty your bag."

Her backpack contained her uneaten lunch, a pair of socks, a box of loose pens, a few scribblers, and three textbooks.

"What's important in your desk? In your locker? Do you have a locker?"

"We don't have lockers."

"In your desk, then."

"I don't know. There's some stuff."

"Can you live without it?"

She shrugged. The textbooks lay on the sidewalk, soaking up filth from the not-quite-melted drifts.

I picked them up.

"Stuff anything you want to keep back in."

She left the scribblers and her lunch on the ground. I picked them up, too.

Apartment blocks were our friends. I missed the days when everyone had garbage cans all the time, in the alley, constantly accessible. As it was, I had to watch for the metal bunkers marked *Private* behind each low-rise flat stack.

There.

I ran. Skidded on black ice, fell. Got up. Hurled the contents of my arms into the bin.

I lost my purse. I had to crawl in after it.

In the old days, I had carried a backpack or a messenger bag, and it stayed strapped to my body, and there wasn't any problem at all.

I said, "Fuck that shit."

Hanna stared at me. She was crying again, but almost without self-consciousness. Her expression was so flatly shocked that I wasn't sure she could feel the tears on her face.

"I always thought school was bullshit," I told her. "I just hoped things might have changed by now. I'm sorry."

We went back to the street. Walked.

"You threw my books away."

"You don't need them. You're not going back there."

"They kicked me *out*?"

"I'm kicking *them* out. That was some bullshit. You beat some bitch's face in and suddenly she's all innocent?"

Hanna said, "She said if my family died, it was because of me."

"I hope her nose stays crooked for the rest of her life."

"He said maybe it was me that killed them."

"Show me your fist," I said. There was a gouge in it, the shape of adolescent front teeth. "We'd better clean that up. If it still looks bad tonight, we'll get you rabies shots."

"He had *rabies*?"

"All boys have rabies," I told her.

I liked our neighbourhood. It would have been too far a hike to reach something that I could ethically set on fire. It was another reason to want a car.

I wondered if Wayne had sold Ethan and Claudia's cars already. Whether he could send me one. For Hanna.

"Why aren't you mad?" she said.

"I don't look mad?" We were walking faster. I'd dodged us away from high-traffic streets, though it meant a longer route home. Too far. I changed course, taking us down an alley.

"You're, like, scary-mad."

"You're god-damn right."

"But you aren't mad at *me*."

I stopped. Turned. "No way."

"I hit those kids."

"I should hope so."

"We don't solve problems by hitting."

"I used to have a T-shirt," I said. "Back when we mostly made our own T-shirts with markers. It said, *I know violence isn't the answer. I got it wrong on purpose.*"

She was still crying. I made her smile anyway.

"A lot of the world is bullshit. They tell you that it's important to be a really nice person, especially if you're a girl. That's a giant fucking lie. Being nice turns you into ugly, miserable hamburger. If it's important, you go ahead and take the bastards apart."

The alley was impossibly long. I hadn't realized the shape of these blocks; I'd lived on one for years without ever crawling behind the scenes.

"There's shit you have to do, but you don't ever have to go back to that place."

I was crying too, I realized.

"Allison?"

"Yeah?"

"You're really scary."

"God, I hope so." I scrubbed at my face. "Jesus, what a day. Give me your bag. I'll carry it."

There were old, galvanized cans lying against a fence. Mostly unused, but still thick with garbage. I kicked one. It flew across the alley, spewing brightly coloured tiny bags of dog shit and old drink cups.

~ 18 ~

Tour Bus

I said, "Rabbit, can I ask you something?"

"Sure."

"What are we?"

"Um. People. Artists. Freaks who don't like other people as much as we like each other. Two crazies in a big, messy house that has a kid in it, and were you going to get a cat like you threatened?"

"What are we to each other?"

He sighed. Rolled closer to me. I reflexively turned away and curled in on myself. I'd crawled in with him in the night, still half-dressed, and poked him with my foot until he roused enough to talk.

"Hey." He rolled even closer. Spooned me from behind. "Hey crazy."

"Hey crazy."

"I've been waiting for years for you to ask me that."

"Have you got an answer?"

"Sure."

"Will I like it?"

"I have no idea. But here it is. I don't think you want to marry anybody. You have some serious baggage there, and layers of trauma that I don't want to dig up for you."

"Essentially correct."

"But if you leave, I'm going to go all to shit. I file my taxes separately from yours because my taxes are hella complicated compared to yours. But I will file them jointly with you if you want."

I shook my head.

"No, it's true."

"You're not my husband."

"I'm not your boyfriend, either. But I love you. I know I don't say that a lot."

He'd said it seventeen times since I'd known him. I'd never answered. I had said it a few times on my own. A couple of times, at least.

Three.

"What did you do?" he asked.

"I thought about burning Hanna's school down."

"Fuck the patriarchy."

"I didn't say that."

"Yeah, you did."

"Bitch thinks she's so fancy."

"Hanna?"

"Never. The principal."

"Did you take her down a peg?"

"Only in my head. But I trashed Hanna's textbooks. And I told her she didn't have to go back."

Eden nodded. "I hated school."

"You have a Master's degree."

"That's different. School is shit." Pause. "Leave her with me."

"You're not a good influence."

"No, but you have a job that you like, and if you don't keep showing up, they might give your job to someone else. So you go to work. Hanna and I will be fine. And then it'll be summer." Pause. "Oh, hey."

"What?"

"You know that thing I'm doing this summer?"

"Sure."

"You guys should come too."

His concert-video tour. "I hate motorhomes."

"We'll get a bus."

"I'm not that kind of rock star."

"A VW bus. I've got a line on one, but I couldn't justify it to myself. But if you guys come, it's legit. Family travel, business expense. Saves on subsistence."

"I hate camping."

"I know. But you love music. Isn't it ironic?"

"That doesn't make any sense."

He got up. "How much clothes have you got on?"

I checked. "Cami and panties."

He threw me a shirt. Went across the hall. Came back with Hanna. Said, "Do you want to get in?"

"You don't have to if you think it's weird," I said.

"Are you naked?" she asked.

"No."

"Okay."

Hanna crawled over me, wedging herself between my hipbones and the wall. Eden spooned up behind us. He'd left the window uncovered. There were seeping streetlights and motion lights outside, and only the faintest sliver of a moon.

∼ 19 ∽

Innocents

I spent six years almost constantly on tour.

We formed The Innocents in 1993 in Kara's Winnipeg basement. Me and Kara and Mary-Beth. Our first months were almost wholly acoustic. This because we played on the discarded instruments of a lesbian commune almost two decades old.

Those old dykes saved my life. I'm sure of it. They made it clear, too, that they were *dykes*, and that I should call them that: "*Les*-bians live in River Heights. You live in the North End, you better be prepared to be a dyke."

I came home from that first punk club with Kara, bruised after the night, and they gave me breakfast and said I didn't have to go back where I came from. They put it that way: back where I came from.

I said, "I don't think I'm a lesbian."

"Dyke."

"I don't think I'm a dyke. I mean, I don't know. I never thought about it?"

"You scared of dykes?"

I said, honestly, "I'm scared of Christians."

"You'll fit right in."

I shared Kara's room. It was a crowded building, almost a dozen people living there, but it had been a near-mansion, and then it had been a boarding house, and they made it work. Older women with brush cuts left long in the back had reinforced the foundation and framing, built a garden, rigged a cold cellar and pantry full of canning and whole grains.

I didn't develop a real taste for their cooking, which was mostly vegetarian and grimly organic, but I was prepared to be grateful to be fed.

Kara showed me the basement. Days we didn't feel like going to school — a different school, less interested in the things I wrote on my body — we stayed in the basement and messed around with the leavings of twenty years of women who'd moved on to permanent relationships or radical activism or compromise marriages. There were endless out-of-tune guitars, a drum circle of percussion, ferocious brass instruments that we had no idea how to play. A pump organ in the corner.

I knew how to play that.

You grow up in the church, you learn music. I'd met women who couldn't balance a chequebook, but they could lead a choir and back it on any keyboarded instrument. I could play the harp, even. The only time it came up seriously, though, was 2002, when we did a series of songs for vanished Elizabeth Smart, who played the harp too.

Church girl who fell through the strings and disappeared.

They found her, of course, and she was even alive, but I got to understand that, in many ways, I'd been lucky.

I settled on the battered stool, pumped the organ's feet to find its breath, and played the simplified version I'd learned as a child. *Jesu, Joy of Man's Desiring*.

Kara stared at me.

I said, "I can play the tambourine for a choir. And I almost know how to play the clarinet and the piccolo. And the flute."

If I'd been able to finish a full curriculum of homeschooling, if I hadn't met Ethan, I'd have gone on to some private college, taken an unaccredited degree in church music. Married some boy with a calling and played for the congregation and homeschooled six children of my own until I drowned them all, one by one.

I'd have drowned my husband last, pushing him under the water with all the weight of my body.

I'd have needed to be very, very strong. But I'd have had years to practice.

Instead, I played out the music I knew from memory on that wheezing premodern instrument. It must have arrived there before the current incarnation of the house and simply been too heavy to move. I never saw the organ shift from that corner of the basement.

I said that if Kara was serious about us forming a band, I wanted to drum. She said maybe, but her friend Mary-Beth was in band at school, and she'd spent years putting up with bullshit boys in the percussion section, and couldn't it be her?

I wanted to meet Mary-Beth first.

Mary-Beth was the first girl I knew who wrote *RIOT* onto her skin. She'd shaved chunks of her head and most of her eyebrows, drawing them back on with blood-coloured lip-liner. Her backpack was full of riot grrrl zines that she'd cadged from people who'd carried them to Winnipeg from Seattle and Portland and Washington.

I said, "I wanna do that."

"You're goddamn right."

I flinched.

Kara said, "Alli's a church refugee. We haven't entirely deprogrammed her, yet."

It was Mary-Beth's cue to blaspheme around me constantly, until I stopped flinching and picked up the habit. Then she moved on to language reclamation.

"Say *bitch*."

"Why?" I demanded.

"Because you need to own it. Say it. Say *bitch*."

"Bitch."

"Say, *I'm a bitch*."

"Mary-Beth."

"Say, *I'm a bitch*."

"You're a bitch."

"I already know I'm a bitch. Say *you're* a bitch."

"You're — "

"Allison's a pussy girl."

"You *are* a bitch."

"I'm a fucking cunt is what I am."

I stared at her.

"Why, does it bother you?"

"Yeah."

"It makes you feel bad because boys used those words to talk about you." She stood up. "They used them to take away pieces of you."

"Not just boys."

"Yeah, I know. But the point is, they used them against you. It's like a knife. You want to protect yourself, you pick it up."

I lay on my makeshift bed on Kara's floor. Mary-Beth's sheer ferocity was the sexiest thing I'd ever seen. She walked around completely clothed looking as gorgeous as Ethan had naked, and I thought maybe I'd been wrong when I said that I wasn't into that, but I couldn't imagine having sex with her.

I wanted to cut her open and wear her skin. I said that out loud.

She grinned. "*There* you go."

"What?"

"You wanna wear my skin?"

"Oh yeah."

"Good. 'Cause I'm a bitch. I'm a whore and a slut and a cunt and a pussy and a fat freak and a cunny hole and a bleeding cut, and people are *scared* of me."

It was that. I wanted them to be scared of me.

I said, "I'm a bitch."

"You're goddamn right. I mean, you are a seriously messed-up little bitch. I like you."

Mary-Beth had nice, married, heterosexual parents and went to a fancier school than Kara and I did. She bragged that she'd ruined three sets of Christmas photos in a row. They wouldn't print her picture in the yearbook.

"This year, I'm gonna write *CUNT* on my forehead in magic marker for picture day."

I thought about that. "How?"

"In the mirror, I guess."

I had some experience writing on my body. But writing anywhere other than my arms was hard, hard to see, hard to do, hard to make coherent. When I'd realized I was pregnant, I'd locked myself in the bathroom and written *No* all over my belly with a ball-point pen, pushing until I broke the skin. It was unreadable. Illegible. I could have just cut myself up and made a clearer statement.

"How about I do it? That way it'll look better."

And she knew about the intricacies of being an actual band. How sounds should merge. She studied jazz and joined drumming groups in parks, where they called her *percussion pussy* and then she had to start fights.

We were trying to be a band. Trying to make a song out of scribbled lines in a notebook and our non-intersecting experiences.

Kara's mom came downstairs and watched us. She was a skinny woman with long hair that she kept braided straight down her back. Hand-beaded earrings. She was femme by the standards of the commune, though sporting the requisite plaid shirt at all times.

Really, though, we were all wearing plaid shirts, so why was that important?

She watched us trying to simplify. Years of music lessons had made us useless for punk.

One-two beat. Three chords. Scream.

She said, "Oh my god. You guys are such innocents."

I thought it was funny. I'd practiced saying *cunt* all afternoon, and *Eat Me* was back, not just on my arm but across my breastbone too. Mary-Beth had given up on her patchy scalp and shaved the whole thing, then pushed a pair or three safety pins through her ear cartilage (it got infected, later, and we spent a night at emergency with her, laughing like we were high and terrifying the Christian nurses). Kara was experimenting with kinderwhore, so that you could see her panties under her skirt all the time.

We were fucking scary.

We were innocents.

It stuck. When Mary-Beth hauled her drum kit over and we dragged it to the basement, she let us stencil our name on with spray paint and a cut-out.

We played every afternoon. Ferocious little high school girls.

We went to punk nights. I started fights that Mary-Beth and Kara had to drag me out of or help me finish.

We wrote songs.

They were, to be clear, terrible. They were the songs you write when you're a furious high school kid, that rage multiplied by the sheer force of girlhood we'd been forced to put up with.

Three of them survived.

> *Knit myself a knife*
> *Kiss me, bite me, eat me*
> *Queen of the girls' room*

Kara's school and mine had pep rallies. The video for "Smells Like Teen Spirit" hadn't reached the administration, though they'd noted in passing that the children appeared poorly groomed and increasingly layered in salvaged clothing. They didn't get why we thought the whole thing was so funny.

At the rallies, which were compulsory, they announced school sporting wins, upcoming drama club performances, and dances for which tickets were now available.

I did go to the dances. I told Kara that I'd been warned, after my eerie wedding, never to make love standing up.

"Because it might lead to dancing."

"Is that a joke?"

"Yeah."

"Good. But I kind of wish it was true."

I liked the dances, but they weren't sure they liked me. The girl who was raised to sing only in the worship of the divine was the same one who knocked blood out of faces in punk club mosh pits. At dances, Kara clung to me with her friends, working to keep the bloodletting to a minimum until I learned to dance like someone sane. We went as a group, moving through the city in low-slung, too-big jeans and tank tops that showed off the tops of our breasts, layers of flannel to keep out the chill. I don't remember ever owning a real winter coat then, though I'm sure someone offered to buy me one. I had a salvaged 80s jean jacket, once very fashionable and now markedly alien, but lined in a way I appreciated, and a motorcycle jacket that I won from an asshole who didn't think that I could throw a knife so that it would stick in a dartboard.

I remember being cold all the time. I never wore anything really designed for winter. I had runners and denim and boxes of discarded clothes, and I cut the fingertips out of all my gloves.

For the dances, sometimes I abandoned plaid. Instead, I took men's dress shirts, pinned patches to the back with text I'd created with markers and glitter glue.

> *my mother doesnt let me go out looking like this*

We hung out mostly with girls. Kara had so many friends. And then we'd meet up with all the girls Mary-Beth had as friends. They'd been friends all their lives. They were Brownies together. They took gymnastics and ballet.

We formed a pack. I remember, once, they didn't want to let us all into the dance.

"But we have tickets."

"Too many girls."

We stared.

"We don't want you starting fights. Lots of these girls already have boyfriends. They won't be happy if you steal them."

We wrote a song about it later: *I don't want to steal your boyfriend (you can keep him)*

I said, "We just wanna dance. Like, in a group. No slow songs." They pushed me to the front. I'd buttoned the shirt over my tank, up close to my chin. I still hadn't cut my hair, then, and I opened my eyes church-girl wide.

I leaned in close to the table, where the two girls were sitting. "We would *never*," I said. "We took a pledge."

"To the flag of the United States of America?"

I reared back. "To Jesus!"

Mary-Beth, standing in the back, gleamed in the hallway light. Her piercings were clearly visible.

"What about her?"

I looked back. "Oh, don't you worry. She's born again."

"She has pins in her face."

"The doctor said that if we take them all out at once, she might die. Toxic shock. It's why you should never, ever use tampons. That, and," I leaned in, confidential, "they break your flower. No man will want you."

"Christian girls don't dance."

"Our church dances. We bring the light of Christ with us, and we are pure. May we, please, please, go in?"

They let us in.

I was good at that.

We did dance together, as a group. A mob. We occupied half the dance floor and pushed the steady-dating couples off to the side. We shifted around, absorbing other groups of girls and waving and laughing when they stared at us.

We didn't grab boys for the slow songs, but no one could make us surrender the floor. We owned it, shouldering out those cute-hetero couples. What were they going to do? This wasn't the kind of place where you could throw down. It was only a gym, marked up by decades of running shoes and gum, and dark-lit with a mirrorball for the occasion. They had punch, but it was in a McDonald's orange-drink cooler so that no one could spike it.

Mary-Beth and I got up on the edge of the hardwood theatre stage and danced, wildly, to the Cranberries.

They stopped the music. Turned on the lights.

"Please get off the stage."

I said, "We're The Innocents! Come see us play!"

They threw us out, still screaming, "We're The Innocents! You know you want us!"

All over the city. We went to high schools and community centres and church dances. We dressed like nice girls to get in the doors. We made leaflets. I put up posters in the bathrooms with Fun-Tak, explaining how to take back your cervix.

Come see us play!

That year, none of us were old enough to drink, and the city cracked down on clubs letting in kids. If we were going to do shows, we had to find a new venue. We played the Red River Rec Centre, in the gym.

Ten people came. Most were guys.

"We're the Innocents!"

"Show us your tits!"

Kara came off the stage first. I was behind her. We flattened those guys. The Rec Centre manager helped us push them out the door and said we could keep the rental fee, just for letting her see those piles of crap get what was coming to them.

"Tell people to come see us."

"Next Friday. I promise."

We were kids. We played guitars that weren't in tune, struggled with amps whose wiring surrendered to corrosion in mid-song. Power grids blew. Our mics were too loud.

We played every song we knew, and then we started playing the angry-girl folk songs Kara's moms knew, in raw 2/2 time, as fast as we could scream them. Girl group 60s songs from a tape Mary-Beth got for her twelfth birthday.

> *You don't own me*
> *It's my party*
> *She-Bop*
> *Bad Reputation*

It was important: when you play for kids, you play songs they recognize. If they know a few words, a melody line, they'll scream for you. You can have two, maybe three songs of your own.

Adolescence is the land of the punk cover.

I learned *Boys of Summer*, and we played it every show. Changed the parts we wanted.

> *Out on the road today*
> *I saw a Bikini Kill sticker*
> *On a Cadillac!*

144

NONE AND THIS IS THE CURE

Wait.

Most of our audience only had a basic grasp of punk, but theirs wasn't much less complex than ours. We knew our sound, and we knew we were sarcastic and possibly angry. We ripped our clothes, messed with our makeup, screeched.

Somebody phoned Kara's house to ask if we wanted to play a grad party.

We moved our gear in a 1986 Chevy Nova. It belonged to Cynthia from the collective. Cynthia's last name was on the car registration, and it was normal, but if you asked her, she'd say her last name was Van Dyke. She was thinking about changing it legally. She was newly out, newly divorced, and she'd come into the house from Kara's mom's Womyn-Loving-Womyn support group.

Cynthia had come out of Mennonite country. She was the closest thing to one of my own people that I'd met in the city. She'd burned that version of herself, but her mother-instincts were still present. Kara and I met some need in her that she'd decided not to name. She'd drive us places, pack us lunches.

I remember walking down the hall to bed one night in my oversized T-shirt, and she leaned out of her bedroom and said, "How bad are the tangles?" Pointing to my hair.

I still hadn't cut it. Kara and Mary-Beth were both aggressively short-styled, but my hair ran down my back. It was long and smooth if I took care of it, but I didn't. Most of the time it was twisted into rats' nests.

"It's okay." It wasn't. I had mats at the base of my skull that I couldn't dislodge. I was afraid of what would happen if I cut them out myself.

"Can I take care of it for you?"

Cynthia had a full brush cut, not even long at the back. She cut it herself, with clippers, in the bathroom, and then carefully cleaned up the mess. We lived like that, in the commune. It was full of ex-housewives. They were aggressively dykey, but very, very clean. You could have eaten off our baseboards.

I sat in Cynthia's room on the floor while she sat on the bed. Braided the untangled hair up into a complex structure on my head, leaving the snarls exposed.

"Let's see what I can do with those."

She got them loose. It took a week, sitting at night with a brush and comb, and peanut butter to slick each strand away. When it was free, she said, "Go wash it." Waited until I came back and combed the wet into a long, silky plane. "Okay. Go to bed."

She was there when I got up in the morning. Comb in her hand, flanked with bobby pins and elastics. She braided me from my scalp to hair-tips. My bangs had grown out. They still straggled loose of any braid, but they obscured my eyes whenever I ceased battling them.

"Sit." Trimmed them with nail scissors.

It looked alright. Not high fashion, but it fit with the state of me. She said, "I never had girls. I haven't done this since I left my sisters." She reached for my shoulder, and I flinched back, suddenly terrified she'd ask me to pray with her. Instead, she asked, "Did they hurt you?"

"I just had to leave." She didn't need to know everything about me.

"Glad you're okay. Do you want a snack?"

"No. Thanks."

I didn't want the mothering she offered, but she was persistent. She gave me things. Gave us, but mostly me. Gave me food, haircuts, rides places. Took me to an abandoned parking lot and taught me to drive.

"I don't *need* to drive."

"You don't drive, you're always going to depend on some man to take you places. Now. This is the clutch."

I was the only Innocent with a driver's license. I drove Kara and our gear. Mary-Beth showed up by bus, snare strapped to her back, because there wasn't room in the car for her or the rest of her kit.

I hadn't been to Tuxedo before. It was almost another city. We crossed rivers, ducked around the nature preserve and sound barriers, and into the deep trees that Kara told me used to be a whole other town. In the before, that block of time previous to the now, but not exactly historical. The houses were massive, story-book buildings that I'd only encountered in Gothic romances and John Hughes movies.

All of us stared at the paper in our hands and then at the address.

Rich kids, we learned, didn't go to Rec Centres to hear bands. They had their own parties and the bands came to them. Played in their basements.

It wasn't like any basement I'd seen before. Decades later, I read about the Iceberg Houses of London, where what you could see above ground was only a tiny symbol of what's hidden below. This wasn't as vast as that, but it was huge enough to have a room designed just for parties. Soft carpeting and raised areas for bands to set up. The stage was hardwood, carefully aged and maybe salvaged from some real venue in the earlier version of its life, but there were Persian carpets laid out to cushion the resident drum kit.

We stared. We loved it.

It wasn't a high school grad party, though. Even we were older than our audience. They had, elegantly, just completed grade 8.

They were having the best party in town.

Their parents were there, with a list of rules. I think we were prepared to leave. Blow them off. *You can't censor us!* But the rules were almost entirely about what we could drink and what we couldn't take pictures of. None of us owned a camera.

Rich girls and their boyfriends danced until two in the morning. We hadn't played that long at any point in our lives. We had eight songs of our own; the rest we summoned from our girl-pop repertoire. When Kara's knees gave out, our host mother stepped in. Activated a sound system that fit seamlessly into the gap we'd left.

"Do you want to go outside?"

The outside was full of kids. They'd hung the back yard with lights. There was a pool.

There was another pool, inside.

The kids' parents came to take them home. We sat on the curb and watched. I thought I saw women in BMWs wave to Mary-Beth, but I wasn't sure. I was almost asleep, leaning on Kara's shoulder. I whispered, "I didn't know places like this were real."

She nodded.

We loaded into the Nova even deeper into the small hours of the morning. The buses had long since ceased running. Any remaining house staff in the surrounding homes either stayed the night or lived in.

They had *staff*. Not just someone to clean the house, or a gardener, but people who drove the kids, cooked, polished. Managed details.

We weren't all going to fit in the car. Mary-Beth said she'd walk. It seemed wrong. There was a vast undeveloped tract and a set of industrial buildings between us and where I thought her universe might begin.

"I'm okay," she said. She claimed she was wired on Diet Coke. I hadn't learned to drink it, then, or anything harder, and I didn't have enough caffeine in my body to keep my eyes reliably open. I wasn't sure I could remember the route home.

"No," I said. Insisted, the way girls do when they're entirely unsure they're doing the right thing. "I'm going to take you home first, and then I'll come back for Kara."

"I can kick the ass of anything that gets in my face."

"I'm taking you home."

"Alli."

"Mary-Beth."

Kara said, "Just let her drive you, jeez. I wanna go home."

Kara sat on the hosts' lawn, thick and perfectly even at the edges, and watched us get in. I drove to the end of the street and looped around, heading for Roblin Boulevard and arterial roads leading to the outer world.

Mary-Beth stopped me. "You don't need to go that way. Turn right."

I nodded. Turned. Paused, sure I was turned around, moving west instead of east, but I was almost asleep. I had to trust her.

147

"Turn up there. Left."

I turned.

"Okay. Stop for a sec." I pulled in and waited. It occurred to me that I could close my eyes while she was figuring out what her point was. "Alli, I need you not to say anything about this."

"Sure."

"No. Like, don't."

"You pregnant?"

"I'm home."

She nodded up the street. In between the streetlights and massive trees, there were a few houses with porch lights on.

"Was I asleep? Like, while I was driving?"

"No. We're down the block."

I pondered this. "You live here?"

"I really could have walked."

"So what am I not telling Kara?"

"Where I live."

"I'm too sleepy to care." I thought. "How do I get back?"

She told me. I went back. Kara stood, stretched, and checked her watch. "What the hell?"

"What?"

"You were, like, five minutes."

She was already in the car. I turned us again, looking for Roblin, for bridges. Needed to go home. "She decided she wanted to walk."

"God. Wish you'd saved the trouble, then."

Later, I asked Mary-Beth about it, her home in the land of mansions.

"It isn't me. It's just where they live."

I nodded.

"My parents, I mean."

"You go to Vincent Massey," I protested. The Collegiate was miles away, in a different pie-slice of city. I'd expected to take her there, into treed, quiet suburbia.

"My parents wanted to send me to Balmoral." She said this like it was toxic.

Balmoral Hall was an entirely theoretical entity to me, though I'd heard its name. It was associated with money, and snobs, and I understood that it was private, too impressed with itself to merely be a Catholic school sporting fetishy uniforms.

When Mary-Beth told me, I shrugged. "How bad could it be?"

She said, "You don't understand." So we had to go there, to Balmoral, and look at it.

It wasn't particularly the preppie school of my imagination. Yellow brick buildings behind a simple fence, like a lot of schools, in Wolseley, which I didn't associate with the kind of wealthy sheen Mary-Beth seemed to.

"I said I wouldn't go. You can see why, right?"

It seemed to be important to her, so I nodded.

"They wanted to get me boarding, I think. Just go home on weekends. That way they could do less supervision, and more of their own thing. They could pretend that they don't have a daughter at all."

We walked down Westminster Avenue. The neighbourhood mixed old houses like the one where I lived in with Kara with brick apartments, and the sidewalks were crowded with girls my age pushing strollers, and slightly older women with two or three kids, one usually on a filthy big-wheel, racing towards nothing in particular.

We turned onto Sherbrooke Street and found a diner. I didn't have any money, but I'd since realized that I could trust Mary-Beth to buy me a coke and fries, or possibly a new guitar, or a tour van so we could go on the road.

She told me about the things her parents wanted her to be, that she didn't want to be. "You understand," she said. She was so certain. Because I knew about parents, the way they could make you do terrible things, things that would kill your soul.

In retrospect, I'm shocked by her gall and my own acceptance, but when you're a teenager, the line between private school and forced marriage doesn't seem vivid. They were both things we needed to not do. Mary-Beth was my friend, maybe a better friend than Kara, if only because I'd never had to share a bedroom, a bathroom, and a mother with Mary-Beth.

"I made it so they wouldn't take me." She gestured to her shaved skull. "I wanted to get tattoos, but I'm not sure if there's anybody in town who'll do it for me while I'm underage that also won't give me AIDS."

"But why are you travelling so far just for school?"

"It was my choice. I'm not going to go to school with snobs." She sighed into her Diet Coke. "I love Kara, but she's got this town in her blood. She knows where I live, she's going to think I'm a poser."

"Did you set up the grad party?"

"I babysit for them. The kids like me. I mean, they're too big to be babysat now, but I used to. And they wanted something different, you know?"

I said, "I won't tell Kara."

We didn't tell Kara. We didn't tell her then, or later, when we were invited to Grand Beach to play a party at somebody's "cottage" that turned out to be less a log cabin and more an architectural magazine exploding across the shore of

Lake Winnipeg. There were cars parked in the yard that I'd only seen before in magazine spreads tacked up on boys' bedroom walls.

That needs to be said. I didn't live with Kara bone and blood. She went to school with me, and she had friends I didn't have, and I did my own thing. I liked boys.

They liked my hair.

I kept a list, in the notebook full of lyrics that lived in my backpack. Boys I'd made out with by the track equipment shed, who kissed like their tongues were in convulsions. Hands up inside my shirt. It was important to them, I realized, that I put up a fight. Tell them no.

Over the bra only.

No way.

Can't we just kiss some more?

There were boys in my grade, and above it, and some below it, who hadn't hit their growth spurts yet; those ones were pushy. They made a point of my recognizing their erections. They liked holding onto my wrists.

The bigger ones, I could push around. They weren't so touchy about it.

I loved the ones who moaned. Closed their eyes and leaned back into it or whimpered until I kissed them harder.

I think there were girls who'd fuck on the school grounds, but I wasn't one of them. I held the line strictly at *you can kiss me*, on campus and out into the streets and down to the 7-Eleven and past that into the alleys. I kept apart from them until we were halfway to their houses, and then I said, *Okay.*

Take me home.

Not all of them understood what I meant. One of them took me in the front door, introduced me to his mom, and asked her to make us a snack. She did: peanut butter and jelly, cut into angled quarters, and grape Kool-Aid. He took me down to the basement, turned on the TV. I think it was showing something Disney-flavoured, possibly animated, with a cheery theme-song.

He wanted to make out, there. Open stairs between us and the kitchen, where his mom was cooking supper.

I remember snorting, grabbing my bag. Jogging up the stairs.

Flicker of terror as his mother turned to look at me. I was conscious of the licks of grape sugar rising at my mouth's corners. I held out my empty plate. Muttered, "Thank you, Kyle's mom." Fled.

I wanted to tell Kara about it. About Kyle, his mom, the completely normal ridiculousness of it. I stood in an alley and laughed, and a block later I threw up.

I caught a bus. Rode across the city to sit on Mary-Beth's front lawn until she came home so that I could tell her instead.

～ 20 ～

Fridays I'm in Love

I got up early, tuned again into my work schedule even in the absence of my phone. I was nearly wedged against the wall, Hanna and Eden behind me. Still dark, and achingly cold. I'd lost the covers.

I wasn't fully conscious, but I needed to move. The streetlight through the bathroom window illuminated taps and towels. I'd done this before, showering without the lights; it let me ease into wakefulness. Shivering in the cold, and then the full-body shudder of hot water.

Lights on, after that. I blow-dried and smoothed my hair, did makeup, walked towel-wrapped down the stairs to select clothes from the piles of black in the chair of my home office.

Dark lipstick, dark clothes, bright eyes.

I went to work.

Good morning, Gander.

Good morning, Charlebois.

Good morning, Mount Forest.

Good morning, Flin Flon.

Good morning, Grande Prairie. This is The Cure.

The Wrecked Butterflies came in to play live. They arrived just half an hour after I did, sliding in out of the dark with their instruments and greasy hair. They were professional, sober. They took the coffee we offered, and a couple of the standard pastries, and got to work.

They tuned, warmed up. The studios buzzed. Producers brought me scripts and monologues. I checked my makeup and then stepped in for photos with the Butterflies.

Hello, Instagram, we're on The Cure*!*

They don't tell you this when they book you, but Allison Winter is really pretty!

The opening monologue was ready. We had a producer and sound engineer in their seats. We had levels check, and beautiful carpets to muffle the drum kit.

I accepted a Wrecked Butterflies T-shirt. They'd called ahead, asked for my size. It was lovely. Hand-written fonts and damaged insect graphic art. I paused.

"Can I swap you?"

"Too big?"

"Good fit for me. But, like, I'm trying to teach my daughter about decent music. We need to get her off her boy band diet. I think she'd like your stuff."

They found a second one, x-small. Told me I could keep mine.

"That's perfect. Thank you."

"I had no idea you had kids."

"I have one."

"How old?"

"Eleven."

"That's a great age." He dug his phone out. Keyed up pictures. "Mine are twelve and nine. Watch out for twelve, I'm telling you."

Six minutes to air. We cued the national news and let it run over the studio speakers. Expense scandals in the Senate. Refugees drowning in the Mediterranean. The price of oil falling, falling. Hockey scores. National energy conference. Explosive conditions in Syria.

That's the news for this hour. Stay tuned, now, for The Cure*, with Allison Winter.*
Cue music.

On Mondays, we opened with "Boys Don't Cry." Tuesdays were "Lovesong." Wednesdays arrived "From the Edge of the Deep Green Sea." Thursdays drawled out "Just Like Heaven."

Fridays I'm in Love!

We used an acoustic version of the day's song, rather than the traditional full-electric one. Once, we got Robert Smith on the line, and he sang "Friday" for us acapella, sent over a file with the rights. That one we saved for special occasions.

Simple chords, befitting a band with punk roots, and when the electronica New Wave edges were stripped away, they were easy to hear: D, G / D, A / B-minor, G / D, A.

I don't care if Monday's blue
Tuesday's grey and Wednesday too

The opening music was the first alteration I made to the show, even before we truncated the name. Originally the song was going to be a one-off. When I suggested a permanent change, we had to get permission up the chain of command. They didn't object, aesthetically, but we were using previously recorded material by a non-Canadian band, and the lack of national content was.

.   Well.

A concern.

Public Broadcasting was dedicated to Canadian content. If we used British music, scandal might follow. Parliamentarians weren't above using such lapses to attack our funding. Small decisions mattered.

We made some trades. Limited the number of international acts we talked to in any given week, and I did more on-camera publicity to please the administration.

I covered the Olympics in London for Public Broadcasting Radio, just as if I knew anything at all about sport. The summer Olympics lasted seventeen days, which was longer than the functional period of my marriage. I almost melted, got lost in traffic, appeared on television once or twice for featurettes.

I came home; we cued music, carried on.

The Wrecked Butterflies played five tracks from their about-to-drop album, told jokes, lurked and napped while I talked to other, off-site parties, danced madly during the news breaks.

Later, they sent me a flash drive containing their covers of the five weekly theme songs, the first in what later turned into a trend of cover versions.

No one cares if Monday's blue!

The show was good. Better than that: synergy and human energy and sound fused and travelled across radio waves and digital space across the continent. We got good chatter online in the first hour afterwards, and the downloads off our website ticked up.

Good job, *Cure*! You're gaining new listeners in Uruguay and South Korea!

At 11:28 a.m., we were out. On the control panels, a previously-recorded and -mixed piece on francophone culture across the country went to air. The Wrecked Butterflies gave their goodbyes and vanished.

During the afternoon, word got out that I was re-wardrobing Hanna, and the swag started to roll in.

Sleater-Kinney couriered over a smoke-grey T-shirt with the broken-flowers image for *No Cities to Love*. Adult XS.

The Arcade Fire and The Reflektors sent shirts.

Then the Frocklettes.

Then Wunder Princess.

By late afternoon, I realized I'd opened a door in the floor, and bands were falling upwards through it. I was going to be able to dress every tweenaged girl in Toronto.

I was five hours at work before I checked my phone. A text from Eden: *we're fine do your thing.*

I wrote back, *really fine, or fucked up insecure neurotic emotional?*

Really fine. We're going to see a friend of mine. He has some cool slides of a trip to China that I think H might get a kick out of.

How long will you be?

Don't wait up.

Vending machines fed me caffeine and sugar. I went into planning meetings and stayed there.

Movies to be released: which did we think might be worth discussing? Promo packets littered the table, filled with glossy photos of the kind that hadn't withered with the advent of a digital world. Some sent along stickers, buttons, massive posters rolled for protection.

Someone had printed out dozens of hopeful emails from bands' agents and unrepresented indie kids. "Allison, you know any of this bunch? What do you think?"

I flipped through. Pulled out five. "These, maybe."

We considered pop culture panelists for next month. Selected comedians and jazz performers and avant-garde dance productions.

Two file boxes full of books were guaranteed to be conversation-starters.

The world is loud. There was a point, a few centuries ago, when you could read and know everything, and understand most of it. Collect all the books, meet all the people. Hear the music night after night and look at a hundred productions of *Macbeth* or *She Stoops to Conquer* and learn to be bored with all the art that was in the world.

That ennui turned impossible such a long time ago. I'd read a book in which a woman sleeps through the end of the eighteenth century, and at the beginning of the Victorian age orders copies of all the books that might be important and finds herself unable to enter her own home for the books choking it. In the two hundred years since then, we hadn't slowed down.

Before I was fifteen, I heard the equivalent of maybe three albums worth of music, plus organ and piano lessons, and liturgical performance. I read carefully-curated Christian books. I saw no movies. I crocheted a lot of pot holders.

I was never, ever going to catch up.

I wasn't alone. The show had a staff of eleven people, three working full-time just to select and book our guests. *The Cure* wasn't the biggest pop culture show in the world, but it was, for whatever that was worth, the biggest in Canada. Americans were listening, too. It was an anomaly, a weird glitch in the culture flow. Normally, Canadians sucked down American media and hurled our own into the void.

We did that, if I'm honest, because so much of what Canada made was shit: all those shows about pinafores and pony races and beavers in the creek.

The Americans produced stunning shit, too, but theirs filtered a little by the time it reached the border. And there were more of them, producing more work, some of it good, and the statistical result was that they looked like they were better than us, always.

And then there was the rest of the world, making media without considering Canada at all. Britain howled with music. Ireland rattled and hummed. Sweden hurled out sweet pop melodies that shimmered eerily danceable on the world stage.

Mexico and South Korea made better soap operas than we did. Nigeria and India swept musical theatre across movie screens. China exploded a billion people's ideas into its restricted airspace.

In the midst of the howl, someone, somewhere said, *Have you heard this yet?* The Cure. *Not the band, the radio show. You can podcast it. Download it for free. It's good. Give it a listen.*

Out we went, moving the wrong way through the osmosis filter, into the global consciousness.

I stretched. Got up from the table and bent low over it so that my cheek rested against the laminate and studied the paper mountains. "How late it is?"

"Five-something. You're not usually here this long. You feeling better, Alli?"

I paused. "Was I sick?"

"You were quiet."

They weren't wrong. I felt better. Depression had been carrying me like a low-grade illness for weeks, not quite contagious or bad enough to retreat to bed, and it had taken the day off. Stayed in bed while I got up.

I didn't feel good.

I felt ecstatic.

So, *so* good.

I took music home. Books. Went back and got stickers and posters and pieces of everything to give to Hanna. I was vaguely aware that my mood was swinging, but it wasn't violent enough for me to need help, not yet. This was the good stuff that off-balanced the dysthymia. When the pain vanishes, you bounce *up*, you feel *good*.

The snow was melting. In a few more weeks, I'd be able to skateboard to work if I wanted.

I came back to the house and both Hanna and Eden were there. They'd made spaghetti, and were eating it at the table, like a civilized family. Hanna had her legs knotted up around her, one knee between her body and the table. There was sauce on her thigh. She looked happy enough.

I said, "What do you fools want to do tonight?"

⦙⦙⦙⦙⦙

We took Hanna's bedroom back from the clutter, cleaning the remaining boxes away and establishing her desk by the window.

I stared at the computer on her desk. Articles that popped into my news feed periodically debated how much internet access to allow children. I'd hosted a debate about it with *The Cure*'s pop culture panel. The chorus insisted, *not in their bedrooms, not while they're kids.*

Eden nodded.

The tiny back bedroom, the one I'd never broached, was emptied out, too. Hanna acquired her own office, matching Eden's and mine, with an Ethernet port and a desk. The curtains were improvised from cashmere thrifted scarves, but when I got up close to them, I saw they'd been hemmed with hot glue.

Tacks went in all the walls, through the vintage paper, covering it with her pictures.

I went to work, and they went out, for days at a time, to museums. They had a list and a map in the kitchen. A plan. Notebooks and phones.

When I asked, Eden introduced me to Hanna's online presence, logging her education: carefully-designed pages for each gallery and exhibition. I called it up from time to time and tried to parse what Eden and Hanna were doing. How they spent their days on transit, wired into separate ear buds, playing out the household music archive, wandering the halls of archival institutions.

They went to the Bata Shoe Museum at least twice.

They went to flea markets. Came back with a heavy 1963 Pentax and a collection of lenses.

Film cameras.

I said, "Where are you even going to get film for those?"

Hanna opened the box at her feet. Unexposed rolls, hundreds of them. Someone's hobby, neglected since before I was born.

The basement emptied. A dark room generated itself next to the laundry room.

I went to work, chose guests, attended meetings, phoned home and nobody was there, so I stayed through dinner. Went to shows.

Came back at one in the morning with two guys from The Inopera Company, to find Hanna and Eden were both awake, at the dining table, with curl-edged photos scattered between them.

Hanna nodded to the band like she'd met them a dozen times. Went into the kitchen and came back with a bowl full of grapes and a Coke for Eden.

They stayed almost all night. I stayed up, too wired to sleep for just an hour, and carried Hanna upstairs, finally. She'd gone boneless on the couch. Skinny kid, and getting, I thought, taller. If she grew as tall as I was, she was going to need new clothes. Different ones.

I thought I should take her shopping.

Hanna got up, hours later, and rejoined us. She took pictures with the band in the early-morning glow, solar twinkle-lights luminous at the house's edges. How long had we had those?

Walls of the stairwell were covered in Hanna's photos. Fewer of museums than of the city. She and Eden had gone walking through the Don Valley, looking for homeless camps. Guys peered out of bushes and ragged nylon shelters at her lens. This peculiar expression on their faces as they looked back at a pre-pubescent white girl studying them through a piece of antique tech.

Pictures of the men sleeping on the sidewalk outside the broadcast building.

Women panhandling on the streets. Dirty and hunched. Holding out coffee cups. Women with no legs sitting in cheap, folding wheelchairs.

No photos on the refrigerator. It stayed bare. Eden's gesture, I thought: telling her those were not little-kid pieces to be hung up for a day. Her pictures went up on the wall, because they were art.

The pictures on the wall rotated, changing rapidly enough for me to worry about chemical burns on preteen lungs.

"I do the prints for her while she's reading," Eden said. "She hasn't really got the steady hands."

"I could get her something digital and she could just print them out."

"No way. Too much waste. You can take a thousand pictures with a digital camera and none of them mean anything. It's messy. She went through a couple rolls of film before she figured out that she had to make a shot count. She's doing better, now. Good framing."

I took photos down, randomly, and carried them to work. Used sticky-tac from the dollar store on the corners to hold up the massed images.

The bass player from Onyx Systematix stood in my office, stroking the images with both hands and leaving long oily smears.

"These your husband's work?"

"My daughter's."

"I need these. Does she sell them?"

I had no idea. "Come to the party on the weekend and ask her."

He took shots of the collage with his phone, and he came to the party armed with beer and a contract for digital design that Eden had to intercept.

We hadn't had a full-on party in months. Not since Ethan and Claudia. I hadn't been in good shape, then. Now, rising into ecstatic mania, I wanted everyone to come. I passed messages through the city's music scene. Texted friends.

People followed me home, or they knew where to find us. They showed up with acoustic instruments and bottles and random vegan dishes of food and an entire karaoke machine.

Shook the neighbourhood.

The Annex on Saturday nights was fully-gentrified and awake with music and shining hipsters. They didn't mind if we stayed up late. People came in cars, but overwhelmingly they came on foot, tangling the sidewalk and ruining parking, shouting up the street.

Dance!

The vintage hi-fi rang out in the living room. We cleared the floor. People jammed in the kitchen and the basement. They were singing in the bathroom upstairs, enchanted by the watery acoustics of the room.

Eden issued wind-up 8mm cameras with short streams of film to outstretched hands.

Scene kids swept Hanna into their Brownian motion and leapt into the tiny, paved back yard. They'd brought guitars, hand-drums, tambourines like it was still 1968. They'd taken to braiding feathers into their hair, even wearing headdresses, and I was going to have to remind them to knock that shit off.

You should know better. Go appropriate someone else's culture.

Salt and alcohol. I was vaguely aware that I shouldn't be drinking, not while I was that close to mania, but I was at least in my own home. I could do what I wanted.

The musicians shifted to other floors and surrendered the living room to karaoke and let us knock down all the walls of independent music with pop anthems from other periods.

Sing Bryan Adams. Sing Mariah Carey. Sing Olivia Newton John!

Allison, get up and sing. Come on, girl. Pick something good. Something funny. Go for it!

I flipped through the digital catalogue and said, *Yes. This one.* Celine Dion power-ballad, in French, circa 1995.

My church-girl voice didn't get much exercise in my adult life. Careful practice with scales and hymns and diaphragmatic control had disappeared in the punk scream of The Innocents. My voice was there, though, lurking. We used to break it out just to shock our audiences. Reinforce the name. We could stand there, in full kinderwhore, and sound like beautiful children.

Belt it out.

It was easier to sing those words in French than it would have been in English. Self-abnegation to the unnamed lover, the need to become anything that would make you loved. We'd made a rule, in early songwriting, to never, ever promise that to any audience at all, ever.

The oddity of my almost-perfect French accent startled people. In interviews, I told them I took French-immersion in early childhood.

People at Quebec shows, sometimes, heard the Burundian intonations, the Haitian echoes.

Anything, anything, said the song, *if you'll only love me again.*

I will invoke the magics of African mystics. I will cover the world in gold.

Anything, anything, if you'll love me again.

I adored the shock. Half of the audience only recognized it as an old, corny pop song. Refugees from Montreal grew up with it on the radio, though, and they were laughing.

Hanna stood in the doorway and stared at me while I sang.

Audience shrieking, flipping through the book. *What else of hers have we got? Oh my god, Alli, what else do you know?*

I sang a Meatloaf song. Somebody opened the window so the curtains would billow. Hanna stared.

I couldn't maintain that level of histrionic sincerity for a whole song. I cracked up and stopped. "Oh my god."

No, it's awesome! Do it again!

"Nope. That's as much irony as I can take for one night."

Hanna was gone, back outside. When people finally drifted out, the house was chaotic, and Hanna was sitting on the stairs in full makeup, glittering faintly. Almost asleep.

I said, "Bed."

"I'm not tired."

"*I'm* tired." I held out a hand. She took it and let me tow her upwards. "I hope I sleep for a week and never have to clean that mess up."

Hanna said, "Come in with me?"

Her pajamas were old university wear, maybe Ethan's. Her bed had developed odd, damaged stuffed animals.

"Would you sing to me?"

"What?"

"You sing really good."

I was so tired the room was spinning. I thought Eden was probably already asleep, somewhere, or out on patrol with his photo people, looking at the pre-dawn city through multi-era lenses. "Sure. What do you want me to sing?"

"Whatever."

I tried a few bars of the Jonas Brothers. It came out flat, tuneless. I was too tired to manage a song I'd only heard a few times and barely remembered.

Hanna curled up. "It's like you're unplugged now."

"Good metaphor."

"What?"

I said, "Can I sleep here?" Eden was elsewhere. I was getting worse at sleeping on my own.

We'd left Hanna the guest room's double bed. I remembered, vaguely, that she hadn't had one, before, in the other house. She slept on the edge of it and filled the rest with stuffed creatures.

They slid into the crevice between bed and wall. Little fuzzed bodies.

Too tired to sleep, I listened to Hanna breathe and thought about boy bands.

The genre's pixie boys were so femme. An unthreatening queerness radiated from them, making them safe, passive objects of desire for the first wave of female sexual love. They sang about love entirely in the abstract. They made promises that were susceptible to liquid sentiment.

Every word I say is true . . .

Daylight emerged. I slid out the bottom of the mattress and went back to my own room and slept there until Sunday afternoon.

～ 21 ～

Naked Girls

The Innocents were in Windsor the first night I said, "If you think a naked girl is that exciting, well, here." And did the show naked.

I hadn't planned it. I didn't warn the others. I was only singing lead about half the time we played, and I'd stepped up at that moment and shifted Kara away from the microphone with my hip. I was playing bass, by then, because punk bands don't tour with pianos, or they didn't then. We only had what we could carry. It was decades before you could crowd-source a show.

I stepped up with the bass still slung across my chest, and when I went to take it off, I hit the mic, triggered an arc and burned out one of our speakers. Ripped the ears out of the audience.

While they were reeling, I toed off my shoes and peeled away my clothes. This part I'd imagined before. I'd been reading Madonna's *Sex* book and thinking about how I'd never for a second in my life looked like that, but so far it hadn't stopped me from fucking in more places than the book imagined, and getting knocked up accidentally, if only once.

(Once, at that point in my life. A second time later. I keep wondering if there's a third time, the charm, coming up.)

I put my shoes back on, after, because the stage was gritty and my feet were raw.

There were photos. I could see them happening, faint flashes from the back of the club, but.

Well.

I told people, later, that in those days, we didn't worry so much about what some idiot with a camera was doing.

Kara stared at me. Then laughed.

Mary-Beth counted off two basic four-beats and Kara knocked out a chord and I understood that we'd changed the set-list.

"Knit Myself a Knife" later. "Naked Boys" now.

Innocents' Naked Girls play "Naked Boys."

The student paper had people on scene. They took the kind of terrible pictures that college kids armed with their first SLR cameras take, but someone developed them carefully, and the staff kindly sent us the negatives. A gift.

They were grateful. Our issue was the first one they'd ever sold out.

Behold, Alli Winter in her naked-ass altogether, hairy and flat-footed.

Tits and a bass guitar.

Kara stepped back, finally. Motioned for me to step up and sing. I finished out the set, growling songs I knew but had only sung backup or in the shower.

I kept waiting for embarrassment to hit. It didn't: some magic force arising from my body at that age protected me. I had bruises across one shoulder from a fight I'd had three nights before. My knees weren't all that clean, and my nails were short.

I screamed, "Tell me this isn't the worst present you've ever had."

Howls. Somebody threw a shirt at me. A guy at the back shouted, "Put it on! Put it aaaalllll back on!"

If we'd been heading back up the 401, homewards, I think that would have been the end of it, but our tour was planned to run down through Michigan so that we could play the Midwest and swing back to Winnipeg through North Dakota. We toured in a shitty van that looked like we were out to kidnap children. It had enough seats to be legal for the three of us, but no more. We had to pick up techs on-site, and our gear rode shoved to the side so that whoever wasn't driving could sleep. We were only all awake at the same time because we were crossing the border. Dressed like well-behaved children with our documents at hand.

We were refused entry.

Pulled aside, first, for secondary inspection. That had happened before. We always looked like we were smuggling drugs, so we made a point of not carrying anything that had been contraband in recent history. When we wanted angry feminist zines from the States, we got friends to bring them in. No one would let us through customs with anything like that.

We just *looked* like people carrying obscene material. That's what they claimed.

What the guy actually said, while we were sitting on the curb, fully-dressed and looking as much like college girls maybe headed to the Michigan Womyn's Music Festival as we could, was that they didn't need extra whores in America.

Denied entry. No feminazis allowed. No whores, strippers, or lesbian cunts needed on the Detroit side of the river. Thank you.

They said we were welcome to use the payphone while we made alternate plans.

Kara phoned her mother. Ranted in sheer fury about the dickheads who wouldn't even admit they'd come to our show. Mary-Beth picked up the next phone over in the bank and called her parents.

I considered whether I should phone my parents. Tell them I'd been denied entry to America for running around naked on stage. I didn't think they'd have helpful suggestions, but I did think it might brighten someone's day. My mother could phone Elaine, and Elaine could have been right about me all along.

We called the news, instead.

We left the border station, carefully turning around and returning whence our whorish asses came. Went to the Windsor library to find the numbers we needed.

We called the student paper first. They'd left us a number, scribbled on notebook paper. I let Mary-Beth talk. I'd run out of words. I sat with the phone books and fed Kara numbers: the Windsor *Star*, the Toronto *Star*, the Toronto *Sun* (who said they'd print my pictures, if I wanted, but that was the limit of their interest), the Detroit *Free Press*.

They took notes, said they'd see what they could do.

I got up and phoned the local radio stations. Called community radio. I called Detroit.

I phoned Public Broadcasting. They kept the archive version of that call. Someone played the recording for me, years later, when I came to work in Toronto. Public Broadcasting is the memory of the nation.

It was just me, by then, on the phone, running through all the change I'd been able to gather.

We held a press conference on the side lawn of the Windsor Public Library. If we'd been thinking, we'd have gone back to the club, the scene of the naked crime, but I was exhausted, shaking, and we had to be in Detroit in three hours for our show.

We didn't make it. We did get to be on five radio stations.

Television showed up.

Were you really naked, Miss Winter?
Yes.
What do you have to say about that?
That it's super funny. And anybody who thinks it was a sex show wasn't there.
Would you say it was performance art, then?
Pause. *Oh, definitely.*

That bought us another interview, with a Michigan affiliate broadcaster who came across the border just to take footage of me in my wrecked jeans.

> *This woman is not allowed into America!*
> *The most dangerous grrrl in Windsor-Detroit!*
> *Canadian girl-rockers too sexy for America!*

We crossed the border eighteen hours after we'd been stopped. There were cameras.
What are you going to do in Detroit, Miss Winter?
Play music.

We didn't have a TV or friends in the area, so we assumed that the local-news footage was lost to history, but years later I found out there were home recordings of a surprising amount of what aired. The video was grainy, filtered through low-quality magnetic recordings, but nearly complete: clip after clip put together by the riot grrrls of Detroit and mailed to us one day, years later, as a kind of love letter.

We played that night, a booking we hadn't had before we were banned from the country. I hadn't been prepared for the wrecked scenery of Detroit, or the mismatch between the outside and the inside. Black people on the street, white girls in the club, running in from the suburbs in their parents' cars. It was the scariest places they'd ever been.

Art kids drove up from Ann Arbor to play in bands as shitty as ours. Riot grrrls, but punks and university rock-snobs and community radio kids and high school kids who'd heard something from somebody, too. Frat boys came to see the naked chick. Photographers came from everywhere.

Kara fronted the show. I played behind her, lower-energy, aware of the hours Kara's fury had been building. The pictures of the band that had turned into pictures of just me.

They howled until she stripped too, to satisfy them. Just, not entirely. Kara never, as far as I can remember, played a show in less than a bra and granny panties.

Off stage, she never wore a bra. I'd been surprised she still owned one. She told me she'd picked one up at K-Mart, for the occasion. Soft-cupped and floral. She'd spilled coffee on it and washed it out in the washroom sink to give it the necessary level of age and filth to move against her body in a plausible show of discomfort.

The boys yelled, "Show us your tits!"

Kara yelled back, "They're right here! If they're too little for you to see, I can buy you a microscope!"

That grinding bra and her sagging, ragged boy-jeans. Runners and gel holding her bangs back out of her face.

We finished at 2 a.m. Loaded out surrounded by girls and art-boys in the alley. They were standing guard.

"We can take care of ourselves," Mary-Beth said. "I promise we've done it before."

"We don't want anything to happen to you." Chin gesture at the streets beyond.

They were empty. Occasionally, an almost-dead car ground over the pavement and slid away.

"How long are you here?" they asked.

I thought we were moving on, out to the Upper Peninsula before looping back down, but Kara said, "We're playing the Grande Ballroom the day after tomorrow."

"Got anywhere to stay?"

We were introduced to the Detroit mansions. These streets full of decaying Victorians, almost completely empty and surrounded by burned-out shells. We were new to the city, enough that we hadn't encountered the mythos of Detroit and its grinding death.

I write about "we" like I was talking to Kara, or to Mary-Beth. I think they were talking to each other. They'd called back home and found bookings for us. They weren't angry at me. I didn't think they were angry. I was braced for a fight, but they handed me sandwiches and Diet Cokes and just didn't say much of anything, and the arthouse kids kept pulling me away.

We had two free days in Detroit.

Mary-Beth went to the Art Institute. Kara went thrifting. I went out into the industrial mess with a pair of photography students from Wayne State.

I'm not naked in any of those pictures, but the shoot penetrated magazines in a way I'd never been pictured before. There were magazines in the States that I hadn't heard of, sold just in anarchist bookstores and art venues, and my face showed up in them. Little write-ups about The Innocents went with photo spreads. They didn't always tell us we were being featured. Or that I was featured and the others weren't. I ran searches, later, when the internet took over, and found photos of myself from magazines I'd never heard of.

Someone said, *Do you guys have an agent?*

I said, "Uh-uh."

Mary-Beth said, "No, we do. Here." Handed over an actual business card, crisp-edged and looking entirely real.

She phoned back home. Talked for a long time. We were in somebody's suburban basement. I'd had a real shower and painted my fingernails the eeriest shade of pink that I could find in St Clair Shores. Mary-Beth said, "We're re-booking."

"Okay."

"No, don't be like that. We have actual money. It's a miracle."

"We're out of tapes."

"More coming. And T-shirts."

I said, "Is this what it feels like when you get discovered?"

Kara said, "It feels like shit, so, yeah, probably."

We had it out, eventually. We left the eerie, elegant house and stalked our way to a perfectly-groomed park and Kara tore my skin off. Screamed in perfect girl-fashion about who the *fuck* did I think I was?

I may have said something about a chick with a whiny bitch of an ex-best-friend who couldn't fucking stand it if anybody else got attention, and did she want the money or what, exactly?

She said, "I don't think it's fair that you act like such a slut and everybody fucking loves you."

"You say *slut* like it's a bad thing."

"You love it when guys drool over you."

"It was a *joke*."

"Try spending just one day not trying to catch a dick, maybe, and see how that works out for you."

She took off. Wandered, I think, all over the non-city that night. Girl in the dark in the perfect security of white flight. I went back to the house, found my wallet, and went out and got drunk.

I started a fight with some girl with razor-nails about her awful, frat-boy boyfriend and got the skin yanked off my cheekbone, and then her friends bought me Jägermeister, and in the end I couldn't find my way home.

I had to call for help. Long distance. To Kara's mother.

"Diane?"

She said, "What did you do?"

"I took off my clothes on stage and got in a fight with Kara and then I got in a fight with somebody else and now I'm lost in this rich-person town and I think the guy across the parking lot thinks I'm a hooker."

"All right."

"I think I should quit and come home."

"And then what?"

"I mean, I think I'm going to go home. Do you think they'd take me back?"

If I was going to show up in rural Manitoba at my parents' gate, I'd need a dress. The jumpers I'd worn for years were long gone, but the malls were full of long, floral dresses that might work.

Or they might prefer me as I was. Prodigal daughters should look the part.

The whore is back. How shall she atone?

This fantasy, when it played out, involved blood sacrifice. I'd been watching horror movies for weeks, to the point I wasn't sure how much of my childhood was memory and how much was the gaps in my recollection being filled by French Extremist cinema.

Diane said, "How about you tell me where you are, first?"

"How?"

She sighed. "You were less trouble when you were a teenaged runaway. I can't believe I'm saying that."

The guy sitting in his car got out, started to approach me. I dropped the receiver and yelled at him, "If you get close enough to touch me, I'm going to rip your balls off."

He got back in his car.

Diane said, "Tell me where you are."

"I don't *know*."

"Read the street signs."

She hung up on me, finally. I had eight dollars left, and I ate breakfast out of the 7-Eleven's selection of miserable sandwiches. Slurpee in electric pink. It was the most Winnipeg food I could imagine. I stared at the sky.

Mary-Beth came to find me, driving too-slowly down the adjoining streets like she was looking for a lost dog. "Get in."

"How mad is Kara?"

"Well, she cried most of the night, and I'm not sure which one of you is the bigger cow, but if you can both knock it off, we have a gig at CBGB."

I stared at her.

"That's right, bitch. You're going to New York. And you're going to have to pull that shit again, so paint your toes up good."

~ 22 ~

Glass

I was cooking. In the kitchen, making pizza — dough, pesto, tomato slices, hot stone — when Hanna walked in. She stood by the cupboard for a while. Watched while I searched our decrepit plant for basil leaves full enough to spread over the rest.

Something exploded next to my head. What was it?

A jar of whole cloves. This little, strong glass vessel. *Exploded* wasn't the right word, though, because it was still mostly intact, spilling out over the counter with just the lid gone. The stone was hot, though, and the cloves that hit it sparked and exploded. They exploded. Yes.

Something else came at me. A mug, I thought, sailing by my ear and hitting the cabinet. *Crack.*

Thud.

I turned. I saw Hanna reach for the wine glass.

It was behind the sink, lurking there since the last party with a quarter-inch of unidentified red at the bottom. She took it like she knew that this, finally, was the right object.

She threw it at my face.

This was all too fast. Impossible. The raw pizza filled with glass shards, and the plant broke behind me, and I reared back and burned my hand on the pizza stone and shrieked. Knocked the stone to the floor, where it cracked. There was thunder, distantly, upstairs, that was Eden descending toward us.

Hanna screamed, "Why aren't you crying?"

I stared at her. Still trying to decide whether there were cheap glass shards in either of my eyes.

"Why aren't you ever crying?"

She was sobbing. Angry.

"How did you cry it all out and get to be normal and why did you think I could do that and why aren't you crying, aren't you scared or something?"

I needed to speak, but when I opened my mouth I realized I'd been hit. There was nothing in my eyes, but there was glass embedded in my cheek, pushed through deep enough to scrape against my teeth on the other side.

Eden said, "Oh my god, what happened?"

Hanna said, "She never cries. She isn't *real*."

I said, "I think I might have to go to the hospital." Very calmly. Only a little muffled by the effort not to move my teeth or face.

I wanted a taxi, but Eden called an ambulance, and probably he was right. We would all have had to go in the taxi, and I would have been the logical one to sit up by the driver. It would have been unfair to confront some poor Eritrean cabbie with our domestic gore.

Paramedics arrived to find me sitting in the living room. I had a tea towel against my chin because I was afraid to touch the glass. If I was bleeding, it was only a little. They said I was in shock.

"Can you just pull it out?"

"That close to your eye? I think we'd better take you in." The nearer guy was shielding me with his body. "I'll get your coat. Can you walk?"

"Of course," I said. "I'm fine."

They drove with the siren off and curled around corners to Toronto Western. There were other bodies coming into the Emergency bay on gurneys. I saw the crowd inside and wished I'd brought work. Maybe a book.

They walked me in. Gestured someone over. Whispered.

I didn't sit in triage.

I heard other people muttering. There was a black woman — east African, I thought, maybe from around the Horn — with a massive, bloody towel on her hand, and she was waiting. Kids coughed tearing sounds out of their lungs. Someone might have been holding a finger. Arms were broken. People were drunk, aching, sick, shouting at the people walking me by them, into the linoleum throat of the hospital.

Not into medical care, exactly. Just onto a curtained bed. The medic put my feet up, dug my phone out and handed it to me.

"You'll be okay," he said. Then, "I love your show."

I said, muffled, reflexively, "Thank you. That means a lot."

I kept waiting for it to hurt. I thought that if I could see my face, look in a mirror, I'd realize the extent of the mess. Or realize there was none. I considered looking for a bathroom, but when I sat up the curtains spun around me.

Selfie. I had my phone. I could look at myself. I could look at anything.

I held the camera at arm's length and studied myself. It didn't look that bad from that distance, but my skin was fading to the shade of the curtains. When I held the phone close enough to show detail, my eyes wouldn't focus.

I took pictures. Different angles. Tried to study them. Failed.

I think I slept for a while. I woke up, holding my purse like a clutched pillow, to a nurse checking my pulse. Palpating my face.

"What time is it?"

"Someone will be in to look at that shortly. I think you're going to need a plastic surgeon. I'm not sure whether we have one on call tonight."

When they cleaned my face, I was almost unconscious. They'd given me painkillers, at some point, and something else, maybe Ativan or Xanax. The tranquilizer sea was gorgeous, warm, full of jellyfish, and moving like Eden's footage from the Keys. I rolled into a tighter ball, letting the injured cheek press upwards into the antiseptic air.

I thought, vaguely, that I should text someone and tell them where I was.

Later, I realized they were moving me. They needed the bed, the curtained space, but I was immovable, too inert to discharge and too healthy to admit. My fan base was gone, and I was left to doze in the corridor, purse half-under my chest, with everyone else.

Like sleeping on the road. Don't let go of your things.

When I got up to pee, I realized I was lost. Someone in scrubs – a nurse or an orderly – found me. Ushered me through rooms into a counselling-green space of plastic chairs. I said, "Bathroom." Muffled. My face was stiff. I tried to think how many hours until I had to be on air.

"Over there."

I looked awful. The mirror was minimal, metal polished to almost-reflection but with a prison-edge that unnerved me. I was swollen, bandaged. One of my eyes was black. When I came out, the scrubs-wearer was waiting. I had people to talk to.

I met with two police officers. A social worker.

I tried to explain. Sort through details in my head.

They must have talked to Eden, maybe to Hanna, but whatever version had come through, they thought he'd hit me. Stabbed me.

No, please, officer, it was the little girl.

She didn't mean anything by it.

It's been a strange day.

A strange week. Months. When did I bring her home, exactly?

It was customary, I was told, in domestic disturbances, to keep the partners separate. They could ask him to vacate the house while I retrieved my things.

I said, "He didn't hit me."

"Ms. Winter . . ."

"My daughter . . . a glass broke. There was a mess. This was an *accident*."

"Just take a minute."

I said, "There's a place in hell for people who lie about this shit. It was an accident. Things happen. They must be so scared."

The recording angels nodded. I waited alone, and other people came and studied me.

"Ms. Winter."

"Yes."

"Your story confirms the other ones we've gathered. That your partner did not harm you. I'm sorry for the pressure — we get the most horrible cases. But . . ."

"Yes?"

"Your daughter was previously reported for violence."

"What?"

"At her school."

"Jesus." I tried to rub my eyes. Regretted it. "She got in a fight."

"How's her counselling going?"

"People were *picking* on her."

"Could you give me the contact number for her therapist? I'd just like to liaise."

It occurred to me that I'd meant to do something, maybe take Hanna to my psychiatrist, but then I'd remembered that the pills that resurrected adults killed children, that Hanna probably shouldn't be medicated, and then I hadn't had any idea what to do next.

"She doesn't have one."

These were words of doom. I imagined telling the woman in front of me that Hanna didn't have a bed. No shoes. That she went hungry.

"I think I can help you with that." She left. Returned. "I've made calls. To-morrow at eleven."

"What day is it?"

"The tomorrow in question is Thursday. Here is the information. I will also contact your partner. Ms. Winter, please understand that this isn't optional."

"What time is it?"

"It's about seven."

I was late for work. I nodded. Accepted her papers.

I took a cab, this time. We moved across town at raw, exciting speed.

That's a lie. We moved through the snarls of Toronto traffic until I got out, walked to the subway, rode the rest of the way to work like that.

Late. Hours late. Fifty-seven minutes to air.

They stared at me. James walked out, reached towards my face. Recoiled.

"Can you even talk?"

"What?"

"You sound like you lost your teeth."

"It's not that bad."

"Alli, it is. Sit down. I'll call a sub."

I sat. My office was too far from things for my taste, but when I went to the sound booth the producers looked at me in horror, and the guest-host went pale. It made me miss the punk scene. We'd opened once for a band whose bassist had stage-dived, laid his thigh open, and played the rest of the show like that, blood streaming down and yellow fat showing in the gouge in his body, and no one ever told him to sit down.

In my office, I stretched out on the couch. Called up Public Radio on the house speakers.

"Good morning Port-aux-Basques. From the edge of the deep green sea, I'm Linda Jansen, and this is *The Cure*."

Cue music.

I couldn't go home. I'd texted with Eden through the day, and dozed on my office couch, and wandered the streets half-conscious, looking for food. Every restaurant I approached made me nauseous. I couldn't imagine chewing and swallowing anything as nutritious as a vegan sandwich. Not even fruit.

I walked until I found a McDonald's and sat in it. Found myself eating McNuggets like a kid. Salt and fat somehow eased my stomach. In the over-lit venue, I didn't even look alarming. I thought I didn't. Guys sharing the newspaper looked like they slept outside. The girl on the register had a black eye.

Eden wrote, *she's sleeping. she was up all night.*

Should I come home?

. . .

His flickering ellipsis of a half-written message lingered for five or more minutes. I wanted a milkshake but didn't think I could suck hard enough to consume one without popping my stitches.

Two girls slid up beside me.

"Excuse me, are you Allison Winter?"

I shrugged.

"Can I take a selfie with you?"

I hadn't looked hard at my face in hours, but I could guess enough to want fewer public records of it than already existed. I said, "No."

She stared at me. Like she thought I didn't understand that she'd only asked as a courtesy. Walked away, four or five feet, then turned and shot a picture of herself with me in the background.

Trending Twitter post: Allison Winter, her face.

Eden's dialogue box still showed the ellipsis.

I threw my dipping sauce away. Tried to think where I was going. The girl came swooping in for another photo.

She didn't grow up in a punk club. She was a hipster grad student, maybe, or a dilettante journalism major. Slow reflexes.

I took her phone.

She wasn't prepared. I was out the door before she reacted, and even then she was steps behind me.

"Bitch!"

"I said, don't take my picture."

"Give me my phone back."

I studied her. The space between us.

Threw her phone to the pavement as hard as I could.

The screen cracked. It wasn't enough. I dived for it a second ahead of her, grabbed the phone and elbowed her face, and threw the half-dead mechanism into traffic.

One hit. Two. Tires rolled over it.

Gone.

Digital footprint intact, but I felt better.

I said, "Next time don't fucking take my picture."

She said she was calling the police. I told her to feel free. Walked away.

Wondered how long it would be before she realized she didn't have her phone to call them with. How far she'd have to walk to find a public phone she could use.

▮▮◈▮▮

From my office, I keyed through my own contacts.

Eden said, . . .

Tina. Erin. Lacey. Mary-Beth.

Kara.

Kara was, I thought, still in Winnipeg. She'd known I was there — I couldn't think she hadn't noticed — but she hadn't called me, and I hadn't called her. Two years into no calls, I wasn't sure which of us was due to break the detente.

Mary-Beth was in Vancouver. I called her.

"Babe, I think I'm homeless."

She said, "Well, you're welcome to stay with me, but it's a long commute."

I tried to explain the night. Trusted that she could decipher my cursing and drug-induced vagary.

"Is she okay?"

"Trust you to take the kid's side."

"I saw her lifted out of a slit in your belly. I guess I can worry about her if I want."

"Eden said she's sleeping."

"Why haven't you gone home?"

I didn't answer. Eden's dialogue still held at an unfinished response. I wished he'd erase or send.

"Fine. Who's the sanest single bitch you know that I know, too?"

"Do you know Lucy?"

"Lucy C with the nipple piercings?"

"I was thinking the one with the cats."

"Same Lucy. She got her nipples pierced. Posted photos. Girl has no fear."

I remembered being able to do that. Alter my body and take photos, share them with a calm fuck-you-here-I-am. Lucy's route was still easier — fetish model, playgirl, private therapist to people who posted their own mutilated photos. I'd met her at a party, a good one, and she'd introduced me to the dancers, people who'd come just to dance and not for anything else. Girls in thongs and heels and nothing else. She travelled to fetish parties all over the continent. Lucy had met Mary-Beth before she ever met me.

I said, "I owe her two phone calls. Three. I can't show up on her doorstep."

Sigh. Mary-Beth said, "If I phone her, will you at least phone home?"

"Will you call me back?"

"Yes, baby girl. Now hang up."

I looked at my phone. Eden's hanging text waited.

I keyed his name.

"Hey."

"You didn't answer my question," I said.

"What?"

"Hanging text. Hour and a half."

"Oh, shit, sorry. She woke up. I sat with her for a while."

"Is she okay?"

"She's . . . I was thinking I might call my mom."

"Jesus. Please no."

"Just to talk to. Alli, I don't know from upset kids."

"Are the police still there?"

"No. But we have a family court date."

"I have a lawyer." I thought I probably had a lawyer. "We'll deal. Am I coming home?"

Silence on the line. I waited.

. . .

I said, "Right. Call me later, okay?"

Mary-Beth texted, *lucys coming to pick you up twenty minutes outside bring your shit*

you said youd call

ive used up all the fucks i had. get some sleep and call me when youre sane again, girl. love you.

Lucy drove a tiny two-door car with shredded upholstery. The odometer looked to be rolling over.

She said, "Get in."

Down through the city to Corktown. Underground, and then through cement hallways like the set of a police shoot-out. Up the stairs.

I thought about Lucy's condo as often as I thought about her, but I was still amazed by its beauty. It was nicer than the one I had when I imagined my life without Eden. Her building had been gutted and re-made into nests for single adults. Not quite studios, but the units were each only about the size of our living room. They had glossy enamel kitchens and gleaming appliances.

Cats. Three. Four. Crying around her feet and leaping into her arms.

She moved furniture into a sleep formation. Brought out sheets and a T-shirt — too big for me, probably small on her — and dropped the shades. "Go to bed."

Like it was that easy. I couldn't imagine sleep.

Instead, I took a shower in her tiny, glossy bathroom. The cats wandered in to shit in the box I'd moved out of the shower stall. I washed my hair. My face burned under the soap. I kept sucking at my teeth to see how many were present.

She'd made up the exquisitely expensive couch for me. I lay on it, letting my wet hair weep into the flat guest pillow. Towels pooled around me.

I woke up in the middle of the night, burrowed in scramble of damp terrycloth and random blankets and animals.

Two cats had joined me, one at my shoulder and the other behind my knees. Streetlight pushed through the blind slats.

God, I was hungry.

The fridge was septic, but I found edible yogurt. Ate some and gave some to the cats and went to the bathroom, where I found Lucy standing at the second access door that I realized after led to her bedroom.

"You better?"

"I don't know."

"Wanna sleep with me?"

"Yeah."

It wasn't a massive bed — it couldn't have been, in that apartment — and it was crowded with animals. She shifted them unceremoniously. Pushed until there was room for me to get in.

Away from the street windows, her apartment was profoundly dark. The world stank of cat and girl and I slept for a while.

Still dark when I woke, but I thought it might be morning. The bedroom lacked windows, and there were blackout curtains across balcony doorway. The cats had vanished, off hunting or feeding on unwary neighbours. Lucy sat up in bed, naked, reading off a tablet.

"How are you?"

"I hurt less. I'm not too impressed with the state of my life, though."

"You're going to take her to therapy, yes?"

I ground my teeth. "Children survived millennia without therapy."

"They killed and ate their parents. What's your therapy issue?"

I shrugged. "Too *New Yorker*. Freud and shit."

"That is not even a thing." She handed me my phone. "Call your family and tell them you're not dead."

I took it to the bathroom. Didn't call. Left my phone beside the sink and walked into the kitchen half-naked to see the animals.

Lucy came out, later, with my phone activated and glowing. She said, "Alright. Do you want her back?"

"No, she's here. Communing with the zoo. Let me talk to Hanna."

Pause.

"Hi. I'm Lucy. Can I talk to you?"

"No, Alli's okay. I don't know if she's mad. I'll ask her." Pause. "Hey Alli, are you mad?"

The cats were long, skinny creatures. I'd never met a cat lady with thin cats before. The barn cats from my early life were leaner than these, but no one fed them. Every band-house cat I'd encountered was a massive thing, ready to steal food from our travel bags. These were sleek creatures that she fed precisely according to their needs. They had no collars and vivid eyes.

"Alli, are you mad?"

"I don't know."

"Your daughter is on the phone. I need you to give me a real answer."

"That is a real answer."

"I need you to give me a kid-ready answer. She's what, eleven? You can't tell her that you don't know if you're mad."

"Why not?"

"She won't know what that means. Kids are direct. They can be wrong about what they feel, but they're almost always sure."

I said, "Tell her I'm not mad."

"Good girl. Hanna, honey, she's not mad. And I asked her twice, so I'm pretty sure she means it.

"I mostly talk to grownups, but maybe we can work something out."

Lucy said, "Get dressed. We'll get brunch and you can take me home with you. Maybe I can keep you out of court."

‖◌‖

Lucy was a single woman in a city that worshipped brunch; it was a meal she'd perfected. She asked me twice what I wanted, and when I didn't answer, she gave me options: vegan, fruit-based, down the street, or filthy diner on the way across town.

I ate cholesterol for breakfast and she had steak and eggs and told me that I was doing everything wrong.

"I mean, how many people have told you that your daughter needs help?"

"Four. Ish."

"If four people told you she had a sinus infection, what would you do?"

"That's not a fair question."

"It is from where I'm sitting. You took a glass through the face and it's your own damn fault. She doesn't have to be all stoic and punk-rock just because you are."

"I never met a therapist I'd trust with my own sanity, let alone hers. No offence."

She wrinkled her nose at me. "If you say shit like that, *no offence* loses its meaning."

"You *know* what kind of people go into therapy. Preachy assholes with their own ideas about normal who couldn't think their way out of a paper bag."

"You're not helping yourself."

"I don't want them to take her apart."

"She's taking you apart."

"She's a little girl. I think I can cope."

"Yeah, but you have a thick skin, most of the time. And this is really funny, because you're the queen of medication."

"When your brain chemistry's off, resetting isn't the wrong thing to do. But you can't give pills to little kids. It makes them worse."

"Well, thank god you figured that out, at least. Tell me you weren't going to give her your meds."

Lucy waited for me to pay for breakfast. I dug through my bag for a credit card. Suppressed my memories of the impulses I'd had to grind a pill or two into Hanna's breakfast.

"Of course not."

"Okay. Now, I'm going to take you home and you're going to let me talk to her."

I shook my head.

"It isn't negotiable."

"She doesn't have to talk to anybody she doesn't want to," I said. "House rule."

"She already asked me. That's consent." Lucy punctuated her statement with a sharp right turn that knocked my head against the window.

"Ow."

"Baby. You have two black eyes and a hole in your face. *That* didn't hurt."

I sat for a while, watching the Saturday traffic. "I hit a girl yesterday and smashed her phone because she took a picture of me after I told her not to."

"You should probably talk to someone about that."

"I told her not to take my fucking picture."

"And yet you bring it up now, suggesting that you're aware this isn't the behaviour of a high-functioning adult."

"Or at least that I'm probably going to be arrested for it at some point."

"I expect you'll live. What's your address again?"

I paused. "Don't put it in your phone."

"What?"

"My address. Don't write it down. Or list it under Eden's name instead."

"I'm a confidential counsellor for people with fairly extreme kinks. I think you can trust me to be discrete."

"Still."

"Fine. But you have trust issues."

I said, "Turn left up here. There."

Lucy in daylight in our living room looked shockingly normal. Almost exactly like a therapist — wide-assed and dressed in polyester slacks and a fitted button-down slashed with pale and darker green lines. Hair up. Glasses. With her clothes on, you couldn't see a trace of her piercings. All her tattoos were invisible.

Hanna said to her, "Can I show you the park?"

"Sure." She waited while Hanna grabbed her backpack and shoes. Nodded to me.

I couldn't think of a reason to prevent them from walking out the door.

Alone, Eden pulled me onto the couch and studied my face. "Oh god."

"It's not that bad."

"It's absolutely the worst thing I've ever seen. I'm so sorry."

"Why?"

"I told you not to come home. I feel like shit."

"Yes, you feel like shit. I'm fine, except that a maniac just walked off with my daughter."

"Did you sleep?"

"Passably, under many cats, next to a kinky naked chick." I paused. "Did you?"

"Not much."

He curled behind me on the couch and dozed while I looked at my phone. There were lurking messages there that I'd been avoiding for weeks. Messages from Wayne Cardinal and Margaret. One that I'd simply avoided, left unopened so that it flared an alert every time I opened my mail app.

I thumbed the app closed and went to Twitter. Hashtagged my name.

Her name — my photographer — was Jasmine1993, and she was mad. She'd written an eight-tweet post, linked it to Facebook, explaining exactly how much of a bitch I was. What I'd done to her. In her version, I'd damaged her face, too. She'd been nice. What the hell?

The internet's response was approximately *pix or it didn't happen.*

hey asshole she broke my phone took my pix did u miss that?

Answers. Obscene and non.

Ignore her. She's just doing it for attention.

I shifted to my browser. Visited Kara's blog.

> *She's Just Doing It for Attention*
> feminist media commentary
> riot grrrl web presence
> bitch opinions

Kara kept it low-key. She'd watched the other women who did this work become public figures, then go into hiding when death and rape threats became daily occurrences. When bomb squads had to check the venues of any public appearance they made. When they had to move their kids out of school.

Hazards of the job.

Kara didn't not do her job. She just kept it low-profile. Skipped non-academic conferences. Shifted media requests to someone else in her department.

She had a book coming out. I'd been wondering if I should make sure she got an invite to appear on *The Cure.*

Whether she'd come if I asked.

When I keyed over to consider phoning her, I found I'd actually already missed three calls during the night. Kara. Mary-Beth. Kara again.

The phone vibrated in my hand, a nameless Toronto number that I sent to voicemail.

I went to bed. Woke up later, at twilight, and phoned Mary-Beth back.

"Hey, honey. Your day's improving, yeah?"

I said, "Sleep helps."

"And. . .?"

I paused. "M.B., are you pregnant?"

Pause.

"That was random and intuitive, but no."

"Have you been talking to Lucy?"

"Yes, but that's beside the point. Did you say yes?"

"One more time. From the top. What?"

She said, "Phone Kara. Then call me back."

It's proverbial that we can't predict what's going to be big in Japan. Random fragments of western pop culture sail out to form nebulae in the galaxy of Nippon's own hallucinogenic creations.

On *The Cure* we'd done shows about small-town anime clubs and the kids who cosplayed their way through high school, and all the little kids that look like pixies to survive. Naomi Klein accused them of commodifying themselves, I remembered, before she'd gone on to deal with more pressing issues. The illuminated hair colours were her particular concern. I remember looking in the mirror and wondering if we were seeing the same phenomenon.

The last time I had long hair, it was twists of blue and purple, layered Manic Panic that smelled like stale grape soda.

What they liked in Japan was, at present, not that. Instead, what they liked was us.

Mujitsu no punk!

It wasn't just our music. Something had grown there while we weren't paying attention. Stories. Sketches. Television. Kara sent me pictures. The tiny figurines, and video clips from the series. It was animated, and it must have been in production for years. Angry girls form a band, fight boys and demons, conduct their romances in secret with entities that might only be gutter punks or might be creatures of the night.

The characters didn't look that much like us, and there was one more band member, and I thought their style was more Bikini Kill than anything else. But they'd scored it with poppy idoru covers of riot grrrl anthems, and they *had* given us credit for that. Songwriting lines, plus royalties for the track sales.

Then, because there's always a backlash to sugar, the fans had dug up the original versions.

Riot comes to Kichijoji.

Stores in Tokyo sold posters of all of us. Of Kara. Mary-Beth.

Of me, topless, straddling a guitar and smirking at the camera.

They liked my hair.

They said, back and forth in texted romaji, *Alli-chan, she's a real girl.*

Look, there she is.

She's pretty.

She has a terrible story.

Tell me.

Our old coverage had been carefully transliterated from fan sites in English and German into Japanese. Roman alphabet first — romaji's easiest for texting — but then into kana and kanji. *Here is Sleater-Kinney. Here is Bikini Kill.*

Here is the goddess Kathleen Hanna.

These are The Innocents.

It wasn't something I was prepared to deal with. I had no idea what Kara wanted me to say about it, so I didn't say anything. Put away my phone.

She made it simple. I ignored her calls for a day, so she emailed. Direct.

Do you want to go be big in Japan?

~ 23 ~

Medusa

The Innocents went overseas in 1998. We took off in the middle of the university term, and it was years before I got around to going back. We played England first, and then France, where we were an alien spectacle and the teenagers smoked.

It was existential, even more deeply so than Quebec. France, they told us, was never sure what it thought of punk. They had techno club kids and indie rockers who hated techno, and they hurled vitriolic posters at each other in Lyon and Strasbourg. We played Paris twice, and the second time we had a decent venue. The audience liked that I could speak French. Someone told me she thought my colonial accent was *très subversif.*

We met anarchists at our shows who took us home with them to half-ruined squats covered with graffiti where the women's building was cordoned off and guarded by girls in military surplus gear and kufiyah face scarves. The wiring was jerry-rigged and hung below the sagging plaster cornices. The residents washed on the roof with collected rainwater.

It was incredible. I sat next to the cistern with Kara, head on her shoulder, and stared at the roofs of Paris.

Kufiyah-wearing Delphine said, "Come out with us."

I hadn't realized how small Paris was. You could genuinely walk across it.

Nothing like London's horizon sprawl or any North American city's shape. There were suburbs, tangled neo-brutalist messes, but we were in the city proper, and you didn't even need the Metro to get places. We just walked through the alleys, wrapped in our surplus layers and salvaged flannel. It was raining again. Grey and ozone-smelling.

Up and over and up hills and into buildings older than anything that had existed in my earlier experience.

I told somebody once in an interview that we met Simone de Beauvoir on tour, but that isn't true. She died while I was still proselytizing to people with their own faiths and problems. But we met other *grandes dames*. Lean-faced women with tight ponytails and unimaginable senses of style, whose apartments were full of books and papers. You couldn't not be intimidated by beauty like that.

On that night, they took me out to meet the Medusa.

She wasn't hosting, but the party revolved around her, the way parties do when everyone present is an artist but not everyone has a name that college kids know in other countries. Our host was a magazine writer. There were a lot of black turtlenecks on the attendees, and expensive statement jewelry. Delphine, who brought us, seemed to be a kind of accent-piece, intended to give the event some sense of authenticity.

People talked around us, occasionally asking a gracious question. We were given bits of fruit and cheese. The host gradually migrated us through the kitchen to the salon where the Medusa sat.

She had a magnificent nose and a knack for full, heavy eyeliner. Beyond that, she looked like women I'd met all over the world, senior women in different polities who were certain of their own authority. I think I may have bowed to her.

She thought it was funny. I got shy and sat staring at her, this woman who wrote the books that I'd tried to parse in Diane's bedroom when I was first loose in the world.

There's a surprisingly revered place in feminist thought, at least the vein of it I first dug into, for those severe French thinkers. Diane's project to re-educate me involved reading a lot of those books. If she'd fed me on bell hooks or Angela Davis, I'd be different. Still, I couldn't always make anything of it. Their dismantling of meaning and language, their explications of the structures of gender, made me want to cry. There was something there, present, and I couldn't get to it. Too hard for me. Too complicated.

I was sure if anyone looked at me directly, they'd be able to tell.

We took one picture with her, with a disposable camera, and my face was turned away. I wouldn't look at the lens. Her face was captured perfectly. Mine blurred.

You're adorable, Delphine said. *She asked us to come.*

It wasn't a huge party, and it was quiet by our standards. Mostly women, older and starker-looking than we were, and a few obviously-queer men. People who identified as *journalists* and *theorists.* Kara was in her element. She slid herself down onto the sofa, accepted a glass of wine, and started talking. Asking questions. She got excited, waved her arms, provoked laughter. She didn't even speak French, not as well as I did, but people found her charming, her youth, her rawness. They switched to English to keep up with her.

One of those moments when you see the future forming and don't know what it is.

I sat on the floor, cross-legged, just outside the circle. I could follow the language shifts when clusters of talkers shifted back into French, but I couldn't always grasp the snarled threads of their ideas. They were speaking of the theatre, its modes and levels of meaning in construction. About what we did, in Riot, as *la théatre primitive.*

Kara followed their thread, started to argue for the value of the primitive, to talk about masks and performance.

I felt vaguely like a kid at an adult party, pushed into a second tier of existence while everyone else rushed forward towards an excitement that I couldn't see. I studied my wine glass, contemplating hurling it at the impeccable nineteenth-century plaster, soaking the books piled against the walls with the remains of my drink.

I started to do it. Mary-Beth caught my wrist. Said, "Chill."

I got up. Walked to the kitchen and stood there, then leaned back through the door to see what was going on. That other, thickly-reasoned world going on without me.

Mary-Beth handed me my jacket and a handful of silk scarves that she'd obviously gathered from other peoples' coats. She said, "Time to go."

"Kara . . ."

"Kara's having a blast. You, not so much. Come on."

We walked through the city, draped in silk and expensive perfume, looking for second-hand markets and lacking the sense of direction that might actually have taken us to them. Instead, we found couture avenues so polished I couldn't believe they didn't vomit us out on sight. Furs in the window, and high fashion in a mode that I'd thought was dead, given the length of time it had been suppressed at home. Grunge didn't swallow Paris the way it swallowed Seattle and Vancouver and even Winnipeg. Paris, the city wanted us to know, was un-swallowable. It was uninterested in our rejections of consumer goods or fashion.

In Paris, you stormed the barricades with one hand and styled yourself with the other for infinite grace. The *grandes feministes* carried a beauty that I was never going to be able to manage.

Mary-Beth had looped cashmere around her shoulders over her army jacket. She grinned at me.

We walked around in our salvaged layers through streets full of stores that sold clothes with no price tags on them. We saw the Hermès store in Avenue George V, just from the outside. Like an old book. Not even huge, not impressive except that it was so intensely what it was: expensive, beautiful. There were women in those streets who might have been made entirely of silk and bone. They wore their perfect features without any awareness of the grunge revolution or the synthetic nature of beauty.

I said, "I think I need eyeliner."

"Everyone needs eyeliner. When society collapses, we'll still be wearing it."

We found something approximating the kind of drugstore where I'd have bought makeup at home, and I pocketed an eye pencil while Mary-Beth bought a handful of fashion magazines with a credit card I hadn't realized she owned. She bought me a Coke, which I drank half of and threw away, and said, "I think I need to walk by myself."

"Whatever. Have fun."

I left her in a cafe, reading her prizes, and wondered what kind of girl Mary-Beth was, underneath, and what she'd make of herself when the revolution was over.

When I came back to the squat, people stared at me, incredulous, and laughed. One girl told me that a woman who had perfectly-lined eyes and no brassiere wasn't to be trusted.

She hadn't met the Medusa.

I asked her if she had a brassiere that I could borrow.

She did. It was red and black lace, slightly too small, so that my breasts struggled upwards, out of their traps, and it was exactly what I needed.

I went out alone that night. Punk clubs might have existed in the city, but they were un-findable. Techno blurred its venues' edges, and hard rock and soft rock were everywhere, and I couldn't find my people. The Euro scene was full of skinheads that I couldn't always tell from anarchists until it was too late, and the girls who travelled with them had shadow bruises that were created with makeup more than half the time. *Punk* meant different things here. If I wanted bodies, ones I hadn't already met, I was going to have to dig.

It would have been easier, really, if I could have been a lesbian. I'd already met a dozen women, beautiful and smart and sharp, and I adored them, but they didn't set my body on fire. It was like they had armour that I was missing. Smarter than me. Better.

I didn't find what I was looking for, but I decided that I liked French clubs. They looked me over, wearing my best angry-butch, my boy clothes and still-virgin skin, and let me come in anyway.

Electronic sound swallowed my breath.

The best music was the kind that made me deaf. Metallic synth with limited chords and ratcheted decibel counts that shook the bones of my middle ears. Ringing all over. I'd met musicians who spent enough time in modulated silence to hear skin slide on skin, but they didn't go to clubs like these.

We were in the antithesis of the underground. They'd taken over the top floor of a warehouse, blacked out the windows. The crowd wasn't dancing. No one had designated a mosh pit or staked out slam-dance territory. They just stood, jumping in place, shaking the floor like they could break through some dimensional barrier to vibration and rage. Girls in fishnet and asymmetrical haircuts dodged around me. Too many of them clung to the arms of their guys like they thought I might be out to steal them. Skinny, ratty boys with bad teeth and skin. They all stank. I stank.

We could sweat together until the end of the world.

One of the girls pushed up against me. Hissed *gouine* and shoved hard.

I thought about the box-cutter I carried in clubs in the U.S. The girl who'd knocked me out in New York.

I bit her. She screamed, running backwards.

Skin between my teeth. Just the surface and that thin veil of French hair, but satisfying.

Her boyfriend was laughing at her so hard.

I pushed away from them, into the crowd. The band was French, amelodic, and screaming. They felt good under my skin.

I thought, for a while, that the music might be enough. There were bodies colliding with mine, occasionally, and I was ripped through with endorphins. One more time, the angry girlfriend came after me and I stiff-armed her. She fell, and then I had to dive after her into the crowd of feet, pull her to the edge before her skull caved in. She was bloody already. Spitting teeth. Her eyes tried to fix on me, but they'd developed the off-centre concussion-glimmer I'd seen in men's eyes for years, the momentary aftermath of a steel-toed boot to the head.

I needed to get outside.

There was only a ladder up to the roof, but it wasn't hard to climb. Out in the rain, smokers and weed-smokers talked in groups. Their legs vibrated with the bass from downstairs.

I wanted a cigarette. I had maybe four, in my jacket, but no lighter.

It was a way in.

«As un briquet?»

I wasn't sure it was correct. My French was childish, but I was holding a cigarette, and my breasts showed above the neckline of my shirt, and I think they got the idea.

I'd love to claim I picked him out, but that implies some canny seductiveness I hadn't imagined for myself. He was the one who made eye contact, grinned out of his circle of friends, and pulled a cheap plastic butane out of his pocket. Messy, infected eyebrow piercing. Ugly, skinny face.

Just, you know, a boy. You smile at them and they follow you all night.

I smiled.

It was so easy to have him come down with me, back into the crowd, and fight the bodies while he grinned from inches away, this constant threat that I'd lose my front teeth the moment our balance failed. Stale nicotine and beer breath, and something that I recognized later as cheap candy.

I hadn't expected French boys to taste like processed sugar crap. I didn't know if I was disappointed.

He pushed me up against the wall of the club and licked my cheek, smiled at me like I'd eaten his heart. I said twice, *take me home*, but he shook his head like he was deaf. Like he didn't have a home and lived in the perpetual Paris smog and rainfall.

The bathrooms were packed, too, but I had sharp elbows. Enough to win out a middle stall.

The people who had to piss could go deal in the street.

I took my coat and shirt off after I locked the door. Let him stare at my tits for a second before I pushed his head down to them.

He licked better than I'd expected. His hair, up close, reeked of citrus esters. It was sharp enough in its spikes that he might have used lemon Jell-O to set it.

Mouthing over my breastbone. I was going to give up and go hunting again, but he dug his front teeth, suddenly, against my sternum, and I yelled, shocked, and he was so fucking proud of himself that I dragged his head up and kissed him.

He was pretty, ugly-pretty, and he could have grown up in the next shitty Canadian town over from mine, and he was hard against me and hopeful in a way I hadn't expected.

And he wasn't tall. Once I'd shed my jeans down one leg, pushed aside my panties, he could lean into me, push up into me without having to stoop, and my leg hooked around his hip like he'd been designed to fuck me against a sheet-metal door.

I was never sure about sex in those first moments. There was the after-thought that condoms were a global phenomenon, but apparently we'd both forgotten that. And what was the point? He felt good. The angle pushed back, away from the lines of orgasm, but good, still. He went deeper than I'd expected and leaned into my neck, and I realized that he was whispering that I was pretty.

Jolie. Pretty girl.

He came fast, kissing into my ear. I was furious. I was still aching inside, ages away from what I needed, and he was *finished*? Sliding out, already.

I reached between my legs, caught the wet mess sliding out of me and held it in my palm between us. Tried to look pointed. Like I'd done this before.

He rubbed his fingers in it. Grinned and pressed them up into me.

Better.

He started with two, like he was sure, after his dick, that I could take it. His hands were big, actually. Long, bony fingers with blunt tips. Curling forward towards where I needed them.

I hissed, "Three." In English, but he nodded. Pulled out, adjusted, and pushed in with three fingers together.

This massive stretch, and the pressure of it, and he got me to come like that, spasming around him. Too much, suddenly, and I tried to squirm, but I'd clamped down on him. Locked pussy over bone.

Wild eyes and both of us mostly deaf.

Locked like that for long minutes, maybe as long as we'd fucked for. He wrapped his second arm around the back of my neck and hummed against my skull where I could feel the vibration. Waited for me to relax.

Pretty. Pretty. Shhh.

I did, and I let go of him. He slid his fingers out. Winced like I'd bruised him.

Pushed his hand against my face.

He was right. I smelled good. Better than him.

I thought, really, he should take me home. Not out of any bonding impulse; just because I wanted to do it again, lying down, in half an hour when my muscles had reset. Properly, he should have lived in another squat, less militant and more boy-smelling than the one I was at. He should have had a spot to sleep on a bare mattress with a couple of blankets on it and his clothes shoved into a pillow. Surrounded by candles and tapes from his favourite bands, and maybe he kept spray cans for his graffiti crew, and a bottle of something harder than the beer he tasted like.

He could go down on me, properly. I was swollen, too sensitive, but by the time we'd walked for half an hour or an hour, I'd be ready for that. If he wasn't quite sure how — I thought he maybe wasn't — I could try to explain it.

I'd read two books on what I wanted, and I'd tried a few things on my own, and I was ready to give directions.

Aftershocks tremored through my pelvis. I wasn't sure they weren't triggered mostly by my fantasies of architecture.

He whispered against my ear, «Mes amis m'attend.»

My friends are waiting.

Bye.

He waited, at least, while I crawled back into my jeans and top. The panties were a write-off, but they were still there, bunched around my hips.

I couldn't find him, later, when I walked out of the bathroom alone. I looked awful, probably, but there were no mirrors, and I wasn't interested enough in the expressions on other people to figure it out.

∎╏◉╏∎

The third show we'd tentatively booked in Paris fell through, and we had to keep moving if we wanted money. Lurking at the edges of the discussion was always Mary-Beth's family's money, the credit card she carried, but we left it in the conversational shadows. We travelled in an unlovely Westphalia van from the early 1980s into the mountains on the French-Swiss border where Parisian sophistication was almost entirely absent.

I was reassured, somehow, to discover that small, shitty towns were the same everywhere. The boredom of rural life was a steady creature.

There weren't separate band houses, but some of the bars had rooms in the back where we could crash. The audiences were good. They had no idea who we were, but we were loud and offensive, and their parents would have been moderately horrified if they'd spoken enough English to translate the lyrics.

My tits weren't as shocking to them as I'd hoped, but their ennui might have been a remnant of that beautiful French poise. After the show, a pack of girls invited us to drink with them by the river. They passed around cigarettes, not joints, and they'd invited their boyfriends. There were mountains behind us, but everything else might have been summoned from Steinbach, Manitoba, for our perpetual ennui.

Nothing not to love about discovering that France is disappointing. After Paris, if something hadn't been a let-down, I'd have been absolutely devastated.

One of the other girls peeled off to swim in the river, and I joined her. I was sticky from the show, and it had been days since I'd washed my hair. Underneath, at the base of my skull, it was starting to mat again.

She had a huge tattoo, one of the first like that I'd seen on a woman, and definitely the first on a woman who didn't have the over-dried contempt of an aging biker chick about her. I drew a fingertip along the black, raised line of the image on her shoulder. It wasn't good, exactly, but the line-work was excellent. Aesthetically, it was awful: a skull sporting a pink mohawk, smoking a cigarette. But whoever'd drawn it onto her had done a good job of the transfer.

I said, «Qui l'a fait?»

«Mon beau-frère.»

«Où habite-t-il?»

Walking-distance, apparently, so we went in a group, passing beers around and smelling like river-water. Her sister's place was in an ancient building that had been renovated maybe twenty years earlier, with heavy, industrial linoleum covering what appeared to be a stone floor. They weren't up, but the brother-in-law came down, looked us over, and palmed some lights on.

I got a medusa-head tattooed on my shoulder at four in the morning, mostly drunk, with a handful of French riot grrrls, and a pack of half-interested boyfriends studying my tits while I braced against the arm of a couch to keep from twitching.

He really was good. The lines were clear, and the medusa's face had a faint sneer to it.

«Les cheveux verts?»

"Noir."

He sighed, disappointed. Took my eighty francs and asked if he could bite my nipple.

"No."

«Ensuite, montre-moi ta chatte.»

I dropped my jeans. Half the concert had seen me nude already.

He reached out. Touched just the point where my pubic hair spilled out onto the top of my thighs.

"Ok."

It got infected, the tattoo, but I don't think that was particularly his fault. A medical student at a walk-in clinic in Lyon gave me some antibiotic cream and skipped the lecture, and the blurring that the infection added cut the artistry in favour of a messiness that was more like me, and that marked my back for the rest of my life.

~ 24 ~

Stray Girls

W e're *The Innocents!*
Show us your scars!
We played a bar in the north end of Saskatoon in 1999, just down the road from an enormous trade school that hulked against the railroad tracks. Later, we took off on foot through that industrial country, running into gas-huffers in the alleys and down-coated sex workers who stared at us with big, scared eyes until they were sure we weren't there to kill them. They said, one of them — who was it? I'm trying to remember. A woman with a yellow bruise on her jaw that was amplified by the yellow-orange streetlight — that packs of Pentecostal girls in grunge clothes had been on patrol through the neighbour-hood, kicking prostitutes unconscious, and leaving them in the snow. Police saw sometimes, picked the kickers up and drove them back to nicer areas and never arrested them.

If you were a working girl, you didn't let the police pick you up. They'd take you out into frozen country and they wouldn't find you until spring.

I believed them. Kara maybe did. Mary-Beth never looked like she believed anything. Bracken said, "No kidding." Bracken had run the sound boards for our show, and she said you should believe everything they told you about the police in Saskatoon.

Our show had been full of bar regulars in small-town skid clothes, greasy and mulleted, six years after the last mullet had fallen off the last rocker. They picked up girls in skin-tight jeans and bleached-blonde hair. Collided with other girls who'd come up to see us on the #2 bus or hiked from other parts of town through the lingering snow.

Like oil and pure alcohol, not just not mixing, but both potentially explosive.

Girls who'd come to see our show peeled their shirts off and showed us their bras, incidental to the livid cutting-scars all over their lumpy bodies. Raw skin on arms and legs and abdomens. One of them had a razor-blade just below her breast-bone, held in place with clear plastic tape that iridesced in the bar's gel lights.

Other girls hunted down the groping skid-boy hands and kicked their owner into the floor while we cranked the volume to cover the sound of his whines.

Kick him like a girl
Walk out in the dark
They might see you
They might think you're
Some kind of little hungry kitten, stark
And ugly, come on out with me
We'll break this shit down
When they find us
They can grind us
We'll be toxic all the way to morrrrrrrning
Kick him in the
Morrrrrrrning
Baby I'm a scary
Morrrrrrrning
I'm a scary
Morrrrrrrning
I'm a scary girl

For us, Saskatoon was a big show. We'd played in France and Manchester, but Canada was always hard. We played rural bars and messed-up, tiny venues in towns that we had to track down on the side index of a provincial road map. We played in Wynyard and Melville and Kindersley, where farm girls had layered angry black eyeliner over their country gear.

It was nothing, we were nothing, but we had fans.

We played a show on the Saskatchewan-Alberta border and nearly caught fire. Guys from the oil patch — it was just spiking then, and the guys had come in from other provinces, or up from the States, to lay the wells and pipelines — had occupied our motel, and they howled in the parking lot when they saw us carrying our shit into a ground-floor room. They were there, pressed up against the glass, when we twitched the curtains, and they kicked at the doors while we were changing.

Heyyyyyy bitch. Come out here and playyyyyyy bitch.

We were between sets when Bracken shifted up to us in full cowgirl drag and said, "Don't go back to your room tonight."

"What?"

"They're going to pull something. I'll send some people to grab your stuff. Come out to my family's place. You don't need this from that."

She looked like a rawer-boned version of the woman that I would have become if I hadn't managed to run away from home. At least ten years older than we were. Like she'd smoked since first communion.

We followed her out, three in the morning, into the prairie dark. Her pickup was full of the bags from our room. Panties we'd washed out in the sink were piled on the truck seat. Girl deodorant and markers and Kara's notebook in a plastic grocery bag.

"I'm sorry. We had to go in fast."

We had fans. They'd walked in wearing housekeeping uniforms and rescued our underpants. They left notes tucked under the bumper of our shitty touring van.

Bracken drove ahead of us, so close we had to watch her brake lights constantly, out south and west into the empty country of the Alberta border. Barbed wire intermixed with no fences, just open, blank country with no human lights breaking it apart.

I took over driving when Mary-Beth flagged. Flashed my brights to make Bracken stop.

All of us peed in the ditch, half-drunk and shocky with exhaustion and cold.

This edge of nowhere. Trees rose up, though, marking the farmstead, and we could see the shadows of the abandoned house. A roof sloped too far to the back, like it was getting ready to shed itself and produce some new creature, unrelated to housing, a snake or a large bird or some angry hybrid of drywall and rusted farm machinery. The yard lights were out, and the gate across the road was electrified. Bracken stopped, pulled to the side and opened it, waved us through.

Just the one trailer there, shadowy and sided in cheap aluminum. Bracken had us pull around the back. She said, "Get what you need and come in."

The house was like a wartime space. The windows were covered with black-out curtains, but there was a separate universe inside.

⋮⦿⋮

The farm was a quantum leap from my own life. I wanted to stay there.

I remember someone explaining to me, in a bar in Calgary, how we misunderstand that term. We assume a *quantum leap* is a massive shift, an unimaginable distance spanned in an instant, creating a radical, alternate existence from the moment before. But a quantum leap is infinitely small, almost unnoticeable except in the single, tiny adjustment it makes, with tiny, rippling consequences moving through its universe.

One impossibly small change.

Teenaged me sets out walking west instead of south. Assume my intersection with Child Protective Services is approximately the same. A slightly different, interchangeable boy takes me for a witch in a slightly different town, changing my trajectory marginally further westward, northward.

I arrive at a different punk show.

I'm adopted by a different lesbian outpost in the universe.

I would have slipped in there like an invisible girl. One more plaid-wrapped, odd-bodied chick on a farm on the edge of the world, boyless and scarred.

They had horses. I'd missed the smell.

We'd have formed a country band. Not me and Kara and Mary-Beth. Me and Karen and Bethany. Electric-acoustic fusion and three girl voices building in harmonies seductive to the farm-girl ears of a nation, insinuating ourselves into honky-tonk festivals and jamborees and producing bumper stickers to mark kinship across the grid-road network of the western half of the continent.

> *Skip the boy, ride a cowgirl*
> *Friends in low-flow places*
> *I push back*

They'd keep a couple of half-broke quarter horses in the back pasture for the two weeks a year we came home, and we'd go to places like Austin, where the dykes hadn't been noticed yet in the swirling plaid and denim, and we'd meet the secret lesbians of Hollywood on their ranches in Jackson Hole, surrounded by wilderness that only celebrity helicopters could cross.

That leap, sideways.

:::⦂:::

Fran and Barbie lived sixty-seven miles southwest of Kindersley, in the empty, half-mapped territory along the fourth meridian at 110° west. The farm was a first-wave colonial creation, settled by Barbie's grandparents at the turn of the last century and industrially glorious until the beginning of the Cold War.

The failure of that farm wasn't environmental. There was something else. Alcohol and, they suspected, incest. Something ugly that led an aunt to lock herself in the original family home and set it on fire.

Two uncles died in jail.

Barbie's sisters lived in Toronto, last survivors of an agricultural empire.

They didn't farm. They'd let the land go feral and it was full of horses. Cattle, too, for profit, and they had the infrastructure to handle them. Moldering grain trucks rested against the sheltering trees.

Fran and Barbie met at a music festival in 1972 and left their husbands.

They'd fostered five girls in twenty-five years, raised them all, and they took in strays. The fences around the farmstead were electrified beyond the needs of livestock.

Barbie said, "The cops don't always come when we call." Nodded to the rifles by the door.

That was over breakfast. We'd slept through the morning in their living room, spread out across the area rug in salvaged sleeping bags. I remembered curling tighter into myself when someone stepped over me, smelling like manure and chore clothes. Smelled coffee, later, and didn't move.

We almost never stayed in band houses in the west. The keepers were men, usually, stoners in their thirties, and after Mary-Beth elbowed one guy in the trachea and then had to call paramedics to save him, we made our own arrangements. But the farmhouse was like a band house in an alternate universe where the bodies ranging across the continent in crappy vans were almost entirely female and hung over. It smelled like oily hair and girl bodies and very faintly like period blood.

I got up in the early afternoon and walked in my panties into the kitchen to look for caffeine and painkillers. I had a bruise across my cheekbone where I'd jumped into the audience and taken the heel of a hand to my face.

Grey prairie light stuck to my skin while I stretched. My jaw cracked. I checked the rest of myself for fractures, didn't find swelling, and dug a cup out of the sink to wash by hand.

"You look like shit."

Fran was a different species from Diane and Cynthia, but she was instantly recognizable as a lesbian matriarch from the dark time before the second wave. With long hair, she'd have looked like the women I remembered from my childhood who did field work in ankle-length dresses. She had the same level of UV damage and creeping melanoma at the hairline. Maybe the same Russian-German ancestry.

"I'm okay."

"Good to know." Pause. "Are you cold?"

"I'm okay."

"Again, good to know. I wish I was younger. It's been years since there was a naked girl your age in my kitchen. I'm too old to care, except thinking that if you stay like that you'll chill enough to wrinkle at the thighs."

Bracken wasn't Fran's daughter, or Barbie's. She was permanently resident, coming in at twenty-three with a dislocated shoulder from southern Alberta in the passenger seat of another matriarch's pickup. She arrived on the underground, inter-provincial exchange of bruised lesbian girls coming out of bad marriages to stupid boys with anger issues.

She studied me. "Where'd you come from?"

I told her.

"That's serious Jesus country. Any of us out there?"

"If there were, I never saw them."

Barbie came in from the bedroom and wrapped a shirt around me. Sat cowboy-style on a chair. "How did you get all the way here?"

"I'm one of The Innocents."

"I bet you are."

"I mean." I told her. It was more than five years since I'd walked out of Neuenheim, and I'd had time to give a shape to the narrative, a version of myself I could tell in ten minutes, adding or removing relevant details to please my audience, and vaguely epic in ways that I was only becoming aware of.

Good Christian girl. Winnipeg. Burundi. Haiti. Neuenheim. Ethan.

One missed period. Wednesday night wedding.

"How old?"

"Fifteen."

"Jesus."

How I walked out. Down the highway hitch-hiking and somehow intact all the way to the next town with an RCMP detachment. Walking in there in my long skirt, my hair loose and wind-tangled, and saying, "You have to help me. I was in a cult. My parents sold me. Tried to marry me off. I'm fifteen. I need you to protect me."

I'm a child. You have to do something.

The version I told when I was twenty-one intersected almost completely with the version I told the woman at the police desk, and the first and second social workers, when I was fifteen. I used different details, though. For Fran, I focussed on my parents' horror. Elaine's fury. Getting married in the middle of the night, and the paperwork that lied about my age. I only changed the order of certain events.

It was and is plausible, nearly correct, and legally unassailable. I could tell it a thousand times. If I could believe in the complete impotence of my own mind and hands, I'd believe it too.

Fran was, as far as I can remember, the only person who disbelieved me on the spot.

She said, "What did you do?"

Not like she was angry, or thought I was lying. Like she genuinely wanted to know.

So I told her.

"I wasn't pregnant."

"But you thought you were."

"That would have been good. No. It's easy to convince people that a home-schooled Christian girl doesn't know anything about sex, but we lived in Haiti and Africa when I was a kid, because my parents were missionaries. And my mother was a midwife. There were no secrets. There were always bodies around, you know?"

"No."

"I mean." I thought. "It's not like here. You couldn't pretend that bodies didn't exist. People had babies at home and got pregnant and married and talked about how things happened, and I learned the words for those things in other languages before I learned them in English, but I wasn't as stupid as I told people I was."

"So what happened?"

"They were going back. My parents. They were talking, and then they wrote letters, and they wanted to go somewhere new, maybe Indonesia. Minister to the unsaved.

"They wouldn't have been willing to leave me behind."

The prairie cold wasn't what I loved. I'd spent enough of my early life bare-foot and warm to hate the cold with a lizard-passion that pervaded my being. I dressed in layers all my years in Canada, locked in long underwear and flannel until I could strip down to my skin in the body-warm dark of punk clubs where the air started to approximate my preferred climate.

There are other versions of my life where I didn't say anything, and we moved to Bali and I fled my family on a different day and became a pale-skinned hula girl at resorts for the impossibly rich.

I wanted the reason I stayed to be Ethan. He was so present. I liked his body, skinny teenaged-boy form that he let me touch in the half-light of his bedroom. I liked the music he poured into my body through the cheap headphones wrapped around my skull while he chose the tapes.

We had sex.

It could have been true. It just wasn't.

Only after we'd done it, gotten married, and I thought about having children and a locked-in life in small-town Manitoba, did I start considering other exits.

"You told them you miscarried," Fran said.

I wanted them to believe me. I thought they wouldn't. I was driven by claw-ing anxiety as depression's inertia started to give. No one would believe me, and I'd have to carve an infant out of my own body to prove myself. Steal one from passing families. Become the madwoman in the hospital who waits to steal new-borns from the nursery.

In Burundi, I'd seen three late-term miscarriages. The earlier ones hadn't made an impression on me, so when I staged a miscarriage, that was my model. So much blood.

I made it convincing. I used a paring knife on the inside of my thigh. It didn't scar, much, and what there was looked like stretch marks when my body was too hot for them to be invisible.

In the kitchen, when I tried to show Fran, I could only find the lines because I knew where they were. I had a tough, strong body that swallows its evidence. I look, always, fine.

Fran nodded. "Would you do it again?"

"Sort of. Maybe differently? I don't know. I'm out."

It was something she said, about what I could have done with the blood, that made me think of the uses of it, now. I was level — I'd been level for months — and I'd left the plastic-handled paring knife that I used for carving myself in a box at home when we went on tour. But I still bled, and it had possibilities.

Everyone's scared of period blood.

Barb told me, before we left, that one time when guys came prowling around, she started collecting menstrual blood. Added a bit of water now and then to keep it wet, but she massed it up, chunky clots and mucous and the long, transparent strands of undistinguished tissue that washed out, and kept it in a jar.

The next one who came right up to the house, she opened the screen and threw it in his face.

"He's going to have nightmares about that for the rest of his life."

It was true. You could make a boy throw up just by implying period blood at the right moment. I realized you could use it like defensive smoke, like squid ink, in an emergency.

It seemed like a workable idea, but I hadn't discovered menstrual cups yet, and my tampons dried even if I kept them in a sealed baggie. Kara found them in my duffle, after a concert in Calgary.

"You planning to make tea for a vampire?"

"Just something I've been working on."

"You think you're going to scare anybody with that?"

"I think I might."

"The tampon's good," she said, considering, "but the problem is, how much do guys even *know* about period blood?"

"They think it's gross."

"Still. Seems like you might as well use stage blood and pads if all you want to do is scare them. Save this stuff for the real witchcraft. You could put a serious hurt on somebody if you tried."

Bracken wasn't with us anymore. She'd gone back to Saskatoon, where she guarded her own baby lesbian brood, but Fran and Barbie sent us postcards, occasionally, care of Diane in Winnipeg. Maybe they knew Diane from the old days of the lesbian underground, even. I never found out for sure. I was adult enough by then to be out of the house, and Diane never did tell me her secrets.

We played a show in a half-time cowboy/half-time punk bar in Calgary. I'd tucked a tampon soaked in stage blood into the waistband of my jeans, and when I threw it into the audience we almost had a riot. I'd expected a wide hole to form in the human wall wherever it landed. That happened, initially, but then girls started to circle it. They studied it. One reached out and touched it, experimentally, like a hot stove, and then she sniffed her fingers. Laughed and picked it up and saluted me.

I don't know if it was her who left the tampon under our windshield wiper. There were other girls there who looked like they wished they'd pulled her move. The punk scene in Calgary wasn't huge at the time, so there were guys present, prepared to either dance because they wanted to dance or to complain about chicks who didn't really *get* punk. Some of them actually were stupid enough to try something on the girls in the audience, and we enjoyed watching girls kick the shit out of them.

They were out in the parking lot when we came out. Two groups, one all-girl, one a mix of guys and their girlfriends, had been circling each other all night. They'd been, I thought, more entertaining than we were. And they were ready to go.

The girls won that fight, largely because the guys seemed unwilling to fight women in groups. They'd have happily smashed the face of one woman, but a bunch together confounded them.

They weren't prepared for the blood. The girl who hiked up her skirt, pushed her panties aside, and pushed fingers up inside herself. Covered both her fists with slippery red and then dove into the fray, smearing it on male faces and, wherever she could, shoving it into their mouths.

I sat on the loading dock with Kara and watched. We even tried taking pictures, but the mess and the dark didn't transfer to film, and later I was sorry.

The girl covered in blood came back to the band house with us, and we took pictures with her in the liver-bile artificial light. I pulled my shirt off and let her smear blood on me.

She had pictures, different ones from us, and I wonder sometimes what happened to them, because they've never, never shown up online. Not one popped up in a zine, and if I didn't so vividly remember it happening, I'd assume the whole thing was a manic hallucination, a fantasy of slut-witchcraft that I generated in the course of long-distance driving and the low-grade psychosis that comes from too many nights on the road.

~ 25 ~

Witch

Hanna said, "Allison, are you a slut?"

If I hadn't given Hanna up, if I'd had a decade to rehearse the conversations I needed have with her, would I have pre-planned an answer to that question?

I'd answered it to other people. There was even a picture in circulation, not one of the naked ones, but striking, with my handwriting over it, colour-inverted to shine white across the monochrome image. It says, *Yes. I am. A slut. So fucking what?*

There's cheap video from the Barefoot and Pregnant Tour of me screaming, "I'm pregnant from *fucking*!" in answer to the fifteenth time someone asked me how the hell I'd wound up pregnant.

Jay's fanboys had a forum, for a while, called *Allison Winter is a Fucking Slut*. When they changed it to *Allison Winter is a Fucking Slut Who Deserves to Die*, I got a Cease & Desist order against them, and the forum vanished. I hadn't found it again, yet, but I spent nights looking on every site I could imagine hosting that level of adolescent phallic rage.

To Hanna I said, "Um. Context?"

"I was listening to music on your computer. There isn't much on mine, and I think if I touch that," gesturing to the hi-fi, "I might break it. You have a playlist. It's just called *slut*. So I wondered."

I tried to remember whether *slut* had been reclaimed far enough for a meaningful conversation with Hanna in particular.

"What do you think?" The only answer I could think of, but I was proud of it. It sounded like something a parent might say.

"I think a lot of people call you that."

"True."

"I think you don't look like a slut. But I don't know what old sluts look like." Pause. "What do young sluts look like?"

"I don't know. Eyeliner. You can see their boobs a lot."

"I spent some time wearing a lot of eyeliner. I spent some time with my boobs showing."

Hanna looked worried. She said, "Never mind." Walked out of the room.

I'd been working on the couch, going through pre-interview notes and ignoring tour-planning suggestions clogging my inbox. Texts on my phone, from Mary-Beth, from Kara, asking me to say yes or no to Japan, set dates, get my ass to Winnipeg because Kara had a line on a decent rehearsal space, and we could find our feet in the Exchange in front of friendly audiences of Kara's graduate student friends and the radical baby lesbians.

Pack your shit, girl. The world awaits.

Eden really did have a van. It was a VW, not really restored from its 70s glory. It smelled like a family camping trip.

I could say no. Tell them to pick one of Kara's girls to be the mad, sad woman at the front of the band. Online evidence suggested that the Japanese fangirls were expecting somebody younger anyway.

Anime girls didn't get old enough to have their knees hurt. Their sleep deprivation only showed in heavier facial shading, wider eyes with angry edges.

Eden was going on tour, with or without me. He was almost packed. There was an itinerary on the fridge. The first date was for Cavendish Beach on Prince Edward Island, two-and-a-half weeks away.

Decide.

My phone rattled under the papers. Kara, texting.

DECIDE, bitch. I know you're coming up to your last Cure date. If you don't answer me by then, I'm going to send someone to ask you on camera Alli I swear to god.

Four days.

Decide, bitch.

I got up and went looking for Hanna.

"Why'd you ask?" I said.

She looked up from her book. One of Eden's. *Timothy Leary: The Fugitive Philosopher.*

On the floor, *Why We Hate the Oil Companies, Getting Steamed to Overcome Corporatism, Days of Destruction/Days of Revolt.*

Under those, *Witchcraft: A Very Short Introduction* and *Living with a Wild God: A Nonbeliever's Search for the Truth About Everything.* Off to the side, *Angelsmisfits.* Half under the bed, *Drunk Girls Make History.*

It occurred to me that this must be Elaine's nightmare: Hanna astray, in my house, reading her way out of residual faith. She'd be trouble any day now.

Hanna held up her phone. Thumbed open an icon I didn't recognize. There was an email system inside.

I imagined boys, perverts, internet psychos stalking my daughter out of adult view. Jay, looking for something younger. His minions, looking for an innocent to rip apart.

I reached for the phone. She let me take it.

The message was from Elaine. It said, very clearly, *When that slut hurts you you can always come back to me, baby.* The last line of a long, long email.

I tried to imagine Elaine at a keyboard. Their house wasn't quite pre-industrial, but I couldn't imagine a computer in it. She must have hunt-pecked in the public library, one letter at a time. And found Hanna in the digital world, somehow made her keep it secret, whispered to her like a witch in the woods.

"She said you were a witch, too," Hanna whispered. She was shaking so hard. I stared at the phone.

"Are you mad?" she asked.

"Oh god yes."

"I'm sorry."

"What?" I said. "No. No, not at you. But her I'm going to kill." Pause. Tears all over her. "Not literally. I'm going to yell at her. And possibly do something really scary so she leaves us alone."

There'd been another possibility. In it, I went to Winnipeg alone, and then to Japan, and Hanna stayed with Eden and became a festival circuit photographer while she was still young enough to be excused from any criminal charges.

That dissolved.

Hanna followed me back to my room. I dug through my closet, found bags. I was going to need clothes, gear, meds for months at a time.

"To be clear," I said. "I used to be a slut, but I got tired. It was a lot of work. Your grandmother doesn't like me. But she thinks I'm stupid, and I'm not. Also, I am a witch. And I'm the scariest thing she's ever seen."

I wanted to show up on Elaine's doorstep and set something on fire, but there were logistical problems with that. I didn't have a car. I thought my rage might bleed out on a drive to Winnipeg, and they'd never let me bring my favourite weapons on a plane.

We couldn't blow out that night, because I'd turned into an adult, and I wanted to be able to come back. There were steps, though, that I could take *in situ.*

We hiked out into the ravines. It was fading into dark, almost ten o'clock, and cold in the shade. There were fire sites where people had been camping, and trees where baby Wiccans had tied up bits of cloth and feathers.

Hanna left her good camera behind, but she brought her phone. Stood back. I told her she should stay home. Eden told her she could come.

"I'm going to scare the shit out of her."

"She needs to see you. I think she doesn't understand how you're scary."

We had a three-quarter moon. I took a sheet of printer paper and nailed it to a tree. *Elaine* written on it, scrawled in rough ink. Film canister in my bag that peeled open and poured thick and almost-clotted menstrual blood into my hand. Years of practice and menstrual cups had finally given me the blood-technology I'd always wanted.

When I realized Hanna was coming, I collected the blood in advance. I'd been going to pull it from my body in the moment, and use whatever was in the cup, but I didn't think she was ready to witness me that kind of naked.

Sticky on my hands. I should have mixed water in. It was like phlegm. But it stuck to the paper, ugly and dark, and covered the name with it.

I said, "Go away.

"Leave us alone.

"Go away and never come back."

Banished, witch. You're banished. Disappear, right now, before I track you down.

I spit on it. Swore in English, French, fragments of Haitian creole, and the worst words I'd picked up in Ouagadougou.

I'd gotten to be a better witch in my adult life, but those seeds were planted in childhood. You travel with the saved and you get to know everything, *everything* they fear. The right person can observe that, store it up, use it later.

I spit on the paper, on my hand, smeared it.

Hanna reached up, after, and touched it. Smelled her fingers.

Walking back, in the dark, she said, "That's exactly what I remember you smelling like, when I was little."

I said, "There's no way you could remember that."

"It's what you smelled like. I didn't know you were a witch, though. I wish they'd told me."

I said, "They didn't know. It wouldn't have made them happy. But I won't ever hurt you, baby, and the rest of them are going to run when they see me coming."

～ 26 ～

Jezebel

The Innocents did two festival tours. I remember them as the only periods in which we made money. Mostly, not having money wasn't a problem in the 90s. We were part of a scene of filthy, poor children squatting in the baby boomer wreckage and resisting the heteronormative zeitgeist. We came later than the first grunge wave, who squatted in Seattle, but maybe that made our path easier. At the point where we came in, there were still squats, and semi-abandoned houses divided into illegal suites where you could crash, and the thrift stores of the central plains hadn't yet been fully stripped of their vintage glory. The coastal world had been overgrazed, but the continental centre still had the resources we needed.

You could live on the college rock scene for years, never famous, never seeing radio play, but working and living and grinding in bars full of university kids. They didn't necessarily know who we were. On-campus bars hosted bands three, four nights a week, and kids in the dorms came down every night. They came down to drink and hook up and get high on the steps outside, and maybe dance if the place had any kind of a dance floor.

There was nothing standard about the venues. Bars in the basements of turn of the century gothic piles alternated with echoing caves in concrete Modernist creations of the sixties expansion.

We started keeping notes. Names of bars, and where they were, and what the buildings looked like. Where the band houses were, relative to the venue. What the students were like.

In Winnipeg and Saskatoon and Regina, the audiences looked like us. Sometimes in Edmonton. Calgary was slick with unexpected money, and Vancouver was miles ahead, already finished with the sticky movements we were just learning.

Ontario was like another country. Quebec like another continent.

I loved the Cape Breton punk scene. Going out to Saint Francis Xavier to play a gig, and then meeting people from the wilds of the island who stood out all sharp-rock edges from the university kids. Punk fiddler Ashley MacIsaac was all over the airwaves, and we met people who played in barns and small-town bars where most of the clientele were farmers and coal miners, but they'd come out to see the band because they were all cousins, or friends of someone's parents, and there was always someone to stay with.

Eighteen people out there, maybe, who weren't musicians or older sisters of musicians.

We went to Newfoundland, up the coasts playing for furious kids stripped of their assets and wild with near-arctic levels of Nordic alcoholism.

Down into the States. Four or five times to New York. (It was four. We counted every one. We played CBGB just the once, and we have pictures; and it was transcendent and utterly sane in a way we hadn't expected.)

We went to France. We went across Canada again.

Then this message coming through our booking agent: do you want to join the Jezebel Festival Tour?

That was the second year for the girl-music project: all women singers and female-led bands, moving across the continent in a haze of hemp and third-wave feminism.

It wasn't punk, but aspirationally, Jezebel was everything we'd wanted. I don't think we ever considered saying no.

We were less sure why they chose us. We were three women on stage at the same time, but the other acts were nothing like ours. Most of the girl scene was made up of folk and folk-rock acts, lots of long hair and unshaven legs and acoustic guitars.

Still, if you're a woman of a certain age and you know The Innocents, you probably first heard us on the Jezebel Tour. We sold more albums that summer than we had before combined.

It was a good time. We joked it was possible we'd eat regularly enough to get fat. We had a reliable RV to travel in, and other bands were willing to share instrument techs. We didn't have to manage our own sound boards, or recruit someone on the fly. We had money for the entire summer.

Kara fit the scene like she'd only temporarily stepped out of it. Suburban girls who'd just discovered feminism wanted a sweet, fantasy version of what Kara had been living all her life. Not exactly the same, of course. They wanted it prettier. Eighty per cent more femme. You could stop shaving your armpits, but it didn't mean you had to give up eyeliner. They didn't want dyke-life. They just wanted to be feral-sexy, covered in henna tattoos and hand-made jewelry and wearing bodies new to going braless in public.

The major shift for us was playing during the day. We'd been on tour for years, living nocturnally and playing shows that never started before 10 p.m. and often didn't start before midnight. We had accidental goth-girl pallor. Now we needed sunscreen. Kara got up most concert days while it was still cold. Pulled on a hoodie over whatever she was wearing and went out in the wet world.

Fields like fantasies of nature spread out around us, with electric snakes lurking in the grass.

In between shows it was so quiet. It gave me time to read. On the Jezebel Tour, there were book exchanges set up in the shade of the second stage. You read *The Beauty Myth* or the short stories of Jane Rule and pass them on. Someone had brought a box of small-press poetry that got picked through but remained low on its uptake. Most people preferred memoirs or Vonnegut.

When the festival camp was set up, the bands had a makeshift outdoor kitchen. It wasn't craft services, as such, but if you wanted, you could kick in, take a turn cooking, and join the breakfast club. There was a boom box playing Sarah McLachlan or girl-singers who sounded like her, and breakfast was usually the same: scrambled eggs and toast and fruit salad. The fruit salad was mostly orange slices and banana, but it provided enough vitamins and fibre to keep us alive. There was a separate grill for the vegans. They did potato-and-chickpea scrambles that smelled wonderful, but that I found I didn't much like the taste of.

Breakfast started at six in the morning. There was yoga set up on the grass, but I wasn't going that far.

The exchange was full of vintage Mills & Boon romances from the period before they included sex. I dug, looking for anything readable, and discovered that inside the covers, someone had glued in radical feminist science fiction.

You could have the good stuff, but you had to be willing to get your hands dirty.

Inside *Romance Goes Tenting* I found *Daughters of Earth*. *Come Blossom-Time, My Love* turned into Joanna Russ' *On Strike Against God*.

Cupid in Mayfair was *The Left Hand of Darkness*.

Love's Fantasy was *Woman on the Edge of Time.*

The rest were actual romance novels. If you finished one, you were supposed to sign the inside cover. *We read trash: join the club.*

I read a couple of the SF novels, but mostly I picked the fat old paperbacks that looked like they came from library sales. I read *Jane Eyre.* Then I gave up my pride and made off with the first six *Anne of Green Gables* books and hoarded them for the rest of the tour.

The readers among us swapped books and scuttled back to our vans and busses, out of the sun while the yoga girls baked their tattooed skins on the grass and the crowd-control fences went up around them.

I remember being curled up in the RV, tiny electric fan running, when Erin and May came to find me.

American folk girls with bluegrass-edged voices. They came like sisters in Christ, and I instantly didn't trust them. It was the season of broomstick skirts, but having grown up in a sea of modest dresses, I didn't necessarily trust a sweeping skirt when I saw one coming. I tried to remember who these women were. Checked their albums for songs about Jesus and didn't find any.

They sat at the tiny table while I sat on the slab couch that folded down into my bed at night. I wasn't sure why they were there. I was groping for something useful to say, something polite and vaguely conversational to cover the expectant gap between us.

I said, "Your music kind of reminds me of Townes van Zandt." He'd died the previous year, and I picked up his name through a magazine left behind in one of our more lost venues. Picked up tapes of his stuff at inner-city exchanges and started listening.

"Poor bastard," said May.

Erin asked, "You never played with him?"

"No. Was he trouble?"

"He was a junkie. He'd get handsy and then guilty about it and write long apology poems and stick them under the wiper on my car." *Erin* could have been abbreviated from *Aryan*: wildly blonde and almost six feet tall. This fantasy of an American woman, with the low accent that never quite marked itself as southern but reiterated my own nasal Canadian-ness.

"Anyway." Erin looked me over. "You allergic to sunlight?"

"No." I had sunscreen next to all the doors, and eyeliner that I kept on all night, but I'd been reading in the shade between shows, moving around in the morning and evening and sleeping with my ears stuffed through the loudest afternoons.

"We had a service, this morning, and there's something we want to show you."

There was this problem. The Tour's zeitgeist was heavily lesbian-wiccan, but the American contingent threw back to the Bible belt, and gathered to pray on Sabbaths. They'd gathered women around them who were baptized summarily in shallow creeks across the Midwest.

"I'm not Christian," I said.

"You were."

"I can't help how I was born. And I don't want to be rude, but I don't want to talk about the invisible man, either."

Sigh. "Come down to the river anyway. We promise not to re-baptize you without permission."

I decided it was worth it. Every tour had an ongoing war with bodily marination. It was blazing hot, our venues were rural, and hotel rooms occurred only when we had intersecting money and time. In between, people set up solar showers and washed at cold hoses. Dry shampoo traded like heroin.

Heroin traded more quietly. But it was the 90s, and it was the scene. Goth edges included a few tracks up your arms.

Suburban girls were learning to simulate them with theatrical makeup.

You could, really, always run away to Vancouver-Seattle for a year, spend some time addicted and hooking, and then vanish, but it was hard to maintain your music scene cred in your absence and subsequent death.

Easier to go on tour with wholesome girls. They'd feed you, lure you into the sunshine. Come down to the river with us, not for Jesus, just for the water.

Minnesota was a spatial repudiation of the coastal scene. We'd moved into the state at night, crossing from Michigan-Wisconsin in a single long haul that I'd driven so that the others could sleep. Navigation wasn't strictly required, as long as I didn't lose the bus in front of us, carrying Wild Strawberries forward into the Midwest. It meant I didn't watch the world. I emerged shocked into the dense not-quite-prairie lushness that had lurked throughout my childhood in books and taped performances mailed to us over international borders.

It has been a quiet week in Lake Wobegon, Minnesota, my hometown, out there on the edge of the prairie, out where I'm from . . .

We weren't that far west, but we were more than an hour from the Twin Cities, and there were Lutheran churches visible along the roads May drove, and farms like fantasies of American family life.

What we came to wasn't the kind of water that you could really bathe in, and it wasn't a river. I don't know what the local term would have been, but it's stuck in my memory as a creek. The banks were muddy, and the water was overgrown with plants and soil. A relief, really: it seemed free from any temptation to baptism. You could dunk me in it and I'd come up in the same condition I'd descended.

They'd brought suits. That shouldn't have surprised me. I hadn't, but it wasn't going to stop me. I stripped to my panties, left my shoes on the bank and slid in. Mud ran up the backs of my thighs. It wasn't deep, not even really deep enough to swim, but I stretched out in the water, floated vaguely downstream with my nipples pointing up into daylight. Closed my eyes.

The water was cooler than the air. It occurred to me that if stayed floating there, I could drift to the Mississippi.

I sat up in the water. Erin and May were upriver, washing their hair while standing hip-deep. Walked back. I said, "It this it?"

"What?"

"Is this the place that the Mississippi starts in Minnesota? At a place that you could walk across with five steps down?"

Erin shook her head. "No, that's north of here. I like that song too, though."

"What did you want me to see, then?"

May said, "I wondered what you were like, without the other two." Her eyes stayed at shoulder height. She pointedly ignored the tattoos.

"I'm like this."

"You aren't like them. I've read about you. You have the most amazing origin story."

She said it like I was a superhero. The Innocents were still building our mythology, then. We'd only ever had a handful of interviews, and half of them were in hand-created zines that circulated in college towns. A couple of fanzines collected and self-published by kids in Winnipeg, where we'd be playing again next winter. Profiles of the band in punk magazines showed us unified, only fragments of personal data leaking through. Kara, who was raised by lesbians. Allison, who was raised by cultists. Mary-Beth, who'd set fire to her prom dress.

"I'm not the pyro. That's Mary-Beth. And the thing about the prom dress is a lie. Prom isn't really a thing, where we come from. But she did buy one at a thrift shop and burn it, for a thing we did when we were kids."

"We know."

"So?" Mud around my thighs. I realized I had to pee. Sat down in the water and pulled my panties aside to let it happen.

"We work with this group, out west," Erin said. "We'll be moving into their territory in about eleven days."

There was no approximation in *eleven*. They were both ignoring my mostly-naked body. I crawled out of the creek-bed, hauling myself up on a branch without considering the height first. Balanced for a second between ascension and falling, then made it up. Lay down on the bank grass to watch them, two and a half feet higher than their eyes.

"It's a thing that we felt like we could help with, because we travel."

"Are you running drugs?"

"What? No. Girls."

I snorted. "Planning on starting your own bordello?"

Erin ducked down to rinse her hair and stood, streaming. Her suit was pale pink with white lines through it, an odd fabric, and the brown water stained it unevenly. "We help girls who've grown up on compounds. Save them from forced marriages. It's hard to get them out, but we have some contacts, and the ones who want to leave the stronghold states are pretty determined."

"All you'd have to do is provide them with rides. We'll be heading for Portland and Seattle, and a lot of them would like to go up there. But it's something you have to be up for, you and your whole band, because there are prosecutors who'll claim you're violating the Mann Act."

I tilted my head. I remember doing this, like an interested cat and not like an irritated punk listening to crazy women.

"Moving women across state borders for immoral purposes," May explained. "Usually, it's prostitution, but if you're a lesbian, they'll usually stretch a point, especially if the girl's a minor. And the thing is, most of them are. Hence the forced marriages."

"Jesus. Why me?"

"You were Mormon, once."

Oh. I ran a set of terms through my head, tried to keep from laughing. Failed. "Oh, no."

"What, baby?"

"I'm not Mormon."

"I know," May soothed.

"I mean, ever. I'm *Mennonite*. Whole different kind of missionary."

"You were raised in a compound."

"In Burundi. Where lots of people live in compounds."

They looked at each other. Fragments of *we've made a terrible mistake* flew between them.

"So, you're suggesting that, since I came from . . . Mormon cultists . . . that I help you kidnap child-brides and transport them to the land of grunge for lesbian purposes?"

"We didn't say that."

"Your pitch is terrible. Next time, skip the Jesus part and ask me if I want to help weird girls run away from home, because the answer to that is always, *always* yes. Extra points if they're stuck wearing prairie dresses, because those things are uncomfortable as fuck.

"I don't know if Kara and MB are up for it. I can ask them. Otherwise, I think you might be on your own. But I won't tell anyone you're secret lesbians. Do I have a sunburn on my breasts?"

I didn't, but later, on stage, I said, "I have a sunburn on my tits!" and the audience ate it up like ice cream.

⫶⦿⫶

It wasn't, I decided, safe to be known as a Christian, even a lapsed one. They'd recruit you, one way or another. If I wasn't a Christian, then I had to visibly be something else. It meant I had to get up earlier, and then move. Learn yoga. Sun salutations at sunrise.

I wasn't fully medicated at the time. This is important. The meds we had, then, were mostly awful, and I wasn't functional when I was on them. Kara's mom fed me a lot of herbal supplements, and everybody in the band was enlisted to keep me from drinking, and there were pills in the RV's glove box in case I totally went off the rails. Mary-Beth got a pair of fuzzy handcuffs from a femme-positive sex shop to ride in the glovebox next to them, to keep the pills from feeling like a threat, but the cuffs shifted almost immediately to ride on the rear-view mirror, and then when we were playing Michigan and left the doors open for air, somebody stole them.

The girls from Mixed Megaphone bought us new handcuffs and had them delivered in a decorated box.

We were the only punks on the tour, and that made us everyone's pets. The girl-folk scene at the time was in full earth-mother mode, and they were determined to care for us. Not just feed us, but make us happy.

Kara and Mary-Beth took to it immediately, but for the first tour stops I'd stayed nocturnal, coming out in daylight just to find food and exchange books.

I had to go outside.

I showed up for yoga with a full-sleeve tattoo and heavy eyeliner on, and people just shifted over to make room. Showed me the basic poses and helped me adjust my posture.

I liked it more than I expected. Yoga changed the inner lines of my body. I stayed at the edges of the group, away from the hippie-girl believers, but it seemed to reassure them, to have me there. I ate breakfast with them, too. Some-body's girlfriend drew, and I let her sketch me, dressed and nude, and in return she designed a lotus mandala tattoo for me that stretched across my hipbone and lower abdomen and held beautifully until seven months into my pregnancy with Hanna, when its skin split into lightning stretch-marks that ruptured the ink and never fully pulled together afterward.

:::•:::

We had lunch, all of us, at a surprisingly cute restaurant in a town off the tour route. Two country girls and three punks eating hearty sandwiches and sprout-heavy salads in a room marked by oiled dark-wood floors and local art hanging over each table.

Mary-Beth wanted logistical information. And she wanted to call a lawyer on the Canadian side of the border, to consult hypothetically, and maybe have someone on retainer, just in case.

Kara didn't know about the compounds.

"Okay, you know about Mormons?"

"Sure."

"You know that modern Mormons dropped the polygamy thing a long time ago?"

"I don't think I ever thought about it."

"It's a major point for them, that they don't practice 'plural marriage.' Part of their mainstreaming. Any Mormon you can find will explain this to you. That it's not who they are."

"Are they lying?"

"They're not. Most of them wouldn't lie to you about anything, except maybe they'd tell you they thought your shirt was cute when they actually hate the colour, because they work on being really nice people, you know?"

"Okay."

"It's a bit creepy, the niceness. It's all the time. But, you know, people get to decide how to live."

"Agreed."

"So you know there's got to be some asshole who's going to go exactly the other way, just to be difficult."

There were other churches, run by men who couldn't accept being limited to just one wife at a time, living out in the hills. In compounds and isolated towns, old men married teenage girls and bred mega-children.

"If they're so isolated, where are you even finding these girls?"

"Networks. Most of them are already out of the compounds, but they need to get out of the area, because everyone there is related, and they're not really safe. Our church helps girls move to other towns. Or, if they want, other countries."

Mary-Beth found a payphone and spent half an hour on it. Said she had to make some more calls, but she thought, yes, maybe.

Kara loved the idea.

"Why didn't we think of this years ago?"

I shrugged.

"I thought you'd love this."

"I feel like we're being set up."

"You think we're going to be arrested?"

"I think we're gonna be converted. When they're baptizing you, you'll know I was right."

And maybe I was, because Kara got to be friends with Erin, and the next time they all went down to the river, she went along and I stayed behind. I suggested she use *I'm a lesbian* as spiritual armour.

"That's not really how it works."

"It might with them."

"I'll tell them you're a witch, and I'm working to save you, and I can't be distracted," she said.

I nodded.

If I'd wanted to be a witch in the girl-collective sense, the Jezebel Festival would have been my conversion site. Vendors sold pentagrams and crystals, and there were probably as many tarot cards as tampons in the attendees' tapestry purses. But even in that girl country, there were boundaries they wouldn't cross.

Shit and blood and fury didn't mesh with the folk scene.

Even our audiences at the Festivals were softer core than we were used to. They were easier to shock. They'd decided they were feminist, but their feminism was softer than ours, and involved more jewelry and fewer zines detailing how to perform your own cervical exam. They were back at *pussy* while we were screaming *cunt*.

It meant that I performed in cut-offs and a bikini top instead of naked. That we played "Drugstore Princess" but not "Fuck Your Friday Panties."

If we hadn't been recruited to the rescue project, given some kind of outlet, we'd probably have done something terrible and scarred those children for life.

We played the festival outside Denver, and went south to Santa Fe, west to Phoenix. Then the tour split. Some of the acts were going down to play the Inland Empire, and normally we'd have gone with them. The endless suburbs of

Los Angeles were friendly territory, and there was a girl-rage well there that we hadn't yet fully tapped.

Instead, we turned north, through Flagstaff and then Hopi country, to the Utah border. Mary-Beth climbed down to make phone calls whenever we found service stations, and Erin came dashing down the convoy line in her broomstick skirt to bring us scraps of paper.

The convoy turned west. We kept going north. Lost maniacs in the desert, following old maps and a set of directions scribbled on the back of a tourist pamphlet: go to this secondary-road intersection, arrive at that time. And wait.

Two in the morning, in southern Utah, Odanna climbed into our rig.

Someone had already freed her from her prairie dress, but her posture that of a girl who'd been wrapped up in awkward quilting cotton for years longer than she should have been. Her steps were short. Her hair was quintessential, loose and curly like someone's virgin fantasy.

She had two fantasy novels with her, and she commandeered my Walkman as soon as she'd determined that she had property rights in our space.

We picked up Veradeane a day later, north of Salt Lake on the border with Idaho. She'd been out longer. Her look was fugitive, sharp. Newly-discovered eyeliner smudged the too-open girl-eyes she was sporting. She'd acquired a pentacle choker, like camouflage.

Odanna and Veradeane hated each other on sight. Mary-Beth made phone calls, and Erin's rig met us near Spokane so that we could give Vera to her.

"I thought you might get along with her," Erin said.

I said, "She already knows how to be a witch. We thought we'd corrupt the nice one instead."

Odanna slept through the crossing at the BC border. We were searched, but not intensely, because they were looking for drugs and not children, and the only psychoactive substances riding in the van were legally prescribed. Dogs sniffing underneath found nothing.

We'd been careful. We didn't even smell like incense, just girl-deodorant and period blood.

The border agents backed out of the rig and waved us through.

Odanna let us play with her hair, but she didn't particularly want to talk to us. She picked up new books when she finished the ones she'd read, and commandeered my Lucy Maud Montgomery paperbacks. She read them with a pencil in her hand, like they were Bible-study guides.

We were pulled over, stretching our legs, when she said to me, "Would you cut my hair?"

I said, "Sure."

"Sort of, well, like this."

She held out the book. Anne had dyed her hair green, and they cut it, and then she wore it held back with a black velvet ribbon. That was what she wanted.

I said, "Can I dye it green first?"

She wasn't a redhead, but she was fair. Kool-Aid would do the job.

She considered. "Do you have to?"

I sighed. "No. Come on."

So I cut her hair, and Kara found her a velvet hair band, and she was happy. She'd picked up a broomstick dress and T-shirt that seemed to satisfy her sense of modesty, but I kept expecting her to whisper *puffed sleeeeeeves* into the space between us.

I told her, "Anne Shirley was a lesbian, you know."

She stared at me.

"Deeply, deeply in love with Diana Barry. Go read the books again if you don't believe me."

We intersected with the rest of the convoy in Osoyoos, in British Columbia. Veradeane had swapped rides twice since we'd last seen her. Someone remarked, on a day off in Kelowna where we were shopping and showering and getting girl drinks that we'd have time to sleep off, that Vera was the kind of stray that'd go through four homes before someone decided that she'd make a great barn cat.

"Just feed her occasionally and give her somewhere to sleep and don't try to pick her up, you know?"

Her rage was something like what I'd had when they first brought me into Winnipeg, the first time, but without the psychiatric containment that made me presentable. If I'd been that sharp when they picked me up, I'd never have been re-homed. I'd have fought until the group home was sick of me and I had to stay in one of the downtown hotel rooms.

Social workers get tired and go home, and then you're all by yourself in the Winnipeg core. You go looking for friends, but you aren't really friendly.

You're easy meat.

You spend a few months, or just a few weeks, turning tricks, and then you drown in the Assiniboine river, and they call it an accident, and everyone forgets you ever existed.

Veradeane's ride was seriously considering just leaving her in Kelowna and letting her fend for herself.

Kara said, "I'll trade you Odanna for her."

How many girls were riding with the convoy, by then? Five or so. We'd been quiet, picking them up, and by then the tour wasn't moving in a single group, so there might have been others that I didn't know about, and not all of them had come across the border. Two were going to meet with us again in Seattle. Fangirls had come out by fried-out Subaru to ferry them across the wilds of eastern Washington state.

Odanna hadn't forgiven me for pointing out her Prince Edward Island fantasy's lesbian undertones, and when we packed her up she didn't protest. The Christian-country singers had found her a family in the Lower Mainland, faithful but not polygamist, who'd be happy to finish raising a pretty, well-behaved refugee. She had good manners, and she could already read; she'd be no problem.

Veradeane was harder to place. Mary-Beth had relaxed once we came across the border safe, but Kara worried. I did, too.

I phoned Diane. She said, "Lack of gratitude, yeah?"

I said, "Yeah."

"Somehow, it'd all be worth it if she'd just act like she was grateful to you."

Vera felt less like a rescued princess than a resentful teenager on a forced road trip. She didn't like the food. She borrowed our clothes, mostly mine, without asking. If we met up with other groups, she wouldn't talk to them.

"Congratulations. You have a teenager. Is she pretty?"

"I don't know. She isn't hideous."

"Too bad. Pretty or hideous would probably help her along." She sighed. "I don't think I could deal with that again." Pointed silence. Diane didn't say it explicitly, but she did strongly imply that if we brought Veradeane to her, we would be in everlasting disgrace.

Mary-Beth said, "We can't keep her."

"I don't know. I kind of like having a baby pit bull."

"She's too young to drink, so she can't work venues with us, and also, I'm pretty sure that keeping kids out of school to work unpaid for you is a violation of international law."

Vera said, "I'm not a kid."

Kara said, "Fine. If you're not a kid, come up with a plan."

Vera hesitated. She'd developed protective sarcasm, but her sense of how the non-compound world worked was barren. We weren't sure she could count reliably enough even to make change.

Kara stayed up at night, worrying. We talked. Went outside so Vera couldn't hear us, and when we'd come back, found that she was now referring to us as Mom One and Mom Two.

"I can't be Dad?"

She shrugged.

We thought about it. Kara thought of phoning Fran, but I was the one who actually did it.

"We need a home for a really angry girl."

"On a scale of one to you, how bad?"

"On a scale of one to her," I said, "I'm a seven."

Nobody thought we should send Vera to Saskatchewan. One compound replaced by another one, crazy girls in both and no shelter. But Fran and Barbie made some calls, and while we were camped in the deep grass of Abbotsford, the rescue Volvo arrived.

Old hippies in sweaters got out and paced around us. They weren't ancient, but I was young enough to still have no sense of people other than that they were older than I was. These two had silver hair, messy, and surprisingly neat clothing. They wore complex jewelry. Him too.

"We have a cabin up the coast. We thought you might like to try it for a couple of months."

Vera said, "I don't want to be alone."

"It's not isolated. It's an artist's colony. Some people's . . . there are people your age. Difference is encouraged."

Vera didn't go with them, but she was quiet, and later she helped tech for the show. Like me, she'd been raised on church music, and she could tune guitars by ear. Moving instruments back to the trailer, she said, "I think they could be . . . I don't know. They don't seem dangerous."

I said, "Full disclosure?"

"Please." Pause. She'd forgotten not to be polite. "Yes."

"They lost their daughter. They'd like another one, but filling that role is strictly a volunteer job."

"She died?"

"She killed herself."

"Oh."

"Somebody knows somebody who knows them. The daughter was . . . complicated. Hard to deal with. So, you know," I said, "they've had practice."

She fitted the cases together, coiled cables. "I think I could screw that up."

"It's my understanding that all you have to do to succeed at this is not die."

She went with them. We went southward, down to Seattle, to finish the tour in old grunge country. Two or three people came by after our set to say that we sounded good. Almost like the real thing.

～ 27 ～
Unusual Meats

I made a digital shift, moving my office home so that I could be there sometimes, running prep for the next show while I was still physically in the
house. It was part of Lucy's plan to make me function as a mother. When
Hanna came to find me, I was working. Listening to layers of audio we were
experimenting with, for a possible different intro for *The Cure* come fall.

Noise-cancelling headphones whispered a hipster-acoustic cover of The
Cure's "Lullaby."

Hanna sat on the floor, flipping through a tablet, mine or Eden's.

She probably needed underwear. I didn't know what girls her age wore, or
where it came from. I thought they might have developed training-underwear for
pre-teens, so that they'd be fully prepared to wear sexy lingerie as soon as they
had anything to sexy with.

I took off the headphones. Held them out to her.

She shook her head.

I said, "What?"

"What happened to the first baby?"

"Ever?"

"Your first baby. With my dad. You guys got married because you were pregnant. So what happened to the first baby?"

I said, "It died."

She stared at me for a minute. Then she started to cry. I thought that I should have thought of a different word, to soften it for her. I'd avoided actually saying the word *die* to her, as much as I could, since we landed in Toronto. Dead houseplants *dried out* so I *moved them outside*. The batteries on the small sound-hearts of our phones and her iPod got *very low* and then *went to sleep*.

I'd thought about getting a cat, but I couldn't have anything in the house that was so fragile. What if it got out and was hit by a car? Would Hanna survive feline death so soon after the failure of human existence?

She didn't fully get up. Instead, she crawled across the floor to me, wrapped her arms around my legs and laid her head in my lap.

"Oh, honey." I'd been working on words like these. "It's okay."

"It's *not*. You lost *everybody*."

Cold all over. I pulled her up toward me, but we off-balanced and both fell to the floor. "Oh no. Oh honey, no. It died because it was never a baby at all."

"I don't understand."

"It died because it wasn't really . . ." I paused. Tried to articulate it for her and failed.

Hanna's grief felt sticky against me. It was more misery than I'd ever poured out for that same bodily failure. I'd managed wholly to imagine the pregnancy as a transformation of myself, and only twice had I even successfully fantasized it through to a full human being. The other times, it was as it was: imagined, present, disruptive. A catalyst for the second half of my life.

※◉※

Lucy texted me while I was at work. *Talk to me.*

In person?

Please.

Friends or work?

It's about Hanna.

Am I paying you, then?

Bitch. Come have lunch with me.

Lucy had fabulous taste in restaurants, in the sense that she could instinctively find places that served breakfast all day, and had surprisingly cheap deals on steak and eggs. Most of them wouldn't serve her steak blue, but she'd settle for rare. She ate her bleeding meal under the eyes of "local artist" paintings of asymmetrical parrots and sad girls. Every restaurant she and I had ever eaten lunch at had those terrible paintings in it. The canvases hung on stretchers with ragged threads hanging down, and watercolours hung from binder clips tacked to the wall, like no one could imagine framing those creations, and they always had prices next to them in case someone desired one of the horrors enough to take it home.

Lucy had bought three of those paintings since I'd known her. None of them hung in her condo, suggesting that she either threw them away or displayed them in her professional office as defensive colouration. Their vivid brush strokes might have entranced her clients, the ones who self-described as perverts and came for therapy that had little or nothing to do with their sexuality at all.

She didn't usually treat children, she reminded me. This was a favour.

Lucy saw Hanna twice a week, usually while I was at work. I never took her.

I said, "When do girls start needing lingerie instead of underpants?"

"Not yet. You're right that she needs clothes, though." Lucy's steak had arrived with fried tomatoes instead of potatoes, suggesting that she'd gone low-carb. The mix of blood and nightshade on her plate was striking enough that I asked her to stop eating so I could photograph it.

"Hanna would like that, too," she said.

"I'm glad to know you think we're related."

"Don't get distracted. She needs clothes."

"She has clothes."

"She has clothes she's grown out of, and she has clothes that Eden buys her."

I tried to picture Eden buying clothes for a little girl. He was an alien creature in almost any environment, let alone a mall. "Value Village?"

"I expect so. I think Hanna would appreciate it if you spent some time with her. Take her shopping. Maybe fix her hair."

"Hanna's hair is fine."

Lucy snorted. "Look underneath. God, she reminds me of you. She tells everyone she's fine and storms around like she's going to break thing and tells people it's her personal style."

"Good for her."

"You guys are going to keep therapists busy for generations."

"Hanna has a therapist. I just have a psychiatrist."

"So you take pills and repress everything."

"It's good for my art."

"Take your daughter shopping, Alli. And pay for my lunch. I won't bill you." She gave me a hug before she left. "Your face looks a *lot* better. Soon you'll be able to pretend you have a kid who hasn't stabbed you even once."

:::◉:::

I'd been leaving Hanna to deal with her own hair. When she was out with Eden, she kept it in a ponytail, and I helped by keeping her supplied with no-snag elastics. Around the house, she let it fall loose around her face. Like mine, her hair resisted both the wavy glory of the Christian fantasy girl and the sleekness of current fashion. Hers was two or three shades lighter than mine, I thought, but I'd been colouring my hair for long enough that I couldn't be absolutely certain.

Since asking about the baby, she'd taken to sitting closer to me on my office floor and occasionally leaning against my legs, like a house pet. The more she butted against me, though, the more I thought she might be actively imitating a cat.

I said, "If I pet you, will you purr?"

"Maaaybe." She was smiling.

I was utterly charmed.

I tried to pet her like I would a cat, to please her. I scratched behind where her cat ears would be. I did long strokes.

When I moved down to the base of her neck, though, there were tangled lumps. I pushed my fingers through to palpate them, and Hanna pulled away. Got up and left the room.

I went online and searched for cat ears.

The ones that arrived on my office desk were disproportionately large for Hanna, and too furry to feel fully "cat," but the hair band that anchored them had a nook for batteries, and when you pushed a barely-there button the ears twisted to follow sound. Made in Japan, like every whimsical thing, though discontinued for reasons the website had declined to elaborate on.

I offered them to Hanna when I got home, in a shopping bag with a Punk Daisies band T-shirt and a handful of pairs of Korean novelty socks that the gutter-punk teenagers downtown had been selling on the sidewalk. She accepted the lot without looking inside. Vanished upstairs to Eden's studio.

I went back to my office. My own bag was clogged with summaries of upcoming books that we might feature on *The Cure*. An actor's struggle with a family history of abuse in the face of fatherhood. A memoir of disordered eating. An intensive survey of the surviving honky-tonk bars of western America in the age of generic corporatism. A collection of zines by queer indigenous women, re-bound and distributed by a tiny Edmonton press. It looked promising, and I made a note on the summary that I wanted to see the whole book. The next summary was of a journalist's account of eating unusual meats in hipster cities, and it should have been garbage, but the marginal notes said he was funny, good on the radio, and we should consider it, so I looked at his webpage.

Twelve minutes max length. Remote phone interview.

Find someone who can contest the category "unusual meats" with him on-air.

Hanna came in wearing the ears and sat on the floor by my desk. She made an approximated purr.

"I'm glad you like them."

I kept working. When she leaned in, she was still enough that I could feel the mass at the base of her skull: matted hair, vaguely sticky, hidden underneath the mostly-brushed upper layer.

I let it go. Let her play with her tablet. Got up, wandered to the kitchen, and chopped vegetables to stir-fry for dinner. Waited until Hanna followed to say, "Are you trying for dreadlocks?"

She glared at me.

"It's a real question."

"It's fine."

"Oh. Happened by accident?"

She shrugged.

"Is this one of the things I should have been paying attention to?"

"You don't have any No More Tangles in the bathroom."

I sighed. "Sorry." Pause. "How long has your hair been like this?"

"A while."

"Did you tell Lucy?"

"I don't have to tell you what I tell Lucy."

"That's true. Did you?"

"No, but I think she knows."

"Did she offer to fix it?" I asked. Hanna cocked her head. "Never mind. Can I fix it?""

She hesitated.

I said, "I used to get those. It's our wavy hair. It's not really your fault, it's just something that happens in our family."

"My mom didn't say that." She meant Claudia. Realized that she meant it and waited for me to react.

"She had really nice hair," I said, "and probably didn't have to worry about this kind of thing. But I bet I can get the worst of that out with peanut butter. Why don't you let me try?"

The peanut butter made her laugh, but when I looked in the cupboard all we had was an ancient jar of chunky, almost dried to a single mass, and we had to go out for more. Hanna came with me, still wearing her ears. She showed them to the clerk at the corner shop while I looked for something appropriate.

They had jars of sugar-sweetened legume paste of the kind I hadn't had in the house in years. They also had No More Tangles. I bought both, flinching at the mark-up. Carried them home.

Hanna said, "I've seen these online." Meaning the ears. "Don't they come with a tail?"

"The tail is sold separately." It was. The tail was supposed to respond to the wearer's mood, and most of the marketing materials had been overtly sexual.

Disappointed. "Oh."

"We can talk about it."

Hanna walked beside me down the sidewalk, using the curb as a balance-beam. Every so often she flinched.

"Are your shoes too small?"

"A bit."

I was going to need a separate list just for her clothes. I wondered if she could use her phone to send me updates, reminding me of the things she needed.

I said, "I'm sorry I'm not good at this."

I thought she'd say *it's okay*, but she didn't.

I said, "I grew up in a weird family. We didn't have a lot of things that you think are normal, so I forget they're important. That doesn't mean you can't have them. It means that I don't look at you and think, *Hanna needs shoes*."

"You didn't have *shoes*?"

"We mostly didn't wear shoes, because it was hot where we lived. If we did, it was mostly sandals, and you can wear those for a long time after they're officially too small."

"Oh." She paused. Eyed the curb like she was thinking of trying something more gymnastic.

I said, "On the grass if you're going to risk your neck."

She crossed in front of me. Tried for a cartwheel on the neighbour's lawn and failed. Got up and walked along.

She said, "I'm sorry you didn't have shoes."

"It's really seriously not your fault. It didn't even occur to me to be mad about it until a lot later."

"Is that why you became a witch?"

I thought about it. "Not just because of that, but a bit, yes, probably."

"Okay."

The peanut butter helped loosen the outer strands of the mats in Hanna's hair. As I freed segments, I pinned them to the top of her head. Then peanut butter stopped working and I switched to olive-oil and tweezers.

It got late. I hadn't been watching the stove clock, but when Eden came to find us he was in his pajamas.

"It looks like you're mixing potions in here," he said.

Hanna announced, "We're being witches."

"Do witches stay up all night?"

It wasn't quite time for the bars to close, but I thought it might be worth my just staying up until work, then going to bed afterwards.

I said, "Make me coffee, hon. We're staying up all night."

"Can I have coffee?" Hanna asked.

"No."

"Why?"

"Because I'm a very bad mother, but I don't give coffee to people who are eleven."

"Who do you give it to?"

"Established witches."

"Will you teach me how to be a witch?"

"Maybe. There's some other stuff you have to do first."

"Like what?"

I sighed. "Like learning to brush your hair all the way through. This isn't coming out. Can I cut it?"

Hanna pulled away. "No more kitchen haircuts."

"I have never once cut your hair in a kitchen before."

"When I was little, Grandma Elaine used to cut my hair in her kitchen, and I always looked *awful* after."

"That I believe. I'm better at this than she is, though."

"Because you're a witch?"

"Because I spent most of my life in a punk band, and in those days you couldn't get the look in a salon."

Hanna said, "Pictures or it didn't happen."

I said, "Pictures I've got."

In the period before I met Eden, when my medications weren't balanced, I made some bad decisions, like sleeping with Jay and waxing my eyebrows. In the early stages of recalibrating my meds, I also went through a period of compulsive organization. I cleaned my shitty apartment with heavy chemicals and sorted all my clothes. I organized my papers. I threw things away.

I made actual fucking photo albums for every year of The Innocents, and separate "Rock Star" albums for Kara, Mary-Beth, and me.

Hanna looked at the pictures very seriously, like she'd been presented with someone's baby book and was supposed to appreciate it. Some pages in, I remembered that her parents, her other parents, had locked this part of my life into a box, and that Hanna had almost certainly never seen most of these images before. The nude shots were there, on upcoming pages. The ones that had been shot on ordinary grocery-store film and developed in commercial labs were tucked behind more fully-clothed versions of me. Only the odd oversized print was on full display.

"I don't like your hair in these."

Oh. "All right."

She said, "Who cuts your hair now?"

In Toronto my hair was cut by a heavyset girl in elaborate makeup who worked on the third floor of an anonymous office tower and mostly styled people who worked in second- and third-tier media.

I said, "Let me cut your hair and I'll buy you the cat tail."

She thought about it. Found a nude shot of me and flipped the page over as if it was blank. "Okay."

I gave her the best jagged bob I could manage. I hadn't had hair-cutting scissors in years, and the ones I used weren't as sharp as they should have been. It wasn't my best work.

Hanna slept on it, washed it, and let me comb it out after work. I tugged the remaining knots free and cleaned the rest up with scissors I'd bought from a beauty-supply store in the Eaton Centre. I brought her lip gloss as an apology.

"You went to the mall."

"Yes."

"Can I come next time?"

"Why?"

"If we're going to music festivals, I need some stuff."

"You're planning to style yourself for the festival scene?"

"I looked online."

She had. Her phone was full of bookmarks for Urban Outfitters and Forever 21.

I said, "This or the tail."

"This. You can get me the tail later." She paused. "And we have to get you some stuff. I don't think you can go to festivals looking like that."

"I've been to festivals before."

"Not since, like, goth was a thing. You have good army boots, you can wear those. But you need some flowers. Like, in your hair. And a different version of you to wear with them. Why don't you try actually looking like a witch, and see what happens?"

～ 28 ～

Animal Rescue

Jay was never my "boyfriend," but he used to put the word in air quotes and laugh at it. I laughed too. I was too cool, too sophisticated to want a *boyfriend*. I knew the score. I was doing my own shit, obviously, and if I happened to always be available when Jay texted to ask if I was *dtf*, well, he just had good timing.

Down to fuck?

Sure. Wasn't busy anyway.

In spite of that, he could be intense about things. He liked to show off his access. Once, after sex, he said, "Get dressed," and we went out to three clubs, and then he talked to someone and took me out on the roof of a twelve-storey building surrounded by low-rise industrial and parking, where I thought we might be swallowed by vertigo and dragged out to the wilds of suburbia or Kitchener before the wind let up.

The club was in a neighbouring building. This was, I think, a hotel. Some nameless airport-style creation. But he expected me to be impressed, maybe that he could ask strangers for keys and they'd just hand them over.

He said, "Name a band and I'll put them on the show."

"That's okay."

"Go on."

"The Innocents."

Pause. "I don't know them."

There's a slim chance he actually didn't, though at the end I found out he had a whole file of information on me. Stranger that he'd say that, though, because he claimed to know more about the Canadian music scene, "such as it is," than anyone else in the office.

"It was worth a try."

"You have shitty taste in music. Pick someone good and I'll introduce you to them."

"I'll think about it."

"Want to blow me out here?"

I studied him. "Only if you stand at the edge."

Jay snorted. "Going to push me over, Winter?"

"I figure if you die I can have your job."

He stopped. Dug in his pocket for his phone and studied it for a while, and then said, "I have somewhere to be. Can you get yourself home?" Walked away into the building so that I had to run after him to catch the door before it locked behind him.

Saturday night nowhere, trying to get a cab in a world of empty spaces and fragmentary cell phone reception, trying to explain where I was when I finally tracked down a payphone.

▮▮▮◉▮▮▮

I showed up on Monday before he did, in the early hours of producers preparing show notes. Jay came in hours later, drinking coffee like he hadn't been home since Saturday night, and said, "I could fire you, you know."

"I'm unionized."

"I'm the host. You're fucking *nothing*." He dug around in the top drawer of my desk, between his knees. He sat on my desk whenever he talked to me, pushing me back out of the space and creating a vague blowjob pose that it was my prerogative to back out of, or not. "And even if I died, they'd *never* give you my job."

I'd been cold all that night. I stared flatly back at him. "Why don't we kill you and see?"

Long pause. The other cubicles could hear us.

Then Jay laughed. "Fuck, Winter. You want to be on air today?"

I checked the show notes. Our guests were two filmmakers with a documentary about Chinese dissidents. An American journalist with a new book about his years as a war correspondent. Jay hadn't read the book; I'd read it and made crib notes for him.

"Absolutely."

"Too bad. Next time, try pushing harder."

⋮⋮⦂⋮⋮

But then he'd call and tell me about his wife. He was still married, then, though they'd been separated for a while. She'd taken the dog when she left, and then the dog had died, and she hadn't told him. He went to her place, to see the dog, he hadn't seen the dog in ages, and she just stood there like an ice witch and said, "It died."

"*It died*," Jay said. "Bjorn was never an *it*. Not while he lived with me. She changed that. Did I tell you she had them cut his balls off?" He said it like *they* were a pack of cold-eyed enforcers who came to the homes of unsuspecting men and animals for castration purposes.

"I'm sorry your dog died."

"Thanks. He was my friend, you know?"

Jay talked for ages, until I put him on speakerphone. Jay was an asshole, but he did love that dog. I shifted from the couch to the computer, working in a T-shirt and panties, making feminine listening noises and not acknowledging his occasional voice-catches.

Jay did monologues before I was hired, but after I joined the staff, I wrote most of them. His dog monologue was the best work I did before I started writing for myself.

I didn't get credit for it, of course; Jay did. His name is still on the book they made of it, illustrated by a handful of art photographers and published officially to fundraise for animal charities.

It's a gorgeous book. It went out of print after Jay was convicted, and now it's collectible, though not wildly so. Second-hand copies on Amazon sell for forty or fifty dollars. Less for a signed copy. He did a mass signing of the books, and sketched a stick-dog into each one, distinctive. Later, he started using the stick-dog instead of a signature in autographs, and when he "signed" things online.

He drew it on my abdomen with eyeliner when he stayed over at my apartment. He'd avoided that part of my body before. The stretch marks and c-section scar both reinforced the parts of me he didn't like — my sexual history, the fact that I wasn't younger than he was, the places where my skin didn't fully adhere to every connective tissue. That night, though, he used the scar as a ruler line, drawing the dog running along it. Sketched and rubbed and refined. Sat back and studied the result.

"Your womb's under there, right?"

I flinched at *womb*. "Yes, that's where I keep my uterus. The zipper's for easy access."

"You should have puppies or something. You could grow extra nipples, nurse them."

His way of calling me *bitch*, but nicely.

My relationship with Jay was mostly sharp edges, but he wasn't always a total shit. If he had been, he'd have been an easier person to deal with. He was creepy and an asshole, and a sweetheart, and smart and interesting, and he loved animals. After Bjorn died, Jay ranged out through Toronto, finding animal rescue centres and walking dogs for them until he was recognized, then moving on to the next one. His condo building didn't allow dogs.

"You could move."

He didn't. He went online and made friends with the ruthless people who did active rescue. They scouted the city with eyes open for neglected pets. If animal protection wouldn't intervene, they went in. Climbed fences, broke into houses, liberated half-starved German Shepherds and limping Pit Bulls and carried them out. Big dogs they cradled like children.

They weren't well-organized. Not a gang or a society with a central meeting-house. What they did was illegal, but, Jay said, "Only technically. Like, the animal protection people want to do this shit, but it's against the law, so they can't, or the city gets sued. Instead, we go in."

He'd bring me dogs, "Just overnight," because his place wouldn't take them. Huge, silent animals, or restless and howling. I'd never coped well with dogs, and the sheer size of some of them terrified me. He came one night in his Mercedes with a pair of Huskies in the back seat, strapped into safety harnesses that they fought against like leg-hold traps. He said, "Just for tonight."

"My landlord's going to kick me out if they catch me with another dog."

"Just one night."

"Take them to your place."

He growled. Then said, "Only if you come, too."

There were too many bodies in that glossy space. He'd rescued wolves, essentially. They were muscle-bound and enormous, and they'd been confined for too long. He said there were people coming to take them out of the city in the morning. Early.

The dogs wouldn't let us sleep. They stared and paced, and one threw itself repeatedly against the windows until we wrestled it into the bathroom.

It bit Jay. He wrapped his hand in a towel, and it wasn't until after work the next day that I saw how bad it was. The rescuers were supposed to arrive in the pre-dawn hours, when I usually went to work on my own. Jay said, "Stay. I'll give you a ride in."

"I need to be there before you."

"I'll vouch for you. Take the dogs for a walk, okay?"

The dogs were too big for me to take both of them. Even one pulled me off my feet. I was in flats and jeans, but I ran with it, just to calm the animal, down procumbent concrete in the glass tunnels of downtown. The Husky veered intermittently toward the smell of the lake, into the paths of single cars that veered away.

It took most of my body weight to drag it back. There was a commissionaire in the lobby, watching me bring the dog through. She didn't say anything. I remember her as a big, stocky woman with traditional braids pinned against her head and a mighty moral judgement that lingered for weeks after she saw me walk through. I don't suppose she knew who Jay was, either, if only because I never heard her listen to anything but Christian radio. But she wouldn't have known I was with Jay, or at Jay's, because when we arrived together he escorted me in from underground parking and only ever sent me through the lobby when I was travelling by myself, because he was busy or I was sick of him or because animals were dismantling his home while he read show notes and tried not to sleep.

Jay's hand got infected. Dogs' mouths aren't as septic as cats', but he left the wound for hours, and then picked up something antibiotic-resistant at the hospital.

Lindsay Avon came in to cover for him, and we had guest journalists come in to read "Jay's" monologues, written "from his hospital bed," so the audience wouldn't forget him.

I wanted to ask him why he didn't rescue cats, but it would have been a stupid question. Cats weren't his animal. Rescuers saved them, too, but cats didn't have the machismo of big dogs, and their injuries weren't largely borne in silence.

And, really, you didn't want to start rescuing cats. There were just so damn many of them. People didn't drown kittens, anymore, so the cats spilled over, eating birds and occupying streets and the homes of madwomen, and it wasn't noble at all. Just cats.

During Jay's trial, his lawyers made the point that he hadn't done anything as obvious as actually draw the stick-dog onto his ex-wife's body. They referred to her, in the newspaper and in Public Broadcasting reports, as Alice Goreszeki, leaving off the "Beaton" suffix. She hadn't actually changed her name back, after their divorce, but the newsroom had a meeting about it, and the staff of *The Cure* were invited. They said we had "a stake" in the proceeding.

The official policy was that Alice would be referred by her maiden name, "out of respect," but also for clarity. Jay would be referred to as "Beaton" or "Mr. Beaton," and then, as time passed, "disgraced former broadcaster Jay Beaton."

No one asked me to testify, and I wasn't about to offer. Jay's not-girlfriend's opinion on whether or not Jay killed his ex-wife over the neutering and subsequent death of their shared pet weren't pertinent evidence. The courts had family and friends and forensics, and photographs of Jay's fridge, where he'd stored her uterus in a Styrofoam take-out box.

It was, he allegedly told a friend, much smaller than he'd expected. He'd assumed that he'd need a much larger incision to get it out.

ꜱ 29 ꜱ

Naomi

I never answered the door when I wasn't expecting someone. If Eden wasn't home, or didn't want to answer the door, it simply didn't get answered. In the summer, we hung commercial baskets of wave petunias from the wrought-iron hooks framing the porch so the house would look friendly, but it was a floral simulacrum of hospitality, not only not existing, but having no original source.

Hanna found me in my office behind the kitchen, listening to a Purity Ring album. *The Cure* was in summer repeats, but music labels sent advance copies of albums by artists we might want to have on in the future. (Labels sent advance copies of albums we'd *never* feature. Indie bands sent waves of digital music and links to Soundcloud and messy personal/band pages and BandCamp, and we had interns from Ryerson and the University of Toronto whose summer job was to sort the tangle of it.) It was going to be too hot, soon, to work in my office at home, and we'd have to dig out the window-mounted air conditioners just to survive because the house had never been rigged for central air and the city was unlivable without it.

"Allison?"

"Hey."

"Your sister's here."

I said, "No she isn't."

"She is. She's in the living room. I said I'd come and find you."

Hanna had a notebook where she kept the previously unwritten rules of the house. *Drinking glasses go under the counter, next to the stove, for some reason. Headphones after midnight. Allison goes to bed early or else she stays up all night. Don't move Eden's pills around in the bathroom. Leave the mail on the floor/don't pick it up. If you need your clothes washed, pile them on the dining table. Check the labels before you eat anything in the fridge in case it's bad. Yell loud if we need food.* We hadn't fully impressed on her, yet, that we didn't answer the door.

Hanna grew up in a place without sidewalks. She presumed that if somebody came to your door, it must be important. Eden said he came down from his office once and there were Mormon missionaries in the living room, avoiding the piles of underwear, and watching Hanna while she played with her tablet and ignored them.

I said, "You let her in?"

"She's your sister."

"How the hell do you know who my sister is?"

Hesitation. Hanna flinched whenever I swore, even if it wasn't directed at her. "She said she was."

"People can say anything."

"And she looks like you."

"Oh really."

"And I know her from Neuenheim. It's Naomi."

I got up and pushed past her. Considered, in that second of bodily passage, locking Hanna in my office while I exorcised the parlour. I didn't think I could contain her, though, not that way. I said, "Stay in the kitchen," but she didn't do that, either. Twisted past me, in fact, through the living room and up the stairs, leaving foot-beats that ended on the landing, where she could hear perfectly without being seen.

Naomi didn't look like me, except in the bones in her face. She was heavier, and fairer, and her long hair had the ripples of a carefully maintained and night-braided cult-coif. Her skirt ended at mid-shin, revealing white sweat socks and orange and fuchsia New Balance runners.

Behold your sister. Her face at thirty-three looks like yours at thirty-nine looks like your mother's. You have seen her in recommended but unpursued Facebook posts. You, like Hanna, instantly believe in her. She is that which she says she is.

She said, "You need to come home."

"Get out of my house."

"You don't answer messages and you keep changing your phone number, so I *drove to Toronto* to talk to you. Be polite."

On the other side of the curtains, just visible, there was a minivan parked at the curb with its windows partly down. Children's hands flew in and out of view in the cracks.

"Are those yours?"

"Yes, I brought the kids. They like camping. And it's not like I could, I don't know, leave them by the side of the road and run away with a punk band."

"Oh, you're a fan. You aren't welcome here."

"Mom's sick."

"Good for her."

"Dad died almost two years ago and you didn't bother to come home. Well, now you have to. We're worn out, and there aren't enough people, and Mom's been conducting some kind of feud with Elaine Hoeppner that got out of hand and now everybody's got a side in *that*. You started a *war*."

"I left more than twenty years ago. I think you can handle it without me."

"They started their thing because of *you*. Because Elaine said, after church, that you were a slut and you were going to turn Hanna into one, and she hoped we'd all pray for you to go crazy so you'd have to give Hanna back. And Mom wasn't going to have that. She never, ever did. You should have heard the things she's defended you from."

"I never asked her for that."

"Too bad. It turned into a thing. They've been peaceful for *years*, ever since Mom and Dad moved home, and then this happens, and suddenly Mom's in the middle of a war she's too sick to fight. The ladies who work home-care all took Elaine's side, so I've been taking care of Mom when Carly can't. But I have to sleep sometime, you know?"

"Hire someone."

"With what?"

"You want money?" I started math in my head. How much I could raise, right then, that I could use to make Naomi go away?

"I need you to take over."

"You need lots of things that aren't going to happen. Have Mom move into Winnipeg. There must be city women who aren't part of the Mennonite blood feuds who you could hire to take care of her."

"She says she's not giving up the ground."

"Then I guess she's going to be really lonely."

Hanna came down the stairs again and commenced looking in corners. I said, "What do you need?"

"Charger. My tablet's dead." Without looking at Naomi, "How's Grandma?"

"Which one?"

"Grandma Alma."

"Tell your mom to take you to find out," Naomi said. "You could come with us." An alluring offer from an adult with a better grasp on child language than I had. Hanna pushed towards the window.

"Who came with?"

"Aiden, Gwyn, and Jazz."

Hanna left her tablet on the floor, tripped over shoes, and ran outside barefoot. Let herself into the van via its heavy sliding door and clambered in. I saw car seats, and stuffed animals fell onto the curb.

Naomi said, "At some point, you're still responsible."

"They gave me *away*."

"Yes, I read your book. But you've had a lot of mileage out of that version of things. You owe something for the rest of it."

"I don't owe you anything."

"You owe Mom so, so much. And us. You *left* us. You took off, and you told people that Mom and Dad were monsters and cultists. But you were awful. You made it sound like going overseas again would kill you, and so you slutted around for a while, and even then, Mom and Dad found you a family, and then you blew *that* up."

I said, "You're done."

Naomi said, "You're going to get into that van and come home with me. Or I'll start telling people my version of things."

"Go ahead."

She paused. If she'd been living in Neuenheim as long as I suspected, she'd imagine the internet as a version of the Mennonite social network, interested in whatever she had to say and endlessly interested in me. And it was, but she'd never find the right rabbit holes. Not even Jay's bulldogs would find her, and even if they did, what could they do with her information?

aLISon WINt3r is an ungr8ful slut-daughter!

WinT3r's cult-family both more and less cultish than suspected!

Naomi said, "You aren't even *working* right now."

"I don't owe any of you anything."

Hanna came back, trailing sticky children. They smelled, from a distance, like car-warmed stale cheddar cheese and synthetic banana. Hanna said, "We're going camping!"

"No."

She started at me. Then screwed up her chest and started to scream.

I hadn't heard a noise like that from her since we'd come to Toronto, and only once or twice in the aftermath of the Winnipeg bloodbath. (*Don't think about that. Don't think about the bathroom.*) When she was an infant, Hanna had made sounds that chewed my nerves through, but those were wired into my brain, and this wasn't.

Naomi was unmoved. What I'd thought was her purse was, when she picked it up, a massive diaper bag with a carabiner for keys.

"It's okay, Hanna, honey. If you can't go, we'll stay."

In four and a half months, Eden and I had cleared enough space in the house for Hanna to move. Before dark, Naomi had made room for everyone. She pushed boxes to the side and created a zone of soft, unbreakable objects. Sat her sticky baby there. She pulled alcohol wipes out of her van and disinfected the kitchen, then the dining room. The piles of laundry from the living room vanished upstairs.

I thought for a while, while she was cleaning, about why it was that the house's condition could possibly be a manifestation of my moral failures and not of Eden's. Not of his parents'. It occurred to me that I could hire someone like Naomi to deal with the household chaos, and then it would officially stop being my responsibility.

The two older kids went upstairs with Hanna. She'd given me a death-look on the stairs, toxic as the first day I'd seen her in the Winnipeg hotel room.

I remembered my mother doing this when I was small, overcoming my objections to life changes through joyful, singing housework. Naomi did that too: she sang. Some of her songs were in French; more of them were in the Low German dialect that ruled Neuenheim. I'd mentioned it in my book, that language that no one other than Mennonites spoke, my sense that it was a prison we chose to live inside.

The prison was a sense of our collective origin almost five hundred years ago on the Swiss border, making us seem like one unit. We spread out first to Russia, when Catherine the Great invited the Anabaptists to farm the Steppes, and we kept speaking Low German while our Russian peasant neighbours became more and more furious with us, until they came at the dawn of the Revolution to set us on fire and slaughter our old people, and everyone who survived that came on ships, through Ukraine and Greece, to the U.S. and Canada and Mexico, and then down to Paraguay and Bolivia. There are still colonies there, a century later, speaking Low German in a sea of Spanish and guarding their blonde-haired girls against outsiders.

I knew a little Low German, but not a lot. Less than English, less than French. My parents used to tell us stories, when we were living in the Burundi highlands, about the choice our people made, after the Russians came to burn our houses down. *You can decide the world is against you and build another fortress, or you can accept that you've lived for centuries in dereliction of your Christian duties of charity and compassion. We chose the latter. That's why we're here.*

We will be useful. Not only because it is our responsibility, but because we have centuries of failure to atone for.

Eden came down, prompted by the scent-shift from vague decay to Lysol-freshness. He stood in the living room archway, hugging himself.

I said, "I didn't let them in."

"Who are they?"

Naomi came, held out her hand. "I'm Naomi, Allison's sister. I brought my kids to visit Hanna."

I said, "That's not true."

"It's true enough."

"She wants to *take me back.*"

"I'm pretty sure I can't pick you up and carry you. Therefore I'm visiting. Hi. Who are you?"

"That's Eden. This is his house. So you can stop cleaning it," I said.

Eden said, "I guess you can clean if you want? I'm . . . ." He paused. "Is everything okay?"

Naomi looked him over. "Hmm. Are *you* okay?"

She had that gift our parents did, of expressing pure, Christian empathy. I'd seen it directed toward women coming to talk to my mother, and people in airports, and church members and beggars and strangers in cities we'd never go back to. Eden reeled in front of it for a second, then blinked. He said, "It's not my best day. Things are a bit blurry around the edges. I'm sorry."

"Everything is fine," Naomi told him. "I'm going to take care of things for a while. Is there anything you need?"

Eden took the question seriously. "I think I should probably take something, for the blur. Maybe have a cup of tea. Um, is that your baby?"

"She is. She's Jasmine."

"Can I pick her up?"

"Absolutely."

He hadn't, I thought, expected Naomi not to think about it first. Eden asked people before he sat down near them on the bus, and if they said, *please don't* (and they did, reacting to the rabbinical beard, his height, the absent-mindedness of his self-presentation that varied from artistically charming to implicitly psychotic), he'd move away and sit or stand somewhere else. He crouched, shifting a box away from the baby's play-area so that he could see her clearly. "Hey, honey."

"hi" Breathy little-girl voice.

"Can I pick you up?"

"yes please"

Naomi beamed. I wondered how much drilling it took to instill social graces in a child who couldn't eat without spilling.

"Are you hungry?" I wasn't sure if she was speaking to Jasmine or Eden. He answered.

"Yeah."

"Okay, then." She vanished into our kitchen. Came back.

"Allison, get your purse. We need to go grocery shopping."

She drove us in her van. It was grey-blue inside, with stains on most of the seats, and the back benches were still loaded with bags and pillows. I said, "There's a market down the street."

"That's fine if you eat like a skinny hipster. You look good, by the way. But the kids aren't going to eat that stuff. I need an actual supermarket. Give me your phone."

She pulled in to the first available space and parallel parked with the expertise of a woman who spent her life driving. Keyed through my phone. Paused. "Oh, my word. Is that your email?"

"Is it work, or is it bad?"

"I sincerely hope your work doesn't send you that kind of message."

"Eden'll put a new filter on it for me, later." Pause. "Why are you reading my email?"

"My phone's older. Dead, in fact, in the glove box. I wasn't sure which icon was the location search."

"That's cute. I'm not sure I believe that you can't tell the difference between Mail and Google Maps, but it's a good excuse. Can I use that the next time I want to go through someone's phone?"

"I was under the impression that you just threw people's phones into traffic when you were done with them."

"That made the news all the way out in Neuenheim?"

"I keep a Google alert running for news of you. For mom. I don't tell her everything, but she likes to know how you're doing."

I tried to imagine Naomi reading fragmentary media mentions off a dying phone screen to my mother, wherever she lived now. It wouldn't be in the same house as before. What kind of furniture would my parents have adopted when they ceased to be nomadic?

The obvious answer was, whatever came through the charity shop. They'd have bought it for more than it was worth, to put the money back into mission work, and lived on other people's velour floral discards. They'd have thick wall-to-wall carpet that was too much trouble to replace and pictures of the grand-children on the wall in heavy, thrifted frames.

Oil or pastel portraits of the kids, done by a neighbour, or by my sister Carly, if she'd taken that up. Eerie-looking things, the eyes too big and the faces peering up from the uncanny valley.

Table covered in papers and mission work. Aging computer in the corner of the living room, and no TV.

Naomi drove us out of my territory, far out of Toronto's civilized core, first on Davenport, then St. Clair, and finally Weston Road. It was disorienting for me. These weren't streets I ploughed through in a car, going from point A to B without regard for transit schedules or other human bodies. We were miles out of my way, and when I re-oriented, I had a sickening feeling that she was taking me to the airport, to be bundled luggage-less onto an airplane and collected in Win-nipeg before I could mount serious opposition. Maybe Eden had demonstrated marginally enough adult skill to be left in charge of her kids as well as mine. Or she could be reaching out through the eerie network of Mennonite women to find someone who'd descend and take over while we were absent.

The problem with the anxiety that underlay everything else in my brain was that it didn't need rational problems to trigger it. Random thoughts about money, or family, or work, or sex, or Jay, or Ethan and Claudia (*don't think about them, don't think about the bottom of their kitchen table*) could jumble my brain chemistry, triggering fight-or-flight.

I realized that I was seriously considering jumping out of the van and running away. Naomi still had my phone, but if I kept moving lakeward, I'd approach home, eventually.

I dug in my purse. In the bottom, with bottles of expired meds that I'd been meaning to take back to the pharmacy and over-the-counter painkillers and lip-stick, I found the one still-shiny bottle. Twisted the cap, licked my finger, caught a single Ativan on the sticky tip and thrust it under my tongue. Put the bottle away.

Naomi pulled across three lanes of traffic and into the parking lot of what I realized was a Superstore, massive food-mart and purveyor of fast fashion and mid-range household items. She had loonies in the ash tray, for the carts. A bag of reusable bags in the van's overstuffed back hatch. She said, "Get out. I'd rather we weren't gone all night."

When I climbed down, though, my purse tilted, and the Ativan bottle spilled across the grungy footwell carpet, joined by earrings and mints. The pill hadn't fully kicked in, and the mess was a temptation to palm a couple more, sticky as they were, and dry-swallow those as well.

"Move." Naomi pushed me aside. Took my purse and set about collecting small items. "You can't leave that stuff in the car. The kids will eat anything. Oh. I didn't think. Is your bathroom safe?"

"I haven't killed myself in there yet."

"You aren't funny." She found my phone, held it out for my thumbprint to unlock it, then took it back. "Hi, Eden, honey, I need you to make sure there isn't any medication at kid-level, okay? Maybe just put it all in a grocery bag on a high shelf? I'll do something more permanent when I get back. Is there anything you want, while we're at the store? Okay." She handed back my phone. "He wants carrot cake."

I trailed after her through the warehouse like a resentful teenager. It wasn't a random simile. The store was full of brisk women trailed by resentful teenagers who alternated studying their phones and demanding to know how soon they'd be finished.

"You can wait in the car, if you want," a passing mother said.

I didn't have that option. Naomi had questions for me involving cookware and dry ingredients and the contents of a pantry I seldom paid attention to.

She bought house brand macaroni and cheese, frozen vegetables, rice and canned mushroom soup and family packs of ground beef. A life of church pot-luck dinners flashed before my eyes.

"If you're going to look like that, just pick out something you'd want to eat," Naomi told me.

"What?"

"You make faces like a kid. How are you forty?"

I tried hunting for food for both of us, me and Eden. Frozen edamame, sticky rice and spicy tuna and nori for homemade Korean sushi. Daikon radish. Soba noodles. Whole artichokes.

That part was easier than I'd expected. The produce was grouped together by culture, with massive Chinese selections near the back of the store, and the WORLD FOODS aisle, hideously marked out, was actually fully stocked and crowded with families loading their carts. Hijabi women with toddlers considered spice selections and compared cooking oils. I found a range of Japanese and Korean junk foods that had become my addiction over the years, at a third of the price I usually paid, and had to consider whether migration to the edge of the urban world, through the automobile stampede, might be worth it for the savings.

No one was interested in me. I wondered vaguely if Public Broadcasting had ever penetrated as far as Etobicoke.

I stayed invisible until we circled back, because Naomi said she was out of underwear, and we dove into clothing and housewares, and there, on the edge of fast-fashion lingerie, was the book aisle: cookbooks, self-help, fantasy sagas, murder mysteries, and memoirs, including mine. It sat halfway down a table, four or five hardcover copies that must have been remaindered at some point, then salvaged. A bright sticker marked the top one *40% OFF!*
BESTSELLER!

Naomi picked it up. The book crushed the handful of rayon underpants already in her grip. "I have a copy of this. I've underlined the parts you need to apologize to Mom for."

I said, "Nothing for Dad?"

"After he died, I burned the first copy. Then I got another one at the charity shop and re-did it, just for her. So I wouldn't have to think about him."

The expected *I'm sorry* hung on a line between us. I ignored it until she'd put the book down and pushed the trolley away, toward the massed lines of shoppers waiting to pay. I walked away from her, toward the scattered drinks coolers. Found two ginger ales and brought them back. Waited.

I said, "It was fast, wasn't it?"

"Whatever gave you that impression?"

"I think a week elapsed between the first *come home* and *he's gone.*"

"You really don't check your email, do you?"

"Eden sorts my email. You've seen what's in it."

"What did you ever do to get that kind of hate?" Pause. "I say that as your abandoned, half-orphaned, slandered, and impoverished sister, by the way."

"Oh, *please* don't."

"What did you ever do?"

"I'm a woman in media. That's all it takes. But it's mostly because of Jay Beaton's fanboys. They didn't appreciate my taking over for him. Some of them think I set Jay up for murder, just to get his job. The saner ones just think I fucked Jay in order to fuck him over."

"Did you?"

"Fuck Jay?"

Just the slightest flinch. "Yes."

"A couple of times. They weren't my proudest moments, and they were definitely evidence that I needed my meds adjusted. But I didn't, you know, seduce and destroy him. He just liked having sex with anything that was female and relatively fresh, so I was probably inevitable." I opened the ginger ale and drank some. The woman in front of us in line turned around and stared at me, scandalized.

"Was it worth it?"

"Sex with Jay, no. But I like the job, and I wouldn't have been able to stay around long enough to have it if I hadn't slept with him, so in that sense, it was worth it. And it sent me to find a psychiatrist and get my meds adjusted, and that's how I met Eden, so maybe that was worth it, too.

"If you want me to apologize, you're going to be really disappointed," I continued. "I've decided that nothing could actually have gone differently than it did. It takes all the choices we make to get to where we are, and we live with that and don't pretend that another version would have been infinitely better."

"It's still possible to be sorry."

"Sorry is a function of brain chemistry. Mine's fairly balanced right now, so sorry isn't in play."

Naomi shook her head. "We're going to have to respectfully disagree about that until after supper. Anyway, you're paying for this, so pony up."

Other Mother

I n her pajamas, sitting on my bed, Naomi could have stepped off a Laura
Ingalls Wilder book cover. *Little House in Toronto*. Her hair was braided for
bed, and she'd arrived complete with ankle-length nightgown. It was sleeveless as a concession to the heat.

I said, "If you were Mormon, you could wear the magic underwear, instead.
Did you know the women put their bras on over it?"

"The idea of a skin of divine protection isn't the worst I've ever heard."

"You're just determined not to judge anyone, aren't you?"

She re-settled, cross-legged under her nightgown. I wondered if it passed for
sexy, in her marriage. In the streetlight, the fabric was translucent, and shadows
of pubic forest and nipple emerged.

There could be a whole fetish devoted to that hyper-innocent sexiness.

There was. I'd only escaped it by the skin of my teeth.

Naomi said, "Dad was sick for a couple of years. But, you know, he wasn't
all that old, and he went to the doctor regularly, and I don't think any of us
believed it was serious. He said they were just keeping an eye on him. Then he
started walking like an old guy, and then his kidneys started failing, and he was
dead before he was seventy. That part was fast. But he kept wanting the radio
on. Wanted to listen to you. It was grotesque. Like you were his favourite kid

instead of the one who suggested to the whole country that he'd sold you into cult-marriage.

"His death hit Mom really hard. She'd been in pretty strong denial, and when he went, she just sat down and didn't move for about two weeks. Her weight dropped hard. I couldn't get her to eat. Then she got up, one morning, and started making calls about going back out on mission. Her bags were packed. She was going to go to the Congo. Do you know what was going on there?"

I did. The civil war in the Democratic Republic of Congo was on the border of Burundi, and that corner of the world had never quite crawled out of my brain. I'd found newspapers, while I was living in Winnipeg, and burrowed into the public library to try to reconstruct what was going on in Rwanda, and then the DRC. When they'd first put up the web pages of survivors, I'd scoured them.

How many of our neighbours were living in camps in Kenya and Tanzania, a generation on?

Everyone in Public Broadcasting was entitled to a good cause. Mine was sexual violence against women in that war, even as I failed to be able to read about it for any period of time. I'd advocated at work for interviews with survivors, but I hadn't been able to conduct them myself. I couldn't even listen to them.

You can live your whole life in fury, never having anything that terrible happen to you. I'd wanted to take off my skin more than once, but stories involving vaginas and machetes were beyond my ability to process.

I said, "They're still doing it."

"She thought a midwife might be useful. Or she could run an orphanage. Deliver babies and take care of the ones the mothers couldn't stand to keep."

"What stopped her going?"

"All of us. Mom's good in a nice, friendly town, and she's brave as heaven, but none of us had the courage to go with her. Carly and I had panic attacks every night, thinking about her going alone. We got her fundraising, and we called Ethan and Claudia, and they sent Hanna to stay with Mom for a while. That helped a lot."

Hanna was down in the living room, unconscious in a nest of blankets and sleeping bags with her cousins. Gwyn, all of eight, had carefully combed out Hanna's tangled hair, and they'd shared a book with a bright, suspiciously megachurch-branded cover. Some kind of nineteenth-century colonial adventure for girls that I'd have to talk through and dismantle for Hanna later.

I said, "Was that the first time?"

"Of course not. Ethan and Claudia were up all the time. They only had Hanna, you know, and grandchildren are currency in Neuenheim. Mom and Elaine shared her pretty peacefully, most of the time. She was at Hoeppners', mostly, but Claudia used to bring her to visit."

"I guess she was entitled to one good kid."

I hadn't meant to say that. I'd tried, for months, not to think about Claudia at all. She'd been present in my brain for a decade or so as the brighter, better, more stable version of me. She'd survived a divorce from a perfectly nice man and married another one, taken on his daughter without the level of side-eye I'd have given in the same circumstances, and proceeded to live a happy domestic existence until her horrific, completely random death.

Except, that couldn't be correct, because she was Collin's mother, and Collin had always been present, from his birth until the afternoon he killed first his mother, then his step-father, and then himself, leaving just Hanna alone in a gore-coated McMansion. Collin had always been Claudia's son, and he hadn't, really, been okay for a long time before they all died.

Collin had lived with his father most of the time, but he must have visited Claudia from time to time. Maybe he'd even had a key to the house.

It occurred to me that, since Hanna and I had left, that David was more or less alone. I wondered whether he'd changed the bedding, after I pulled myself together and left, or whether he kept sleeping in the bed laced with my sweat and anxiety, if only for the symbolic human connection soaked into the fabric.

It occurred to me that I should have called him. Sent an email. Something.

Naomi said, "And there it is."

"Fuck you."

"Keep going."

"I can't be responsible for everyone's agony. There isn't enough of me to absorb it all."

"You only think that way because you've locked yourself away from all of it. If you expose yourself to enough, you build up an immunity."

"Why would I ever want to do that?"

She leaned forward and tilted my face so that she could, I thought, make out my jawline in the dim light. "Because you're a woman, and it's your bloody responsibility."

"That's Mennonite talk. I'm not interested."

"It is, but whether or not you're interested isn't important. It's part of you."

"I cut that part out."

"Well, it's invading your house. We need you. I do, and Carly does, and Mom does, because — this is what you keep forgetting, Allison — if women don't do this, absorb the misery, it just keeps floating around, poisoning the air, and making it impossible to live."

She sounded completely reasonable. I pulled her arm toward me.

It looked like mine had looked. There were thin, white lines running horizontally along the inner skin like the markings on a cat.

"You call that absorbing?"

"I call that an ongoing family problem with bipolar disorder that I have medication for. And a side-effect of the floating agony. Too much misery and not enough women."

I said, "I can't go back there."

"It doesn't have to be permanent."

"They'll take Hanna."

Naomi nodded. "Yes, she might. That's a risk. So is breathing, and driving, and eating. I'd say Elaine's less of a threat than, say, climate change. Did I tell you we went full solar, at home?"

"No."

"House and barns. Greenhouses too."

"You farm?"

She said, "Allison, don't you know anything about us at all?"

I tried to think if I knew Naomi's husband's name. I said, "Those are all your kids, downstairs, right?"

"Nope. I have two more. You need to come home. You can make an inventory of everyone, and show off how glossy you are, and help Mom move into Winnipeg, and tell everyone to go to hell if it makes you happy. But we really, really need you."

I said, "I'll think about it."

It was still hot in the house. We both lay on top of the covers, head to foot, and stared at the ceiling. I wondered how long we could go on pretending that we were both dolls, able to sleep rigidly on our backs, faces to the sky and eyes wide open.

Naomi said, "Claudia was wonderful, you know? I'd rather have her, but you might have noticed that she's gone, and you're it. The other mother."

I said, "Hanna has that book. The one about the Other Mother. I swear to God I'm not her."

"No, not if you don't steal souls and replace children's eyes with buttons. But you might have to be the evil fairy godmother for a while. You can be the bad witch. Scare everyone. It'll give you material for another book. If you do this, do it right, I'll tell you every awful story I can think of, and you can write another book about all the terrible things that happen to Mennonite girls, and half of it won't even be made up."

I said, "I didn't make that stuff up."

"You made up your version of it. It would have been fairer if you'd let some-one else make up another version, to balance it out."

∷∶⦂∷∷

Hours later, Naomi said, "Get up."

I wasn't actually asleep. In the summer, I still kept radio hours, up before full sunrise. July sun curved over the world's edge and into the house, creating daylight while everyone else slept. Naomi had still been sleeping in my bed when I'd crawled over her and gone to make coffee.

In my office, where I'd been creating program notes before she'd descended upon us, there was at least a boundary. Winter territory. Good morning, Annex, and happy Thursday. This is the cure for familial invasion of your home. We have six new albums for your review, coming books by riot grrrls-turned-bloggers, a proposal for a panel discussion on the gender politics of haunted-girl horror movies.

I liked that one. We could plug it into any show in the second half of Octo-ber that was low on content.

Naomi let herself in. Took my headphones off me.

"What?"

"It's time to go."

Her version of *as long as it takes* was four days. Then she gathered her chil-dren, mine, and a bag of things from my bedroom, and simply pushed me toward the door.

Eden hugged Hanna and gave her a tote bag of film stock and lenses. To me, he said, "I'm going to come after you, okay?"

"What?"

"I'll skip the first couple of dates on the concert tour. I'll get my license renewed and come rescue you in a few days. As long as it takes me to do that and drive."

Naomi's van still smelled like old food and children, but I had first claim, at least, on a front seat. Naomi said, "Navigate," like it was a complete instruction in itself.

"Winnipeg?"

"We won't make Winnipeg in one day, unless you want to drive tonight. When was the last time you drove at night on the highway?"

"I don't know. Innocents Abroad, maybe?"

"So, not likely. Not with this bunch. Aim us up the 400 and we'll reassess in Sudbury. Does anybody need to go to the bathroom?"

Everyone did. I considered, then went back and peed when the kids had finished. Walked back to my bedroom and collected electronics chargers and medications. Found Eden and told him to get me more before he came after us.

"Glad you remembered those."

"I don't want to do this."

"Yeah, but it's important, I think. I love you. Hold together, and don't kill yourself before I catch up with you."

He said it so seriously. I said, "I promise not to kill myself right now. I don't want to leave you with the paperwork."

"Thank you."

Naomi's kids were eerily well-behaved in the car. She'd armed them with colouring books and juice boxes, but I wasn't prepared for them to simply settle into their seats and shut up.

"Don't get used to it. It's early; they're still tired."

Our exit from Toronto's mega-sprawl echoed the stock visuals of an apocalyptic film, but in reverse. Millions poured into the city; we alone moved out of it. It probably wasn't that extreme, in fact. There was traffic — it was morning — but I hadn't seen the normal multi-lane commuter flow before, and I found it overwhelming. Long segments were essentially locked down, with cars inching forward.

It wasn't that I hadn't been aware of Toronto's car problem. *The Cure* did three shows a year on gridlock. Other shows, and the *Star*, and city blogs, devoted hours a week to it: the failures of transit, the horrors produced by amalgamation, the absurdity of having left urban planning to a crack-addicted redneck, however much support he had in the outlying areas. But the way I lived, it was difficult to grasp the problem's scale. I'd lived for half a decade in the warm, smug core of the city, embedded in its hipster street-culture that eschewed cars in favour of bikes and boards and transit, and nodded faux-sympathetically at commuter woes.

If I'd had to buy my own house, I wondered, where would I live?

Winnipeg, likely. I'd be a string reporter on local issues, or trying to run some kind of alt-weekly newspaper on a shoestring budget out of a house-share in Wolseley.

Had Wolseley gentrified while I'd been away?

"Allison, what lane should I be in?"

"I don't know. This one. This one's fine, as far as I can tell."

"Don't fall asleep on me."

I didn't. I fell asleep only once we were safely on the highway, with a chosen lane, and the children were only starting to rouse and complain about the distance.

∷∶◉∶∷

Sleep is the best tool we've yet developed to compress time. I woke up like a displaced traveller fallen into a different part of the map. Naomi had pulled into the massive parking-field of a Walmart.

"I'm getting McDonald's for everybody. What do you want?"

"Nothing." I'd adapted away from road-food after I stopped touring. I wasn't sure my body could take that kind of a sodium-fat blow and survive.

"I'll get you a Happy Meal."

Hanna said, "I need sunglasses."

I needed sunglasses. Naomi looked at us. "Sunglasses come from Walmart. It's over there."

The oldest of Naomi's children, Aiden, said, "I want to go with you." And so I found myself with two children in the grubby, glowing world of a Highway 400 Supercentre, pushing a cart that kept filling with objects I couldn't fully explain. Hanna needed clothes, a hairbrush, deodorant, which I couldn't remember having bought for her before, underwear, a glittering hat. I found sunglasses in a maze of costume jewelry. Mine, hers. Aiden looked at me hopefully.

Children's sunglasses were elsewhere. Hanna had chosen enormous movie-star sunglasses that covered half her face. I found plastic-framed ones sized for children at Naomi's familial increments.

The kids piled up food in the cart. Masses of pudding cups. Cereal. Granola bars. Bananas. I said, "Naomi's buying you guys food right now."

"This is for later. Can we have bubble bath?"

"I have no idea when you're next going to have a bathtub."

"Just to smell."

Bags of things, all grey plastic and consumer disposability, crossed the parking lot with us. Naomi surveyed the wreckage. "I don't usually let them have that stuff."

"Yours asked for it."

Not the lipstick; that was mine, part of a face cobbled together out of teen-aged brands I hadn't exposed my skin to in a decade. I hadn't found anything like the sunglasses I really wanted, but I had a matching pair to Hanna's. Naomi captured the snack foods and processed sugar and stashed them in the trunk, then righteously handed out cheerfully boxed lunches of fried dietary murder.

"I got you chicken nuggets."

They tasted like travel. My toy was a clip-in piece of green hair. Aiden received a small plastic rabbit wielding a toilet plunger. Hanna's clip-in was purple. Naomi's was pink.

"Back in the car, everybody. We've got miles to cover."

It felt more like being on tour than I'd expected. Hanna took my phone and ear buds, leaving me staring out the windshield at the asphalt world.

~ 31 ~
Snake Knot

Winnipeg was ringed by a highway that somehow, unlike every other city I'd lived in, hadn't seriously been overgrown. It captured the Trans-Canada like a planet's gravity well, whirling cars around the city and hurling them outwards again at increasing speed in different directions. Go west to Calgary, south to Grand Forks, north to the spreading Bible belt and the snake pits of central Manitoba.

That part was true. Manitoba was full of snakes. Garter snakes, mostly, but tens or hundreds of thousands of them, sleeping together in knots underground in the winter, then dispersing. Now and then invading a seniors' residence and settling into the warm, dark ventilation shafts, only to fall from ceiling ducts onto frail grandmothers in the night.

I said, "You need to drop us off in town."

"What?" Naomi said.

"Give me my phone, Hanna. Is it dead?"

"Um. No?"

"I'll get us a hotel room."

Naomi said, "You can stay with me."

"I'll rent a car. We'll come out tomorrow." It was getting on for dusk.

"Your car's at my place."

I cocked my head.

"Well. The car from, you know, Hanna's house. It didn't get sold with the rest of the estate. It's a decent car, and we thought you'd probably need it. You can't really have kids and not have a car."

"We live in Toronto."

"Even so."

"I still want a hotel room."

She sighed. "Fine. Where do you want to go?"

She left us at one of a line of almost-nameless hotels near the airport. Our suitcases had plastic-bag supplements of detritus acquired on the road.

I'd been prepared to walk, but the first place I chose had rooms, and, they proudly informed me with a glance at Hanna, a pool and waterslide. "Would you like a room overlooking it?"

I hadn't realized hotels were still being built like that, with a central "tropical paradise" space of pool and decking surrounded by sturdy plants and a poolside restaurant. It echoed the "good" hotels The Innocents had occasionally been able to afford on tour.

Hanna said, "I don't have a swimsuit."

"Do you have panties?"

"Allison."

I said, "I'll lend you a tank bra. You can swim like that. Tell them it's one of those mismatched bikinis." I needed a car. I didn't want to go shopping again.

Hanna refused.

The hotel was airport-affiliated, and they had car rentals. I paid for one, and at seven at night, we slid into a Value Village parking lot. I said, "Whatever you get is just for now. Pick something."

This was what my childhood was like, when we were in Canada — second-hand swimsuits and short-notice shopping. It triggered a moment of realization that, in spite of twenty-five years of struggle against it, I'd turned into my mother.

I picked myself out a bikini. It had probably been designed by a teenager to be worn by a teenager. I found a black T-shirt to wear over top. It said,

I love my husband with all my ass

I'd say 'heart'

But my ass is bigger

It was a Tuesday night, but it was summer, and at eight-something the pool was still crawling with screaming children, with and without parents. On the far side from us, there was some kind of church group having a pizza party, inspiring Hanna to demand pizza.

She only liked Hawaiian.

I ordered from the same service I'd always called when I was still a Winnipegger. One Hawaiian, one tomato artichoke. Airport Rest House. Room 147.

I ate pizza in my swimsuit, watching Hanna swim with a whirl of girls who seemed to have absorbed her. They moved in a single body out of the pool and up the three flights of stairs to the waterslide, reappearing intermittently. The pizza got cold waiting for her, and I fell asleep on the deck chair. She woke me up, eventually.

"The pool's closed."

"Okay."

"Can I watch TV?"

"Go nuts."

I took a shower. Walked out drying my hair and watched her stare at me in horror. "Put clothes on!"

"I just need to air dry for a bit."

"You're naked. And you're old. Put clothes on."

I went back into the bathroom.

I looked objectively good, something reaffirmed by the still-unsigned contract to host a still-in-development talk show on television, Saturday nights, next year. They'd taken pictures and done screen tests. We were close to finalizing.

I was, in the proposal text, "direct, subtly glamorous, and sexy in a still-got-it Gen-X way." Likely to appeal to male viewers as well as female. Good voice, good face. Nice tits under an expensive, understated black pullover.

Happy Saturday, Canada. This is . . . title pending.

I found a T-shirt and panties in my bag, and a book from the Value Village haul. Went back out.

I said, "I'm going to read, and then I'm going to sleep. You can watch TV all night if you want, but try not to make it so loud that they send security to tell me to tell you to turn it down."

If there'd been a mini-bar, I'd have considered a drink. There wasn't. The fridge was simply an amenity, holding leftover sodas and cold pizza. The room smelled like chlorine and garlic.

"Also, I think breakfast ends at 10. I'll be up at my usual. I'm hitting the road at ten-thirty. Time your sleep accordingly."

Hanna hadn't turned her bedside lamp on. When I turned mine off, the room was lit only by the television and light seeping from around the curtains that blocked the atrium view.

Sleep in motel rooms had always been a translucent thing for me. I'd toured for years with my sleep fractured by the light that seeped in under my eyelids. I woke up and went back down and dreamed television shows, too strung-out to demand that the screen extinguish its programming and settle into pre-industrial silence.

Years of childhood spent with nights as dark as a town where the generators shut down at 8 p.m.

I woke, hours later, from dreaming about snakes. Hanna was asleep with the TV on. I turned it off, opened the curtains and stared at the pool deck, desperate for unavailable for fresh air.

The pool wasn't open, officially, but I could unlock the door. The chair I'd commandeered the night before was still there. I settled into it with my phone, digging through work messages and watching the minutes slide out of the sixth hour of the day.

When I flicked over to text messages, Kara's question still hung there: *Do you want to go be big in Japan?*

I typed, *yes*. Went back into the room and took another shower, used the machine to make terrible coffee, then turned the TV back on. Watched it on low volume until Hanna stirred.

She said, still buried in covers, "I want to go swimming."

"So go. There's a lifeguard. You can have an hour."

My phone buzzed. Kara calling.

In Toronto, it was an hour later. Still early. I picked it up.

"You've decided to stop ignoring me?"

"I was just . . . it's been an awful couple of months."

"You could have told me about it."

"I don't know. Maybe. I wanted to say something. And then I didn't, and then I started to feel sick every time I opened my text messages. And then I read them in the middle of the night and I just said *yes*, you know?"

"We're going to need to talk."

"Okay. Do you want to come over?"

"You're funny."

"I'm hilarious. I'm also in Winnipeg. Airport Rest House. Come up and I'll smuggle you in for complimentary breakfast."

∷◌∷

Since the last time we'd seen each other, Kara had become the proud owner of a

1997 Honda Accord. It was oddly sporty, a red little two-doored thing that managed to conceal its age and rust. She showed it to me when I met her outside. The back seat was full of papers and library books.

Dr. Kara Campbell, PhD in Women's Studies, established freeway-flier, moving from campus to campus covering other people's classes to keep herself fed, looked as ragged as when we'd been stray children. I wondered if I'd have needed to buy her breakfast, if we hadn't been planning to steal it. Whether I should have met her somewhere that I could buy her breakfast properly. Ask her to conquer my family for me. Introduce her to Hanna when she wasn't chlorine-laced and soaking wet.

As it was, Hanna didn't have to put on real clothes. The breakfast buffet was served in the restaurant next to the pool deck, and she wasn't the only kid in a wet suit, sitting on a towel.

I thought, *This is nice.* As though it were entirely usual, eating warm, rubbery eggs in a chlorinated faux-tropical atmosphere, and I was just acknowledging the pleasantness of my life, Vonnegut-style. Kara had lit up at the buffet, which was a little better than I'd been expecting, and had made herself waffles on the only-slightly-dodgy machine. The fruit tray had given her a range of toppings, and from somewhere she'd raised canned whipped cream to go on the lot. Hanna's eyes widened, and she pushed away her half-eaten bacon and eggs.

"I want what she's having."

Kara raised an eyebrow. "Yeah?" I remembered hours she'd spent practicing that move, learning to move her eyebrows independently.

"Yes, please."

"Okay. Go pick your fruit."

I went with them, abandoning my plate, and made myself a new mug of coffee. Kara said, "You still do that?"

I'd learned early not to go back to an abandoned drink. I couldn't remember what town we'd been in, but I did remember not remembering anything after reclaiming my rye-and-coke during the interval of a show, and Mary-Beth holding my hair out of my face while I vomited the next day.

"Habit."

"It's not a bad one. Watch me walk out of here with half this buffet in my purse."

"Are you okay?"

"I'm fine. I'd just rather be touring, even in Japan, even for shit tour money, than working as a sessional lecturer."

"I should have come to your thesis defense."

"You sent me a stethoscope. That was nice."

I had. The florist had sent me a picture of the finished product, medical rubber wrapped around hideous orange lilies, and the card that said *Congratulations "doc"*.

"I didn't tell them to put 'doc' in quotation marks. I'm aware that you're a real doctor."

"Yeah. What in the name of God are you doing here?"

"My sister kidnapped us. I managed to jump and roll on the Perimeter Highway."

"Your sister?"

"The younger one. Naomi. She had this whole thing about our mom, and emotional labour, and the word *responsibility* got used a lot, and then she just stuffed me in a car with her sticky, sticky children."

Hanna, coated in fruit juice, zipped up to deposit a double-handful of melon onto the hot waffles. "Thank you!"

Kara snorted.

"I'm aware I'm a terrible mother."

"You're not that bad."

"You speak from a stunning lack of knowledge."

"Yeah. But I do still love you." She looked at our table. "Jesus, she's huge."

Kara was Hanna's godmother, though I suspected that Ethan and Claudia had arranged for a more conventional one, later. Kara and Mary-Beth had been with me when I went into labour, and she'd read a book and alternately helped me swear through the first five hours. When I'd been wide-eyed and unable to make decisions, Kara had explained the necessity of the caesarean to me. After, we'd stared together at tiny, warped infant Hanna. I'd said, "I have no idea what to do."

Kara studied the baby without picking her up, then grabbed the brown plastic water cup from the nightstand. Took the baby's hat off and sloshed a little on her. Replaced the hat. Said, *Welcome to the world, tiny bitch. Hang in there.*

"If we go to Japan, what happens to Hanna?"

"You don't think she'd like touring? We could demand a tutor as part of our rider. They must have loads of them for all those child-star *idoru*."

"She's not actually in school," I said.

Pause. "What?"

"I have some problems with authority."

"What's she doing?"

"Home schooling. Un-schooling. She goes to museums with Eden. He gets her to write. She seems okay."

"Didn't she put a glass through your face?"

"Who told you about that?"

"Mary-Beth. Anyone would think she was your daughter, the way she breaks shit."

I said, "I actually do want to go to Japan, I think. I just don't have any idea how I can."

"Name the barriers."

"Work. Hanna. My godawful family that somehow tracked me down."

"Anything else?"

"I think Eden would miss me?"

"You could bring him. Maybe he could get a grant to make a movie about us?"

"You said *grant*. You're such a grad student."

"I graduated, thank you, but I still believe in making the government pay for things. Especially art. Fuck, someone should pay for it."

A vacationing family looked up from their group prayer. They gathered their plates and moved away from the buffet, ironically toward Hanna, who sat alone, devouring whipped cream and waffles.

"How big of a problem is work?"

"I don't know. A lot? I mean, not for them. I think there's a line of people out the door who want my job."

"Anything else on the horizon?"

"A TV show, maybe. Not this year. Maybe next year."

"Then you have time."

"Naomi says my mom's sick."

"Good for her."

"Sick and it's my turn to take care of her."

Kara snorted. "Do you want me to ask my mom to look in on her?"

I tried to imagine Diane in full social-worker drag, facing my mother.

"I shouldn't ask that."

"Go to the bathroom and I'll ask her while you're gone. Then you can take me out and buy me things, glamour-girl."

I said, "If I go to the bathroom, don't ask her. I'll think of something."

I went to the bathroom. Looked in the mirror and considered that if I didn't go myself, Kara might actually send her mother in my place.

When I came back, I said, "Did you call?"

"No."

"Thank god. So I guess I owe you one. What do you want in return?"

"I want you to take me thrift shopping and buy me things."

"Hell, I'll buy you things that haven't even belonged to anyone before."

"Tempting, but against my anti-capitalist principles. Ask Hanna what she wants to do. We can go from there."

Hanna wanted to go to Waterfalls. She said it was a waterslide park. Kara said, "But I don't have a swimsuit."

"You can wear bra and panties. Allison apparently thinks that's okay." She darted away.

"Alli, I haven't worn a bra in *years*."

"I'll lend you one. Or you can go topless and tell them it's a political statement." She grinned. "We'll be kicked out in no time."

"Well, if it makes the news, you can call it free publicity." Pause. "Do you think we should tell Mary-Beth?"

"I phoned her already. You were in the bathroom for ages. Steal me a towel from the bathroom, girl. Take me to the beach."

~ *32* ~

Consumption

Waterfalls lay outside the city, northwest of the Perimeter Highway. Winnipeg was centred in the flattest imaginable country, a floodplain that extended for almost a hundred miles along the two intersecting rivers, and when the city didn't block the view you could see forever, see the lines of towns dotted along the paved roads and the clumped farms spreading out towards the planet's curve. It was a place for vertigo. Waterfalls loomed, there. They'd built it into a garbage hill, so that the slides weren't raised above the ground so much as ranged along an artificial ridge. The primary-coloured plastic tubes were visible from a long way off.

The parking lot wasn't as massive as I might have expected, and it was only half full. It was still early.

Hanna was the kind of unearthly pale that only comes from living nocturnally, almost entirely indoors. One shoulder had a faint sunburn from her hours in Naomi's car.

My watch said 10:37. Neuenheim was back ten minutes down the highway, up the Perimeter again, and northward.

I'd promised. I imagined Naomi marching in to Waterfalls in a knee-length swim-skirt, followed by a line of children, hunting me down if I didn't show.

I dug money out of my wallet — all my cash, then a plastic card to go with it. A Sharpie.

I said to Kara, "Give me your arm." High up, near her shoulder and on the inside, I inked a four-digit code. "Use that."

"Alli."

"If I don't go now, I won't go. And then Naomi will come after me. But there's no reason Hanna should have to go, or you. Take my bikini and have a day of it. Buy yourself terrible food and take pictures of Hanna and we can have dinner later."

"You'll have my car."

We were miles from anywhere. I wondered if a cab company would come out this far, just to collect two wet people.

"I'll come back. Three hours. If I'm longer, call an airport limo or something and make me pay for it."

"You're just going to give me your daughter?"

"If I'd given her to you in the first place, I think we could have prevented a world of hurt."

"Alli."

"It's true."

"She's in the car. And she isn't deaf."

Hanna gave every impression of being deaf. She was focussed on my phone's screen, listening with headphones. When I reached for it, she glanced at me blankly. I said, "We're here. Go with Kara and I'll be back in a little bit."

"Where are you going?"

"To talk to some people."

"Are you going to see Grandma Alma without me?"

No. "Yes. She and I need to talk. Go swimming. I promise I'll be back." Implacable girl-look. "I'll buy you things."

"Yes, you will." She gathered her things.

Kara said, "I shouldn't take your money, but I'm going to, and I'm going to buy overpriced lunch for both of us, and maybe surfing lessons if they're selling surfing lessons."

She got out. I watched them pad across the asphalt to the turnstile gates. Backed the car up, carefully, and turned back toward the highway.

I missed my exit and had to pull out at a service area, program my phone to navigate me, and try again. I had to drive out, down into the city, loop around a block, and come out again, just to legally turn around. Kara's car smelled like chlorine from the hotel pool, and I sat for a while pulled in by my turnaround, considering whether I wouldn't rather go swimming, burn my skin hard enough to shed layers, and disappear with Hanna and Kara into Winnipeg until Eden could catch up with us.

You can, if you want, avoid confrontations with some people forever. I didn't suppose that Naomi was strong enough to physically carry me into my mother's house. But it was ridiculous, too, to have travelled passively all the way from Toronto only to melt into a terrified puddle at Winnipeg's city limits.

I did go north, finally. I took the main highway, the one I'd come down in a social worker's car after I'd walked away from the Hoeppners' farm, into the town and then into the police station, and told them they had to save me. That I'd been given away, turned into a child bride, forced into marriage, and fled. That I wasn't safe.

That if they sent me back I'd kill myself.

I don't know if I meant it, but they believed me. It was close enough in time to cult scandals across the country that they weren't going to risk my becoming the cover story of a national news magazine: *Sex cult escapee returned to bondage by police, killed.* Below that: *New investigation reveals infant corpses, possible victims of human sacrifice!*

I was good. I'd heard "witch" stories in a half-dozen countries. If you told those same stories just right, people anywhere in the world would believe you.

They gave me new clothes and a new home to flee from, and I went into Winnipeg like a newborn girl, an innocent waiting for a place to happen.

I texted Naomi from the edge of Neuenheim: *where does she live?*

I'll take you. Where are you now?

Where does she live?

She doesn't know you're coming.

Feel free to warn her. Where does she live?

She gave me an address. Neuenheim was bigger than I remembered, with new cul-de-sacs of massive houses on its edge. The interior, though, was still a simple grid, with Railway Avenue running parallel to the tracks, and 2nd Avenue east of that, moving sequentially up to 8th. Cross streets named for trees and fundamental concepts and family names. The house we'd lived in when I'd last been home had been sold and subjected to what I supposed must pass locally for gentrification: intensely coloured paint and container gardening. Someone had blessed it with a gazebo.

I went past that, and around the trailer park to the small houses that hadn't yet been expanded beyond their original frames. Their hedges had grown into massive walls of caragana and lilac that overwhelmed the sidewalk. Driveways, where driveways existed, were almost lost in that forest. No flowers, now, but in spring, I thought, the smell must be sweet to the edge of nauseating.

The house looked like one that had never met a gardener. In the back, because I did walk around the place, still avoiding the door, there was a vegetable garden cordoned off with orange twine, but with as many weeds as potatoes, and deep, mosquito-laded grass all around it.

It occurred to me that, in Naomi's absence, our mother had simply died. Some other family member had arranged the removal of her corpse, and the yard had been forgotten.

"Naomi?"

"Do I look like Naomi?"

"You look like a burglar."

She was as obviously my mother as any person could have been. I didn't look like Naomi, but Alma looked like me. If I'd aged into a slightly dazed hippie living alone at the edge of the civilized world, surrounded by vengeful matrons and slowly degenerating, I would look exactly like that. I would wear those inappropriately-bejewelled thrift-store jeans, and the T-shirt that said *Martyr Masochist or Maniac*, that I remembered from a nurse who'd worked relief on the famine in Ethiopia. We met her at a mission retreat, swapped clothes and stories, and she'd had that shirt.

I remembered, because I'd been learning to sight-read, and I'd asked, loudly, "What's a may-zo-chist?"

And the nurse had said, "Masochist, baby. Someone who loves suffering. It's *martyr, masochist, or maniac* because anyone who does relief work is one of those things. I'm a maniac. Your mother is a martyr."

"I don't want to be a masochist!" This absurd memory of tearing up, ready to scream that this was the only job still available.

"Try not to be one," she told me. "Maniac is always best. There's room in that camp for you, too."

She'd said my mother was a martyr, but my mother thought the T-shirt was hilarious, and swapped the nurse a good skirt for it. The shirt had lost its yellow brilliance, and it was stained, the sleeves long gone, but she still had it, and I thought, *I'd never give that one away, either.*

"Did Naomi tell you I was coming?"

My mother cocked her head, thinking. She stood there for a long time. Too long. Said, "Oh, I think I missed a call from her. Wait a minute." And went back into the house, leaving the door open and me standing in the swirl of insects and daylight.

I followed her inside. The house wasn't dim, but dust hung in the chunky light pouring in the dirty windows. It was a mess. The floor had clothes on it, and dishes, and insects. There were ants trailing into a half-eaten sandwich, slowly dismantling it and removing fragments under the sideboard and into the walls. The television was on.

She had a television. I tried to process that.

Behind me, she said, "Naomi says you're Allison, but I think she's wrong about that. Allison's on the radio at this time every day."

My watch said 11:17. She was, technically, correct. *The Cure for Summer* ran excerpted interviews in our time slot, framed by a fill-in host who sang my praises and reminded listeners that I'd be back in the fall. The interviews, though, were still me, pieces of the past come back to fill in the blanks in summer media. I thought, *We're going to have to stop doing that. Nobody does seasons anymore. We'll lose people if we don't start broadcasting year-round.*

My mother pointedly turned on the kitchen radio. It was an old thing, leather-bound object straight out of the '60s.

My voice came out of it. The radio played my interview with The Inopera Company. They'd played a song live. We'd followed that up with a recording from their new album. What did they think fed their current wave of creativity?

Well, Allison, we came to this project with a real enthusiasm. . .

"It's a rerun, mom." I paused, flinching. The eeriness of my recorded voice made me wait for electronic feedback, or an electrical arc. None came. I was reminded of why I didn't listen to myself when I could avoid it. "Naomi said you were sick."

She didn't look terrible, but there was a pill caddy by the sink, and a hand-drawn schedule on the fridge full of doctor's appointments and medication reminders.

"I'm doing alright."

"What do you have?"

"I have nothing to do. I'm." Deep breath. Cough. "I'm glad you came to visit. How are you?"

"I'm good." She nodded, sat down at the table, and looked at me. "Did you want something in particular?"

"You were following me," I said.

"I beg your pardon?"

"Last time I was in Winnipeg. You were following me. I saw you outside the house." In the snow in her old-lady coat. Waiting for us to come out, like a paparazzo.

"You'd had such a terrible loss. And you didn't call. I thought it might have reminded you of Burundi. It would have reminded me. All that death. I thought you might need comforting."

The counter under my hands was gritty. Absently, I found a cloth in the sink and began wiping at the mess. "Nothing awful happened in Burundi."

"So many people died."

I thought. "Not when I was there. You went back without me."

"We had to fly you kids out. You were in Frankfurt for weeks without us. I was so scared for you. For us. For our friends. It didn't really spill across the border, but we kept waiting ... "

Again, I said, "Mom, you went back without me. You left me behind."

"No, that was later."

"It's not the sort of thing I'd forget. You went. Without me." It came out sharply. I had my back to her, rubbing hard at the laminate. There were ants on the counter, too.

"No, it was definitely when you were little, Naomi."

"I'm Allison, mom."

The shift into clarity was sudden, like a breaking window. Dementia, as simple as television.

"Oh. Okay."

"I'll be outside."

I went and sat in the front yard. The grass there was a little shorter, so the insects were less aggressive. I was still there when Naomi pulled up the curb. She got out and looked at me.

I said, "Why is she living on her own?"

"I've never been able to tell mom anything."

"The place is awful. I'm pretty sure there's a law against people living like that."

"It's not that bad. It's just an old house, and she leaves food lying around. That's how you get ants."

"If I pay for residential care in Winnipeg, will that make us even?"

Naomi snorted, "Oh, she can't go into residential care."

"She's demented."

"Is she weird?"

"She thinks I'm you."

"She forgot her meds. Rats. Hang on." Naomi let herself in the front door. Came back counting pills. "For ... I don't know. Looks like a week. Ohh." The word like a sigh. "Yeah, she probably seems demented."

"Is there a difference between *seems* and *is*?"

"Officially, yeah. Clinically bipolar is what Dr. Marwari says she is, but when she doesn't take her meds, it mimics dementia. She goes out for walks and disappears. We lost her for a week, once. That happens less often since I 'lost' her car keys. She went to Winnipeg and abandoned the car. Started hanging out with homeless people. She'd sit with them downtown while they were panhandling, but if anybody gave her money, she'd be all, 'Oh, no thank you,' like it was a green bean casserole or something. That's what the police told me. And we think that's how she got sick."

"Bipolar isn't contagious."

"Nope, it's hereditary, so she might have got it from you. How are you doing, by the way?"

"I brought my meds with me. Thanks for packing them."

"I didn't . . . oh. Oh man, I'm so sorry."

"I got them when I went back to pee. I'm okay. What does she have?"

"She has, wait for it."

I waited.

"TB."

"My mother has *consumption*?"

"Yeah, we caught that one just before it was bloody handkerchief time. It's really common if you're homeless. She was sleeping in a boarded-up house with, like, ten people, and they all had it. Public health workers came in to check if guys were taking their meds and found her. She still had her purse — no money, of course, or anything useful — but she still had her purse clutched in both hands, and they called me to come get her. By the time I got into town, though, they'd taken her up to Health Sciences for tests, and they wouldn't let her go for three days. After two, she definitely had TB, and that she had to take these pills *absolutely every day* for six months. Hilariously, she's been really, really good about it. She leaves her antidepressants in the box and just takes the TB meds."

Behind her, our mother said, "Creating drug-resistant tuberculosis is a serious thing. No sane person would fail to take her medication."

Sane, I thought, was arguable. My mother had pulled some fragments of herself together and made, apparently, coffee. She held out heavy white mugs. "Why don't you girls come in?"

I said, just to Naomi, "I go into convulsions if I miss too many days in a row. How is she standing up?"

"Different pills, I guess. But she broke a window, once, and she laid on the floor in the bathroom for a whole day, another time. I'd take her home with me, but if she comes to live with us, we all have to take TB meds. The kids, too."

"Is this why no one will come take care of her?"

"No, that's because she cursed Elaine out at church. I don't think that was symptomatic, by the way. Elaine's degenerating into witchery at a ferocious rate. But Ethan's dead, so she gets to be the martyr. Mom's the maniac. I've been the masochist for ages. It's your turn. She has six more weeks on her meds. Then, if her tests are clear, I think she should go live with you."

∽ 33 ∾
Red Velvet

Hanna and Kara were both sunburned. I'd collected them from the same parking lot and driven us to a Redbird restaurant, because I thought Hanna might enjoy it. She told us, cautiously, that she hadn't ever been.

I said, "That's practically a tragedy."

Hanna looked at me pointedly.

"No, I know. But this is a separate tragedy. Go pick out a booth."

Hanna poked cautiously at her coleslaw, but seemed to think her burger was edible. I got up and looked at the black and white photo posters of heritage moments in the city.

They'd re-styled Red's since I'd last eaten there. The new look was pointedly retro-diner, but with a glossy difference and a more stylish-looking menu than the one I remembered. Most of the booths were gone. In the absence of cracked red vinyl, only the photos of early restaurants and hockey games lingered. They'd added new photos, though, in the process of trying to make the chain hip. The Guess Who, circa 1970, peered down at our table. Down the wall were snapshots, grey-scaled and blown up to poster-size, of Bachman-Turner Overdrive, The Watchmen, Propagandhi, Crash Test Dummies.

They'd placed The Weakerthans on a different wall. Below that photo, someone had sharpied graffiti:

The Guess Who sucked

The Jets were lousy anyway

Someone else had replaced *were* with *are* in ballpoint pen. A retro-polaroid of some guys, presumably hockey players, eating in the restaurant, was tacked up with a pin. I took a picture of it with my phone, for posterity.

I said, "Good band photos."

"Is there one of you guys?" Hanna asked.

Kara shook her head. "I doubt it."

Our waiter came back to see if we needed more Cokes. He studied us for a minute. He reminded me of the madmen they used to have on the night shift when we came in for food after shows at three or four a.m., who'd be half an hour late with your fries but didn't care if you waited until morning. This one had more of a hipster sheen, complete with soft-focus tattoo sleeve, but he was a mess in a way I appreciated.

"Do you want dessert?"

I said, "I need red velvet cake."

He said, "Because that would make this the most Winnipeg scene ever?"

"Why?" Hanna demanded.

"The Innocents in Red's eating red velvet is pretty Winnipeg. If it was snowing, that'd help, and maybe if someone was stealing your car," he said.

"Did you do the graffiti?" I asked, nodding to the Weakerthans lyrics.

"Yeah. I'd tell you not to tell my manager, but I'm the manager. Don't tell head office. This place needed some grime so it wouldn't suck."

It seemed only polite, so I asked. "Are you in a band?"

"I'm in a shitty band. But now that we're friends, can you get us on *The Cure* anyway?"

"Hardly seems fair when there isn't even a picture of us on your walls."

He grinned. "Oh, we have one of *you* up in the kitchen. Not for public consumption."

"You're talking yourself out of a tip."

"I'm joking." He wasn't joking. I could tell.

"Get a good photo of us. Something from the high school days. Put us next to that one of the drive-in girls on roller skates. Or next to the women's washroom. Then we'll talk. And take that photo down or pick one of me with clothes on, or I *will* tell your head office and ruin a perfectly good terrible diner just for spite."

He walked away abruptly and stayed gone for a long time. Came back with extra cake, four pieces, and sat down with us. He said, "You're really as much of a bitch as they say you are, aren't you?"

Hanna said, "She's a witch. You talk to her that way and she'll cover your house with period blood."

I was a little startled. Then thrilled. Hanna's delivery was deadpan, flat, eerie. I was filled with an urge to take her shopping.

He said, "Who the hell are you?"

"Allison's my fairy godmother. The kind that comes and eats people I don't like while they're sleeping."

Kara, I realized, had been recording the exchange on her phone. She looked up, and said, "Dude, push off. Seriously."

He got up and walked away. Came back with the bill. "The cake's comped. And we're Hot Meat, my band, I mean, in case you ever care. Thanks for the experience."

Kara's apartment didn't really have room for both me and Hanna, but Kara shifted piles of books and clothes aside and hung the reeking swimsuits up in the tiny bathroom. The hall light beyond the bathroom was burned out. The kitchen table was buried in loose-leaf paper and books. Hair mounded in the corners, apparently without source. I looked around, "No cat?"

"Whitney died. Two . . . almost three months ago." Kara bent and gathered some of the drifting hair near her foot and threw it away. "She was old. I guess."

Like an inversion of our lives in university, when I'd been desperately poor, and she'd only been moderately. I had as many new clothes in my suitcase as Kara had in her apartment.

You can be the first riot grrrl with a PhD, but that won't buy you a tenure-track job, or a living cat, or a car that runs in all weather.

Emotional backwash knocked me over, and I retreated to lie down. I could hear Kara and Hanna in the kitchen, messing around with something.

"You didn't tell that guy she's your mom."

"Allison's . . . okay, I know she's my mom, like, my birth mom. But she's not my *mom*. She's just the crazy lady who came and took me away."

Pause. Pots and pans noises. Then, "Do you remember me at all?"

"No. But you seem nice."

"I was there when you were born, so I can guarantee, for whatever it's worth, that's she's your mother."

"Ew."

"Someday you, too, will have a friend you love enough that you'll watch people cut a hole in her and pull a baby out and you won't even barf, little girl. God it's hot in here." I heard her turn on the small air conditioner by the patio doors. "I'm not sure that helped, but. Well. I was there before you were born, too. You went on tour with us."

"I did?"

"Sure. You're the reason we called the tour *Barefoot and Pregnant.*"

"I don't understand."

"Because she was pregnant with you."

"But why *barefoot?*"

"Because they used to say that women should stay in the kitchen, barefoot and pregnant."

"Who said that?"

"I don't know. People. Your grandmas, probably."

"What do you think Allison and Grandma Alma said to each other?"

"I can't begin to imagine. Do you want a diet soda?"

"Yes please."

I rolled over in the bed. "No caffeine."

Kara came and shut the door, leaving me in stuffy shade. Her bed smelled like her body, and vaguely like cat. I tried to picture us living in a tour van again. If we were big enough in Japan, would we rate a bus, or was Japan too small for tour busses? Would we just take the subway from gig to gig?

Maybe from Japan we could go on some kind of extended tour of Asia. Play shows in Kazakhstan and Georgia. Sneak into Iran and play the underground punk clubs where girls tore off their government-mandated headscarves and started fistfights with strangers just because they could.

Vanish, accidentally, into the post-Soviet night, leaving Hanna to be scooped up by the wicked witch of the north.

I texted Eden. He answered, but not immediately, and in the meantime I did fall asleep. Woke up in fading daylight and found Kara and Hanna eating scrambled eggs and watching Netflix on Kara's laptop. I said, "Can Eden come with us to Japan?"

"Who's going to Japan?" Hanna asked.

"We are, maybe. The band. They've invited us."

"Why?"

"Because we're popular there, apparently."

"Why?"

"They're using our music in a TV show."

"Which one?"

We told her.

"Oh! I think that's on Sweetroll." Hanna took over the laptop and navigated. She keyed in a password and brought up a world of east Asian TV, neatly lined up for viewing. "Anime, Korean soaps, Japanese game shows. All subtitled in English. You have to pay to get stuff dubbed, and I don't have a credit card. Here it is."

We watched the show. It was live-action, most of the time, but sequences loaded with emotion shifted into watercolour animations. A girl in a baggy hoodie and knee socks went to a concert. It was full of boys who pushed her to the back of the room so that they could howl closer to the wall of sound. A guy walking past her said, *Too bad she's not pretty. Why did she come here?*

No one knows why ugly girls do anything.

The two men dissolved into a parody of laughter, became cartoons, and vanished. The heroine, too, had turned into a cartoon: a tiny, massive-headed gnome screaming into the air. Her animated rage pushed her forward, into the crowd again.

The band played on, in live-action. As the heroine regained her body, another girl, this one in jeans and a tank top approached. She held out a hand. She said, *I don't think you're an ugly girl. I think you're pretty.*

I hate boys like that!

Everybody hates boys like that.

I never get to stand at the front.

Me either. Do you think it's nice up there?

I think we should find out.

A swirl of action. The girls arrived at the front. The band paused playing to stare at them. Female faces looked around. *This is disappointing.*

The girls climbed up on stage. One took up the microphone. She sang, acapella. The crowd was mesmerized. End credits rolled.

"What did they call it?" Kara asked.

"*Girls to the Front,*" said Hanna.

"That's not even original."

Hanna said, "I like it, though. I like the song. What band is that?"

I said, "That's us. I mean, it's our song. They've re-recorded it in Japanese, and those vocals are godawful, but it's definitely us." To Kara, "Did we get paid for it?"

"You bet. It's paid two months of my student loans. Don't you read your bank statements?"

"Almost never. They make me feel sick."

"If you can live without looking, you have a sweet life, baby girl."

Hanna said, "You sang that?"

"Originally, yeah. And we all wrote it."

"What's it called?"

"*The Very Best Daughter.*"

Hanna looked like she had a question, but she didn't ask it. Her mouse-cursor hesitated over "add this show to my list," but she didn't click that either.

"What did Grandma Alma want?"

"Not much," I said. "She's been sick, I guess, and she isn't all there, right now."

"Did you talk to Auntie Naomi?"

"Yes."

"And?"

"Never mind."

Kara said, "Actually, I'd really like to know, myself."

I said, "Naomi thinks Alma should come and live with us. Me and Eden. But she isn't going to."

Kara nodded. Hanna asked, "Why not?"

I said, "She never came looking for me. Not once. I was on a plane sixty-seven minutes after I got the call about you. I made them hold a flight so I could get on it. I can do that. I'm famous. She only had to drive into Winnipeg to find me, and she never did."

Hanna said, "She came later."

"Twenty-odd years later. I don't owe her anything."

Later, in the car driving north through the city, Hanna said, "What do I owe you?"

"You don't owe me anything. That's not your job. I owe you things. Everything. I might be a shitty mom most of the time, but I know you're important. You're a whole person, and I made you, and I'm not going to let you get lost."

"What if you and Eden go to Japan?"

"Then you can come too, if you want."

Immediately, "What if I don't want to?"

Panic tingled through my forearms, convulsing my fingers around the wheel. I said, "I really, really want you to. But if you really didn't, then you could stay with your Auntie Naomi."

"What about Grandma Elaine?"

"Nope. Not ever. Not Grandma Alma, either. Only with people who'd care where you were, and make sure you were okay. Every single time."

I realized I was shaking. Traffic flowed around us, too thick to pull over, and I wondered what would happen if I fainted. Century Street mercifully split, creating exits on both sides, and I pulled left into the parking lot of some home-improvement business and parked.

Hanna was watching me, but only out of the corner of her eye. She reached for my phone, and I didn't knock her hand away. We sat for a while.

I held out my hand for the phone and checked it. Said, "Are you okay?"

"Uh-huh."

"I'm glad. We have to go to the airport, okay?"

"When?"

"Right now."

~ 34 ~
Shrine

Mary-Beth flew in from Vancouver and descended on our hotel room. Hanna studied us balefully, apparently trying to determine which one of us was going to force her from her bed. I told her, quietly, that Mary-Beth would either stay with Kara or get her own hotel room.

"Why don't we just all stay at the house?"

I cocked my head.

"You know. My house."

I had, just for a second, a vision of all of us in that house, pointedly ignoring bodily fluids still left on porous surfaces and sharing the main bathroom while keeping the master bath locked. I breathed through my nose. Nausea pushed at me; I pushed back. Reminded myself that I'd actually seen the cleaners restore the house, put it into pristine condition and turn it over to lawyers and realtors for a new existence as someone's undisrupted family home.

"They sold it, honey." That was true. Wayne had called me, then sent a letter showing the money safe in Hanna's trust. He'd apologized, pointed out that murder houses don't fetch high prices. I'd only stared at the number.

Ethan and Claudia had had mortgage insurance to go with their life insurance. Hanna's trust contained more money than I'd had cumulatively in my entire career.

"Then where's my *stuff*?"

Hanna's voice was high and sharp. Mary-Beth looked up from her phone conversation and stared at us.

"What?"

"Where's my stuff? My room stuff?" She paused. "Did they sell that too?"

"Your stuff's at our house in Toronto."

"That's, like, one bag's worth. I had things. Where are they now?" Her face had turned red. Now it was screwing up. If she'd had a glass object within reach, I'd have ducked.

Mary-Beth said, "They won't have thrown it out. I bet Allison can find out where it all is. Right?"

I said, "Sure."

"Why don't you go do that right now?"

Go where? But I gave them the room. Walked out to the parking lot, where it was hot and dusty and car exhaust hung over the pavement, and started making calls.

I came back in. "Your Grandma Elaine has it."

"Has what?"

"Everything, apparently. She took all the stuff from your room, and everything else she thought you might want. It's all safe and waiting for you."

"I want it."

"Okay. We can deal with that."

"Now."

I'd been out to Neuenheim that day already, to deal with my mother. I wasn't sure I could deal with Ethan's. Mary-Beth avoided my look, but she said, "We'll all go," like it was a completely reasonable idea. She left her bags on my bed and told me to get my purse.

"They might not be home," I said.

"So call."

I shook my head. "I don't think that's a good idea."

"Oh for fuck sake." Mary-Beth took my phone into the bathroom. She came back and handed it to me and said, "You weren't joking."

"How bad?"

"She said bring Hanna, yes, definitely, right now. And I can go in, but apparently you have to stay in the car. Who *is* this woman?"

"The witch who ruined my life."

"Melodramatic. I don't think your life's ruined, so try again. I mean, she's Ethan's mom . . . "

"She took his body and banned me from the funeral. That isn't nothing."

"Mmm. She definitely doesn't like you. Did you set her house on fire?"

"I didn't even sleep with her husband."

"Just her son. Well, I'll see if I can defuse this a little. Come on, you're driving."

I said, "I'm too tired. It's practically the middle of the night."

"It's 7:30. And last I heard you slept all afternoon. You'll be fine."

∷◦∷

Elaine and Marshall still lived on their farm, but the yard had acquired a second, prefabricated house, apparently occupied by one of Ethan's older brothers, his skirted and kerchiefed wife, and multiple children. The wife was a brighter, more stylish version of Naomi.

Stylish was the wrong word. She was a better seamstress, certainly. I suspected she'd sewn the dress herself, adapted from a 90s or 80s sewing pattern. But her makeup was flawless, complete with contouring and highlighter, so maybe *stylish* was right.

The space was schizophrenic. Elaine's garden was the garden I remembered, sprawling and efficient, with vegetables bordered by insect-repelling marigolds, and faux-marble pots of geraniums near the step. Across the yard, there were miniature lights strung from a wooden overhang, descending to a garden that most reminded me of the Mormon hipster housewife style blogs that we'd featured on *The Cure* the year after I took over hosting. Gorgeous, do-it-yourself with a designer's eye, intended to create the over-lit vision of a perfect domestic life.

Want to know the secret to our happiness? Feel free to click on the link at top right. Learn more about our church and community!

It was a new phenomenon to me, hipster Old Order Mennonites. *Prairie dresses: they're back! Long hair, don't care! Blog now for a place among the elect.*

Mary-Beth had taken Hanna in, leaving me in the car with the windows down. The evening fizzed with insects and alfalfa flower-scent.

I waited. Played with my phone. Got bored.

Behind the new house, there was a wall of flowering trees and an immaculate patch of grass that must have taken half the well's production to stay so lush. On that, she'd set up two white, wood-framed tents edged with pompons (hand made). Little girls in long dresses had crawled inside and now peeked out while their mother photographed them with a surprisingly massive, multi-lensed camera.

I stepped up behind her.

"What's your blog?" I asked.

She smiled. "Love Light Ana." Smiled wider when I stared. "The *Ana* is for Anabaptist."

Not, I thought, to be confused with the rest of the internet, where it was short for *anorexic*. But she might have created the confusion deliberately. Her face was narrow to the point of frailty, all while the youngest visible child was still crawling. How many more children in the house?

The girls dashed out of a tent and past their mother to the other side of the garden, passing under a clothesline hung with printed-out photos of flowers. They returned with a tiny frog, holding it up to their mother for examination.

"Hang on," she said. "I should shoot this."

"Who's she, momma?"

The girl studied me. "I think she's a friend of uncle Ethan's."

"Oh. It's sad he died." Pause. "Oh! Is Hanna here!"

"Yeah," I told them. "She is."

"Momma, can we go see her, momma?"

Momma. Keep your children away from the world beyond Pintrest and Instagram and they'll never call you anything that isn't perfectly picturesque.

"I bet she'll come over in a bit. Can you come back to the tents for a minute? I thought you could play with this," holding out a balloon, "by them."

To me, she said, "We made a bunch of these, me and Scott. They'll sell for more if the pictures are good."

That, at least, was familiar, the hand-crafted hustle of border Christians was generations old, and only a step removed from Amish quilting.

"Did you want one?"

I said, "Hanna's a bit big. And we don't really have a back yard."

"Oh. Are you in an apartment?"

"No, it's just mostly pavement."

"In Toronto." She thought. "I'm Innogen, by the way. Would you send me pictures?"

"Of Toronto?"

"Of your back yard. I might have some ideas."

"I don't think we're going to become outdoor people."

"Still. If I could get a foothold in Toronto…." She nodded. "Send me pictures."

"Excuse me, can I steal Allison?" Mary-Beth had a knack for inserting herself into conversations, but I was startled; I hadn't heard her come up behind me. "Alli, you need to see this."

I hadn't planned on going into the house, really, ever again, but Mary-Beth kept a hand clamped on my bicep and walked me through the door. She avoided the kitchen and basement, at least. Steered me down the hall to what had been Ethan's room.

I'd been expecting a shrine, but it wasn't to Ethan. Elaine had re-created Hanna's bedroom in that space, even to the paint on the walls. Posters were where they'd been, and stuffed animals in the same order on the bed. I couldn't have sworn to its accuracy, but Elaine was a woman to take pictures before she started a project, just to ensure that everything was perfect.

Hanna sat on the floor, silver-white carpeted like the house in Winnipeg, and a total mismatch to the house around us, and held up a T-shirt. She said, "None of my clothes fit."

It looked like she'd tried on a half-dozen outfits. I wasn't terribly attuned to what she wore, but even I could tell they were smaller than she was. Some of the clothes on the floor looked new.

I said, "Okay."

Elaine, in the doorway behind me, said, "We can get you new clothes, baby." Then, to me, "I'm glad you brought her here. It was the right thing."

"I'm sorry?"

"You know we'll be good parents to her."

I hadn't realized that I was actively afraid of Elaine. I knew I didn't like her, and that she didn't like me. I'd fantasized about screaming at her, but not seriously. I tried to speak and failed.

"Allison. Mom?" Hanna was still on the floor. "Are you ... do I have to live here now?"

"No," I told her. "No, we just came to get some of your stuff. As much as will fit in the car. Your grandma can send the rest to us, so we can get your room the way you want it."

"How much stuff will fit in the car?"

"I have no idea. Why don't you start loading up and find out? Try to leave room for the people to fit." I sounded, maybe too obviously, exactly like my mother when she was terrified and being rational about it, the way she'd sounded when we were carjacked in Lagos and had to get all of us kids out, with our passports, at gunpoint.

Elaine let Hanna pass, but she blocked me at the door. "You need to think about this. You aren't prepared to be her mother. You barely know her. Marshall and I have known her all her life. And we know about raising children." She smiled. Sweet, like a church-lady in a TV show. "Let her stay here."

"No." It wasn't something I had to think about. My skin hurt from the idea of her trapped in that house.

"Allison. Be reasonable."

I said, "You stole Ethan's *body.*"

"'Stole'? He was my *son.*"

"He was Claudia's husband, too." And mine, briefly.

"I'm sorry you never developed a sense of what family is," Elaine said, brittlely.

I pushed past her. Actually pushed her back against the wall and walked to the door. Made her chase me down the steps. *"Allison."*

I said, "I'll come back tomorrow with a truck. For Hanna's things. She's right; it's her room. I should have taken all of it when we left for Toronto the first time."

"Tomorrow?"

"I'll be here at ten. Earlier if I can get a truck earlier."

Hanna was there, by the car, watching us. She had the high-shouldered posture that built up preceding tears.

Elaine said, loudly, "Why don't you pick Hanna up tomorrow?"

Hanna blinked. Refocussed without tears and took a step forward.

"She could stay overnight. Just one more, in her room the way it was."

I said, "No."

"We're her grandparents. We should get to see her for one more night before you take her away forever."

Hanna said, "I don't have pajamas that fit."

"I have something you might like." The daughter-in-law had slipped over. She had the fading light behind her, and she glowed like an angel. Whirled and disappeared and came back from the house with her arms full of white.

The nightgown was sleeveless, and otherwise a Victorian fantasy of eyelet cotton. It was long, maybe too long, but Hanna was fascinated by it. Held out her hands and held the thing up to herself, letting the hem trail through the dirt.

She lit up. I'd missed Hanna's princess phase, or most of it, but its traces were still present. Elaine must have loved that, dressing her up, making a frozen-time doll she could capture in pictures.

Hanna said, "I want to stay over."

"What?"

"Allison, please," Elaine said. "One night. You can make whatever arrangements you need to, and Hanna can have some quiet time with her grandparents and her things. You can bring whoever you want in the morning." She paused. "I won't help you, but I won't stop you from taking whatever Hanna wants."

Mary-Beth said, "That's reasonable."

I didn't particularly want to be reasonable. Kara lurked behind the car, not commenting. Then she raised her hand and I saw she was recording the conversation on her phone. It hadn't occurred to me to do that.

I said, "She has to be ready to go at ten." It was almost ten at night. It was going to be dark as soon as the light finished bending over the horizon. Then I held out my phone to Hanna. I said, "Call Kara if you need *anything.*"

"Okay." Very serious.

I said, "If you call, I'll be here so fast you won't even believe it. I love you."

"Okay."

I waited.

"I love you, too."

My skin hurt all the way back to town, but Kara handed me her phone and I had a truck reserved before we reached the Perimeter Highway.

Mary-Beth never did get her own room. We'd shared two beds among the three of us for a quarter of our lives. Mary-Beth stayed up with me, packing clothes and sorting papers, while Kara read in the bathtub. Her sunburn was bothering her.

When had she had time to be sunburnt?

She'd spent the morning in the sun, with Hanna, and showered Hanna in sunscreen but forgotten herself. "Still today, Alli," she said. "You just forgot because you slept in the middle."

I said, "I don't even know how long I've been here."

"In Winnipeg or on earth?"

"Either one. I don't know. How early can I reasonably set the alarm?"

"You're wired. Stay up and read or something. Watch TV. We'll sleep, and we'll fill you full of coffee in the morning, and you can sleep after we've rescued your daughter, and then you'll be fine."

I did that. Without my phone, I felt vaguely naked. Nothing to play with while I watched television. Eventually, I probably did sleep a bit, stretched across the foot of one bed. Kara and Mary-Beth slept in the other one, curled slightly around each other unselfconsciously, as if they'd never been apart.

∷◉∷

When I was a kid, just once, we had to leave in the night.

I remember my mother waking me up while it was dark. I had a flannelette nightie on, with Care Bears silkscreened on the front, and socks, because I'd recently learned that there were people who wore socks to bed, and I wanted to try it.

I think it was just one sock, actually. I'd kicked off the other one. By the end of the day I only had one sock, but both my shoes. If I'd only had one sock on to begin with, it would explain one of my early-childhood mysteries.

My family had a van, ostensibly for church use but most of the time it func-tioned as a bus for the town, ferrying food and people through the mountains and southwest to Bujumbura when our passports had to be inspected or some-thing governmental sorted out. There was no formal Canadian embassy there, but there was a small office, and the Americans had a consulate we could work through, as long as we were helpful and polite. I suppose I thought when they loaded us into the van in the pre-dawn that we were headed there, for medical checkups or new paperwork. I had a level of faith in my parents, then, that I had trouble comprehending later. Enough that I fell asleep again without questioning why they were packing our things.

We spent three weeks in Kigali. There'd been a coup in Burundi, and the Catholics had crept over to our house to warn my parents that we should run. Just in case. Because they had small children. The priest, the couple of resident nuns, they would stay. They had no children except the ones in the village to worry about. They would guard our house.

They did guard our house. They even sent word to my mother, while we were in Kigali, to let her know that individual people were safe.

We'd only ever converted a dozen or so people away from the Catholic church, and I suppose we were more adorable than threatening. Or the ones who stayed behind really were filled with the kind of compassion that every church person I'd ever met pretended.

It was what I thought about when we showed up with the truck in Marshall and Elaine's yard and everyone was gone.

~ 35 ~
Border Christians

Eden wanted to take me back to Toronto, but he also wanted to be on the road, shooting music festival footage, and neither of those things happened. He met me in Winnipeg and sat in the police station and shook while I shook, offered up his phone to the investigators as proof of his location for the past four days. They let us leave by a service door so that we could hide from the cameras or flee or go and fix our faces and give a prepared statement to the press.

Public Broadcasting covered it, of course. Everyone did. Six months after Ethan's murder, and here was Hanna, gone. Hanna Winter-Hoeppner, daughter of *Cure* host and erstwhile punk musician Allison Winter, was formally missing, the subject of an Amber Alert.

That part had taken hours. I'd needed to prove that I had custody, and to do that I had to find Wayne Cardinal, and he had to find Ethan's papers, and we had to formally swear that Elaine and Marshall weren't Hanna's legal guardians before Hanna could formally become a stolen child. Eden was still on the road, coming in under RCMP escort along the slowest, narrowest stretch of the Trans-Canada highway. Mary-Beth was on the phone, looking for a lawyer.

I said I had Wayne.

"Wayne is Ethan's lawyer, Alli. You need your own."

Kara changed hotels for me. Once the police had dismissed her, she found my things, signed me out of the airport room and moved me downtown, to a tower half a block from the one where I'd found Hanna waiting for me in the winter.

I told her that. She said, "Shit. Do you want to move?"

"No. This is good. Can I pretend that's where she is? Over there?"

Elaine didn't take my phone. It was sitting on the farmhouse steps, screen smashed and battery melted, when we came to pick up Hanna.

Eventually, Mary-Beth fed me a pair of desperate-housewife-strength tranquillizers, and while I was asleep, gave a brief and dignified press statement asking for help, privacy, and Hanna's safe return.

I woke up with Eden wrapped against me. I had to ease myself free from his grip, and at the edge of the bed I found he'd clamped one hand around the hem of my T-shirt. I left it with him, got dressed out of my messy suitcase and watched him gather my abandoned pajamas back to his chest.

Mary-Beth was settled at the table. In better focus after sleeping, I could grasp that she'd made arrangements with the expertise of an international fixer. We were in a suite, simple brown upholstery and a kitchenette, with branching bedrooms. Mary-Beth had piles of paper and two phones.

The kitchen was full of casseroles.

Mary-Beth muted her phone and looked over. "Your sister's here. She brought food. And her entire church. They're a bit freaked out."

"Do you have any more tranquillizers?" I asked.

"Not that you can have right now. Eat something. There's breakfast casserole, lunch casserole, dinner casserole. There's, like, six kinds of cake. That machine in the corner makes coffee. How's Eden?"

"He's asleep."

She nodded. "He can't leave until the police talk to him." I blinked. "Marine arranged it so he could sleep first, but they do want to question him when he's coherent."

"I don't know Marine."

"Marine is your lawyer. She's lovely. She and I did undergrad together. She does family law, and weddings, and criminal consultation but only for people who aren't charged with anything, so she's perfect. She used to come to our shows, actually. She had the stoplight hair."

The hair pulled me into focus. Marine had had to bleach her hair white to get that colour to work, and it was so vivid you could see it a block away. She once bit a guy once who groped her while she was dancing.

"In other news, I bought you a new phone. You're welcome." She pushed the box toward me. "The sim card was salvageable from your old one. If anything was in the cloud and you remember your passwords, you should be able to get maybe eighty per cent of your stuff back. After you've got that set up, and eaten something, you need to call work."

"I'm on holiday."

"You're news now. And you're a cultural property that more or less belongs to them, so they need to talk to you, and you should talk to them, and you need to be prepared. The documentarians are already on the ground. There are going to be in-depth reports, probably as early as tonight. I hope you didn't have any secrets left."

⦙⦙⦿⦙⦙⦙

The messages waiting when my phone awakened were mostly from legal at the broadcast office. Two others were from Linda Jansen. We weren't friends, exactly, but she'd given me her go-bag on what had been, then, the worst day of my life, and she treated me with the respect of a journalist instead of a fluff-broadcaster, which had left me more or less permanently grateful.

I called her back.

"Are you alright?"

"No."

"No, of course you aren't. Listen. There's no way we can treat this as not-news. We'd get in shit from the ombudsman, and anyway it would be wildly unethical. So we have to cover you. But none of us wanted to do it, here in the office, because we know you, so they're bringing in a couple of freelancers and some Winnipeg people who came in after you left."

"Okay, that's out of the way. What can we do for you?"

I said, "I have no idea. I just woke up." That was a lie. It had been more than an hour, but I'd locked myself in the bathroom with Eden as a buffer between me and the crowd forming in the kitchenette, and I was prepared to plead sleep to anyone who asked.

"How about information? What do you know?"

"Nothing, basically."

"Right. That's where we can help you. Obviously, I can't always tell you everything we know, but I can tell you more than the police will, because we have people on the ground. If this keeps up for more than a day, we're going to have to create a sub-page on the network site just for your stuff."

I had no idea how long Hanna had been gone. Had they taken her and run as soon as we left the yard?

Was the lifestyle-website pixie still there, fielding police questions and taking artfully-filtered pictures of the chaos in her yard, or had she gone too?

I said, "You won't need to."

"Allison. Realistically, we probably will."

"We have seventy-two hours, right?"

There was a pause on the other end of the line. "If you're right and your in-laws took her, this isn't a murder case. It's just custodial interference, jacked up with celebrity appeal. There's no time limit on that."

I hung up. Linda texted me an apology, brief and professional, then commenced sending me files.

There were no Hoeppners left in Neuenheim. It wasn't clear whether they'd all left together, or gone separately, but they were nonetheless gone, their houses locked up and the contents of their fridges left in the church kitchen for redistribution to the poor. Animals had been left with water and messages for neighbours to feed them/take them/keep them. A note at the church expressed a wish for field crops to be harvested by anyone with facilities and devoted entirely to the church's international relief program.

Gone in the night.

My mother had told me, when I was little, that Mennonites were people who'd survived by learning how to leave a place without crying over it. It wasn't a statement that matched the lamentations I heard as a small kid regarding grandparents slaughtered in the Russian revolution, or violence in France in the seventeenth century, but it motivated our family's tenure in a half-dozen countries. I'd been fooled by Elaine and Marshall's farming and their stable, furniture-owning life. It hadn't occurred to me that they knew how to run.

Of course they did. Elaine came from a closed colony. She had cousins in Mexico and across central America and deep in the Paraguayan interior. Anabaptist colonies lurked in countries that didn't regulate them, filled with women in prairie dresses even in tropical heat and men who ensured that no one learned Spanish in addition to the collectively-spoken Low German. We sent them aid, sometimes, but they never sent missionaries out to join us, and my mother had said they were reproducing the culture that nearly saw us wiped out in Russia, and if another holocaust loomed, we were going to be faced with a lot of work to save them.

She never once suggested letting them die on the grounds that, really, it was all their own fault.

I called up a map on my phone and studied the number of international boundaries between Paraguay and Canada. It would have been more comforting if we hadn't swept Odanna across the border with no more than a passing glance.

After my first meltdown, I didn't cry again. We found me a doctor who offered a scrip to suppress panic attacks, and carried on. Time passed, and the churchgoers retreated north to tend to their own families. The police officially released us to go our own ways.

Mary-Beth had another lawyer waiting for me in the Lower Mainland, one who specialized in international child abductions, a friend of the entertainment lawyer who'd been sitting with a performance contract for weeks while I searched for my daughter and news services investigated ever more intimate corners of my life.

Marine tracked where the lines of inquiry were headed and got a judge to formally lock my mental health records. They weren't legal to publish in Canada, but a handful of American media outlets had been caught up in the whirl, and they were less likely to be bound by court restrictions.

We waited for explosions from that corner that didn't come.

Instead, they found my mother.

Naomi's church women had softened on my mother after Hanna and her grandparents disappeared. They were dubious of Winters generally, but none of us had stolen a child and fled the country. Her home care resumed. Community members volunteered to look in on Mrs. Winter and ensure she was well.

They probably talked to reporters. Or else the reporters simply found her. Neuenheim was small. Second-string journalists might simply have been stretching their legs, noticed the witch-house in the trees, and asked after it.

Under pastoral supervision, my mother was back on her meds and coherent enough to legally consent to an interview. Not with Public Broadcasting, but Linda got wind and let me know, and I dispatched Marine to see if we could stop them from going to air.

We couldn't.

My mother had certain things to say.

They aired her interview on the third network, on television, and then websites picked it up. On film, my mother looked serenely Christian: long skirt, long hair, slightly elevated expression of absolute forgiveness for others.

"I don't think most people can imagine the kind of pain they were going through," she said. So calmly, like it was about people in a Bible story she was interpreting for an unfamiliar reader. "To have lost their son. I wish that they had made other choices, but I know that Elaine is a woman fiercely protective of her family."

"Do you believe, then, that Mrs. Hoeppner was right to kidnap your grand-daughter?"

"Well, no. But I understand *why* she did it. I hope that she will reach a point where her heart can comprehend something beyond her current grief, and then she will return to us."

"How do you respond to reports that Mrs. Hoeppner orchestrated a shunning campaign against you in the months leading up to the kidnapping?"

"I think the rumours of her malice are exaggerated."

The end of the interview was the part that pundits sampled into mini clips and shared online.

"Do you think your daughter deserves to get her daughter back?"

"I think Allison has been deeply troubled for much of her life. But perhaps I have too, and no mother should suffer as she is suffering."

"Is your daughter a good mother?"

"I don't know. No. Maybe."

It repeated on social media. Hot takes exploded online: is kidnapping ever the right thing to do? Should grandparents have rights? Who dares to name the bad mother?

My mother sent me a letter, since I wouldn't take her calls, in which she explained, carefully, that she had corrected herself afterwards, only they hadn't aired that. She didn't mean that I was a bad mother, only that she didn't know me well enough to judge.

I didn't answer. We were in Vancouver by then, staying in a bungalow in New Westminster while we rehearsed.

The music seemed like a good plan, and it was the only one I had. I was unable to persuade myself to go back to Toronto without Hanna, and going to Japan provided a block of time when I could avoid the vestiges of my regular life.

We did everything we could in Winnipeg before I left. I'd made a video at the church's Central Committee office, in which I sat in a chair with a high-necked blouse on and my hair pinned up, and recited a script we'd prepared about the agony of a mother and the loss of a child, reiterating the importance of our bond and reminding Old Order folk peering at community computer screens that a lost child affected all of us. That Hanna was mine, my daughter. That I missed her.

We had me repeat the words my mother said later, too, about feeling compassion for Elaine's grief. I asked them to pray with her, if they met her, and help her to understand that she wouldn't heal her heart by separating another mother from her child. That God's love could mend families, but only by acting through us.

I called child-find agencies. They took all of Hanna's information, and said they'd try, but that it would be slow. If I was frantic, if I was really serious, I should consider hiring a private investigator.

I looked into private investigators. Their fees, even the moderate ones, made me nauseous, especially when I calculated them over months or years. There were no sliding scales for celebrities, even tax-funded ones with limited means. They might easily be looking for Hanna much longer than the months of her life she'd spent with me in total thus far. When they found her, if they could dig through the immovable Anabaptist wall, would I recognize her?

I couldn't remember Hanna's face. She'd changed a half-dozen times since I'd met her, and she wasn't stable in my mind. She was growing. Changing. She was going to be twelve in seven weeks.

I needed something to do. Public Broadcasting placed me on compassionate leave and informed me after the fact. They were deeply sympathetic, and would maintain my salary in the interim, but the new season of *The Cure* would open without me.

They couldn't imagine that I would want to disrupt the search for my daughter with day-to-day production concerns. Nor did they expect me to.

It would, of course, be better for the show if my personal tragedies didn't disrupt it. *The Cure* had survived one scandal already, but two might destroy it. Someone online had referred to the show already as *The Curse*.

In any case, the administration wanted me to know that they wished me the very best.

I had nothing to do. I needed something to do. A different skin to wear until I could find my mortal one and crawl back into it.

So: sign the contracts. Change cities. In Vancouver no one knew me, and I could move as though invisible.

Japan was waiting. Our audience there was getting older by the week. If we didn't dive through that window, it would close.

～ 36 ～

Borges' Psychosis

den's rehearsal footage of us was gorgeous.

The Innocents had never been live-filmed before, but I'd spent half a decade living with Eden, and I'd come to perceive the camera as an unavoidable extension of his mind. He'd filmed me around the house when we first lived together, edited together footage that he explained was his way of persuading himself that I was really there.

He kept taking pictures of me, still and moving, while we were in Vancouver, but I asked him not to show them to me. I was losing weight again, and I looked awful. Too old to be that thin without carrying *haggard* on my shoulders.

The agent who dropped in to check on us said, loudly, "Tell her to eat something."

I didn't want to eat anything. I'd been counting food, mouthful by mouthful, for weeks, almost since Hanna's disappearance. In the hours after we found the house empty, I'd tried to centre myself. I counted my breaths. I imagined my skeleton, chakras, my calm psyche beneath the screaming mind. What finally worked was tracking food, back to the last meal Hanna and I had shared. Fried late lunch at Red's. I'd recounted it, bite by bite, and meditated on that until the grease suddenly repeated on me, and I vomited.

Since then, everything made me sick. I ate when I could persuade myself to, but it had to be food I'd never eaten with Hanna present. Food with no connection to her.

Vancouver made eating easier. I made runs to the Japanese market on Clarke Drive and loaded bags with cold dumplings whose names I didn't know. I bought food with no English on the packaging, sodas with flavours I'd never imagined. Tried to eat it mostly in the night, and kept down half, and vomited when I couldn't remember what Hanna looked like while I ate.

In comparison, music was easy. I hadn't played, except jokingly, in years, but bass was simple, and the vocals were etched into my brain. Producers came in to look at us and said, after, "Not so fierce, please. Angry, yes, but happy too. Can you bring happy?"

I said, "No."

"We'll try," said Mary-Beth.

Mary-Beth had spent the years since The Innocents working as a session musician and small-time producer, and then as the connecting web for other musicians and techs throughout the Lower Mainland. She knew everyone. She stayed with us most nights, but her home was a condo high up in the downtown glass spires.

After they told me to eat more, Mary-Beth took me home with her. She'd found an app that let Eden monitor my pulse through an odd plastic wristwatch, and she promised I'd stay in the city, and alive, until morning.

We went by car into the depths of underground parking and then up by elevator while my ears popped. There was no exterior view, at least. I could feel the altitude changing and the proximity of the ocean. The hallway into which we disembarked was anonymous, a carpeted anywhere-space at odds with the building's sense of itself. Doors stood close together, each apartment pushing outward toward its glass face.

The apartment itself was tiny. Hard to internalize that a tower manifesting this kind of money could be so cramped, but I'd never before faced the ugly mechanics of the real estate market. One bedroom, one bath, one bonus room, a view of the city that extended nearly to Coal Harbour, refracting off other shards of glass.

I said, "Jesus, you're good at being rich."

"Thanks. I mean, I know you more or less meant that as a compliment, so. Welcome to mine."

Her furniture was singular, gorgeous, and someone had dusted it, but she sat on it like it didn't matter, and she fed me the same raspberry-vodka coolers we'd drunk as broke twenty-something band girls.

I said, "I should move out here."

"You think?"

"Definitely. Maybe. I'd have to get up so early. For the east coast feed."

"I thought you were shifting to television."

I nodded. "We could live here. Can you have kids in a place like this?"

"Not in this building. I had to sign a document. They probably would have demanded an ovarian scan if they could. Kids can visit for a maximum of thirty-six hours." She paused. "I could move."

"We'll see. Put Kara where?"

"She can live with you."

"Hanna's going to want her own room."

"Hanna's going to like the benefits of coastal living. How drunk are you?"

"Barely buzzed by tour standards. Why?"

"Let me show you something."

▚▚▚

We didn't descend as far as the street. On the fifth floor, accessible by key card, the elevator doors opened into saline half-darkness.

The deck lights were barely present, but the pool was lit from below, creating a sense of endless water, enough to drown in, fifty-seven feet above sea level.

It was cold. Designed for aggressively dedicated professionals who maintained their swimmers' bodies in the pre-dawn and then forged out into the city's humidity to generate the swarms of money they needed to continue living here.

I plunged, shallow, not careful enough of the *no diving* warning tiled into the deck, and jammed my fingertips against the pool bottom. Ripped a fingernail down deep and stayed under the water anyway, letting the salt sting my eyes and the blood trail faintly out from the wounded edge. Held my breath for twenty, twenty-eight, thirty-one seconds, and then pushed upwards, kicked for a breath and a second one, and went under again.

The water wasn't as deep as it looked or as I wanted it to be.

Mary-Beth said, "It's not supposed to be deep. You're only supposed to use the top of it."

"I'm not sure I like it."

"Flatten out. Feel free to float face down. If it looks like you're going to drown, I can flip you over."

"You could leave me."

"That's a bit melodramatic even for you, and if I let you drown, the residents' association is going to have me out of here for good."

She read on the deck and I swam for an hour. Breaststroke pulled at my shoulders.

Muscles tore microscopically. I loved how much it hurt.

I came out of the water freezing. The hot tub stood to the side, ready to be activated, but I left the cover on.

I said, "I'm going to get us a place like this. I'll tell them she's eighteen."

"The security's good. But if you get her a fake ID you know she'll be out at night before you can turn around."

"I don't think so."

"You were."

"I was a horrible child." A shower nozzle pushed out of the wall. I could warm myself whenever I chose. My bathing suit hung off me, fitted for Mary-Beth's chest instead of mine. "You weren't."

"I did my best."

"You were a very nice girl. I never figured out why you wanted to hang with us."

"You think there are a lot of punk bands that want a conservatory girl from Tuxedo?"

"Probably some. You're good in a fight."

"Tae kwon do lessons." She threw a towel at me. "If you get pneumonia we'll be out a lot of money." Got up and turned on the hot tub and watched it swirl, then peeled her clothes away. "Get in."

"Those things are septic shock looking for a place to happen."

"Good. You'd love to go out that way, and it'll look good in your posthumous biography."

"I'll start writing it tomorrow."

I stepped into the tub with her. We weren't, I thought, most people's fantasy of naked girls in a hot tub. Not girls, just naked. Hairy legs on her – she'd maintained the riot grrrl look with more militancy than I'd expected – and armpit hair on both of us, and stretch marks turning livid in the hot water. Not everywhere, but my belly and her breasts.

"Didn't they used to be bigger?"

"I had them reduced five years ago. My back hurt."

"They did a good job."

"I know. The scars are barely visible, both nipples stayed attached, and they're practically tacked to my collarbone. I won't sag again until I'm eighty."

"Lucky bitch."

"Tell me what we're going to do with Hanna."

I said, "I think she'd want to go to Japan, with us. She knows a lot about it, even watches *Girls to the Front*."

"Yeah?"

"It's, like, for her. Girls that age. When being sixteen sounds mature and mysterious and you're capable of doing whatever shit you have planned."

"Eleven-year-olds have to think that way. They're only half of twenty-two. How are they supposed to imagine forty?"

"I didn't imagine forty. It just kind of showed up."

"I thought you weren't forty until next year."

"Ever since it started being in range, I just described myself as forty to get it over with. I've been out as being forty for, like, three years."

"And you still talk like a valley girl."

"I don't think that's something that goes away."

"Hanna likes Japan?"

"She's seen those art-house cartoons that are all forest-conservation-fetishy, with spirits popping out and creatures coming to avenge pollution. So she knows where Hokkaido is. How far it is from Tokyo, and, apparently, how to get there."

"Has she got a place to stay picked out?"

"She's eleven."

"Have you got a place to stay picked out?"

"Eden does. He says there are villages where the only residents left are old people, and they'll pay you a stipend to live there and take care of the old folks. I think it's his fantasy to go do that, if he could get decent internet there."

"Would you go with him?"

"I could get him to videoconference with the psychiatrist every few months, probably, but we'd have to get his scrips filled internationally. Mine too."

"Would you move him out here?"

"If he could take the house with him. Just move it across the country and settle it down in whatever neighbourhood is comparable."

"Are you expecting a garden with that?"

"No."

"We could, maybe, get you guys a spot on one of the inner islands. It could work. Could you get the house up to earthquake code?"

"I can't even get the crap out of the basement."

"You got really married for somebody who said she wasn't going to do that again."

"I know. Hanna likes him. Better than me, most of the time. I'm too hot." I got out and sat on the deck. "Can I use your phone?"

"Use your own. We'll go upstairs."

I called Eden from her bathroom. Sat on the bathmat naked and said, "Where do you think she is now?"

He said, "I keep thinking about your Utah trip. The girls you picked up. Not like I think she's in one of those compounds. It's just that a couple of years ago when I was in Utah, I really loved how beautiful it was in the mountains, and I think Hanna would like that. She could take really interesting pictures."

"I don't think she has a camera."

"I think she has a camera."

"Eden."

"Alli. Listen to me. This is what I tell myself. Your in-laws aren't monsters."

"They're monsters."

"They're not monsters. Not the kind that eat little girls. They're awful, they took her, we'll get her back, but I keep saying it to myself. They're not monsters. They're not going to hurt her. They'll give her a camera and buy her good music to listen to and take her places she can climb on things and maybe skateboard."

He was wrong. In my head, she was somewhere in the desert, in Arizona or south of there, in long second-hand dresses with her hair tucked up, wandering by herself toward indistinct livestock that she'd be responsible for hauling water to.

Chores are good for children. And you contribute, if you're going to eat.

Marshall, I realized, would buy her a camera. It would be a third-hand 35mm automatic, and he'd find a box of unexposed cheap 200 ISO film for it. She'd shoot until she ran out of film and then they'd hoard the exposed rolls in their black canisters in a box for some unspecified future time that contained both money and a film-lab that could make prints from technology that was archaic but lacked the cachet to attract hipsters.

"Are you okay, Alli?"

I'd taken off the watch while I swam. It was supposed to be waterproof, but taking it off had been a reflex. I picked the rubber out of my pile of clothes and put it on.

"I shredded my fingertip. Rehearsal tomorrow's going to hurt. Also, Mary-Beth has a sky pool and I may have turned it into a biohazard."

"Are you staying there overnight?"

"I think so. I don't know the way back well enough to drive myself. Also, we came in her car."

"Is it nice?"

"It looks like rich people live here."

He said, "When you go to sleep, call me? I want to just sit with you for a while."

I thought Mary-Beth would want me to sleep with her, but she transformed the couch into some miracle of industrial design that resembled a bed, and coated it in guest sheets. I lay in it with my finger swathed in toilet paper. Listened to her talking in the next room.

She said, "Are you going to hold it together?"

"I'll try."

"Hanna would like Tokyo. Get ready, and we can go take pictures to show her."

Eden in the back of my head said, *They're not monsters.*

I said, "They're monsters, M.B."

"I know."

She established a kind of silence that mimicked privacy. I counted to two hundred, then dialled Eden. He didn't say anything when he picked up.

I set the phone on the bed, curled against it half on my stomach so that my chest leaned in close, and slept like that.

⁚⁚⦙⦙

What does the monster under your bed look like?

Eden tried, when we were first sleeping together, to explain to me that his monsters weren't recognizable in the way that the monsters a child fears are. His monsters were mostly sound and occasionally colour-flashes that pulled at the edges of his mind and destabilized the real.

I said, *You don't get to use Borges to define your psychosis.*

You asked what they look like. I told you. What they look like, anyway, isn't important. I don't usually hallucinate. If I do, you know things are really bad.

Things had been bad for a while when he was fourteen. He'd been scared to leave the house, and he'd cried like he was four when they dropped him off at school, and he chewed on the inside of his arms. He spent three months in residential care, and later, his parents took him on long streetcar journeys to Sick Kids, where his brain was imaged with magnetic resonances and his symptoms charted and his diagnosis was classed into the schizophrenic pseudo-clan.

It's probably not all one thing. Schizophrenia. Just, if you're partially psychotic, you wind up under that umbrella because they don't know where it comes from.

A different night, I asked him, *What would you be like if it went away?*

That's not a question I think I can answer. I try to keep it in its box, but it's so much a part of who I am. I like pictures because they can warp, mimic how my eyes work when they go atypical.

Like someone who'd found Jesus, Eden was gorgeously reconciled to his own madness. It lived near him, through him, and didn't break things like people expected it to.

If he'd been someone else, born without a trust fund, it would have been different. Like it would be different if he'd been born with a standard brain. He didn't really distinguish between those possibilities.

Things are.

Like, I went to the doctor for a meds update and there was this girl sitting on the steps, waiting for them to open the office, and she has sex with me, and she's a rock star, and I'm kind of in love with her.

How do I separate that from everything else?

～ 37 ～

Night Market

I stirred later, in the glass glow of Mary-Beth's apartment, to my name echoing in my breastbone.

Allison. Wake up.

Eerie half-moment of childhood doubt. If I'd been younger, less certain, there might have been the instinct to answer, *God, is that you?*

"No, but I'll take it as a compliment. It's Kara. Your phone kept going to voicemail, so I checked Eden's on a hunch."

"Is he okay?"

"He's fine. He's sleeping. I checked on him a couple of times."

"Thank you."

"He's your guy. Anyway. Wake up."

"What?"

"I figured out what to do."

I sat up. Bare shoulders and spine against the skyline. "What?"

"We need her to call you."

"I don't understand."

"I know. You're not awake. Get up and go to the bathroom or something."

The bathroom adjoined Mary-Beth's bedroom. If I woke her, I'd have to explain what I was doing. I'd need to put on clothes.

I smelled like pool water, salinated rather than chlorine-laced, but vivid and Hanna-like. Stood and paced the laminate. "I'm moving."

"Okay. The girl from their yard. The hippie chick." I nodded. She couldn't see me, but she treated the pause as appropriate and went on. "What was her name?"

Think. "I don't know. I don't think I asked her."

"Shit. Did she go with them?"

"I don't know."

"Find out."

"Kara, what are you *talking* about?"

"You said she was a blogger."

"Hipster mommy shit."

"Is she still posting?"

"I don't know. Why would I know that?"

"Pull it together. What was the name of her site?"

I thought. Thought about her cheekbones, and eating disorders. Pro-ana, the girl-slang for pro-anorexia. We'd done a show about it. Inspirational (*thinspirational*) web communities for girls and women urging each other on to disordered eating. They had affirmations about the beauty of your bones, if you'd just let people see them.

Nothing tastes as good as skinny feels.

"Like starving yourself to death for God."

"That's not helpful. Focus. You're awake. We're looking for Hanna."

I said, "*Love light Ana.*"

Kara vanished from the phone. Soft finger-rub sounds emerged through my earpiece, what must have been her looking the site up.

"She's posting. Two in the last week. Cute girls she has."

"Picture-perfect."

"Allison. She knows where they are."

"The police will already have talked to her."

"I bet. They might even be monitoring her phone. But you met them. Elaine and Marshall. They took Hanna and ran. Those kids on the site, those are their grandkids too. You think they don't check in?"

I said, "You think she knows where they are."

"I think you need to ask her."

My sleep-brain shifted. I said, "Her name is Innogen."

"See, you're already making progress. Now call her and ask her where your daughter is."

⁙⁙⦿⁙⁙

Innogen didn't have a phone number I could find, so I emailed her. I used my professional account, the one that echoed my own name: *allison @ winter.*

I wrote, *You don't have to tell me where they are. I just want to know if she's alright.* Silence.

I messaged Innogen once a day, steadily. We rehearsed and I wrote drafts of four-sentence emails that Kara proofed and Mary-Beth studied and Eden ignored.

Eden, I realized, was writing to her, too, but he didn't tell me what he was sending.

Please

This is my new number. Tell her she can phone me anytime. She can reverse the charges.

Tell her im not mad at her

Please please please

The Innocents got more coherent as we practiced. I wasn't happy, but I was manic, awake for days-long hours at a stretch, and it translated to something that the show backers found appealing.

A producer in the hallway said, "She looks beautiful. Haunted. Too old, but it's good. I didn't think she could look like that. Someone should take pictures of her."

"The thing with the camera is taking pictures of her."

The music people didn't know what to make of Eden. He didn't look human to them. Somebody sketched him like a hair-coated forest spirit on a napkin and left it on the ratty rental coffee table, and it looked exactly like him, bestial and camera-ready. He saw it and snorted. I took the sketch and kept it in the folder with Hanna's search documents and my loose papers.

We played clubs around the city. Punk dives. Student bars.

It rained all the time. Cold.

They booked us into the Tidal Flats Night Market.

Saturday night in October. Teenagers from across the lower mainland poured out to the Fraser River delta in over-loaded cars and on the SkyTrain. Parking stretched for miles, mixing ancient Toyotas with the megacity's notorious Maseratis.

At the Night Market you could buy anything that comes out of a shipping container, straight from the Pearl River Delta and branded with Japanese-Korean characters and fashion trends. The world was grey and raining, but the market was lit up with LEDs imitating the retro-neon of Roppongi echoing a *Blade Runner* fantasy that had been undercut for three decades by anime aesthetics.

Half the audience only spoke Mandarin Chinese. You could buy dim sum on a stick and kill half the night for twenty dollars.

It was a free show. We hadn't played a free show in years, but the producers said we needed the exposure. Needed fan contact. They told us, *This is your audience, now.*

They weren't wrong. We were, somehow, utterly recognizable to the swirling mass of children out for the night feeding and shopping. They held up their phones to us, watching.

Eden sat in the back, watching monitors. He said we cracked the iTunes Top 50 tracks sales, just for a few minutes, in mid-concert. Trended up the pirate systems.

Footage went out on YouTube, unauthorized and smeared wet with the night. The audience crawled closer. Held out their phones.

They cut up the images between songs and reposted them.

She looks like a dead woman. I love her cheekbones.

They stole her daughter, you know.

Who says?

Everybody knows. She's gone, taken. They look for her everywhere.

Why is she singing?

Why? What else would she do?

What does her daughter look like?

I'd worked to keep Hanna invisible, but they found her face in Instagram photos of our house parties. Blurry, small. A creature of pixels.

We stayed up until dawn after the Night Market. I wasn't even drunk, just wired on the performance. My phone buzzed on my hip to inform me that it was Sunday morning, almost 6 a.m. That it was Hanna's twelfth birthday.

I pushed that idea back into its box. I couldn't have a twelve-year-old daughter, because I was myself only fifteen. I would have given my fingertips to find a place like the Night Market when I was fifteen. It would have given me a clear destination when I was running away. Girls didn't run away to join punk bands anymore. They dove into the line-drawn fantasies of Japanese television and stayed up all night making their own versions of those stories to share with people they haven't really met.

The Night Market audience went home, watched *Girls to the Front* again, and got to work. They created whole myths for us before the middle of the week. Fangirls drew pictures of Hanna, pictures of me.

The Innocents had a fan base.

I sent emails to Innogen every night.

Please send me something. Anything. A trace. A fingerprint.

A picture. Is she taking pictures? If she has film, send it to me, send it through re-mailers and I'll get it developed and save all of the prints for her.

We were going to Japan. We had concert dates, a schedule. A mass of little girls suddenly fascinated, sincerely, by the idea of seeing a twenty-something year-old riot grrrl punk band play live while they watched.

Please. Please

Please

I'm sorry. I don't know why you think I know where she is.

I wrote, *You don't have to tell me. If I get a phone, one just in Japan or with a pre-paid number, if I wire money to you to wire wherever you want, would you ask someone to ask someone to borrow a phone from some stranger and just have them call me, just once, just so I can believe she's still alive please. Please.*

please

Innogen wrote, *Please don't send me money.*

I was supposed to fly out in the morning. I tried to think of some action I could take, based on that one short emailed response, and couldn't generate anything that would delay the trip.

I did get a new, extra phone, an ancient model with a Nippon sim card. Emailed Innogen the number.

I couldn't take calls in flight. Even if regulators had allowed it, there were no cell towers over the Pacific, over the Arctic, because you don't cross the Pacific Ocean, not really. We watched our progress on a 16-bit map on the seatbacks between movies. You fly north, along the coast to Alaska and across the Bering Strait and down, never really over open water and using the planet's curve, somehow, to shorten the trip, and you land in Japan with a day missing and thirteen hours of non-sleep clogging your brain, and your phone links up to the new system and shows no missed calls. Absolutely none.

∾ 38 ∾

Electric Town

W hen we met with the first wave of Japanese media people, we were
still in Vancouver. The producers booked us into an East Vancouver
fusion restaurant with communal tables and menus delivered on
clipboards, which felt alien to me but which seemed to be what the media people
expected. Their sense of Canada, we realized, wasn't strong. There was no easy
way to express that Vancouver was thousands of miles away from our natural
habitats. What would they have made of Winnipeg, its flatness and low-rise de-
termination not to be too impressed with itself?

There were other media lunches, though I didn't go to all of them. Kara and
Mary-Beth went out while I slept off panic attacks. They'd worked on a formal
statement, rendered in Japanese so that the subtleties wouldn't be lost, explaining
that Allison was grieving, unable to speak.

They had new pictures of me to share, put together to match that statement.
We'd photographed me in the morning's small hours. I routinely woke at 3 or 4
a.m. and wasn't able to get back to sleep. I'd go online and look for her, site by
site, mention by mention. I emailed the police. I sent Marine suggestions about
steps we could take, all of which she apparently read, patiently, and sent me back
cautiously-worded emails acknowledging every emotion I'd vomited onto the
screen and gently explaining unlawfulness or physical impossibility.

I sent Innogen pleading notes that went unanswered.

My mother and Naomi sent me emails that I deleted unread.

Mary-Beth and a makeup artist found me at six in the morning. In the photos they took afterwards, I looked raw, greasy-haired, all eyes and cheekbones. It was achieved with a fusion of heavy makeup and digital filters. Grief and terror aren't beautiful looking, but they can be synthesized into a recognizable caricature.

Allison is out searching for her lost girl. She is sorry she couldn't meet with you today. Have you seen the footage of her singing from two nights ago?

We had press contacts in English-language media, too, but they were easier to navigate.

There were press waiting for us in Japan, too. They gave us seven hours to sleep, first, and two hours for makeup before we had to appear.

⦂⦂⦂⦂⦂⦂

I'd been expecting a hotel, low- to mid-range, with a lingering fantasy of the vaguely futurist high-end hotels that I'd seen in film and in the pages of some postmodernist writers. I was prepared for the archetypal anonymous space.

Instead, we were housed in something similar to a private house, if a private house had been generated by a set-decorating team to fuse unexpectedly traditional Japanese design with a 90's grunge aesthetic that had run hard through an anime filter. Futons and tatami-rooms dominated, with limited off-floor furniture, but the soft floral textiles I associated with Japan had been replaced with layers of faux-thrifted flannel and knits. Someone had produced, then carefully aged, a set of afghans that sat folded in a corner as extra bedding.

They were impossibly soft when you touched them, completely free of the greasy hand of over-washed acrylic.

I'd been with *The Cure* for years, and we had stylists for on-camera work. They worked for Public Broadcasting, though, or at least with us. I had a style-card on file.

Allison Winter

Height. Inseam. Waist. Hip. Bust. Length of back.

Colour palette: greyscale, shading dark.

No dresses. Black trousers or jeans (black or dark denim) generally acceptable.

Low-femme in clothing.

High-femme in hair and makeup.

Happy to show skin.

The Japanese stylists had no experience of our preferences, and they made us up based on a synthesized version of our media existence, producing effects that startled me. We looked younger, less like ourselves and more like a television fantasy. I thought that if I could capture that version of myself, I could feel better, more numb, than I had in weeks.

We took pictures of each other, for posterity, and then a girl in a black velvet baby-doll dress came in, and photographed us again for the marketable simulacrum of our trip.

Welcome to Tokyo. What would you like to see?

I said, "I need internet access. Can someone help me?"

Ask and receive. A tablet appeared at my elbow, with a keypad that toggled from kanji to roman characters. I took it to the corner.

Camera-clicks continued.

Allison is looking for her daughter. Nothing else can bother her.

Do you know, Allison, that there are stories about you? That girls write stories about you looking for your daughter?

I looked up.

Stories wasn't the right word. They'd produced comics of all of us. There were commercial manga of the show, but fans had gone through the band archives and created separate fan-manga just for us, The Innocents and the women whose lives left traces on the web.

In fan art, I was rendered as an almost curveless figure, face hidden behind shaggy dark hair. I walked city streets and dream-world spaces, consulting with hackers and magicians and spies, looking for a girl who was always just out of reach, outlined as a tiny dreamchild. I thought they must never have seen Hanna, then realized that, except for the photos we'd released to help the search and the handful of blurry Instagram moments, no one had seen her. We'd made her so invisible.

The artwork ranged from weirdly sexual to quite good and looked nothing like either of us.

I said, and then was translated: *Thank you. That's very good.*

Media face, media voice.

We weren't hostages. We had a half-dozen shows to play, three in greater Tokyo, then northward. Tokyo lurked on our phone-maps, as large as southern England, spread over the lowland plains. One of the global wonders you were supposed to want to see. So we went out. I had my travel phone and the burner I'd purchased in Vancouver both pressed against my body.

Everyone told us the same thing: there was nowhere you could go in Tokyo that wasn't safe. With the subway and a phone, you could go anywhere.

I had trouble imagining such a city. In Paris, we'd always been running on the border between tourist beauty and the suburban violence that came pouring into the city proper only after we left. In Berlin, still rawly unified when we played there, you could step into trouble with both of your eyes open.

You could go out Mary-Beth's door in the early morning of Vancouver and trip over people overdosing on synthetic opiates, more explicit now even than during the heroin epidemic of twenty years earlier.

Tokyo wasn't, as far as we could tell, that jagged anywhere. Its hazards lurked in the sheer dullness of its sprawl. Massive areas lurked, residential and bland like the outer, white bread rings of Chicago waiting for Emo to burst forth, filled with low-rise residential ordinariness that featured nothing worth exploring or photographing if you were only in the country for a week. If you were looking for something more interesting, though. Well.

Ginza awaited, polished and full of art galleries. Harajuku, fashionable and dead at mid-week, was close by.

We were guided. Not, we were told, because we were in danger, but because almost no one in Tokyo spoke English, and if we wanted to do anything interesting, we'd need an interpreter. They'd found someone from the scene. Manami was female, twentyish, aggressively boyish in her dress with a resistance to fashion that looked more like violence than anything else we saw in the city.

She said, *Girls come in from the suburbs, from as far away as Chiba, on the weekends and do cosplay shows on the Harajuku streets. They look like dolls.*

Kara said, *Lolita girls?*

Yes. And others. Fashion students. Fans. They bring suitcases of costumes and change in the public toilets. Anyone can take their pictures, anytime.

Is it worth seeing?

It depends, she said, carefully, *on what you want.*

I couldn't decide if she actually didn't care, or if she was sure we'd judge her if we thought she did. There was something in Japan that we couldn't penetrate, a boundary between the real and the unreal that had shifted and that carried meaning in ways I was unfamiliar with.

I said, *Take me somewhere really awful.*

She lit up.

Mary-Beth and Kara split off, acquiring a second guide after a series of phone calls. They wanted to… something. Something without me, probably. They'd been watching me for weeks. They wanted to shop and eat lunch and maybe visit a shrine or something.

Manami stayed with me. She said she thought she might know want I wanted.

She took me to Akihabara Electric Town.

We rode the train for half an hour, or nearly. She'd warned me in advance that if my phone rang, I couldn't answer it. I could text, but trains were voiceless spaces, free from phone calls, and my being foreign wasn't going to break that rule.

I thought, *I should call home.*

My wristband measured my pulse and sent its low signal back across the Pacific to Eden, travelling in his same fragile van back across the continent to our house, to edit footage and fish for projects.

Manami calculated for me. "You said he's where?"

"Close to Calgary, I think."

"It's after ten, his time."

I checked my other phone.

"Elsewhere in America, it's later. Do you think she'll call now?"

"I don't know when she'll call."

"Do you think she's going to call you now?"

I said, "If this phone rings, I'm always going to answer it. If I get arrested, they can chalk it up to punk ethos."

"They won't arrest you," she said. "Probably."

"What happens, then?"

She wrinkled her nose. Implied something socially-coded and far enough from my own cultural nest that I couldn't recognize it.

We took the train.

Akiba was the nearest place I'd encountered to a physical manifestation of the internet. The rail station played its own song, interrupting the train's silence. You descended into the street, which was quieter that day than on weekends but still filled with the massed bodies of men shopping for sex and computer parts, and women dressed in alluring cartoon costumes to lure them in.

These were not, Manami told me, the Harajuku costume girls. "This isn't for fun. It's a job."

Crowds of men pushed in to take selfies with them, or else photographed the girls from a distance.

I thought that *girls* was right. I had trouble parsing Japanese ages, but the Lolita-style teenage design of anime nymphs ensured that adult women were locked out of this industry, though I had trouble imagining them wanting to break in.

There were multi-storey markets, but Manami walked me along commercial streets and then alleys, down to narrow doors and then through crowded shops that sold both computer chips and collectible sets of the small plastic toys that you could buy singly, randomly from vending machines, apparently everywhere.

The shops sold flash drives and CD-ROMs, which I hadn't seen in years, and even books full of apparently amateur manga of the kind that most people traded online for free.

I saw old computer-coding books with coffee stains on them. Coffee pods.

Some of the mini-figures from vending machine eggs were almost-naked girls in elaborate rope bondage, millimetre-sized bulges of flesh showing against the raised plastic string.

It was disorienting until I shifted my brain out of physical existence. We were, I decided, temporarily digital and browsing the edges of misogyny in a digital world.

It made sense. We had come to visit Internet Rule 34: *If it exists, there's pornography of it. No exceptions.*

Have you ever wanted to go into a warren-basement room and buy pornography of yourself?

Manami didn't find what she was looking for immediately, but we searched stores with a kind of blank detachment, and in the fourth one, downstairs in a low-ceilinged room that made me think of earthquakes, we found printed, fan-produced art for *Girls to the Front*.

The first piles were just individual nude renderings of characters. Off-style for the show, which eschewed hyper-cute design in favour of a rougher aesthetic. Here, romantic softness had reasserted itself. Each woman's edges had been softened with a series of filters, and there were soft flares of almost-light obscuring the characters' vulvas. Whiteness where their genitals would be, only enough space left to make clear an absence of pubic or other body hair.

There were a handful of pictures that had been done of The Innocents, filed in behind. There, the artists had been restricted by human anatomy, and the attempts to anime-fy us had largely failed. Only I had nude photos in circulation for artists to work from, but someone was clearly fascinated by those pictures. My tattoos were carefully sketched out, as well as the scarring on my ribs and thighs. Pubic bones present and correct, and the messy hair I'd been photographed with in my twenties, reminiscent of Mapplethorpe's Patti Smith, though wider across the cheeks and shoulders. My body hair had been removed. Underarms exposed in a classic pin-up reach, hands behind my head. Long, bare white legs. Pussy naked to the imagining eye and nothing, I realized, like my own. Nothing like anyone's. Tidy outer labia concealed all.

I said, out loud, "They'd be so disappointed."

Manami said, "When I started wanting to go places that I wasn't allowed, I began here. They all stared at me when I came in."

"No girls building computers."

"If they do, they buy their parts online. I had a man put his hand down my pants back here, once." Like she wanted me to understand the validity of her full experience.

"I believe you.:

"He wiggled his fingers around. I think he didn't know what he was looking for."

"Makes a girl long for vagina dentata."

She cocked her head. "I don't know those words."

I spelled them. "Look it up."

She keyed the letters into her phone. Laughed for the rest of the afternoon.

I was tempted to buy copies of the images, but when I did the currency conversion, I was vaguely shocked at the price. Manami reminded me that the shops in the district only took cash.

"What?"

"Westerners are always surprised. They want their cards to work everywhere."

I said, "We're in *Japan*."

"Yes, but the real one. So, cash only."

I flipped through the pile again, idly.

The book at the back of the display must have been less popular than the other works. It barely qualified as a book at all. Someone had printed out 8.5x11" sheets and cheaply coil-bound them. The ink looked vaguely blue, like mimeograph.

The artwork was strange. It was anime-influenced, like the rest of what was out, but merged that simple line-aesthetic with high school art classes in basic shading and silhouettes. These weren't digital creations: they were scans of physical drawings, erased pencil lines still barely visible in the white spaces.

Most of them had been cropped so that the artist's signature was missing, but one or two of them still had it. *C. Hardee-Wilson*.

Rock-star pinups. Pretty girl in the bathtub, one hand's fingers combing her pubic hair. Naked on stage.

Collin.

~ 39 ~

Riot grrrl Ink

The guides and producers assured us that no one expected us to speak Japanese. They'd hired translator-avatars who dressed like us to come to the shows and provide local-language commentary. Mary-Beth had practiced a greeting for the audience, but when she tried it the avatars giggled, hands over their mouths. Told her that it was good, really good, but maybe she shouldn't.

It meant that interviews were conducted in stages, with the three of us seated at a table so we could be photographed as a group, but our answers were dubbed in later. Like dolls.

Handlers crept forward between photos and ruffled my hair, pulling it over my face as much as they could.

"I don't look that bad."

"No, it's . . . it makes you look ghostly."

Manami had purchased the book of Collin's drawings and burned it in the courtyard of our guest house. She brought me the ashes in a cheap ceramic bowl and asked me if I wanted them.

"No."

"I looked elsewhere," she said. "It was the only copy."

It wasn't the only copy, because nothing dies on the internet. I said, "Thank you."

Manami handed the ashes off to someone to be disposed of, and later they showed up on fans' faces, smeared like melodramatic makeup. They shared selfies of their ash-smearing on the fan-feed, where they were sure we could see them.

It gave the makeup artists ideas.

Allison, prepared for the stage, wore two makeup-induced black eyes and glared at the audience as a personal insult. She looked wonderful, bleached-out, fodder for fan writing. Those eyes and the hair made me, I was told, look like I'd come back from the dead.

The producers asked us not to come onto the club's stage as a group. Instead, Mary-Beth and Kara went on first, picked up their instruments from prepared stands, and I came on after, with separate lighting.

We did the concert in a single set. There'd been an opening act we hadn't heard, playing Japanese covers of other riot grrrl songs. We were supposed to be something special, unseen since before our audience was born.

They looked, every one of them, like Hanna.

Set List for Tokyo Show, 4 November 2015
Drugstore princess
Crazy/Innocent
Kiss me, bite me, eat me
Miss Winnipeg
Fuck your Friday panties
Knit myself a knife
Precious memory box
Girl Jesus

- - Break - -
(drink some water, bitches)

Bite your head off
Running after the rain
Bleeds and doesn't die
Dance with my best friend
Lost girls
Queen of the snow
The Very Best Daughter
I don't want to steal your boyfriend (you can keep him)
- - Encore - -
Not allowed to take off all my clothes

We hadn't planned for a second encore, and we didn't need one, but the audience was better than we'd thought they might be. They were nearly all female, very young, dressed in ways that didn't even slightly match Tokyo street style. They looked comfortable. Ready to be angry, if an outlet for that anger could be readily provided. They knew the words and were prepared to sing along.

Like listening to child-aliens sing. They knew all the words, but there was no sense of them *meaning* anything. Just sound.

They were all so *young*.

When we played *Lost Girls* and paused, I realized the audience was crying. We weren't singing sad songs. Our songs, especially from that first album, were angry and adolescent-wired. They'd become part of a different version of our lives, one reconstructed for a media-saturated audience, while we weren't around.

They sang with us, raw-throated, to *Bleeds and Doesn't Die*.

Offstage, pre-encore, we were well aware we'd chosen the wrong song for a last round. It was too silly. The audience wasn't primed for irony.

The handlers said, "Go on. They're calling you."

We played it anyway, *Not Allowed to Take Off All My Clothes*. We'd been reminded, early in rehearsals, that, along with being "not so angry," I really, seriously was not to take off all my clothes.

Like they were daring me or something.

It was only after I'd thrown my shirt into the audience that I realized that most of them would never have seen a grown woman who had tattoos before. Our band photos for the Japanese tour had been done with all of us covered throat to wrist. Mary-Beth had played the night in a baby-doll dress, but dark tights under that concealed ink and forty-year-old knees at the same time. Kara wore nude sleeves, reverse-punk, over her apparently bare forearms.

They got an eyeful of my skin.

Here is the Medusa in the middle of my back. This, my upper right arm, reads, in oversize typewriter font listing downward,

bitch

slut

dyke

cunt

whore

Little girl with pigtails skull on my left shoulder. Angry little girl with a microphone screaming up my ribcage.

I didn't have tattoos everywhere, but it was more ink that you could legally walk the streets with in Japan. The producers had put us in a guest house, we'd been told, not just for our privacy, but also because we couldn't expect to use the public baths in a real hotel, not even a western one, not looking like we did.

We wore our skins with smeared colours and pin-up girls armed with wire-wrapped bats and stick-figures fighting the boy-monsters of patriarchy.

Not allowed to walk around like that.

The audience was startled, almost silent. Cameras trained on us. I stopped peeling at my waist, stood with my jeans open and panties showing at the zip. Shirts sailed past me.

All of us, topless, braless on the stage. Forty-year-old breasts exposed to twelve-year-old girls.

We weren't arrested. Our producers had, we were told, nothing to say to us. They had to think about whether they wanted to continue.

In the van, driving through the night city, Kara said, "Those babies are all going to get tattoos and it's going to be *all our fault.*"

"We can only hope."

My phone flicked on when I picked it up from my folded clothes. The house staff had laid our beds out for us, maybe not trusting us to do it correctly by ourselves. Kara and Mary-Beth were showering.

Eden had called twice. The other phone, the burner, when I picked it up, was dark. Dead battery.

I plugged it into the wall. Waited.

I smelled like sweat and the absence of cigarettes, a wrongness that had emerged since the smoking bans in Canada, but heavier in Japan, where we played for fascinated children. Their age stripped away the entire scent-palette I'd associated with shows.

Nobody was drunk here. Nobody was smoking, because you couldn't smoke in bars anymore, and anyway, this wasn't a bar, just some kind of perverse all-ages club full of preteens high on their own adrenaline, screaming louder than any audience we'd played for since we were in high school too. Just loud, loud girls.

The burner phone roused itself. It said, *missed call.*

The little screen informed me that I'd missed a call, but not who from, and there was no message. The twelve digits of a North American phone number linked to its country code flashed up and I wrote them down on my arm in ballpoint pen.

Googled them. Got nothing. Keyed them into my other phone and called.

Eden said, "Hello."

"Hey. I missed a call."

"Yeah. Hi."

"Why didn't you call my main phone?"

"I didn't call you. I'm just holding the phone."

It wasn't, I realized, his number. The area code was somewhere south of us, the digits of an unknown state. 011. 52.

"Where are you?"

"Juarez."

"What?"

I only knew of Juarez from the half-dozen audio documentaries I'd listened to about it, and the interview I'd done with artist-activists doing a Toronto installation commemorating women's deaths in the city's ongoing drug war. It was indexed as the most dangerous place in the world. Border city of El Paso.

He said, "I need you not to panic."

"I have too many tranquillizers in my system to panic. Also, I just got back from playing. Tell me why you're in the death city."

"I found Hanna."

I stared at the phone.

"She tried to call you earlier. I wanted to prove to her that you'd been waiting for her. It wasn't great, honestly, that your phone was dead. But I said you'd call back, and you did."

"How the hell are you going to get her over the border?"

"About that."

"What?"

"We need you to come to Mexico. With Hanna's birth certificate."

"I'm *on tour*. In *Japan*."

"Yes, but."

"I know '*but*.' *But* I don't have it with me. *But* I'm on the wrong continent. *But* I'm supposed to play another show tomorrow night. *But* I need to get you out of there. *But* I don't know what to do."

"Allison, you're screaming."

Kara had appeared beside me, soaking wet and naked except for a towel around her hair. I handed her the phone. Dropped my head between my knees.

They talked. Mary-Beth came out, too, and was handed the phone. Kara brought me a wet washcloth for my face.

They handed me the phone. "Allison?"

"Hi baby."

"You didn't say it."

I snorted. "Can I at least get a 'hi, mom'?"

"Yeah, that."

"Well?"

"Hi, mom."

"Are you okay?"

"Yeah. You didn't answer the phone."

I started to cry. Hard, through the pills that were keeping me level, unable to speak. Kara took the phone away.

I curled onto the floor. Rocked there.

I could have, I thought, brought the phone with me. I could have charged it. I could have had it on stage. I'd worn jeans. I'd had *pockets.*

You *don't* take your phone with you on stage. You lock it away. It's not *polite.*

"Alli, I need you to calm down."

Like words out of another dimension. I could feel my breastbone cracking from the force of my lungs trying to escape my body. I couldn't remember what calm felt like.

Kara hit me. Less of a slap than a punch, rattling my jaw and resetting my breathing. "Freak out later. You've scared Hanna. She thinks you're mad at her. Calm the fuck down."

I held my breath. Counted to twenty. Thirty. Gasped and tried again. Took the phone stretched out to me.

"I'm sorry," I said.

"I'm sorry!"

"You don't need to be sorry."

"I made you cry!"

"Lots of stuff makes me cry. I just usually do it in the bathroom where you can't see me," I said.

Hanna paused. "Actually, I've seen you cry lots of times. Four."

"Plus that day I went to bed at David's house and didn't get up again."

"Yeah. You're actually kind of a crybaby."

"I'll keep that in mind."

"Are you coming to get us?"

I wanted to say *no. Maybe. I need a lawyer. I need time.* "Yes. Fast as I can. Do you know where I am right now?"

"Tokyo. Eden told me. Can I go there too?"

I said, "Definitely. Tokyo needs to meet you."

"Okay."

Kara took the phone back, handed it to Mary-Beth. She finished the call, hung up, made other calls on my phone and hers.

Kara took me into our little bathroom with its square tub and shower. Ran the water and put me under it.

Outside, it was almost morning. It was raining a dense, cold drizzle that reminded me how close we were to the ocean. How far, separated by traffic and the ocean and the causeway-bridge that linked us, from Narita Airport.

Sixteen hours to Canada, twenty if I left right now. Five and a half more to Winnipeg, where Hanna's birth certificate was in Marine's office, part of our official file and available 24/7 to the Winnipeg police.

Two hours back and forth to the airports. Two for security. Two and a half to Toronto, the nearest major international.

Change airports. Change cities. Jump borders. Establish parentage, custody, identity.

Jump.

~ 40 ~

Aesthetics

Naomi said, "Thank you. Thank you for asking me."

"It's not like I have anyone else I can ask."

"Still. I'm grateful. I'll call you every hour."

"I'll be here. Until I'm not. Call away."

I had hours to wait until my flight, but I'd taken the train to Narita just after 5 a.m., when the first one ground into our nearest station. Someone had roused Manami out of bed to go with me. She was makeup-free and shivering in the predawn damp. Men in suits surrounded us, and women in their own version of suits, and kids in school uniforms headed for early-morning tutoring, and the odorous bodies that marked the city's homeless, those who'd ride the trains for hours and those who slept in the train stations in complex shelters rigged from cardboard and tarps. I'd taken just my carry-on.

One of Mary-Beth's people worked on the tickets from Vancouver, texting me updates about thickly-booked flights and unavailable tickets and layers of standby.

In the interim, they let me through security. I was left with my passport and a flight still seven hours away to wander the clean airport expanses. Manami waved and disappeared back into the city.

I couldn't remember what time it was in Canada, any city across the mess of time zones. Mary-Beth's people in Vancouver couldn't raise Marine in Winnipeg, or Wayne Cardinal, and they couldn't go to Winnipeg themselves.

I needed bodies on the ground, in the city.

I phoned Naomi.

She answered. I wondered if she'd given me a special ringtone in case I was stricken with Christian mercy and decided to forgive her. She didn't ask. She said, "What do you need?" and I gave her a list. Hanna's birth certificate. My custody documents. Ethan and Claudia's wills. Hanna's passport, if she had one.

Did she have one?

"Ethan and Claudia took her to Costa Rica for Christmas two years ago, so I'd assume yes."

I needed the details of Hanna's life, none of which I had recorded and few of which I could summon. I hadn't slept yet. My hair had dried straw-like. It crackled in the air-conditioning.

In spite of her promise, Naomi didn't call me back, and I slept on a couch-ledge in the airport until a quiet attendant touched my shoulder and ushered me into a boarding lounge.

I hadn't had occasion to travel first-class internationally, before. Public Broadcasting didn't pay for executive-level travel, and when I'd travelled on my own, I'd counted the dollars and rejected the idea. On short notice, business class (*not* first class, I'd had it explained to me) was what Mary-Beth's people could book. I had, therefore, access unbecoming the state of me.

A beautifully-assembled woman in a whispering, expensive suit suggested that I might want a shower. She paused. *Another* shower. Did I need beauty products?

She took my credit card and brought me a concierge catalogue. A nail technician could be summoned if I wanted one. A select range of products could be provided. The passive voice had enormous power, brought to bear to arrange my re-establishment in the physical realm of the elite.

Botanicals for my skin and hair. Modest pans of achingly expensive nude-toned makeup. A straightening iron was provided. Body products were procured.

The Uniqlo outlet in the airport was on the other side of the security gates, but armed with my with credit limit, another quiet woman fetched clothes. Black denim and cashmere, somehow more preppy than punk.

Remaking myself took hours. When they were satisfied with me, I was fed orange slices and sparkling water.

I was, I realized, enormously hungry.

They released me, finally, satisfied with my return to business-elite form and sculpted-neutral face. I had, by my count, forty-five minutes until they called my flight. Unable to locate a steakhouse or any other food-service outlet to satisfy my craving for red meat, I found a McDonald's and gorged.

Flew in vivid awareness of the skin eruptions forming under my glossy makeup coating. Trying not to think about the fiscal damage I'd done myself in the six hours in Tokyo's international hub.

◉

Naomi texted me a half-dozen times to explain that she hadn't yet accomplished anything before I turned off my phone. In the airport in Vancouver, I had a kiosk-monitor change my SIM cards and called her again.

"Did you find anything?"

"I have almost everything on the list."

"Almost?"

"No passport. I'm sorry, I have no idea what happened to Hanna's passport." Pause. "Do you think they took it?"

"I don't think anything. Can you meet me at the airport? I'd like to get the docs and get back in the air."

"About that."

"What?"

"I can't come. The kids are sick. But I'm sending someone." Pause. "Tell me what your flights are after this."

I didn't have flights booked. I had thought the document-hunt would take at least a day, and reservations for 6:18 wouldn't help me if I needed four days or a week to turn up what I'd travelled across the Pacific to find.

"Can you," another pause, "let me talk to your friend's office directly?" She meant Mary-Beth's people. "That way I won't have to keep bothering you, and I can have that info for you at the gate, too."

I was tired. I'd slept a little, in the air, but restlessly, and I'd only tried because sleep was the best method I knew to collapse the intervening time. The tranquillizers I'd been taking had worn off. Coffee, I thought, could keep me awake. Airports ran on it. I could find some anywhere.

"Fine," I said.

In transit from international arrivals to domestic departures in Vancouver, I bought a gel-filled sleep mask. I was already cold under my sweater, but short on time for another shower. I phoned Naomi back.

"I need a coat. I don't know where mine is."

"I can do that. Did you gain weight?"

I thought, *fuck you.* I said, "No. I think I lost it. Probably. I haven't picked out my own clothes for a while."

"Okay. I was just thinking about sizes. I'll send you a couple."

"Thank you."

"I didn't mean to say you're fat."

I hung up. "You never mean anything," I told the phone as it turned off.

∷∺∷

Winnipeg's airport triggered a panic-spike in my animal brain. If I could take Hanna home, I was never going to fly through there again. Not until they demolished this new, glossy terminal in favour of another one that couldn't evoke murder and terror in my private universe.

Naomi hadn't come, but she'd said she wouldn't. Instead, she'd sent the reification of my terror to meet me, wearing my mother's skin.

She was coming with me.

Two tickets from Winnipeg to Toronto, and then Toronto to Juarez via Seattle-Tacoma, taking me back across the continent for some vicious reason known only to the arcane routers of bodies through the air. Two passports, a case of documents, two overnight bags (mine containing exquisite cosmetics in travel-sized flasks), two parkas.

I said, "I just needed a coat for Toronto."

"You never known when you're going to need a coat."

"We're going to Mexico."

"It gets cold at night. Or you can sleep on it. Under it. Take your coat, Allison."

She sounded nothing like the woman I'd stiff-armed three months before. More matter-of-fact even than the woman interviewed on national television regarding my fitness as a mother.

"Take it back with you. I'm not going to need it."

"We need to go through security now. Come on."

In line, I said, "You're not coming with me."

"You are going to need someone familiar with the red tape of foreign governments. I have more experience in that than I would like. I had to legally prove that you were my daughter on four occasions. Also, I speak Spanish, and I suspect that you don't."

"Go home."

"Allison. I have apologized to you. I am coming to solve your problem, and you need my help. You can fuss when we are past security. You can cry through the flights if you want to." She dug in her purse. "I have pills if you need them."

"I have my own pills."

"I brought two months' worth, just in case. I'm sorry about the earlier scene, too, by the way. The one at my house. It wasn't something you should have been subjected to, though I suspect you've staged a couple of scenes like that in your life. So you should understand."

She had methodically stripped off her coat and boots. She emptied her pockets into a plastic bin, then peeled away her jewelry. She'd returned to wearing the long skirts I remembered and a paisley turtleneck that might have come out of a donation bin. To the security agent, she must have looked unutterably ordinary.

They let her pass. Me, they looked over.

"I thought you were on tour in Japan or something," the agent said.

"I am," I said.

"I'm sorry about your daughter."

"Thank you."

"I saw you play the Pyramid Cabaret, once, in the nineties."

"Good show?"

"You bet. I'm glad you guys are back together. When's your next show here in town?"

"Not sure. Watch our website — they have the updates."

"I'll do that. You travel safe."

My mother said, "You're a celebrity."

"A very minor Canadian one."

"I suppose it's more or less what you wanted. They are nosy, though, aren't they?"

We had an hour and ten minutes until boarding. I said, "I'm going to get my nails done."

It wasn't an invitation. Post-security was a world of food, souvenir-purchases, and beauty-shopping. Nails could be done while you waited, without an appointment.

There was nothing wrong with my nails. They'd been lacquered by Japanese experts before our show to ensure they wouldn't chip against the bass strings, and at the time I'd wondered if they'd seen the original version of The Innocents, where any nail polish we'd worn was always chipped. I'd worn polish mostly so that the dirt under my nails wouldn't show.

If I couldn't sleep, I could have beauty. It cost money, but it filled time. When we'd been younger and touring, I hadn't understood women who invested money and time, so much time, in their appearances. We wore T-shirts that railed against it. Decried the industries that fed on female insecurity. I'd said once, in an interview, that I thought the women in niqabs had the right idea: they could walk in public without being subject to the constant aesthetic scrutiny that every other woman in Canada suffered. There were days when a long black veil sounded less like a Johnny Cash song and more like a good idea. If I'd worn a veil here, though, in the world-spanning air travel dimension, I'd never have reached my first transfer-station.

Makeup, then. Nails. I thought maybe I could pick out perfume, choose another soft, enveloping sweater from the endless, anonymous boutiques.

My backup phone rang while they were painting my nails. My mother stepped over, reached into my jeans pocket with parental intimacy, and took it.

"Hello, honey. Yes, it's Grandma Alma. Yes, she's here."

She held the phone to my ear. Hanna said, "Are you better?"

"I'm better. I'm happy you called."

"Are you coming?"

"You bet. We're in Winnipeg. I have sixty pounds of paper to prove I'm your mom."

"That's a good idea. Eden should have brought that with him."

I thought about that. "It wouldn't work. Eden and I aren't married. Unless he adopted you, they wouldn't treat him as your dad."

"What?"

"I mean, he's not your dad. But he could adopt you if you wanted. But the papers wouldn't have been enough for him."

"No, the *other* thing."

"We're not married?"

"Why *not*?"

"Yes, Allison. Why not?" My mother took the phone back. "Honey, you can discuss that with your mom later. Are you okay?" She listened. "Okay. How's your Grandma Elaine?"

⁑⦂⁑

In the air above Seattle, my mother said, "Why aren't you married?"

We didn't have business-class tickets for this leg. The trip was on my credit cards, and I could feel the pressure on them like pleurisy inside my financial ribcage. I'd locked myself into a music otherworld against her, but my mother simply plucked out my earbud whenever she wanted to talk.

"I got married once. I think that was enough."

"Your fellow seems lovely, though."

"When did you ever meet Eden?"

"It's my impression that he's spent the past several months taking care of you, and as soon as he was free of that, he went looking for your daughter, through several different countries, entirely on his own."

"I don't know what he's been up to." I didn't. Eden had called once when Hanna was asleep, but he'd asked me just to describe what I was looking at, or hold the phone against my sternum. Whichever.

"You should probably marry him."

"I'll take it under advisement."

"Thank you."

Later, she said, "Being married can be wonderful."

"I'm sleeping."

"You are welcome to claim that you are. But I'm having trouble settling down, and I haven't had a chance to talk to you in years."

"You're only along because Naomi is fucking sneaky."

She flinched. "Language."

"It's not actually illegal to swear. I do it a lot. You're welcome to go home if it bothers you."

"You're being childish."

"It's my prerogative."

"Isn't it just? Anyway. If you won't talk to me, will you play with me?"

The monstrous tapestry bag that she was using as a purse produced a travel *Scrabble* set. She offered up the sack of letters. "The person with the closest letter to *A* goes first."

"If I play with you, we will not talk about my marriage or lack thereof."

"Accepted."

I played with her, ignoring the welling memory of being taught to spell with another, more damaged travel *Scrabble* set. That she'd told me that I was the easiest child she'd ever taught to read. *Words were welling out of you. You wanted to know what they all were so badly. And then you'd take any paper you could find to write on. You wrote on your father's work papers and nearly ruined a project. Once you wrote in a Bible, very carefully in crayon. It wasn't sharp, but you managed several words per page, and you'd reached the Book of Joshua before we realized what you were up to.*

I studied my letters. Hers, and the space between us.

I made *warbler*.

"That's very nice."

"Thank you."

"You take a compliment very well."

"Thank you."

"I am sorry, you know."

"As you've said, you've apologized."

"I had no idea Elaine was capable of kidnapping."

I looked up. "She's capable of anything."

"I can't think of a single time she ever hurt you before."

I said, "One time, after I married Ethan, I woke up and she was sitting on the basement stairs, watching me. She had a throw pillow with her. I think she was deciding whether to kill me."

"You're being melodramatic."

"Ethan's mother is a witch. And she hates me. And she stole my daughter, so we're not going to have a conversation where you try to convince me that I need to be more compassionate. If I wanted to have compassion for people, I'd have stayed a Christian and lived in some tiny farmhouse and had a million babies, and Ethan wouldn't be dead and Hanna wouldn't be alive and I'd still, in case you're wondering, be mad at you."

To the man sitting beyond her, I said, "I'm sorry, I don't seem to be in the mood for *Scrabble*. Would you like to take over my half of the game?"

He looked startled, but he took the cradle of letters from me and introduced himself to my mother.

I put my earbuds in. I missed my good headphones that I'd worn daily to review albums in the safety of our house in Toronto. I could hear subtleties in their noise-cancelling space. Like being in another universe, temporarily weightless and buried in sound.

Our house was still there, alone for months now. Hanna's room and mine and Eden's studio all sitting empty.

It occurred to me that in a more just world, we'd come back to find it taken over by some of the sixty million displaced bodies I kept reading about, all of them making better use of the space than we ever had. Eden, Hanna, and I could make do in his van. If we were stranded in Mexico for months or years, unable to prove who we were, we'd only be a handful more stateless bodies in an upended world.

My mother could find her own way. If I left her on the street, she'd find or form a women's collective by morning. She could mother other people's children and deliver babies and stay far away from me.

∽ 41 ∾

Juarez

Ciudad Juarez was, on some level, just the mirror of El Paso, the city on the other side of the walled American border. It was a sprawl of residences and factories in half-desert, marked with bullet holes and other artifacts of the drug trade, but not the war zone I'd been looking for.

Eden met us at the airport, standing with a man I hadn't met but who he introduced to me as Will. Will, he said, did TV commercials and occasionally documentary films, and they'd met on a project in Mexico City more than a decade ago. He was one of Eden's odd flock of global filmmakers, evidence that he had friends and a life outside of our domestic fortress.

Sane people, un-jetlagged, separated me from my mother, so that she rode in the front of the Land Cruiser while I stayed in the back, leaning into Eden's shoulder. It wasn't a huge distance dividing us, but I could turn inward. Ignore her voice and the traffic-snarl and low-rise buildings running out of the city and into the Chihuahuan desert.

Half asleep, I said, "Why are there mountains?"

Eden waited a long time to answer. "Apparently they predate everything else. And they're technically not here. They're in Texas, on the other side of the border. The Franklin Mountains. I was thinking we could camp there on our way back."

"I'm supposed to be in Tokyo."

"I know. You made good time getting here."

"I've been awake for so long."

"I know. Go to sleep."

I did. Later, he propelled me walking across gravel and into a dim space with a ceiling fan that whirled while I slept.

:::◉:::

Hanna was relatively easy to find, because she was in the pool most of the time she was awake. She and Eden had settled in this compound, assigned to one of a half-dozen shipping containers converted into low-profile houses and outfitted with anonymous Ikea furniture. Except for the mountains in the distance, everything huddled low to the ground; the pool actually sank down into it, a ladderless concrete tank painted incongruous blue and surrounded by white gravel and searing, paint-stripped deck chairs.

The pool was set up for laps, and she swam them. She'd acquired another new swimsuit, or another used one. It looked old, ancient, like a relic from the 80s, before stretch fabrics had quite stabilized, and maybe like it had been sewn by hand.

She had a tan emerging under a sunburn, and muscles forming more clearly in her shoulders, and I thought she was taller.

She didn't acknowledge me when I came out of the container-house at dusk, finally awake, and sat by the pool's edge. It wasn't hot by any means, and as dark settled, I was actively chilled. I waited, and she didn't get out.

I thought about telling her to get out before she froze. Instead, I padded across the gravel quad to the main house.

Eden, my mother, and Will were spread out at the dining table with documents. Birth certificates and the contents of my purse and legal pads covered the placemats. They had what sounded like a lawyer on speaker from Will's phone.

I said, "Is she going to drown out there? Or freeze?"

Will said, "The pool's heated. She might get waterlogged, though. Tell her it's dinnertime."

"Is it?"

"None of us have eaten yet," my mother said, absently. "Why don't you have a look in the freezer and see if there's anything you could throw together."

She had an inherent parental ability to turn me into a furious teenager. I bit back several answers and instead dug through the lower-drawer freezer in the kitchen. It held carefully-stacked boxes of wholesale ethnic food, mostly Chinese and Indian, and giant warehouse-store muffins in individual plastic bags. Up close, I saw they'd been quartered with their wrappers still on, and remembered seeing that in someone's house before. Trays of the things came from Costco, loaded in oil and sugar, and you could microwave them into edibility faster if they were cut like that.

The one I held was half the size of my face. I considered, then stripped away the plastic and stuffed it into the microwave. Took it, burning hot, outside.

I said to Hanna, "I have food. It looks like it's really awful for you."

"It smells good," she said.

"Can you smell it over the pool water?"

"The pool doesn't have a smell." It did, but if she'd been in as long as I suspected, she likely couldn't tell. "Is that chocolate-chocolate-chip?"

"I think it might be."

"Can I have one too?"

I said, "You can have this one, just give me a bite."

It melted onto my fingers and tasted like cheap, excessive dessert. Hanna bolted the rest. Out of the water, I could see her getting colder. No towels around.

I peeled my shirt over my head and handed it to her.

She said, "Allison."

"I have a bra on. Don't freeze. Don't get back in the water. Come and talk to me while I find new clothes."

I didn't have clothes of my own beyond what I was wearing, but there were abandoned clothes in the ragged Ikea drawers near the bed I'd slept the day away in, and some of them fit well enough. Hanna sat cross-legged on the green duvet and stared at me.

"You smell really bad."

"I rode six planes to get here. And I'm pretty sure I'm still living in the day after tomorrow."

"I don't understand."

"I was in Tokyo. It's across the international date line. That means it's tomorrow there."

"That doesn't make sense."

"I know. I'll try to get a shower at some point." I found a T-shirt for the Waco Bluegrass Music Festival, 2009 and pulled it on.

I smelled like myself and travel. She smelled like chocolate and chlorine, gradually soaking into my bed. I said, "Are you okay?"

"I guess."

"Where were you?"

"Out there." Nodding at the window filling the container's narrow end, toward the obscuring desert.

"Are you okay?"

"You asked that."

"I know." I needed clean underwear. Dug in the drawers. "I lost my mind after you disappeared. I haven't quite found it yet."

Wild eyes when I turned around. I wondered if anyone had ever told Hanna what I considered doing to both of us in the weeks leading up to my surrendering her to Claudia and Ethan.

I said, "Not that way. I just … I was really upset. Not hurting me or anyone else upset. I just feel like I've been under really cold water for a while."

"Okay."

After a while, Hanna said, "I'm sorry I called Eden and not you." Pause. "I remembered his phone number better than yours." She looked intensely sincere. I couldn't decide if that meant she was lying. "He took ages getting here."

"How long?"

"Like, five days, almost."

"Did you tell him where you were?"

"In the desert. I think he had to figure some stuff out. He's good with computers, though, you know?"

"I know."

"He picked me up from the gas station, and we drove all night after that. Till we got here. This is fine." She nodded decisively. "There wasn't a pool at the farm."

I let that go, with mental notes.

She said, "Can I have another muffin?"

"I could make you real food."

"I just want a muffin."

I wanted one too. A whole, massive one, all to myself.

⦙⦙⦙⦿⦙⦙⦙

At night, in the shipping container, Hanna said, "I don't think I want to go to church again."

"That's good, because I don't go at all."

"My dad and mom used to go sometimes. They'd bring me, just a couple of times a year. It wasn't like the ones out in the desert, though."

I stared at the ceiling. There were plastic fan blades up there, turning, but it was so dark. Only the dim shine of my phone charger and the luminous empty sky outside showed lighter shades of dark than the room. I said, "Our church is a weird one. It can help people be really good, or it can make them crazy. I've never been good at figuring out which way people are going to jump."

Hanna chewed on something, her nails or her hair. She'd come to the container after supper and settled beside me. I had no idea where Eden was or where my mother was sleeping, though I could imagine her bedding down with an afghan outdoors and talking with God until dawn.

"Is Grandma Elaine crazy?"

"Yes. She is."

I'd spent months trying to say polite words about Elaine to Hanna. I hadn't cursed her out as thoroughly as I'd wanted to even when I'd literally taken blood and cursed her.

I'd read somewhere, once, on the Jezebel tour, that menstrual blood curses could make people crazy, but that the people they made crazy were all men. But maybe you only had to be afraid of the female body to lose your mind.

"I think she might be. Like, Grandpa Marshall isn't. But she is."

"Why isn't Marshall?"

"Because he gave me his phone. And he gave me a set of numbers that Eden said were what he needed to find me."

"GPS coordinates."

"Yeah."

"Well, thank god for that."

Hanna said, "I won't, okay? I don't want to thank God for anything for a while."

I said, "You don't have to thank god for anything ever. You can even get rid of the capital letter if you want. God doesn't live in our house. We're crazy enough without him."

⁞⁞◉⁞⁞

My phone had a flashlight on it, almost too bright to look at. I used it to take a picture of myself, ragged and in strangers' clothes, and Hanna asleep, and sent that to Kara and Mary-Beth.

MB sent back, *Can we tell people?*

Wait till we're out of Mexico, pls.

OK.

. . .

The ellipse lingered, whispering that Mary-Beth was typing, thinking. I wrote, *what?*

How mad would you be?

What?

We have shows still to play. There's a girl, Japanese. She looks like you did when you were 19 except, you know. Japanese. She can sing.

I wrote, *Go nuts.*

She isn't you.

I'm not me either.

Mostly asleep, Hanna said, "Phones are not for using in bed."

I got up and put it back on the charger. Outside, there were thick stars and desert.

┇┇┋┇┋┇┇

My mother came out of the main house wearing one of Eden's button-down shirts, carrying my phone. She said, "Marshall called."

"What?"

"He called. I heard your phone ringing, so I answered it. I think he was relieved to reach me instead of you."

"Mom, what did you tell him?"

"If you've forgotten, Marshall helped Hanna find us."

"What did he want?"

"He said he has some of her things. He thought she might want them."

"Tell me you didn't tell him where we are."

"I don't know where we are, exactly. I'm not as good with these," gesturing to the phone, still held out, "as you are. I told him you'd call him back."

I went inside and told Eden, who talked to Will, who called the lawyer.

"The police aren't likely to be interested in arresting him."

"In an international kidnapping case?"

"A family dispute," Will said. "You realize the local police have some other fairly major concerns?"

It sounded dismissive, but I'd heard distant gunfire in the night. I was aware that there was a low-key war going on, in the city and around it, and on either side of the border. That it wasn't easily repelled by a low-current gate and electric fence.

"I do."

"We called a lawyer. You will not make your position more vulnerable by meeting him. However, I'd recommend doing it in a controllable location, and not in my home."

I said, "Mennonites are non-violent."

Will said, "No one is non-violent."

"They are. Religiously, as it were."

My mother said, "I'll go with you."

"I'll be fine."

"I am going with you." Emphatic.

Marshall met us, finally, in the small food court of the Juarez Costco. Will and his wife were discreetly present, shopping for bulk goods and specifically for the muffins Hanna had demanded, and my mother sat across from me, eating the ubiquitous oversized hot dog. She'd sat there out of habit, or to avoid sitting beside me and risking the infantile stiff-armed push I was still prone to, but it left Marshall standing awkwardly, unable to choose which of us to ally himself with. He had a pair of shopping bags stuffed full.

He said, "I'm sorry."

My mother said, "Thank you."

"We still have some of her clothes. I thought she might want them. Her books. And her camera."

It was cushioned on stained T-shirts, an ancient Leica with a hand-crank to turn the film and a thick neck strap, the camera of a grandfather on vacation in the pre-digital age.

I said, "I thought cameras weren't allowed."

"They aren't, in the colony. Hanna and I kept it in the truck. She could use it if we went for a drive. She didn't settle with the kids down here, and I thought for a while it might help."

"Do they even speak English?"

"No."

"Spanish?"

"Low German."

"Why did you let her go?"

Marshall said, "I don't think you can imagine what Ethan's death did to us."

I nodded.

"It becomes a kind of madness. Elaine...she isn't surfacing out of it. I'd hoped she would. But she was so desperate."

"I understand why you took her, more or less. You aren't, to be clear, forgiven. But I understand it."

"When we were younger, we thought of moving down south. We were discussing it, actually, before you married Ethan."

My skin went cold. "If I'd stayed, would we have wound up down here?"

"Mexico was never the plan. Elaine's family is in Paraguay." He sighed. "I think you'd have adapted. You'd lived in enough other countries."

My mother looked up. "I wouldn't have allowed that."

"Are you going to Paraguay now?" I asked.

"Yes, I think so. It might be a while, though. We can't easily drive that far right now. But Elaine would like to be with family, and we can't go home."

He looked at me. Waiting. Expectant.

I said, "I said you weren't forgiven."

"You could drop the charges."

"I'm fairly sure I can't. But, more to the point, I'm not going to."

"We have other children."

"I just have the one. You can live happily, very far away, and if you can convince your kids they can always come live with you in Reformation splendour. Far away from me."

"Hanna wouldn't have been happy," Marshall said. "She's a remarkable photographer."

"I know."

"We had some of her photos developed. I hope she'll forgive me, but I'm keeping those. There's more exposed film in the bags, though. I hope you can find a developer."

I took the bags. Marshall reminded me, just by sitting there, that my father was dead, that my mother was mad, that my ex-lover was dead. He looked so sad.

I said, "Except for Hanna existing, I wish I'd never met any of you."

"God has a plan. Perhaps this is all part of it."

Will and his wife came back. I'd been fixated on Marshall and couldn't remember her name. She looked like someone I'd know, or Eden would. Tortoiseshell glasses and bangs and skinny jeans, and lines around her eyes.

I said, "Is part of the plan to give back Hanna's passport?"

He didn't answer. He had it, I realized, but he'd wanted me to say something different. He'd wanted forgiveness, formal and legal.

My mother said, "Ten years."

"What?"

She said, "Marshall, will you excuse us?"

He stepped away, to the condiment stand where chopped peppers marinated in vinegar.

"What is it?"

She said, "Tell him, ten years."

"I don't understand."

"I believe ten years is a reasonable sentence."

I'd done research. So had Eden. "It's unlikely, actually, that they'd get a sentence that long, in court. They're old. They probably wouldn't get anything close."

"But would you consider it reasonable?"

"I'm not sure I want them in jail. Just, gone. Very gone."

"Allison, answer the question I'm actually asking."

I said, "Yes. I'd be satisfied with ten years."

"Then tell him ten years. They stay away ten years. Hanna will be twenty-two by then. If the Crown is still holding charges at that point, you can ask them to drop."

I said, "You've thought about this."

"It feels... proper." She had a speech planned, I thought, but she wasn't giving it. Using silence as her own kind of apology.

"What can I demand from you, then?"

"You don't get to make demands. I'm your mother. But your sister will have to accept that, in spite of her fantasies, I'm not coming to live with you."

"She said she wanted me to *deal* with you."

"Sheltered living with you footing the bill is not what I had in mind. I'm going to go abroad again."

"Naomi's kids will miss you."

"They can come to visit. I don't think I like living in Canada very much. Your father died there. They said he'd die abroad, and he didn't, and I think that means something."

I said, "You're not going to Paraguay, though?"

"Heavens, no. My Low German is terrible. Nor do I enjoy the dresses. I was thinking about Columbia. There's a family on mission who could use a companion, and their community needs another midwife."

"That's acceptable."

"I'm so glad you approve."

Will and his wife were still waiting. Marshall was waiting. If I had Hanna's passport, we could leave the country, quickly and easily and without blood tests or hours in front of a judge.

I said, "Offer it to Marshall."

"You need to do it."

"Are you coming back to Canada with us?"

"No, I don't think so. Guillermo has invited me to stay for a few weeks, and I believe I will."

Will looked so sane. I got up and found Marshall. Offered ten years.

He had Hanna's passport. He gave it to me.

~ 42 ~

Continuous

Hanna was in a position to make demands, and she did. She wanted to resume swimming. She wanted to go to school, some kind of school, that had girls in it her own age. She wanted to go to Japan with me. She wanted to be able to text her friends in Winnipeg, which I swore I'd never forbidden but her version of events was different. She wanted to study to be a witch, but not with me. She wanted an allowance, a regular trip to somewhere she could pick out her own clothes, a chance to decorate her room properly. Piano lessons.

She wanted me to sing to her, sometimes.

She did not, particularly, want to live in Toronto for the rest of her life. I talked to people at Public Broadcasting, who said that the television series could shoot in Toronto or in Vancouver. Winnipeg was not a serious possibility. Even if they'd had the studio space in Winnipeg, and they didn't, the kinds of people they expected me to interview so rarely came to Winnipeg that even proposing it as a home base was absurd.

I said to Hanna, *Toronto or Vancouver?* And she said she'd never been to Vancouver, so we went. We flew directly from Juarez, with Eden. His van, beloved but suffering from a broken fan-belt, stayed in Will's yard.

Eden made demands. Next summer, when it was warm enough, we'd go back. Or in the spring, before it was hot. Drive north. All of us. And his cameras.

I pointed out that that was incompatible with Hanna's demand for school, and she said she wanted the kind of school that let girls go places with their families sometimes, so they could learn things, and also to Japan, because she wanted to go to Japan.

Mary-Beth's apartment housed three of us decently, though only just, and I couldn't imagine putting my work and Eden's into it, and then Hanna's things, too.

I said, in the dark, curled against Eden, "We can't move here. We can't afford a house, and I don't think I'm prepared to live in an apartment again."

"I thought you wanted a security system."

"We have ten years."

"It's a long time. Okay."

Eden's body wasn't one I'd spent many nights sleeping against. When we'd first moved in together, I'd claimed my own room, and while I visited him, for sex and to talk, we'd mostly slept apart. In the calculations of total space, now, I was probably going to be sleeping with him for as long as we lived together.

We bought Hanna clothes. Just a few. I said, *wait. Tokyo.*

Right. Yes. I want Tokyo clothes.

The Richmond Night Market ran all winter, so we went there, too, and to the sky-rise pool in Mary-Beth's building, and to the Sun Yat Sen Gardens, which I'd been meaning to visit all my life. They were beautiful, serene even in the winter, and Hanna was fascinated by the slow-moving koi in the water, how they could still be alive.

"It doesn't snow here."

"Not ever?" she asked.

"Hardly ever."

"Weird."

"What do you think of Vancouver?"

"I'm thinking about it."

In bed, Eden said, "We could rent a house. Normal people here don't buy. Not anymore."

I said, "Maybe."

"You don't want to live in Toronto, so."

"Our friends are there."

"Half our friends have moved to Vancouver. And you'll meet people. You know everyone."

"Tell you what. Find a psychiatrist that can take us both."

In the doorway, Hanna said, "I want one."

"What?"

"A psychiatrist."

That woke me up. "Hanna, are you okay?"

"I liked Lucy. She kind of helped. We move here, I need someone to talk to."

"That's not what a psychiatrist does."

"Don't you lie on a couch or something?"

"No, that's a therapist. A psychiatrist is for the kind of crazy that's caused by chemicals in your brain, that you can't just talk out. That might come for you, because it seems to be pretty thick in my family, but there are good pills now. Eden, make a note. Hanna needs a therapist."

"It's on my list."

"Are you the family secretary?" Hanna asked.

"Yes."

She still stood in the doorway. "Can I sleep in bed with you guys?"

I said, "Yes, but not as a long-term thing."

"Allison." She sighed. "I don't like the glass walls out there," nodding back at the living room, where she'd been sleeping on the couch.

"Okay."

In the full dark, she asked, "When are we going to Tokyo?"

"Three days. We'll get you a cool suitcase."

"Is Eden coming?"

"Yes."

■■◍■■

Hanna loved Japan. Outside of Tokyo, the country lost its cool sheen and turned into a mirror-world version of ordinary life, but it seemed to satisfy her. Eden practiced for a day in a right-hand drive car and then took her out into the country while I was performing.

They visited bathhouses and villages with no children left where elders came over to stroke Hanna's hair and tell her things that she didn't understand, but that she recorded on her phone and ran later through a digital translator. She bought thick black-and-white comics in Japanese, and a dictionary. They met up with me at another hotel. She said, "Definitely Vancouver. I want to move to Vancouver. Can we come back here, too?"

"It's only a thirteen-hour flight."

"You're joking but I'm serious."

"Maybe."

Himeko was the substitute Japanese version of me. She looked nineteen, but she was twenty-seven, and she spoke English, slightly American in tone. "Years in San Francisco." She had a second career as a fetish model.

Himeko went back to Canada with us, at the end of the tour. I took my place back, singing for the band, but she played bass better than I ever had, and she could sing structured harmonies. Someone from A&R on a label we hadn't heard of informed us that with Himeko in the band, we had an official offer for a two-album recording deal and tour dates.

Mary-Beth said, "Don't do it. Nobody signs recording deals anymore. We don't need a contract to make music, if music's what you want to make."

I said, "Not full time. I'm too old for this."

"How part-time?"

"Three months a year. Maybe four. Not continuous. I have a show to host."

Eden and I were still in Toronto, contemplating logistics and finances, when Public Broadcasting called. I was rehabilitated, or sufficiently, and if I wanted to return to work, their replacement host was proving…unpopular.

I said, "I have plans to move."

"Finish the season out for us. Please."

I did. I reverted to a pre-dawn broadcasting schedule. Re-greeted the writers, producers, bookers. Walked down the hall to say hello to Linda, but when I stuck my head into her office she was gone, headed overseas on field rotation and replaced with a bruised-looking man who'd gone to university with her and worked, for a year or so, on the same student paper, and who'd have told me about it for hours if I hadn't fled.

We had bands coming in on Thursday and Friday. Actors and authors booked in all week. A panel assembled to discuss Truth and Reconciliation in media.

Live broadcast picked up at 10 a.m. Atlantic time, 9 Central.

The show's Monday theme was still "Boys Don't Cry." Mary-Beth had called to announce she'd found a bootleg of The Innocents covering the song, circa 1998. She'd run it through filters until it sounded almost professional.

Cue music.

Good morning, Canada. Happy Monday. Our eyes are bright and our intentions are pure. I'm Allison Winter, and this is The Cure.

ABOUT THE AUTHOR

Annette Lapointe is the author of two acclaimed novels, *Stolen* and *Whitetail Shooting Gallery*, and the short story collection, *You Are Not Needed Now*. She has lived in rural Saskatchewan, Quebec City, St John's, Saskatoon, Winnipeg (where she earned her PhD), and South Korea. She now lives in Treaty 8 territory, on the traditional lands of the Beaver people, and teaches at Grande Prairie Regional College.